MAYBE YOU CAN AFFORD TO WAIT. *Maybe for you there's a tomorrow. Maybe for you there's one thousand tomorrows, or three thousand, or ten, so much time you can bathe in it, roll around in it, let it slide like coins through your fingers. So much time you can waste it.*

But for some of us there's only today. And the truth is, you never really know.

before

i

fall

LAUREN OLIVER

HARPER

An Imprint of HarperCollins*Publishers*

Grateful acknowledgment is made to Dujeous, LLC,
for permission to reprint their lyrics.

"Tomorrow"
From the Musical Production *Annie*
Lyric by Martin Charnin
Music by Charles Strouse
© 1977 (Renewed) EDWIN H. MORRIS & COMPANY, a division of MPL Music
Publishing, Inc. and CHARLES STROUSE
All rights on behalf of CHARLES STROUSE owned by CHARLES STROUSE
PUBLISHING (administered by WILLIAMSON MUSIC)
All Rights Reserved   Used by Permission
www.CharlesStrouse.com

"Psycho Killer"
Words by DAVID BYRNE, CHRIS FRANTZ and TINA WEYMOUTH
Music by DAVID BYRNE
© 1976 (Renewed) INDEX MUSIC, INC. (ASCAP) & BLEU DISQUE MUSIC
CO., INC. (ASCAP)
All rights administered by WB MUSIC CORP. (ASCAP)
All Rights Reserved
Photos used with permission of AwesomenessTV and Open Road Media.

Library of Congress Cataloging-in-Publication Data
Oliver, Lauren, date
  Before I fall / Lauren Oliver.—1st ed.
    p. cm.
  Summary: After she dies in a car crash, teenage Samantha relives the day of her
death over and over again until she finally discovers why she has been given this
chance.
  ISBN 978-0-06-265632-2
  [1. Dead—Fiction. 2. Interpersonal relations—Fiction. 3. Popularity—Fiction.
4. Self-perception—Fiction. 5. Conduct of life—Fiction. 6. High schools—Fiction.
7. Schools—Fiction.] I. Title.
PZ7.O475If 2010   2009007288
[Fic]—dc22   CIP
                                                                        AC

Typography by Hilary Zarycky
16 17 18 19 20   PC/LSCH   10 9 8 7 6 5 4 3 2 1
❖
First paperback edition, 2011

before
i
fall

PROLOGUE

They say that just before you die your whole life flashes before your eyes, but that's not how it happened for me.

To be honest, I'd always thought the whole final-moment, mental life-scan thing sounded pretty awful. Some things are better left buried and forgotten, as my mom would say. I'd be happy to forget all of fifth grade, for example (the glasses-and-pink-braces period), and does anybody want to relive the first day of middle school? Add in all of the boring family vacations, pointless algebra classes, period cramps, and bad kisses I barely lived through the first time around . . .

The truth is, though, I wouldn't have minded reliving my greatest hits: when Rob Cokran and I first hooked up in the middle of the dance floor at homecoming, so everyone saw and knew we were together; when Lindsay, Elody, Ally, and I got drunk and tried to make snow angels in May, leaving person-sized imprints in Ally's lawn; my sweet-sixteen party, when we set out a hundred tea lights and danced on the table in the backyard; the time Lindsay and I pranked Clara Seuse on Halloween, got chased by the cops, and laughed so hard we almost threw up—the things I wanted to remember; the things I wanted to be remembered for.

But before I died I didn't think of Rob, or any other guy. I didn't think of all the outrageous things I'd done with my friends. I didn't even think of my family, or the way the morning light turns the walls in my bedroom the color of cream, or the way the azaleas outside my window smell in July, a mixture of honey and cinnamon.

Instead, I thought of Vicky Hallinan.

Specifically, I thought of the time in fourth grade when Lindsay announced in front of the whole gym class that she wouldn't have Vicky on her dodgeball team. "She's too fat," Lindsay blurted out. "You could hit her with your eyes closed." I wasn't friends with Lindsay yet, but even then she had this way of saying things that made them hilarious, and I laughed along with everyone else while Vicky's face turned as purple as the underside of a storm cloud.

That's what I remembered in that before-death instant, when I was supposed to be having some big revelation about my past: the smell of varnish and the squeak of our sneakers on the polished floor; the tightness of my polyester shorts; the laughter echoing around the big, empty space like there were way more than twenty-five people in the gym.

And Vicky's face.

The weird thing is that I hadn't thought about that in forever. It was one of those memories I didn't even know I remembered, *if you know what I mean. It's not like Vicky was traumatized or anything. That's just the kind of thing that kids do to each other. It's no big deal. There's always going to be a person laughing and somebody getting laughed at. It happens every day, in every school, in every town in America—probably in the world, for all I know. The whole point of growing up is learning to stay on the laughing side.*

Vicky wasn't very fat to begin with—she just had some baby weight on her face and stomach—and before high school she'd lost that and grown three inches. She even became friends with Lindsay. They played field hockey together and said hi in the halls. One time, our freshman year, Vicky brought it up at a party—we were all pretty tipsy—and we laughed and laughed, Vicky most of all, until her face turned almost as purple as it had all those years ago in the gym.

That was weird thing number one.

Even weirder than that was the fact that we'd all just been talking about it—how it would be just before you died, I mean. I don't remember exactly how it came up, except that Elody was complaining that I always got shotgun and refusing to wear her seat belt. She kept leaning forward into the front seat to scroll through Lindsay's iPod, even though I was supposed to have deejay privileges. I was trying to explain my "greatest hits" theory of death, and we were all picking out what those would be. Lindsay picked finding out that she got into Duke, obviously, and Ally—who was bitching about the cold, as usual, and threatening to drop dead right there of pneumonia—participated long enough to say she wished she could relive her first hookup with Matt Wilde forever, which surprised no one. Lindsay and Elody were smoking, and freezing rain was coming in through the cracked-open windows. The road was narrow and winding, and on either side of us the dark, stripped branches of trees lashed back and forth, like the wind had set them dancing.

Elody put on "Splinter" by Fallacy to piss Ally off, maybe because she was sick of her whining. It was Ally's song with Matt, who had dumped her in September. Ally called her a bitch and unbuckled her seat belt, leaning forward and trying to grab the iPod. Lindsay complained that someone was elbowing her in the neck. The cigarette dropped from her mouth and landed between her thighs. She started cursing and trying to brush the embers off the seat cushion and Elody and Ally were still fighting and I was trying to talk over them, reminding them all of the time we'd made snow angels in May. The tires skidded a little on the wet road, and the car was full of cigarette smoke, little wisps rising like phantoms in the air.

Then all of a sudden there was a flash of white in front of the car. Lindsay yelled something—words I couldn't make out, something like sit or shit or sight—and suddenly the car was flipping off the road and into the black mouth of the woods. I heard a horrible, screeching sound—metal on metal, glass shattering, a car folding in two—and smelled fire. I had time to wonder whether Lindsay had put her cigarette out.

Then Vicky Hallinan's face came rising out of the past. I heard laughter echoing and rolling all around me, swelling into a scream.

Then nothing.

The thing is, you don't get to know. It's not like you wake up with a bad feeling in your stomach. You don't see shadows where there shouldn't be any. You don't remember to tell your parents that you love them or—in my case—remember to say good-bye to them at all.

If you're like me, you wake up seven minutes and forty-seven seconds before your best friend is supposed to be picking you up. You're too busy worrying about how many roses you're going to get on Cupid Day to do anything more than throw on your clothes, brush your teeth, and pray to God you left your makeup in the bottom of your messenger bag so you can do it in the car.

If you're like me, your last day starts like this:

7

ONE

"Beep, beep," Lindsay calls out. A few weeks ago my mom yelled at her for blasting her horn at six fifty-five every morning, and this is Lindsay's solution.

"I'm coming!" I shout back, even though she can see me pushing out the front door, trying to put on my coat and wrestle my binder into my bag at the same time.

At the last second, my eight-year-old sister, Izzy, tugs at me.

"What?" I whirl around. She has little-sister radar for when I'm busy, late, or on the phone with my boyfriend. Those are always the times she chooses to bother me.

"You forgot your gloves," she says, except it comes out: "You *forgot* your *gloveths*." She refuses to go to speech therapy for her lisp, even though all the kids in her grade make fun of her. She says she likes the way she talks.

I take them from her. They're cashmere and she's probably gotten peanut butter on them. She's always scooping around in jars of the stuff.

"What did I tell you, Izzy?" I say, poking her in the middle of the forehead. "Don't touch my stuff." She giggles like an idiot and I have to hustle her inside while I shut the door. If it were up to her, she would follow me around all day like a dog.

By the time I make it out of the house, Lindsay's leaning out the window of the Tank. That's what we call her car, an enormous silver Range Rover. (Every time we drive around in it at least one person says, "That thing's not a car, it's a *truck*," and Lindsay claims she could go head-to-head with an eighteen-wheeler and come out without a scratch.) She and Ally are the only two of us with cars that actually belong to them. Ally's car is a tiny black Jetta that we named the Minime. I get to borrow my mom's Accord sometimes; poor Elody has to make do with her father's ancient tan Ford Taurus, which hardly runs anymore.

The air is still and freezing cold. The sky is a perfect, pale blue. The sun has just risen, weak and watery-looking, like it has just spilled itself over the horizon and is too lazy to clean itself up. It's supposed to storm later, but you'd never know.

I get into the passenger seat. Lindsay's already smoking and she gestures with the end of her cigarette to the Dunkin' Donuts coffee she got for me.

"Bagels?" I say.

"In the back."

"Sesame?"

"Obviously." She looks me over once as she pulls out of my driveway. "Nice skirt."

"You too."

Lindsay tips her head, acknowledging the compliment. We're actually wearing the same skirt. There are only two days of the year when Lindsay, Ally, Elody, and I deliberately dress the same: Pajama Day during Spirit Week, because we all bought cute matching sets at Victoria's Secret last Christmas, and Cupid Day. We spent three hours at the mall arguing about whether to go for pink or red outfits—Lindsay hates pink; Ally lives in it—and we finally settled on black miniskirts and some red fur-trimmed tank tops we found in the clearance bin at Nordstrom.

Like I said, those are the only times we *deliberately* look alike. But the truth is that at my high school, Thomas Jefferson, everyone kind of looks the same. There's no official uniform—it's a public school—but you'll see the same outfit of Seven jeans, gray New Balance sneakers, a white T-shirt, and a colored North Face fleece jacket on nine out of ten students. Even the guys and the girls dress the same, except our jeans are tighter and we have to blow out our hair every day. It's Connecticut: being like the people around you is the whole point.

That's not to say that our high school doesn't have its freaks—it does—but even the freaks are freaky in the same way. The Eco-Geeks ride their bikes to school and wear clothing made of hemp and never wash their hair, like having dreadlocks will somehow help curb the emission of greenhouse gases. The Drama Queens carry big bottles of lemon tea and wear scarves even in summer and don't talk in class because they're "conserving their voices." The Math League members always have ten times more books than anyone else and actually still use their lockers and walk around with permanently nervous expressions, like they're just waiting for somebody to yell, "Boo!"

I don't mind it, actually. Sometimes Lindsay and I make plans to run away after graduation and crash in a loft in New York City with this tattoo artist her stepbrother knows, but secretly I like living in Ridgeview. It's reassuring, if you know what I mean.

I lean forward, trying to apply mascara without gouging my eye out. Lindsay's never been the most careful driver and has a tendency to jerk the wheel around, come to sudden stops, and then gun the engine.

"Patrick better send me a rose," Lindsay says as she shoots through one stop sign and nearly breaks my neck slamming on the brakes at the next one. Patrick is Lindsay's on-again, off-again boyfriend. They've broken up a record thirteen times since the start of the school year.

"I had to sit next to Rob while he filled out the request form," I say, rolling my eyes. "It was like forced labor."

Rob Cokran and I have been going out since October, but I've been in love with him since sixth grade, when he was too cool to talk to me. Rob was my first crush, or at least my first *real* crush. I did once kiss Kent McFuller in third grade, but that obviously doesn't count since we'd just exchanged dandelion rings and were pretending to be husband and wife.

"Last year I got twenty-two roses." Lindsay flicks her cigarette butt out of the window and leans over for a slurp of coffee. "I'm going for twenty-five this year."

Each year before Cupid Day the student council sets up a booth outside the gym. For two dollars each, you can buy your friends Valograms—roses with little notes attached to them—and then they get delivered by Cupids (usually freshman or sophomore girls trying to get in good with the upperclassmen) throughout the day.

"I'd be happy with fifteen," I say. It's a big deal how many roses you get. You can tell who's popular and who isn't by the number of roses they're holding. It's bad if you get under ten and humiliating if you don't get more than five—it basically means that you're either ugly or unknown. Probably both. Sometimes people scavenge for dropped roses to add to their bouquets, but you can always tell.

"So." Lindsay shoots me a sideways glance. "Are you excited? The big day. Opening night." She laughs. "No pun intended."

I shrug and turn toward the window, watching my breath frost the pane. "It's no big deal." Rob's parents are away this weekend, and a couple of weeks ago he asked me if I could spend the whole night at his house. I knew he was really asking if I wanted to have sex. We've gotten semi-close a few times, but it's always been in the back of his dad's BMW or in somebody's basement or in my den with my parents asleep upstairs, and it's always felt wrong.

So when he asked me to stay the night, I said yes without thinking about it.

Lindsay squeals and hits her palm against the steering wheel. "No big deal? Are you kidding? My baby's growing up."

"Oh, please." I feel heat creeping up my neck and know my skin's probably going red and splotchy. It does this whenever I'm embarrassed. All the dermatologists, creams, and powders in Connecticut don't help. When I was younger kids used to sing, *"What's red and white and weird all over? Sam Kingston!"*

I shake my head a little and rub the vapor off the window. Outside the world sparkles, like it's been coated in varnish. "When did you and Patrick do it, anyway? Like three months ago?"

"Yeah, but we've been making up for lost time since then." Lindsay rocks against her seat.

"Gross."

"Don't worry, kid. You'll be fine."

"Don't call me kid." This is one reason I'm happy I decided to have sex with Rob tonight: so Lindsay and Elody won't make fun of me anymore. Thankfully, since Ally's still a virgin it means I won't be the very last one, either. Sometimes I feel like out of the four of us I'm always the one tagging along, just there for the ride. "I told you it was no big deal."

"If you say so."

Lindsay has made me nervous, so I count all the mailboxes

as we go by. I wonder if by tomorrow everything will look different to me; I wonder if I'll look different to other people. I hope so.

We pull up to Elody's house and before Lindsay can even honk, the front door swings open and Elody starts picking her way down the icy walkway, balancing on three-inch heels, like she can't get out of her house fast enough.

"Nipply outside much?" Lindsay says when Elody slides into the car. As usual she's wearing only a thin leather jacket, even though the weather report said the high would be in the mid-twenties.

"What's the point of looking cute if you can't show it off?" Elody shimmies her boobs and we crack up. It's impossible to stay stressed when she's around, and the knot in my stomach loosens.

Elody makes a clawing gesture with her hand and I pass her a coffee. We all take it the same way: large hazelnut, no sugar, extra cream.

"Watch where you're sitting. You'll squish the bagels." Lindsay frowns into the rearview mirror.

"You know you want a piece of this." Elody gives her butt a smack and we all laugh again.

"Save it for Muffin, you horn dog."

Steve Dough is Elody's latest victim. She calls him Muffin because of his last name, and because he's yummy (*she* says; he looks too greasy for me, and he always smells like pot). They have been hooking up for a month and a half now.

Elody's the most experienced of any of us. She lost her virginity sophomore year and has already had sex with two different guys. She was the one who told me she was sore after the first couple of times she had sex, which made me ten times more nervous. It may sound crazy, but I never really thought of it as something physical, something that would make you sore, like soccer or horseback riding. I'm scared that I won't know what to do, like when we used to play basketball in gym and I'd always forget who I was supposed to be guarding or when I should pass the ball and when I should dribble it.

"Mmm, Muffin." Elody puts a hand on her stomach. "I'm starving."

"There's a bagel for you," I say.

"Sesame?" Elody asks.

"Obviously," Lindsay and I say at the same time. Lindsay winks at me.

Just before we get to school we roll down the windows and blast Mary J. Blige's "No More Drama." I close my eyes and think back to homecoming and my first kiss with Rob, when he pulled me toward him on the dance floor and suddenly my lips were on his and his tongue was sliding under my tongue and I could feel the heat from all the colored lights pressing down on me like a hand, and the music seemed to echo somewhere behind my ribs, making my heart flutter and skip in time. The cold air coming through the window makes my throat hurt and the bass comes through the soles of my feet just like it did that night, when I thought I would never be happier; it goes all the way up to my head, making me dizzy, like the whole car is going to split apart from the sound.

POPULARITY: AN ANALYSIS

Popularity's a weird thing. You can't really define it, and it's not cool to talk about it, but you know it when you see it. Like a lazy eye, or porn.

Lindsay's gorgeous, but the rest of us aren't that much prettier than anybody else. Here are my good traits: big green eyes, straight white teeth, high cheekbones, long legs. Here are my bad traits: a too-long nose, skin that gets blotchy when I'm nervous, a flat butt.

Becky DiFiore's just as pretty as Lindsay, and I don't think Becky even had a date to junior homecoming. Ally's boobs are pretty big, but mine are borderline nonexistent (when Lindsay's in a bad mood she calls me Samuel, not Sam or Samantha). And it's not like we're shiny perfect or our breath always smells like lilacs or something. Lindsay once had a burping contest with Jonah Sasnoff in the cafeteria and everyone applauded her. Sometimes Elody wears fuzzy yellow slippers to school. I once laughed so hard in social studies I spit up vanilla latte all over Jake Somers's desk. A month later we made out in Lily Angler's toolshed. (He was bad.)

The point is, we can do things like that. You know why?

Because we're popular. And we're popular because we can get away with everything. So it's circular.

I guess what I'm saying is there's no point in analyzing it. If you draw a circle, there will always be an inside and an outside, and unless you're a total nut job, it's pretty easy to see which is which. It's just what happens.

I'm not going to lie, though. It's nice that everything's easy for us. It's a good feeling knowing you can basically do whatever you want and there won't be any consequences. When we get out of high school we'll look back and know we did everything right, that we kissed the cutest boys and went to the best parties, got in just enough trouble, listened to our music too loud, smoked too many cigarettes, and drank too much and laughed too much and listened too little, or not at all. If high school were a game of poker, Lindsay, Ally, Elody, and I would be holding 80 percent of the cards.

And believe me: I *know* what it's like to be on the other side. I was there for the first half of my life. The bottom of the bottom, lowest of the low. I know what it's like to have to squabble and pick and fight over the leftovers.

So now I have first pick of everything. So what. That's the way it is.

Nobody ever said life was fair.

We pull into the parking lot exactly ten minutes before first bell. Lindsay guns it toward the lower lot, where the faculty spaces are, scattering a group of sophomore girls. I can see red and white lace dresses peeking out under their coats, and one of them is wearing a tiara. Cupids, definitely.

"Come on, come on, come on," Lindsay mutters as we pull behind the gym. This is the only row in the lower lot not reserved for staff. We call it Senior Alley, even though Lindsay's been parking here since junior year. It's the VIP of parking at Jefferson, and if you miss out on a spot—there are only twenty of them—you have to park all the way in the upper lot, which is a full .22 miles from the main entrance. We checked one time, and now whenever we talk about it we have to use the exact distance. Like, "Do you really want to walk .22 miles in this rain?"

Lindsay squeals when she sees an open space, jerking her wheel to the left. At the same time, Sarah Grundel is pulling up her brown Chevrolet from the other direction, angling it into the spot.

"Oh, *hell* no. No way." Lindsay leans on the horn, even though it's obvious Sarah was here before us, then presses her foot on the accelerator. Elody shrieks as hot coffee sloshes all over her shirt. There is the high-pitched squeal of rubber, and Sarah Grundel slams on her brakes just before Lindsay's Range Rover takes off her bumper.

"Nice." Lindsay pulls into the spot and throws her car in park. Then she opens her door and leans out.

"Sorry, sweetie!" she calls to Sarah. "I didn't see you there."

19

This is obviously a lie.

"Great." Elody is mopping up coffee with a balled-up Dunkin' Donuts napkin. "Now I get to go around all day with my boobs smelling like hazelnut."

"Guys like food smells," I say. "I read it in *Glamour*."

"Put a cookie down your pants and Muffin will probably jump you before homeroom." Lindsay flips down the rearview mirror and checks her face.

"Maybe you should try it with Rob, Sammy." Elody throws the coffee-stained napkin at me and I catch it and peg it back.

"What?" She's laughing. "You didn't think I'd forget about your big night, did you?" She fishes in her bag and the next thing that flies over the seat is a crumpled-up condom with bits of tobacco stuck to its wrapper. Lindsay cracks up.

"You're pagans," I say, taking the condom with two fingers and dropping it in Lindsay's glove compartment. Just touching it gets my nerves going again, and I can feel something twist at the bottom of my stomach. I've never understood why condoms are kept in those little foil wrappers. They look so clinical, like something your doctor would prescribe for allergies or intestinal problems.

"No glove, no love," Elody says, leaning forward and kissing my cheek. She leaves a big circle of pink lip gloss there.

"Come on." I get out of the car before they can see I'm blushing.

Mr. Shaw, the athletic director, is standing outside the gym when we're getting out of the car, probably checking out our asses. Elody thinks the reason he insisted his office be right next to the girls' dressing room is because he rigged up a camera feed from his computer to the toilet. Why else would he even *need* a computer? He's the *athletic* director. Now every time I pee in the gym I get paranoid.

"Move it, ladies," he calls to us. He's also the soccer coach, which is ironic since he probably couldn't run to the vending machine and back. He looks like a walrus. He even has a mustache. "I don't want to have to give you a late slip."

"I don't want to have to spank you." I do an impression of his voice, which is strangely high-pitched—another reason Elody thinks he might be a pedophile. Elody and Lindsay crack up.

"Two minutes to bell," Shaw says, more sharply. Maybe he heard me. I don't really care.

"Happy Friday," Lindsay grumbles, and puts her arm through mine.

Elody has taken out her cell phone and is checking her teeth in its reflective back, picking out sesame seeds with a pinkie nail.

"This sucks," she says, without looking up.

"Totally," I say. Fridays are the hardest in some ways: you're so close to freedom. "Kill me now."

"No way." Lindsay squeezes my arm. "Can't let my best friend die a virgin."

You see, we didn't know.

My first two periods—art and AHAP (American History Advanced Placement; history's always been my best subject)— I get only five roses. I'm not that stressed about it, although it does kind of piss me off that Eileen Cho gets *four* roses from her boyfriend, Ian Dowel. It didn't even occur to me to ask Rob to do that, and in a way I don't think it's fair. It makes people think you've got more friends than you do.

As soon as I make it to chemistry, Mr. Tierney announces a pop quiz. This is a big problem since (1) I haven't understood a word of my homework in four weeks (okay, so I stopped trying after week one) and (2) Mr. Tierney's always threatening to phone in failing grades to college admissions committees, since a lot of us haven't been accepted to school yet. I'm not sure whether he's serious or whether he's just trying to keep the seniors in line, but there is no way I'm letting some fascist teacher ruin my chances of getting into BU.

Even worse, I'm sitting next to Lauren Lornet, possibly the only person in the class more clueless about this stuff than I am.

Actually my grades have been pretty good in chem this year, but it isn't because I've had a sudden epiphany about proton-electron interaction. My straight A– average can be summarized in two words: Jeremy Ball. He's skinnier than I am and his breath always smells like cornflakes, but he lets me copy his homework and inches his desk closer to mine on test days so I can peek over at his answers without being obvious. Unfortunately, since I stop before Tierney's class to pee and check in with Ally—we always meet in the bathroom before fourth period, since she has biology at the same time I have chem—I arrive too late to get my usual seat next to Jeremy.

There are three questions on Mr. Tierney's quiz, and I don't know enough to fake an answer to a single one. Next to me, Lauren's doubled over her paper, tongue just poking out between her teeth. She always does that when she thinks. Her first answer's looking pretty good, actually: her answers are neat and deliberate, not frantically scribbled like you do when you don't know what you're talking about and are hoping if you scrawl enough your teacher won't notice. (For the record, it never works.) Then I remember that Mr. Tierney lectured Lauren about improving her grade last week. Maybe she's been studying extra hard.

I peek over Lauren's shoulder and copy down two of her answers—I'm good at being subtle about it—when Mr. Tierney calls out, "Threeeeee minutes." He says it dramatically, like he's doing a voice-over for a movie, and it makes the fat under his chin wiggle.

It looks like Lauren's finished and checking her work, but she's leaning so I can't see the third answer. I watch the second hand tick its way around the clock—"Two miiinnnuuutes and thirrrrty secondssss," Tierney booms—and I lean over and poke Lauren with my pen. She looks up, startled. I don't think I've talked to her in years, and for a second I see a look pass over her face that I can't quite identify.

Pen, I mouth to her.

She looks confused and shoots a glance up at Tierney, who is thankfully bent over the textbook.

"What?" she whispers.

I make some gestures with my pen, trying to communicate to her that I've run out of ink. She's staring at me dumbly, and for a second I feel like reaching out and shaking her—"Twwooooo minnnutttesss"—but finally her face clears up and she grins like she's just figured out how to cure cancer. I don't want to sound harsh, but it's such a waste to be a dork *and* kind of slow on the uptake. What's the point if you can't at least play Beethoven or win state spelling bees or go to Harvard or something?

While Lauren's bent over rummaging for a pen in her bag, I copy down the final answer. I kind of forget I even asked her for a pen, actually, because she has to whisper at me to get my attention.

"Thirrrrttttyyyy seconnndss."

"Here."

I take it from her. One end is chewed: gross. I give her a tight smile and look away, but a second later she whispers, "Does it work?"

I give her a look so she'll know that now she's being annoying. I guess she takes it as a sign I don't understand.

24

"The pen. Does it work?" she whispers a little louder.

That's when Tierney slams the textbook against his desk. The sound is so loud we all jump.

"Miss Lornet," he bellows, glaring at Lauren. "Are you *talking* during my *quiz*?"

She turns bright red and looks back and forth from me to the teacher, licking her lips. I don't say anything.

"I was just—" she says faintly.

"Enough." He stands up, frowning so hard his mouth looks like it's going to melt into his neck, and crosses his arms. I think he's going to say something more to Lauren because he's shooting her a death stare, but instead he just says, "Time, everybody. Pencils and pens down."

I go to give Lauren's pen back to her but she won't take it.

"Keep it," she says.

"No, thanks," I say. I hold it between two fingers and lean over, dangling it above her desk, but she tucks her hands behind her back.

"Seriously," she says, "you're going to need a pen. For notes and stuff." She's looking at me like she's offering me something miraculous and not a Bic pen with slobber on it. I don't know if it's her expression or not, but all of a sudden I remember the time we went on a field trip in second grade, and the two of us were the only ones left after everyone had chosen their buddies. We had to hold hands for the rest of the day whenever we crossed the street, and hers were always sweaty.

25

I wonder if she remembers. I hope not.

I smile tightly and drop the pen in my bag. She grins from ear to ear. I'll throw it out as soon as we're done with class, of course; you never know what kind of diseases get carried through slobber.

On the bright side: my mom always said you should do one nice thing a day. So I guess that means I'm in the clear.

MATH CLASS:
FURTHER LESSONS IN CHEMISTRY

Fourth period I have "life skills," which is what they call gym when you're old enough to be offended by forced physical activity (Elody thinks they should call it slavery instead, for accuracy). We're studying CPR, which means we get to make out with life-sized dummies in front of Mr. Shaw. More proof of his perviness.

Fifth period I have calc and the Cupids come early, just after class has started. One of them is wearing a shiny, red unitard and has devil's horns; one of them looks like she might be dressed as the Playboy bunny, or maybe the Easter bunny in heels; one of them is dressed up like an angel. Their costumes don't really make sense in the context of the holiday, but like I said, the whole point is to show off in front of the junior and senior boys. I don't blame them. We did it too. Freshman year Ally dated Mike Harmon—a senior at the time—for two months after she delivered a Valogram to him and he said her butt looked cute in her tights. That's a real love story right there.

The devil gives me three roses—one from Elody, one from Tara Flute, who's kind of in our group but not really, and one from Rob. I make a big deal of unfolding the tiny card that's looped around the rose stem and acting moved when I read the note, even though all he's written is *Happy Cupid Day. Luv ya* and then in smaller letters near the bottom: *Happy now?*

"Luv ya" isn't exactly "I love you"—which we've never said—but it's getting close. I'm pretty sure he's saving it for tonight, actually. Last week it was late and we were sitting on his couch and he was staring at me and I was sure—*sure*—he was going to say it—but instead he just said from a certain angle I looked like Scarlett Johansson.

At least my note is better than the one Ally got from Matt Wilde last year: *Roses are red, violets are blue, if I get you in bed, it would be really cool.* He was kidding, obviously, but still. *Blue* and *cool* don't even rhyme.

I think that's going to be all of my Valograms, but then the angel comes over to my desk and hands me another one. The roses are all different colors and this one's pretty amazing: cream and pink swirled petals, like it's made out of some kind of ice cream.

"It's beautiful," she breathes.

I look up. The angel is just standing there, staring at the

rose lying on my desk. It's pretty shocking for a lowerclassman to have the balls to speak to a senior, and it annoys me for a second. She doesn't look like the average Cupid either. She has hair so pale blond it's almost white, and I can see individual veins through her skin. She reminds me of someone, but I can't remember who.

She catches me looking at her and gives me a quick, embarrassed smile. I'm happy to see some color rush into her face—at least it makes her look alive.

"Marian."

She turns around when the devil girl calls to her. The devil makes an impatient gesture with the roses she's still carrying, and the angel—Marian, I guess—quickly rejoins the other Cupids. All three of them leave.

I brush my finger over the rose petals—they're as soft as anything, as air or a breath—and then instantly feel stupid. I open the note, expecting something from Ally or Lindsay (hers always say *Love you to death, bitch*), but instead I see a cartoon drawing of a fat cupid accidentally shooting a bird out of a tree. The bird is labeled *American Bald Eagle*, and it looks like it's about to fall directly on top of a couple sitting on a bench—Cupid's original target, presumably. Cupid's eyes are spirals and he has a stupid grin on his face.

Underneath the cartoon it says: *Don't drink and love.*

It's obviously from Kent McFuller—he draws cartoons for *The Tribulation*, the school humor paper—and I look up and

28

glance in his direction. He always sits in the back left corner of the room. It's one weird thing about him but definitely not the only one. Sure enough, he's watching me. He gives me a quick smile and a wave, then makes a motion with his arms like he's pulling back an arrow on a bowstring and shooting it at me. I make a point of frowning and deliberately take his note, fold it up quickly, and toss it in the bottom of my bag. He doesn't seem to mind, though. It's like I can *feel* his smile burning on me.

Mr. Daimler comes up and down the aisles, collecting homework, and he pauses at my desk. I have to admit it: he's the reason I'm psyched to get four Valograms in calc. Mr. Daimler's only twenty-five and he's gorgeous. He's assistant coach of the soccer team, and it's pretty funny to see him standing next to Shaw. They're complete physical opposites. Mr. Daimler's over six feet, always tan, and dresses like we do, in jeans and fleeces and New Balance sneakers. He graduated from Thomas Jefferson. We looked him up once in the old yearbooks in the library. He was prom king, and in one picture he's wearing a tux and smiling with his arm around his prom date. You can just see a hemp necklace peeking out of his shirt collar. I love that picture. But you know what I love even more? He *still* wears that hemp necklace.

It's so ironic that the hottest guy at Thomas Jefferson is on the faculty.

As usual, when he smiles my stomach does a little flip. He

runs a hand through his messy brown hair, and I fantasize about doing the same thing.

"Nine roses already?" He raises his eyebrows, makes a big show of checking his watch. "And it's only eleven fifteen. Well done."

"What can I say?" I make my voice as smooth and flirtatious as possible. "The people love me."

"I can see that," he says, and winks at me.

I let him move a little farther down the aisle before I say, loudly, "I still haven't gotten my rose from you, Mr. Daimler."

He doesn't turn around, but I can see the tips of his ears go red. There are giggles and snorts from the class. I get that rush that comes when you know you're doing something wrong and are getting away with it, like stealing something from the school cafeteria or getting tipsy at a family holiday without anyone knowing.

Lindsay says Mr. Daimler's going to sue me for harassment one day. I don't think so. I think he secretly likes it.

Case in point: when he turns around to face the class, he's smiling.

"After reviewing last week's test results, I realize there's still a lot of confusion about asymptotes and limits," he begins, leaning against his desk and crossing his legs at the ankle. Nobody else could make calculus even remotely interesting, I'm sure of it.

For the rest of the class he barely looks at me, and even then only when I raise my hand. But I swear that when our eyes do meet, it makes my whole body feel like a giant shiver. And I swear he's feeling it too.

After class Kent catches up with me.

"So?" he says. "What did you think?"

"Of what?" I say to irritate him. I know he's talking about the cartoon and the rose.

Kent just smiles and changes the subject. "My parents are away this weekend."

"Good for you."

His smile doesn't waver. "I'm having a party tonight. Are you coming?"

I look at him. I've never understood Kent. Or at least I haven't understood him in years. We were super close when we were little—technically I suppose he was my best friend as well as my first kiss—but as soon as he hit middle school, he started getting weirder and weirder. Since freshman year he's always worn a blazer to school, even though most of the ones he owns are ripped at the seams or have holes in the elbows. He wears the same scuffed-up black-and-white checkered sneakers every day and his hair is so long it's like a curtain that swings down over his eyes every five seconds. But the real deal breaker is this: he actually wears a bowler hat. To school.

The worst thing is that he could be cute. He has the face and the body for it. He has a tiny heart-shaped mole under his left eye, no joke. But he has to screw it up by being such a freak.

"Not sure what my plans are yet," I say. "If that's where everyone ends up . . ." I let my voice trail off so he knows I'll only show if there's nothing better to do.

"It's going to be great," he says, still smiling. Another infuriating thing about Kent: he acts like the world is one big, shiny present he gets to unwrap every morning.

"We'll see," I say. Down the hall I see Rob ducking into the cafeteria and I start walking faster, hoping Kent will get the picture and back off. It's pretty optimistic thinking on my part. Kent has had a crush on me for years. Possibly even since our kiss.

He stops walking entirely, maybe hoping I'll stop too. But I don't. For a second I feel bad, like I was too harsh, but then his voice rings out after me, and I can tell just by the sound of it that he's *still* smiling.

"See you tonight," he says. I hear the squeak of his sneakers on the linoleum, and I know he has turned around and started off in the opposite direction. He starts whistling. The sound of it carries back to me, getting fainter. It takes me a while to place the tune.

The sun'll come out tomorrow, bet your bottom dollar that tomorrow there'll be sun. From *Annie*, the musical. My favorite song—when I was seven.

I know no one else in the hall will get it, but still I'm embarrassed and can feel heat creeping up my neck. He's always

doing things like that: acting like he knows me better than anyone else just because we used to play in the sandbox together a
hundred years ago. Acting like nothing that's happened in the
past ten years has changed anything, even though it's changed
everything.

My phone's buzzing in my back pocket and before I go in to
lunch I snap it open. There's one new text from Lindsay.

Party @ Kent McFreaky's 2nite. In?

I pause for just a second, blowing out a long breath, before
I text back.

Obv.

There are three acceptable things to eat in the Thomas
Jefferson cafeteria:

    1. A bagel, plain or with cream cheese.

    2. French fries.

    3. A deli sandwich from the make-your-own sand-
wich bar.

        a. But only with turkey, ham, or chicken breast.
        Salami and bologna are obvious no-nos, and roast
        beef is questionable. Which is a shame, because
        roast beef is my favorite.

Rob is standing over by the cash register with a group of his
friends. He's holding an enormous tray of fries. He eats them
every day. He catches my eye and gives me a nod. (He's not the
kind of guy who does so well with feelings, his or mine. Thus

the "luv ya" on the note he sent me.)

It's weird. Before we were going out, I liked him so much, and for so long, that every time he even looked in my direction I would get this bubbling, fizzing feeling so strong it would make me dizzy. No lie: sometimes I got light-headed thinking about him and had to sit down.

But now that we're officially a couple, I sometimes have the strangest thoughts when I look at him, like I wonder if all those fries are clogging his arteries or whether he flosses or how long it's been since he washed the Yankees hat he wears pretty much every day. Sometimes I'm worried there's something wrong with me. Who *wouldn't* want to go out with Rob Cokran?

It's not that I'm not totally happy—I am—but it's almost like sometimes I have to keep running over and over in my head why I liked him in the first place, like if I don't I'll somehow forget. Thankfully there are a million good reasons: the fact that he has black hair and a billion freckles but somehow they don't look stupid on him; that he's loud but in a funny way; that everyone knows him and likes him and probably half of the girls in the school have a crush on him; that he looks good in his lacrosse jersey; that when he's really tired he lays his head on my shoulder and falls asleep. That's my favorite thing about him. I like to lie next to him when it's late, dark, and so quiet I can hear my own heartbeat. It's times like that when I'm sure that I'm in love.

I ignore Rob as I get in line to pay for my bagel—I can play hard to get too—and then head for the senior section. The rest of the cafeteria is a rectangle. Special ed kids sit all the way down, at the table closest to the classrooms, and then there are the freshman tables, and then the sophomore tables, and then the junior tables. The senior section is at the very head of the cafeteria. It's an octagon lined completely with windows. Okay, so it only looks out over the parking lot, but it's still better than getting a straight view of the short-bus brigade dribbling their applesauce. No offense.

Ally's already sitting at a small circular table right by the window: our favorite.

"Hey." I put down my tray and my roses. Ally's bouquet is sitting on the table and I do a quick count.

"Nine roses." I gesture to hers and then give my bouquet a rattle. "Same as me."

She makes a face. "One of mine doesn't count. Ethan Shlosky sent one to me. Can you believe it? Stalker."

"Yeah, well, I got one from Kent McFuller, so one of mine doesn't count either."

"He *looves* you," she says, drawing out the *o*. "Did you get Lindsay's text?"

I pick the mushy center out of my bagel and pop it in my mouth. "Are we really going to go to his party?"

Ally snorts. "Afraid he'll date-rape you?"

"Very funny."

"There's gonna be a keg," Ally says. She takes a tiny nibble

35

of her turkey sandwich. "My house after school, okay?" She doesn't really have to ask. It's our tradition on Fridays. We order food, raid her closet, blast music, and dance around swapping eye shadows and lip glosses.

"Yeah, sure."

I've been watching Rob come closer out of the corner of my eye, and suddenly he's there, plopping into a chair next to me and leaning in until his mouth is touching my left ear. He smells like Total cologne. He always does. I think it smells a little like this tea my grandmother used to drink—lemon balm—but I haven't told him that yet.

"Hey, Slammer." He's always making up names for me: Slammer, Samwich, Sammy Says. "Did you get my Valogram?"

"Did you get mine?" I say.

He swings his backpack off his shoulder and unzips it. There are a half dozen crumpled roses in the bottom of his bag—I'm assuming one of them is mine—and besides that, an empty pack of cigarettes, a pack of Trident gum, his cell phone, and a change of shirts. He's not so much into studying.

"Who are the other roses from?" I say, teasing him.

"Your competition," he says, arching his eyebrows.

"Very classy," Ally says. "Are you going to Kent's party tonight, Rob?"

"Probably." Rob shrugs and suddenly looks bored.

Here's a secret: one time when we were kissing, I opened my

eyes and saw that *his* eyes were open. He wasn't even looking at me. He was looking over my shoulder, watching the room.

"He's getting a keg," Ally says for the second time.

Everyone jokes that going to Jefferson prepares you for the total college experience: you learn to work, and you learn to drink. Two years ago the *New York Times* ranked us among the top ten booziest public schools in Connecticut.

It's not like there's anything else to do around here, though. We've got malls and basement parties. That's it. Let's face it: that's how *most* of the country is. My dad always said that they should take down the Statue of Liberty and put up a big strip mall instead, or those golden McDonald's arches. He said at least that way people would know what to expect.

"Ahem. *Excuse me.*"

Lindsay is standing behind Rob, clearing her throat. She has her arms folded and she's tapping her foot.

"You're in my seat, Cokran," she says. She's only pretending to be hard-core. Rob and Lindsay have always been friends. At least, they've always been in the same group, and by necessity have always had to be friends.

"My apologies, Edgecombe." He gets up and makes a big flourish, like a bow, when she sits down.

"See you tonight, Rob," Ally says, and adds, "bring your friends."

"I'll see you later." Rob leans down and buries his face in my hair, making his voice deep and quiet. That voice used to make all of the nerves in my body light up like a firework explosion. Now, sometimes, I think it's cheesy. "Don't forget. It's all about you and me tonight."

"I haven't forgotten," I say, hoping my voice sounds sexy and not scared. My palms are sweating and I pray he doesn't try to take my hand.

Thankfully, he doesn't. Instead he bends down and presses his mouth into mine. We make out for a bit until Lindsay squeals, "Not while I'm eating," and throws a fry in my direction. It hits me on my shoulder.

"Bye, ladies," Rob says, and saunters off with his hat just tilted on an angle.

I wipe my mouth on a napkin when nobody's looking, since the bottom half of my face is now coated with Rob's saliva.

Here's another secret about Rob: I *hate* the way he kisses.

Elody says all my stressing is just insecurity because Rob and I haven't actually sealed the deal yet. Once we do, she's positive I'll feel better, and I'm sure she's right. After all, she's the expert.

Elody is the last to join us at lunch, and we all make a grab for her fries when she sets down her tray. She makes a half-hearted attempt to swat our hands away.

She slaps her bouquet of roses down next. She has twelve, and I feel a momentary twinge of jealousy.

I guess Ally feels it too because she says, "What did you have to do for those?"

"*Who* did you have to do?" Lindsay corrects her.

Elody sticks her tongue out but seems pleased that we noticed.

All of a sudden, Ally looks at something over my shoulder and starts giggling. *"Psycho killer, qu'est-ce que c'est."*

We all turn around. Juliet Sykes, or Psycho, has just drifted into the senior section. That's how she walks: like she's drifting, being blown around by forces outside of her control. She's carrying a brown paper bag in her long pale fingers. Her face is shielded behind a curtain of pale blond hair, shoulders hunched up around her ears.

For the most part, everyone in the cafeteria ignores her—she's the definition of forgettable—but Lindsay, Ally, Elody, and I start making that screeching and stabbing motion from Alfred Hitchcock's *Psycho*, which we all watched at a sleepover a couple of years ago. (Afterward we had to sleep with the lights on.)

I'm not sure if Juliet hears us. Lindsay always says she can't hear at all because the voices in her head are too loud. Juliet keeps up that same slow pace across the room, eventually reaching the door that leads out into the parking lot. I'm not sure where she eats every day. I hardly ever see her in the cafeteria.

She has to shove her shoulder against the door a few times before it will open, like she's too frail to make it work.

"Did she get our Valogram?" Lindsay says, licking salt off a fry before popping it in her mouth.

Ally nods. "In bio. I was sitting right behind her."

"Did she say anything?"

"Does she *ever* say anything?" Ally puts one hand across her heart, pretending to be upset. "She threw the rose out as soon as class was over. Can you believe it? Right in front of me."

Freshman year Lindsay somehow found out that Juliet hadn't been sent a single Valogram. Not one. So Lindsay put a note on one of her roses and duct-taped it on Juliet's locker. The note said: *Maybe next year, but probably not.*

Every year since then we've sent her a rose and the same note on Cupid Day. The only note she's ever received from anyone, as far as I know. *Maybe next year, but probably not.*

Normally I would feel bad, but Juliet deserves her nickname. She's a freak. Rumor has it that she was once found by her parents on Route 84, stark naked at three A.M., straddling the highway divider. Last year Lacey Kennedy said she saw Juliet in the bathroom by the science wing, stroking her hair over and over and staring at her reflection. And Juliet never says a word. Hasn't for years, as far as I know.

Lindsay hates her. I think Lindsay and Juliet were in a couple of the same elementary school classes, and for all I know Lindsay has hated her since then. She makes the sign of the cross whenever Juliet's around, like Juliet might somehow go vampire and make a lunge for Lindsay's throat.

It was Lindsay who found out Juliet peed her sleeping bag

during a Girl Scout camping trip in fifth grade, and Lindsay who gave her the nickname Mellow Yellow. People called Juliet that forever—until the end of freshman year, if you can believe it—and stayed away from her because they said she smelled like pee.

I'm looking out the window and I watch Juliet's hair flash in the sunlight like it's catching fire. There's darkness on the horizon, a smudge where the storm is growing. It occurs to me for the first time that I'm not exactly sure why Lindsay started hating Juliet in the first place, or when. I open my mouth to ask her, but they've already moved on to other topics.

"—catfight," Elody finishes, and Ally giggles.

"I'm terrified," Lindsay says sarcastically. Clearly I've missed something.

"What's going on?" I say.

Elody turns to me. "Sarah Grundel is going around saying Lindsay ruined her life." I have to wait while Elody folds a fry expertly into her mouth. "She can't swim in the quarter finals. And you know she lives for that shit. Remember when she forgot to take her goggles off after morning practice and she wore them until second period?"

"She probably keeps all of her blue ribbons on a wall in her room," Ally says.

"Sam used to do that. Didn't you, Sam? All those ribbons for playing with horsies." Lindsay elbows me.

41

"Can we get back to the point?" I wave my hands, partly because I want to hear the story, partly to take the attention off me and the fact that I used to be a dork. When I was in fifth grade, I spent more time with horses than with members of my own species. "I still don't get why Sarah's pissed at Lindsay."

Elody rolls her eyes at me like I belong at the special ed table. "Sarah got detention—she was late to homeroom for, like, the fifth time in two weeks." I'm still not getting it and she heaves a sigh. "She was late to homeroom because she had to park in Upper Lot and haul ass—"

".22 miles!"

We all bust it out at the same time and then start giggling like maniacs.

"Don't worry, Lindz," I say. "If you guys throw down I'm totally putting money on you."

"Yeah, we've got your back," Elody says.

"Isn't it kind of weird how that stuff happens?" Ally says in this shy voice she gets when she's trying to say something serious. "How everything spirals out from everything else? Like, if Lindsay hadn't stolen that parking space . . ."

"I didn't steal it. I got it fair and square," Lindsay protests, bringing her hand down on the table for emphasis. Elody's Diet Coke sloshes over the side of the can, soaking some fries. This makes us start laughing again.

"I'm serious!" Ally raises her voice to be heard over us. "It's like a web, you know? Everything's connected."

"Have you been breaking into your dad's stash again, Al?" Elody says.

This is all it takes to really get us going. This is a joke we've had with Ally for years because her dad works in the music industry. He's a lawyer, not a producer or manager or musician or anything, and he wears a suit everywhere (even to the pool in the summer), but Lindsay claims he's secretly a hippie stoner.

As we're laughing, doubling over, Ally turns pink. "You guys never listen to me," she says, but she's fighting a smile. She takes a fry and throws it at Elody. "I read once that if a bunch of butterflies takes off from Thailand, it can cause a rainstorm in New York."

"Yeah, well, one of your farts could cause a massive blackout in Portugal." Elody giggles, throwing a fry back.

"Your morning breath could cause a stampede in Africa." Ally leans forward. "And I do *not* fart."

Lindsay and I are laughing, and Elody and Ally keep throwing fries back and forth. Lindsay tries to say they're wasting perfectly good grease, but she's snorting so hard she can barely get the words out.

Finally she sucks in a deep breath and chokes out, "You know what I heard? That if you sneeze enough you can cause a tornado in Iowa."

Even Ally goes crazy at this, and suddenly we're all

trying it, laughing and sneezing and snorting at the same time. Everybody's staring at us, but we don't care.

After about a million sneezes, Lindsay leans back in her chair, clutching her stomach and gasping for breath.

"Thirty dead in Iowa tornadoes," she gets out, "another fifty missing."

This sets us off again.

Lindsay and I decide to cut seventh period and go to TCBY. Lindsay has French, which she can't stand, and I have English. We cut seventh period a lot together. We're second-semester seniors, so it's like we're expected *not* to go to class. Plus I hate my English teacher, Mrs. Harbor. She's always going off on tangents. Sometimes I'll zone out for a few minutes, and all of a sudden she'll be talking about underwear in the eighteenth century or oppression in Africa or the way the sun looks rising over the Grand Canyon. Even though she's probably only in her fifties, I'm pretty sure she's losing it. That's how it started with my grandmother: ideas swirling around and colliding with each other, causes coming after effects, and point A switched with point B. When my grandmother was still alive we would visit her, and even though I was no more than six, I remember thinking: *I hope I die young.*

There's a definition of irony for you, Mrs. Harbor.
Or maybe foreshadowing?

• • •

Technically you need a special pass signed by your parents and the administration to leave campus during the school day. This wasn't always true. For a long time one of the perks to being a senior was getting to leave campus whenever you wanted, as long as you had a free period. That was twenty years ago, though, a few years before Thomas Jefferson got the reputation for one of the highest teen suicide rates in the country. We looked up the article online once: the *Connecticut Post* called us Suicide High.

And then one day a bunch of kids left campus and drove off a bridge—a suicide pact, I guess. Anyway, after that the school forbade anyone from leaving school during the day without special permission. It's kind of stupid if you think about it. That's like finding out that kids are bringing vodka to school in water bottles and forbidding anyone to drink water.

Fortunately, there's another way to get off campus: through a hole in the fence beyond the gym by the tennis court, which we call the Smokers' Lounge, since that's where all the smokers hang out. No one's around, though, when Lindsay and I slip through the fence and get started across the woods. In a little while we'll come on to Route 120. Everything is still and frozen. Twigs and black leaves crack under our shoes, and our breath rises in solid white puffs.

Thomas Jefferson is about three miles outside of downtown Ridgeview—or what you can call the downtown—but only about a half mile from a small strip of dingy stores we've named the Row. There's a gas station, a TCBY, a Chinese restaurant that once made Elody sick for two days, and a random Hallmark store where you can buy pink glittery ballerina figurines and snow globes and crap like that. That's where we head. I know we must look like total freaks, stomping along the road in our skirts and tights, our jackets flapping open to show off our fur-trimmed tank tops.

We pass Hunan Kitchen on our way to TCBY. Through the grime-coated windows we spot Alex Liment and Anna Cartullo bent over a bowl of something.

"Ooo, scandal," Lindsay says, raising her eyebrows, although it's really only a half scandal. Everyone knows that Alex has been cheating on Bridget McGuire with Anna for the past three months. Everyone except Bridget, obviously.

Bridget's family is super-Catholic. She's pretty and really clean-looking, like every time you see her she's just scrubbed her face really hard. Apparently she's saving herself for marriage. That's what she says, anyway, although Elody thinks Bridget might be a closet lesbo. Anna Cartullo is only a junior, but if the rumors are true she's already had sex with at least four people. She's one of the few kids in Ridgeview who doesn't come from any money. Her mom's a hairdresser, and I don't even know if she has a dad. She lives in one of the shitty rental condos right off the Row. I once heard Andrew Singer saying her bedroom always smelled like General Tso's chicken.

"Let's go in and say hi," Lindsay says, reaching for my hand.

I hang back. "I'm going through sugar withdrawal."

"Here. Take these." She pulls a pack of SweeTarts from the waistband of her skirt. Lindsay always carries candy on her, 24/7, like she's packing drugs. I guess she kind of is. "Just for a second, I promise."

I let myself be dragged inside. A bell tinkles as we come through the door. There's a woman flipping through *Us Weekly* behind the counter. She looks at us, then looks down again when she realizes we're not going to order.

Lindsay slides right up to Alex and Anna's booth, leaning against the table. She's kinda, sorta friends with Alex. Alex is kinda, sorta friends with a lot of people, since he deals pot out of a shoe box in his bedroom. He and I have a head-nod friendship, since that's pretty much the limit of our interaction. He's actually in English with me, though he shows even less than I do. I guess the rest of the time he's with Anna. Every so often he'll say something like, "That essay assignment blows, huh?" but other than that we don't talk.

"Hey, hey," Lindsay says. "You going to Kent's party tonight?"

Alex's face is red and splotchy. At least he's embarrassed to be caught out with Anna so blatantly. Or maybe he's just having a reaction to the food. I wouldn't be surprised.

"Um . . . I don't know. Maybe. Gotta see. . . ." He trails off.

"It's gonna be super fun." Lindsay makes her voice extra

perky. "Are you going to bring Bridget? She's *such* a sweetheart."

Actually, we both think Bridget is annoying—she's always really cheerful and she wears T-shirts with lame slogans like *Unless You're the Lead Dog the View Never Changes* (no lie)—but Lindsay despises Anna and once wrote *AC=WT* all over the bathroom right across from the cafeteria—the one everyone uses. *WT* stands for white trash.

The situation is beyond awkward, so I blurt out, "Sesame chicken?" I point at the meat congealing in a grayish sauce in a bowl on the table, next to two fortune cookies and a sad-looking orange.

"Orange beef," Alex says. He seems relieved by the change of topic.

Lindsay gives me a look, annoyed, but I keep rattling on. "You should be careful about eating here. The chicken once poisoned Elody. She threw up for, like, two days straight. If it *was* chicken. She swears she found a fur ball in it."

As soon as I say this Anna picks up her chopsticks and takes an enormous bite, looking up and smiling at me as she chews so I can see the food in her mouth. I'm not sure whether she's doing it deliberately to gross me out, but it seems like it.

"That's nasty, Kingston," Alex says, but he's smiling now.

Lindsay rolls her eyes, like Alex and Anna are both a total waste of our time. "Come on, Sam."

She pockets a fortune cookie and breaks it open when we

get outside. *"Happiness is found when one is not looking,"* she reads, and I crack up when she makes a face. She balls up the little slip of paper and lets it flutter to the ground. "Useless."

I take a deep breath. "The smell in there always makes me sick." It does, too: that smell of old meat and cheap oil and garlic. The clouds on the horizon are slowly taking over the sky, turning everything gray and blurry.

"Tell me about it." Lindsay puts a hand on her stomach. "You know what I need?"

"A jumbo cup of The Country's Best Yogurt!" I say, smiling. TCBY is another thing we can't bring ourselves to abbreviate.

"Definitely a jumbo cup of The Country's Best Yogurt," Lindsay echoes.

Even though we're both freezing, we order double-chocolate soft-serve with sprinkles and crushed peanut butter cups on top, which we eat on our way back to school, blowing on our fingers to keep them warm. Alex and Anna are gone from Hunan Kitchen when we pass, but we run into them again at the Smokers' Lounge. We have exactly seven minutes left until the bell for eighth period, and Lindsay pulls me behind the tennis courts so she can have a cigarette without listening to Alex and Anna argue. That's what it looks like they're doing, anyway. Anna's head is bent and Alex is grabbing her shoulders, whispering to her. The cigarette in his hand burns so close to her dull brown hair I'm positive it's going to catch fire, and I picture her whole head just going up like that, like a match.

Lindsay finishes her smoke and we dump our yogurt cups right there, on top of the frozen black leaves and trampled cigarette packs and plastic bags half filled with rainwater. I'm feeling anxious about tonight—half dread and half excitement—like when you hear thunder and know that any second you'll see lightning tearing across the sky, nipping at the clouds with its teeth. I shouldn't have skipped out on English. It has given me too much time to think. And thinking never did anybody any good, no matter what your teachers and parents and the science-club freaks tell you.

We skirt the perimeter of the tennis courts and go up along Senior Alley. Alex and Anna are still standing half concealed behind the gym. Alex is on his second cigarette at least. Definitely an argument. I feel a momentary rush of satisfaction: Rob and I hardly ever fight, at least not about anything serious. That must mean something.

"Trouble in paradise," I say.

"More like trouble in the trailer park," Lindsay says.

We start cutting across the teachers' lot when we see Ms. Winters, the vice principal, threading between cars, trying to rout out the smokers who don't have time or are too lazy to walk all the way down to the Lounge and instead try to hide out between the teachers' old Volvos and Chevrolets. Ms. Winters has some crazy vendetta against people who smoke. I heard that her mom died of lung cancer or emphysema or something. If you get caught smoking by Ms. Winters you get three Friday detentions, no questions asked.

Lindsay frantically rifles in her bag for her Trident and pops two pieces in her mouth. "Shit, shit."

"You can't get busted just for smelling like smoke," I say, even though Lindsay knows this. She likes the drama, though. Funny how you can know your friends so well, but you still end up playing the same games with them.

She ignores me. "How's my breath?" She breathes on me.

"Like a friggin' menthol factory."

Ms. Winters hasn't spotted us yet. She's making her way down the rows, sometimes stooping to peer underneath the cars as though someone might be sandwiched against the ground, trying to light up. There's a reason everyone calls her the Nicotine Nazi behind her back.

I hesitate, looking back toward the gym. I don't especially like Alex and I don't like Anna, but anyone who's ever been through high school understands you have to stick together against parents, teachers, and cops. It's one of those invisible lines: us against them. You just know this, like you know where to sit and who to talk to and what to eat in the cafeteria, without even knowing *how* you know. If that makes sense.

"Should we go back and warn them?" I ask Lindsay, and she pauses too and squints at the sky like she's thinking about it.

"Screw it," she says finally. "They can take care of themselves." As if to reinforce her point, the bell for final period rings and she gives me a shove. "Come on."

She's right, as usual. After all, it's not like they've ever done anything for me.

FRIENDSHIP: A HISTORY

Lindsay and I became friends in seventh grade. Lindsay picked me out. I'm still not sure why. After years of trying, I had only just clawed my way up from the social bottom to the social middle. Lindsay's been popular since first grade, when she moved here. In the class circus that year she was the ringleader; when we did a production of *The Wizard of Oz* the next year she was Dorothy. And in third grade, when we all performed *Charlie and the Chocolate Factory*, she got to play Charlie.

I think that pretty much gives you an idea. She's the kind of person who makes you feel drunk just by being around her, like suddenly the world's edges are dulled and all of the colors are spinning together. I've never told her that, obviously. She'd make fun of me for lezzing out on her.

Anyway, the summer before seventh grade a bunch of us were at Tara Flute's pool party. Beth Schiff was showing off by doing cannonballs in the deep end, but really she was showing off the fact that between May and July she'd sprouted a pair of C-cup boobs—definitely the biggest of any girl there. I was in the house getting a soda when all of a sudden Lindsay came up to me, eyes shining. She'd never spoken to me before.

"You've *got* to come see this," she said, grabbing my arm.

Her breath smelled like ice cream.

She pulled me into Tara's room, where all the girls had piled their bags and their changes of clothes. Beth's bag was pink and had her initials marked in purple embroidery on the side. Lindsay had obviously gone through it, because she immediately crouched down and reached for a clear zipper case, like the kind we had to store pens in when we were in grade school.

"Look!" She held it up, rattling it. Inside were two tampons.

I don't remember how it started, but suddenly Lindsay and I were running through the house, checking bathroom cabinets and drawers, gathering up all the tampons and pads that Tara's mother and older sister had in the house. I was so happy I was dizzy. Lindsay Edgecombe and I were *talking*, and not just talking but laughing, and not just laughing but laughing so hard I had to squeeze my legs together to keep from peeing. Then we ran out onto the deck and started throwing handful after handful of tampons down onto the pool party below. Lindsay was screaming, "Beth! These fell out of your bag!" Some of the tampons swirled down into the water and all the guys were suddenly pushing and shoving to get out of the pool like they were going to be contaminated. Beth stood on the diving board, dripping wet and shaking, while the rest of us nearly died laughing.

It reminded me of the time my parents took me to the Grand Canyon in fourth grade and made me stand on a ledge to get photographed. My legs hadn't been able to stop shaking and my feet got a tingling feeling in the soles, like they were itching to jump: I couldn't stop thinking about how easy it would be to fall, how high up we were. After my mom took the picture and let me back away from the ledge, I started laughing and couldn't stop.

Standing on the deck with Lindsay I got that exact same feeling.

After that Lindsay and I were best friends. Ally came in later, after she and Lindsay were in a field hockey league together the summer before eighth grade. Elody moved to Ridgeview freshman year. At one of the first parties of the year she hooked up with Sean Morton, who Lindsay had had a crush on for six months. Everyone thought Lindsay would kill Elody. But the next Monday at school Elody was at our lunch table, and she and Lindsay were bent over a plate of curly fries, giggling and acting like they'd known each other forever. I'm glad. Even though Elody can sometimes be embarrassing, I think deep down she's the nicest of any of us.

THE PARTY

After school we go to Ally's. When we were younger—freshman year and even half of sophomore year—we'd sometimes stay in and put on clay masks and order as much Chinese food as we could eat, taking twenties from the cookie jar on the third shelf next to Ally's refrigerator, where her dad keeps an emergency thousand dollars at all times. We called them our "egg-roll emergency" nights. Then we'd stretch out on her enormous couch and watch movies until we fell asleep—the TV in Ally's living room is as big as the screen in a movie theater—our legs tangled together under an enormous fleece blanket. Since junior year, though, I don't think we've stayed in even once, except when Matt Wilde broke up with Ally, and she cried so hard that the next morning her face was puffy, like a mole's.

Today we raid Ally's closet so we don't have to wear the same outfit to Kent's party. Elody, Ally, and Lindsay are paying special attention to how I look. Elody puts bright red polish on my nails, her hands shaking a little so some of it gets on my cuticles and makes it look like I'm bleeding, but I'm too nervous to care. Rob and I are going to meet up at Kent's and he's already sent me a text that says *I evn made my bed 4 u*. I let Ally pick out my outfit—a metallic gold tank top, too big in the chest, and a pair of Ally's crazy four-inch heels (she calls them her stripper shoes). Lindsay does my makeup, humming and breathing vodka onto me. We've all taken two shots, chasing them with cranberry juice.

Afterward I lock myself in the bathroom, warmth tingling from my fingertips up to my head, and try to memorize exactly how I look there, in that second. But after a while all of my features seem like they're just hanging there, like something I'm seeing on a stranger.

When I was little I used to do this a lot: lock myself in the bathroom and take showers so hot the mirrors would cloud completely over, then stand there, watching as my face took shape slowly behind the steam, rough outlines at first, then details appearing gradually. Each time I'd think that when my face came back I would see somebody beautiful, like during my shower I would have transformed into someone brighter and better. But I always looked the same.

Standing in Ally's bathroom, I smile and think, *Tomorrow I'll finally be different.*

Lindsay's kind of music-obsessed, so she makes us a playlist for the ride to Kent's house, even though he lives only a few miles away. We listen to Dr. Dre and Tupac, and then we blast "Baby Got Back" and all sing along.

It's the weirdest thing, though: as we're driving there along all those familiar streets—streets I've known my whole life, streets so familiar I might as well have imagined them myself—I get this feeling like I'm floating above everything, hovering above all of the houses and the roads and the yards and the trees, going up, up, up, above Rocky's and the Rite Aid and the gas station and Thomas Jefferson and the football field and the metal bleachers where we sit and scream our heads off every homecoming. Like everything is tiny and insignificant. Like I'm already only remembering it.

Elody's howling at the top of her lungs. She has the lowest tolerance out of all of us. Ally's got the rest of the vodka tucked into her bag but nothing to chase it with. Lindsay's driving because she can drink all night and hardly feel it.

The rain starts when we're almost there, but it's so light it's almost like it's just hanging in the air, like a big curtain of white vapor. I don't remember the last time I was at Kent's house—his ninth birthday party, maybe?—and I've forgotten how far it's set back in the woods. The driveway seems to snake on forever. All we see is the dull light from the headlights bouncing off a twisting, gravelly path and revealing dead tree branches crowding closely overhead, and tiny pellets of rain like diamonds.

"This is how horror movies start," Ally says, adjusting her tank top. We've all borrowed new tops from her, but she's insisted on keeping on the fur-trimmed one, even though she was the one who was initially against it. "Are you *sure* he's number forty-two?"

"It's just a little farther," I say, even though I have no idea, and I'm starting to wonder whether we turned too early. I have butterflies in my stomach, but I'm not sure whether they're good or bad.

The woods press closer and closer until they're nearly brushing up against the car doors. Lindsay starts complaining about the paint job. Just when it seems like we'll be sucked up into the darkness, all of a sudden the woods stop completely and there's the biggest, most beautiful lawn you can imagine, with a white house at its center that looks like it's made out of frosting. It's got balconies and a long porch that runs along two sides. The shutters are white too, and carved with designs it's too dark to make out. I don't remember any of it. Maybe it's the alcohol, but I think it's the most beautiful house I've ever seen.

We're all silent for a minute, looking. Half the house is dark, but warm light is shining from the top floor, and where it makes it to the lawn it turns the grass silver.

Lindsay says, "It's almost as big as your house, Al." I'm sorry she spoke: it feels like a spell has been broken.

"Almost," Ally says. She takes the vodka out of her bag and swigs it, coughs, burps, and wipes her mouth.

"Give me a shot of that," Elody says, reaching for the bottle.

The bottle's in my hand before I realize it. I take a sip. It burns my throat and tastes awful, like paint or gasoline, but as soon as it's down I get a rush. We climb out of the car and the light from the house surges and expands, winking at me.

Walking into parties always gives me a crampy feeling at the bottom of my stomach. It's a good feeling, though: the feeling of knowing anything can happen. Most of the time nothing does, of course. Most of the time one night blends into the next, and weeks blend into weeks, and months into other months. And sooner or later we all die.

But at the beginning of the night anything's possible.

The front door is locked and we have to go around the side, where a door opens onto a really narrow hallway all paneled in wood and a tiny flight of steep wooden stairs. It smells like something I remember from childhood, but I can't quite place it. I hear the tinkle of breaking glass and someone yells, "Fire in the hole!" Then Dujeous roars from the speakers: *All MCs in the house tonight, if your lyrics sound tight then rock the mic.* The stairs are so narrow we have to squeeze up in single file because people are coming down in the opposite direction, empty beer cups in hand. Most of them have to turn so their backs are against the wall. We say hi to a few people and ignore the rest. As usual I can feel all of them looking at us. That's another nice thing about being popular: you don't have to pay any attention to the people paying attention to you.

At the top of the stairs a dim hallway is hung all over with multicolored Christmas lights. There are a series of rooms, each leading off the next, and all seem to be filled with draped fabrics and big pillows and couches and all are packed with people. Everything is soft—the colors, the surfaces, the way people look—except the music, which pumps through the walls, making the floor vibrate. People are smoking inside too, so everything's happening behind a thick blue veil. I've only smoked pot once, but this is what I imagine it's like to be stoned.

Lindsay leans back and says something to me, but it gets lost in the murmur of voices. Then she's moving away from me, weaving through the crowd. I turn around, but Elody and Ally are gone too, and before I know it my heart is pounding and I get this itchy feeling in my palms.

59

Recently I've been having this nightmare where I'm standing in the middle of an enormous crowd, being pushed from left to right. The faces look familiar, but there's something horribly wrong with all of them: someone will walk by who looks like Lindsay, but then her mouth is weird and droopy like it's melting off. And none of them recognize me.

Obviously standing in Kent's house isn't the same thing, since I pretty much know everybody except for some of the juniors and a couple of girls who I *think* might be sophomores. But still, it's enough to make me freak out a little.

I'm about to head over to Emma Howser—she's super cheesy and normally I wouldn't be caught dead talking to her, but I'm getting desperate—when I feel thick arms around me and smell lemon balm. Rob.

He puts a wet mouth against my ear. "Sexy Sammy. Where've you been all my life?"

I turn around. His face is bright red. "You're drunk," I say, and it comes out more accusatory than I meant it to.

"Sober enough," he says, trying and failing to raise one eyebrow. "And you're late." His grin is lazy. Only one half of it curves upward. "We did a keg stand."

"It's ten o'clock," I point out. "We're not late. I called you, anyway."

He pats his fleece and his pockets. "Must've put my phone down somewhere."

I roll my eyes. "You're a delinquent."

"I like it when you use those big words." The other half of his smile is creeping upward slowly and I know he's going to kiss me. I turn partly away, searching the room for my friends, but they're still MIA.

In the corner I spot Kent, wearing a tie and a collared shirt about three sizes too big for him, which is half tucked into a pair of ratty khakis. At least he's not wearing his bowler hat. He's talking to Phoebe Rifer and they're laughing about something. It annoys me that he hasn't noticed me yet. I'm kind of hoping he'll look up and come barreling over to me like he usually does, but he just bends closer toward Phoebe like he's trying to hear her better.

Rob pulls me into him. "We'll only stay for an hour, okay? Then we'll leave." His breath smells like beer and a little like cigarettes when he kisses me. I close my eyes and think about how in sixth grade I saw him kissing Gabby Haynes and was so jealous I couldn't eat for two days. I wonder if I look like I'm enjoying it. Gabby did, in sixth grade.

It relaxes me to think about things like that: how funny life is.

I haven't even taken off my jacket, but Rob unzips it and moves his hands along my waist and then under my tank top. His palms are sweaty and big.

I pull away long enough to say, "Not right *here*, in the middle of everyone."

"Nobody's watching," he says, and clamps down on me again.

This is a lie. He knows everyone watches us. He can see it. He doesn't even close his eyes.

His hands inch over my stomach and his fingers are pulling at the underwire of my bra. He's not very good with bras. He's not that good with breasts in general, actually. I mean, it's not like I really know what it's supposed to feel like, but every time he touches my boobs he kind of just massages them hard in a circle. My gyno does the same thing when I go in for an exam, so one of them has to be doing it wrong. And to be honest, I don't think it's my gyno.

If you want to know my biggest secret, here it is: I know you're supposed to wait to have sex with someone you love and all that, and I *do* love Rob—I mean, I've kind of been in love with him forever, so how could I not?—but that's not why I decided to have sex with him tonight.

I decided to have sex with him because I want to get it over with, and because sex has always scared me and I don't want to be scared of it anymore.

"I can't wait to wake up next to you," Rob says, his mouth against my ear.

It's a sweet thing to say, but I can't concentrate while his hands are on me. And it occurs to me all of a sudden that I'd never thought about the waking-up part. I have no idea what you're supposed to talk about the day after you've had sex, and I imagine us lying side by side, not touching, silent, while the sun rises. Rob doesn't have any blinds in his room—he ripped them down once when he was drunk—and during the day it's like a spotlight has been turned on his bed, a spotlight or an eye.

"Get a room!"

I pull away from Rob as Ally appears next to me, making a face. "You two are perverts," she says.

"This is a room." Rob lifts both arms and gestures around him. He sloshes a little bit of beer onto my shirt, and I make a noise, annoyed.

"Sorry, babe." He shrugs. Now there's only a half inch of beer in his cup and he stares at it, frowning. "Gonna go for a topper. You guys want?"

"We brought our own." Ally pats the vodka in her purse.

"Smart thinking." Rob brings a finger up to tap the side of his head but nearly takes an eye out instead. He's drunker than I thought. Ally covers her mouth and giggles.

"My boyfriend's an idiot," I say as soon as he lurches away.

"A *cute* idiot," Ally corrects me.

"That's like saying 'a cute mutant.' Doesn't exist."

"Sure it does." Ally's looking around the room, pouting her lips to make them look more kissable.

"Where did you go, anyway?" I'm feeling more annoyed than I should by everything: by the fact that my friends ditched me after thirty whole seconds, by the fact that Rob's so drunk, by the fact that Kent's still talking to Phoebe Rifer, even though he's supposed to be obsessively in love with me. Not that I *want* him to be in love with me, obviously. It's just a constant that's always been comforting, in a weird way. I wrestle the bottle out of Ally's bag and take another sip.

"We made a round. There's, like, seventeen different rooms up here. You should check it out." Ally looks at me, notices the face I'm pulling, and holds up her hands. "What? It's not like we abandoned you in the middle of nowhere."

She's right. I don't know why I'm feeling so pissy. "Where did Lindsay and Elody go?"

"Elody's suctioned to Muffin's lap. And Lindsay and Patrick are fighting."

"Already?"

"Yeah, well, they kissed for the first three minutes. They waited until minute four to start going at it."

This cracks me up and Ally and I laugh over it. I start to feel better, more comfortable. The vodka fills my head with warmth. More people are arriving all the time and the room seems to be revolving just a little bit. It's a nice feeling, though, like being on a really slow carousel. Ally and I decide to go on a mission to save Lindsay before her fight with Patrick turns into an all-out brawl.

It seems like the whole school has shown up, but really there are only sixty or seventy kids. This is the most that ever shows up at a party. There's the top and middle of the senior class, popularity-wise—Kent's just holding on to the lower rung of the ladder, but he's hosting so it's okay—some of the cooler juniors, and a couple of really cool sophomores. I know I'm supposed to hate them, like we were hated when we were sophomores at all the senior parties, but I can't bring myself to care. Ally gives a group of them one of her ice stares as we go by, though, and says "Skanks" loudly. One of them, Rachel Kornish, supposedly hooked up with Matt Wilde not long ago.

Obviously no freshmen are allowed in. The social bottom doesn't show either. It isn't because people would make fun of them, although they probably would. It's more than that. They don't hear about these parties until after they've happened. They don't know the things we know: they don't know about the secret side entrance to Andrew Roberts's guesthouse, or the fact that Carly Jablonski stashed a cooler in her garage where you can keep your beers cold, or the fact that Rocky's doesn't check IDs very closely, or the fact that Mic's stays open around the clock and makes the best egg and cheeses in the world, absolutely dripping with oil and ketchup, perfect for when you're drunk. It's like high school holds two different worlds, revolving around each other and never touching: the haves and the have-nots. I guess it's a good thing. High school is supposed to prepare you for the real world, after all.

There are so many tiny hallways and rooms, it feels like a maze. All of them are filled with people and smoke. Only one door is closed. It has a big KEEP OUT sign plastered on it over a bunch of weird bumper stickers that say things like VISUALIZE

WHIRLED PEAS and KISS ME. I'M IRISH.

By the time we get to Lindsay, she and Patrick have made up, big surprise. She's sitting on his lap and he's smoking a joint. Elody and Steve Dough are in a corner. He's leaning against the wall and she's half dancing and half grinding against him. She has an unlit cigarette dangling from her lips, butt end out, and her hair is a mess. Steve is steadying her, using one arm to keep her on her feet, but he's having a conversation with Liz Hummer (her real name—and, coincidentally, her car) like Elody isn't even there, much less rubbing on him.

"Poor Elody," I say. I don't know why I suddenly feel bad for her. "She's too nice."

"She's a whore," Ally says, but not meanly.

"Do you think we'll remember any of this?" I'm not sure where the words come from. My whole head feels light and fuzzy, ready to float away. "Do you think we'll remember any of it two years from now?"

"I won't even remember tomorrow." Ally laughs, tapping the bottle in my hand. There's only a quarter of it left. I can't think when we drank it all.

Lindsay squeals when she sees us and stumbles off Patrick's lap, throwing an arm around each of us like it's been years since we were together. She snatches the vodka from me and takes a sip while her arm is still wrapped around my shoulders, her elbow tightening momentarily against my neck.

"Where did you go?" she yells. Her voice is loud, even over the music and the sound of everybody talking and laughing. "I was looking everywhere for you."

"Bullshit," I say, and Ally says, "In Patrick's mouth, maybe."

We're laughing over the fact that Lindsay's a bullshitter and Elody's a drunk and Ally's OCD and I'm antisocial, and someone cracks a window to let out the smoke, and a fine mist of rain comes in, smelling like grass and fresh things, even though it's the dead middle of winter. Without anyone noticing I reach my hand back and rest it on the sill, enjoying the freezing air and the sensation of a hundred pinpricks of rain. I close my eyes and promise myself I'll never forget this moment: the sound of my friends' laughter and the heat from so many bodies and the smell of rain.

When I open my eyes I get the shock of my life. Juliet Sykes is standing in the doorway, staring at me.

She's staring at us, actually: Lindsay, Ally, and Elody, who has just left Steve and come over to stand with us, and me. Juliet's hair is pulled back in a ponytail, and I think it's the first time I've ever really seen her face.

It's shocking that she's there, but it's even more shocking that she's pretty. She has blue eyes set wide apart and high cheekbones, like a model's. Her skin is perfectly clear and white. I can't stop staring at her.

People are elbowing and pushing her because she's blocking the doorway, but she just stands there, staring.

Ally catches on first and her mouth drops open. "What the . . . ?"

Elody and Lindsay turn to see what we're both staring at. Lindsay goes pale at first—she actually looks afraid, which is beyond strange, but I don't have time to wonder about it because just as quickly her face goes purple, and she looks ready to rip someone's head off. That's a more natural look for her. Elody begins giggling hysterically until she doubles over and has to cover her mouth with both hands.

"I can't believe it," she says. "I can't believe it." She tries to start singing *"Psycho killer, qu'est-ce que c'est,"* but we're all still in shock and don't join in.

You know how in movies someone says or does something inappropriate and the record scratches and there's dead silence all of a sudden? Well, that isn't exactly what happens, but it's close. The music doesn't stop, but as everyone in the room starts to pick up on the fact that Juliet Sykes—bedwetter, freak, and all-around psycho—is standing in the middle of a party giving four of the most popular girls at Thomas Jefferson the stink eye, conversation drops off and a low sound of whispering fills the room, getting louder and more insistent until it's a constant hum, until it sounds like wind or the ocean.

Juliet Sykes finally steps away from the door and into the room. She walks slowly and confidently toward us—I've never seen her look so calm—stopping three feet in front of Lindsay.

"You're a bitch," she says. Her voice is steady and too loud, like she's deliberately addressing everyone in the room. I'd always imagined her voice would be high-pitched or breathy, but it's as full and deep as a boy's.

It takes Lindsay a half second to find her voice. "Excuse me?" she croaks out. Juliet hasn't made eye contact with Lindsay since the fifth grade, much less spoken to her. Much less *insulted* her.

"You heard me. A bitch. A mean girl. A bad person." Juliet turns to Ally next. "You're a bitch too." To Elody, "You're a bitch." She turns her eyes to me and for a second I see something flashing there—something familiar—but just as quickly it's gone.

"You're a bitch."

We're all so shocked we don't know how to respond. Elody giggles again nervously, hiccups, and goes silent. Lindsay's mouth is opening and shutting like a fish's, but nothing's coming out. Ally's balling up her fists like she's thinking of clocking Juliet in the face.

And even though I'm infuriated and embarrassed, the only thing I can think when I look at Juliet is: *I never knew you were so pretty.*

Lindsay pulls herself together. She leans forward so her face is only inches from Juliet's. I've never seen her so angry. I think her eyes are going to pop out of her head. Her mouth is twisted into a snarl, like a dog's. For a second she looks really and truly ugly.

"I'd rather be a bitch than a psycho," she hisses, grabbing Juliet by the shirt. Spit is coming out of her mouth—that's how angry she is. She shoves Juliet backward, and Juliet stumbles into Matt Dorfman. He pushes Juliet again and she careens into Emma McElroy. Lindsay starts screaming, "Psycho, Psycho," and making the high-pitched knifing noises from the movie, and suddenly everyone's screaming out, "Psycho!" and making the motion of an invisible knife and screeching and pushing Juliet back and forth. Ally's the first to overturn a beer on her head, but everyone catches on to that too; Lindsay splashes her with vodka, and when Juliet stumbles my way, half drenched, arms outstretched, trying to get her balance, I grab a half-finished beer from the windowsill and dump it on her. I don't even realize I'm screaming along with everybody else until my throat is sore.

Juliet looks up at me after I dump the beer out. I can't explain it—it's crazy—but it's almost a pitying look, like *she* feels bad for *me*.

All of the breath leaves my body in a rush, and I feel like I've been punched in the stomach. Without thinking, I lunge at her and shove as hard as I can, and she goes backward into a bookshelf that almost falls over. I've pushed her back toward the door, and as everyone is still squealing and laughing and screaming "Psycho," she runs out of the room. She has to squeeze by Kent. He's just come in, probably to see what everyone's screaming about.

We lock eyes for a moment. I can't exactly tell what he's thinking, but whatever it is, it's not good. I look away, feeling hot and uncomfortable. Everyone's buzzing with energy now, laughing and talking about Juliet, but my breathing won't go back to normal and I feel the vodka burning my stomach, creeping back up my throat. The room is stifling, spinning faster than before. I have to get out for some air.

I try to push my way out of the room, but Kent gets in my face and blocks my way.

"What the hell was that about?" he demands.

"Can you let me by, please?" I'm not in the mood to deal with anyone, and I'm especially not in the mood to deal with Kent and his stupid button-down shirt.

"What did she ever do to you?"

I cross my arms. "I get it. You're friends with Psycho. Is that it?"

He narrows his eyes. "Pretty clever nickname. Did you think of that all by yourself, or did your friends have to help you?"

"Get out of my way." I manage to squeeze past him, but he grabs my arm.

"Why?" he says. We're standing so close together I can smell that he's just eaten peppermints and see the heart-shaped mole under his left eye, even though everything else is blurry. He's looking at me like he's desperate to understand something, and it's worse, much worse than anything else so far—than Juliet or his anger or the feeling I'm going to be sick any second.

I try to shake his hand off my arm. "You can't just *grab* people, you know. You can't just grab *me*. I have a boyfriend."

"Keep your voice down. I'm just trying to—"

"Look." I succeed in shaking him off. I know I'm talking too loud and too fast. I know I sound hysterical, but I can't help it. "I don't know what your problem is, okay? I'm not going to go out with you. I would never go out with you in a million years. So you can stop *obsessing* over me. I mean, I shouldn't even know your name." The words fly out and it's as though they strangle me on the way up: suddenly I can't breathe.

Kent stares at me hard. Then he leans in even closer. For a second I think he's going to try to kiss me and my heart stops.

But he just puts his mouth up to my ear and says, "I see right through you."

"You don't know me." I jerk backward, shaking. "You don't know one thing about me."

He holds his hands up in surrender and backs off. "You're right. I don't." He starts to turn away and mutters something else.

"What did you say?" My heart is pounding in my chest so hard I think it will explode.

He turns to look at me. "I said, *'Thank God.'*"

I spin around, wishing I hadn't borrowed a pair of Ally's heels. The room spins with me and I have to steady myself against the banister.

"Your *boyfriend's* downstairs, puking in the kitchen sink," Kent calls after me.

I give him the finger over my shoulder without turning around to see if he's watching me, but I get the feeling he's not.

Even before I go downstairs to see whether what Kent said about Rob is true, I know it: tonight isn't the night after all. The combination of disappointment and relief is so overwhelming I have to hold on to the walls as I walk, feeling the stairs spiral up under me like they're going to slip away any second. Tonight isn't the night. Tomorrow I'll wake up and be exactly the same, and the world will look the same, and everything will feel and taste and smell the same. My throat gets tight and my eyes start to burn, and all I can think in that moment is that it's all Kent's fault, Kent's and Juliet Sykes's.

Half an hour later the party starts to wind down. Inside, someone has ripped the Christmas lights off the wall and they're trailing along the floor like a snake, lighting up the dust mites in the corners.

I'm feeling better now, more like myself. "There's always tomorrow," Lindsay said to me, when I told her about Rob, and I run the phrase over and over in my head like a mantra: *There's always tomorrow. There's always tomorrow.*

I spend twenty minutes in the bathroom, first washing my face and then reapplying makeup, even though my hands are unsteady and my face keeps doubling in the mirror. Every time I put on makeup it reminds me of my mother—I used to watch her bend over her vanity, getting ready for dates with my father—and it calms me down. *There's always tomorrow.*

It's the time of the night I like best, when most people are asleep and it feels like the world belongs completely to my friends and me, as though nothing exists apart from our little circle: everywhere else is darkness and quiet.

I leave with Elody, Ally, and Lindsay. The crowd is thinning as people take off, but it's still hard to move. Lindsay keeps calling out, "Excuse me, excuse me, move it, feminine emergency!" Years ago we discovered at an under-eighteen concert in Poughkeepsie that nothing clears people faster than referencing a feminine emergency. It's like people think they'll catch it.

On our way out we pass people hooking up in corners and pressed against the stairwell. Behind closed doors we hear the muffled sounds of people giggling. Elody slams her fist against each door and yells out, "No glove, no love!" Lindsay turns around and whispers something to Elody, and Elody shuts up and looks at me guiltily. I want to tell them I don't care—I don't care about Rob or missing my chance—but I'm suddenly too tired to talk.

We see Bridget McGuire sitting on the edge of a bathtub with the door just cracked open. She has her head in her hands and she's crying.

"What's wrong with her?" I say, trying to fight the feeling of swimming in my own head, of my words coming from a distance.

"She dumped Alex." Lindsay grabs on to my elbow. She seems sober, but her pupils are enormous and the whites of her eyes bloodshot. "You'll never believe it. She found out that the Nic Nazi busted Alex and Anna together. He was supposed to be at a doctor's appointment." The music's still going so we can't hear Bridget, but her shoulders are shaking up and down like she's convulsing. "She'll be better off. Scumbag."

"They're all scumbags!" Elody says, raising her beer and spilling some of it. I don't even think she knows what we're talking about.

Lindsay takes her cup and sets it on a side table, on top of a worn copy of *Moby Dick*. She pockets a little ceramic figurine too: a shepherd with curly blond hair and painted eyelashes. She always steals something from parties. She calls them her souvenirs.

"She better not hurl in the Tank," she says in a whisper, tipping her head back toward Elody.

Rob is stretched out on a sofa downstairs, but he manages to grab my hand as I go by and tries to pull me down on top of him.

"Where're you goin'?" he says. His eyes are unfocused and his voice is hoarse.

75

"Come on, Rob. Let me go." I push him off me. This is his fault, too.

"We were supposed to . . ." His voice trails off and he shakes his head, confused, then narrows his eyes at me. "Are you cheating on me?"

"Don't be stupid." I want to rewind the whole evening, rewind the past few weeks, go back to the moment when Rob leaned over, rested his chin on my shoulder, and told me he wanted to sleep next to me, go back to that quiet moment in that dark room with the TV blue and muted in front of us and the sound of his breathing and my parents sleeping upstairs, go back to the moment I opened my mouth and heard "I do too."

"You are. You're cheating. I knew it." He lurches to his feet and looks around wildly. Chris Harmon, one of Rob's best friends, is standing in the corner laughing about something, and Rob stumbles over to him.

"Are you cheating with my girlfriend, Harmon?" Rob roars, and pushes Chris. Chris stumbles and knocks against a bookshelf. A porcelain figurine topples over and shatters and a girl screams.

"Are you crazy?" Chris jumps back on Rob and suddenly they're locked together, wrestling, shuffling around the room and knocking into things, grunting and yelling. Somehow Rob gets Chris down on his knees and then they're both on the floor. Girls are shrieking and jumping out of the way. Someone cries out, "Watch the beer!" just before Rob and Chris roll up against the entrance of the kitchen, where the keg is sitting.

"Let's go, Sam." Lindsay squeezes my shoulders from behind.

"I can't just leave him," I say, though a part of me wants to.

"He'll be fine. Look—he's laughing."

She's right. He and Chris are already done fighting and are sprawled on the floor, laughing their heads off.

"Rob's going to be so pissed," I say, and I know Lindsay knows I'm talking about more than just ditching him at the party.

She gives me a quick hug. "Remember what I said." She starts to singsong, *"Just thinkin' about tomorrow clears away the cobwebs and the sorrow. . . ."*

For a moment my stomach clenches, thinking she's making fun of me, but it's a coincidence. Lindsay didn't know me when I was little, wouldn't even have spoken to me. She has no way of knowing I used to lock myself in my room with the *Annie* soundtrack and belt that song at the top of my lungs until my parents threatened to throw me out onto the street.

The melody starts repeating in my head and I know I'll be singing it for days. *Tomorrow, tomorrow, I love ya tomorrow.* A beautiful word, when you really think about it.

"Lame party, huh?" Ally says, coming up on the other side of me. Even though I know she's only pissed Matt Wilde didn't show, I'm glad she says it.

The sound of the rain is louder than I thought it would be and it startles me. For a moment we stand under the porch eaves, watching our breath condense into clouds, hugging ourselves. It's freezing. Water is falling in steady streams from the eaves. Christopher Tomlin and Adam Wu are throwing empty beer bottles into the woods. Every so often we hear one shatter, and the sound comes back to us like a gunshot.

People are laughing and screaming and running in the rain, which is coming down so hard everything looks as though it's melting into everything else. There are no neighbors to call the cops for miles. The grass is churned up, great black pits of mud exposed. Headlights are flashing in the distance, in and out, on and off, as cars sweep down the driveway toward Route 9.

"Run for it!" Lindsay yells, and I feel Ally tugging on me and then we're running, screaming, the rain blinding us and streaming down our jackets, the mud oozing into our shoes; rain so hard it's like everything is melting away.

By the time we get to Lindsay's car I really *don't* care about the awful way the night turned out. We're laughing hysterically, soaked and shivering, woken up from the cold and the rain. Lindsay's squealing about wet butt marks on her leather seats and mud on the floor, and Elody's begging her to go to Mic's for an egg and cheese and complaining that I always get shotgun, and Ally's yelling for Lindsay to turn on the heat and threatening to drop dead right there from pneumonia.

I guess that's how we get started talking about it: dying, I mean. I figure Lindsay's okay to drive, but I notice she's going faster than usual down that awful, long, penned-in driveway. The trees look like stripped skeletons on either side of us, moaning in the wind.

"I have this theory," I'm saying as Lindsay skids out onto Route 9 and the tires shriek against the slick black road. The clock on the dashboard is glowing: 12:38. "I have this theory that before you die you see your greatest hits, you know? The best things you've ever done."

"Duke, baby," Lindsay says, and takes one hand off the wheel to pump her fist in the air.

"First time I hooked up with Matt Wilde," Ally says immediately.

Elody groans and leans forward, reaching for the iPod. "Music, please, before I kill myself."

"Can I get a cigarette?" Lindsay asks, and Elody lights one for her off the butt she's holding. Lindsay cracks the windows, and the freezing rain comes in. Ally starts to complain about the cold again.

Elody puts on "Splinter," by Fallacy, to piss Ally off, maybe because she's sick of her whining. Ally calls her a bitch and unbuckles her seat belt, leaning forward and trying to grab the iPod. Lindsay complains that someone is elbowing her in the neck. The cigarette drops from her mouth and lands between her thighs. She starts cursing and trying to brush the embers off the seat cushion, and Elody and Ally are still fighting and

79

I'm trying to talk over them, reminding them all of the time we made snow angels in May. The clock ticks forward: 12:39. The tires skid a little on the wet road and the car is full of cigarette smoke, little wisps rising like phantoms in the air.

Then all of a sudden there's a flash of white in front of the car. Lindsay yells something—words I can't make out, something like *sit* or *shit* or *sight*—and suddenly the car is flipping off the road and into the black mouth of the woods. I hear a horrible, screeching sound—metal on metal, glass shattering, a car folding in two—and smell fire. I have time to wonder whether Lindsay had put out her cigarette—

And then—

That's when it happens. The moment of death is full of heat and sound and pain bigger than anything, a funnel of burning heat splitting me in two, something searing and scorching and tearing, and if screaming were a feeling it would be this.

Then nothing.

I know some of you are thinking maybe I deserved it. Maybe I shouldn't have sent that rose to Juliet or dumped my drink on her at the party. Maybe I shouldn't have copied off Lauren Lornet's quiz. Maybe I shouldn't have said those things to Kent. There are probably some of you who think I deserved it because I was going to let Rob go all the way—because I wasn't going to save myself.

But before you start pointing fingers, let me ask you: is

what I did really so bad? So bad I deserved to die? So bad I deserved to die like that?

Is *what I did really so much worse than what anybody else does?*

Is *it really so much worse than what* you *do?*

Think about it.

TWO

In my dream I know I am falling though there is no up or down, no walls or sides or ceilings, just the sensation of cold, and darkness everywhere. I am so scared I could scream, but when I open my mouth nothing happens, and I wonder if you fall forever and ever and never touch down, is it really still falling?

I think I will fall forever.

A noise punctuates the silence, a thin bleating growing louder and louder until it is like a scythe of metal slicing the air, slicing into me—

Then I wake up.

My alarm has been blaring for twenty minutes. It's six fifty A.M.

I sit up in bed, pushing away the comforter. I'm covered with sweat even though my room is cold. My throat is dry and I'm desperate for water, like I've just been running a long way.

For a second when I look around the room everything seems fuzzy and slightly distorted, like I'm not really looking at my room but only at a transparency of my room that's been laid down incorrectly so the corners don't match up with the real thing. Then the light shifts and everything looks normal again.

All at once it comes back to me, and blood starts pounding in my head: the party, Juliet Sykes, the argument with Kent—

"Sammy!" My door swings open, banging once against the wall, and Izzy comes galloping across the room, stepping all over my notebooks and discarded jeans and my Victoria's Secret Team Pink sweatshirt. Something seems wrong; something skirts the edges of my memory, but then it is gone and Izzy is bouncing on my bed, throwing her arms around me. They are hot. She curls a fist around the necklace I always wear—a thin gold chain with a tiny bird charm hanging from it, a gift from my grandmother—and tugs gently.

"Mommy says you have to get up." Her breath smells like peanut butter, and it's not until I push her off me that I realize how badly I'm shaking.

"It's Saturday," I say. I have no idea how I got home last night. I have no idea what happened to Lindsay or Elody or Ally, and just thinking about it makes me sick.

Izzy starts giggling like a maniac and bounces off the bed, scurrying back toward the door. She disappears down the hallway, and I hear her call out, "Mommy, Sammy won't get up!" She says my name: *Thammy*.

"Don't make me come up there, Sammy!" My mom's voice echoes from the kitchen.

I put my feet on the ground. The feel of the cold wood reassures me. When I was younger I would lie on the floor all summer when my dad refused to turn the air-conditioning on; it was the only place that stayed cool. I'm tempted to do the same thing now. I feel feverish.

Rob, the rain, the sound of bottles shattering in the woods—

My phone chimes, making me jump. I reach over and flip it open. There's a new text from Lindsay.

I'm outside. Where r u?

I snap my phone shut quickly but not before I see the date blinking up at me: Friday, February 12.

Yesterday.

Another chime. Another text.

Don't make me l8 on Cupid Day, beeyatch!!!

I suddenly feel like I'm moving underwater, like I'm weightless, or watching myself from a distance. I try to stand up, but when I do my stomach bottoms out and I have to rush to the bathroom in the hall, legs shaking, certain I'm going to throw up. I lock the door and turn on the water in both the sink and the shower. Then I stand over the toilet.

My stomach clenches on itself, but nothing comes up.

The car, the skidding, the screams—

Yesterday.

I hear voices in the hallway, but the water's rushing so hard I can't make them out. It's not until someone starts pounding on the door that I straighten up and yell, "What?"

"Get out of the shower. There's no time." It's Lindsay—my mom's let her in.

I crack the door a little and there she is, her big puffy jacket zipped to her chin, looking pissed. I'm happy to see her, anyway. She looks so normal, so familiar.

"What happened last night?" I say.

She frowns for a second. "Yeah, sorry about that. I couldn't call back. I didn't get off the phone with Patrick until, like, three A.M."

"Call back?" I shake my head. "No, I meant—"

"He was freaking out over the fact that his parents are going to Acapulco without him." She rolls her eyes. "Poor baby. I swear to you, Sam, guys are like pets. Feed 'em, pet 'em, and put 'em to bed." She leans forward. "*Speaking* of which—are you excited about tonight?"

"What?" I don't even know what she's talking about. Her words are all running past me, blurring together. I'm holding on to the towel rack, afraid I'll fall over. The shower is on way too hot and there's thick steam everywhere, clouding up the mirror, condensing on the tiles.

"You, Rob, some Miller Lite, and his flannel sheets." She laughs. "Very romantic."

"I have to shower." I try to close the door, but she wedges her elbow in at the last second and pushes into the bathroom.

"You haven't showered yet?" She shakes her head. "Uh-uh. No way. You'll have to do without."

She reaches into the shower and turns off the water, then grabs me by the hand and drags me into the hallway.

"You definitely need some makeup, though," she says, scanning my face. "You look like shit. Nightmares?"

"Something like that."

"I have my MAC stuff in the Tank." She unzips her coat and I see a white tuft of fur peeking out from her cleavage: our Cupid Day tank tops. I suddenly have the urge to sit down on the floor and laugh and laugh, and I have to struggle not to have a fit right there while Lindsay's shoving me into my room.

"Get dressed," she says, and pulls out her cell phone, probably to text Elody we're going to be late. She watches me for a second and then sighs, turning away.

"Hope Rob doesn't mind a little BO," she says, and as she giggles over this, I start pulling on my clothes: the tank top, the skirt, the boots.

Again.

DOES THIS STRAITJACKET MAKE MY BUTT LOOK BIG?

When Elody gets into the car she leans forward to grab her coffee, and the smell of her perfume—raspberry body spray she still buys religiously from the Body Shop in the mall, even though it stopped being cool in seventh grade—is so real and sharp and familiar I have to close my eyes, overwhelmed.

Bad idea. With my eyes shut I see the beautiful warm lights of Kent's house receding in the rearview mirror and the sleek black trees crowding on either side of us like skeletons. I smell burning. I hear Lindsay yelling and feel my stomach bottom out as the car lurches to one side, tires squealing—

"Shit."

I snap my eyes open as Lindsay swerves to avoid a squirrel. She chucks her cigarette out the window and the smell of smoke is strangely double: I'm not sure whether I'm smelling it or remembering it or both.

"You really are the worst driver." Elody giggles.

"Be careful, please," I mutter. I'm clutching the sides of my seat without meaning to.

"Don't worry." Lindsay leans over and pats my knee. "I won't let my best friend die a virgin."

I'm desperate to spill everything to Lindsay and Elody at that moment, to ask them what's happening to me—to us—but I can't think of any way to say it.

We were in a car accident after a party that hasn't happened yet.

I thought I died yesterday. I thought I died tonight.

Elody must think I'm quiet because I'm worried about Rob. She loops her arms around the back of my seat and leans forward.

"Don't worry, Sam. You'll be fine. It's just like riding a bike," Elody says.

I try to force a smile, but I can barely focus. It seems like a long time ago that I went to bed imagining being side-by-side with Rob, imagining the feel of his cool, dry hands. Thinking about him makes me ache, and my throat threatens to close up. I suddenly can't wait to see him, can't wait to see his crooked smile and his Yankees hat and even his dirty fleece that always smells a little bit like boy sweat, even after his mom makes him wash it.

"It's like riding a horse," Lindsay corrects Elody. "You'll be a blue-ribbon champion in no time, Sammy."

"I always forget you used to ride horses." Elody flips open the lid of her coffee and blows steam off the top.

"When I was, like, seven," I say, before Lindsay can turn this into a joke. I think if she starts making fun of me now I really will cry. I could never explain the truth to her: that riding was my favorite thing in the world. I loved to be alone in the woods, especially in the late fall when everything is crisp and golden, the leaves the color of fire, and it smells like things turning into earth. I loved the silence—the only sound the steady drum of the hooves and the horse's breathing.

No phones. No laughter. No voices. No houses.

No cars.

I've flipped the visor down to keep the glare out of my eyes, and in the mirror I see Elody smiling at me. *Maybe I'll tell her what's happening to me,* I think, but at the same time I know that I won't. She would think I was crazy. They all would.

I keep quiet and look out the window. The light is weak and watery-looking, like the sun has just spilled itself over the horizon and is too lazy to clean itself up. The shadows are as sharp and pointed as needles. I watch three black crows take off simultaneously from a telephone wire and wish I could take off too, move up, up, up, and watch the ground drop away from me the way it does when you're on an airplane, folding and compressing into itself like an origami figure, until everything is flat and brightly colored—until the whole world is like a drawing of itself.

"Theme song, please," Lindsay says, and I scroll through her iPod until I find the Mary J. Blige, then lean back and try not to think of anything except the music and the beat.

And I keep my eyes open.

By the time we pull into the drive that winds past the upper parking area and down to the faculty lot and Senior Alley, I'm actually feeling better, even though Lindsay's cursing and Elody's complaining that one more tardy will get her Friday detention and it's already two minutes after first bell.

Everything looks so *normal.* I know that because it's Friday, Emma McElroy will be coming from Evan Danzig's house, and sure enough there she is, ducking through a clipped portion of the fence. I know Peter Kourt will be wearing a pair of Nike Air Force 1s he's had for a million years because he wears them every day, even though there are so many holes in them you can see what color socks he's wearing (usually black). I watch them go flashing by as he books it down toward the main building.

Seeing all these things makes me feel a thousand times better, and I start thinking maybe all of yesterday—everything that happened—was just some kind of long, strange dream.

Lindsay cruises down to the Senior Alley, even though there's zero chance of finding a spot. It's a religion for her. My stomach dips when we pass the third spot from the tennis courts, and there's Sarah Grundel's brown Chevrolet with its Thomas Jefferson Swim Team sticker—and another one, smaller, that reads GET WET—staring at me from the bumper. I think: *she got the last spot because we're so late*, and I have to squeeze my nails into my palms and repeat to myself that I've only been dreaming—that none of this has happened before.

"I can't believe we have to walk .22 miles," Elody says, pouting. "I don't even have a jacket."

"You're the one who left the house half naked," Lindsay says. "It *is* February."

"I didn't know I'd be *outside*."

We pass the soccer fields on our right as we loop back toward Upper Lot. At this time of year the fields are all churned up, just mud and a few patches of brown grass.

"I feel like I'm having déjà vu," Elody says. "Flashback to freshman year, you know?"

"I've been having déjà vu all morning," I blurt out before I can stop myself. Instantly I feel better, sure that that's what this is.

"Let me guess." Lindsay brings one hand to her temples and frowns, pretending to concentrate. "You're having flashbacks to the last time Elody was this annoying before nine A.M."

"Shut up!" Elody leans forward and smacks Lindsay's arm and they start laughing. I smile too, relieved to have spoken the words out loud. It makes sense: one time on a trip to Colorado, my parents and I hiked up three miles to this little waterfall smack in the middle of the woods. The trees were big and old, all of them pine. The clouds were streaked across the sky like spun sugar. Izzy was too young to walk or talk. She was riding in my dad's baby backpack, and she kept punching her tiny fat fists at the sky like she wanted to grab it.

Anyway, as we were standing there watching the spray of water on the rocks, I had the craziest feeling that it had all happened before, down to the smell of the orange my mom was peeling and the exact reflections of the trees in the surface of the water. I was *positive*. It became the big joke that day, because I'd complained about having to hike three miles, and when I told my parents I was having déjà vu, they kept laughing and saying it really would be a miracle if I'd ever agreed to walk that far in a past life.

I guess my point is only that I was *sure* then, just like I'm feeling *sure* now. It happens.

"Oooh!" Elody squeals, and starts digging through her purse. She knocks out a pack of cigarettes and two empty tubes of lip gloss, plus a misshapen eyelash curler. "I almost forgot your present."

She sends the condom sailing over the front seat, and Lindsay claps her hands and bounces in her seat when I hold it up.

"No glove, no love?" I say, managing a smile.

Elody leans forward and kisses my cheek, leaving a ring of pink gloss. "You're going to be great, kid."

"Don't call me that," I say, and drop the condom in my bag. We step out of the car and the air is so cold my eyes sting and start to water. I ignore the bad feeling buzzing through me, and I think, *This is my day, this is my day, this is my day*, so I can't think of anything else.

A SHADOW WORLD

I read once that you get déjà vu when the two halves of your brain process things at different speeds: the right half a few seconds before the left, or vice versa. Science is probably my worst subject, so I didn't understand the whole article, but that would explain the weird double feeling that it leaves you with, like the world is splitting in half—or *you* are.

That's the way I feel, at least: like there's a real me and a reflection of me, and I have no way of telling which is which.

The thing about déjà vu is that it has always passed really quickly—thirty seconds, a minute at most.

But this doesn't pass.

Everything is the same: Eileen Cho squealing over her roses in first period and Samara Phillips leaning over and crooning, "He must really love you." I pass the same people in the halls at the same time. Aaron Stern spills his coffee all over the hallway again, and Carol Lin starts screaming at him again.

Even her words are the same. "Were you dropped on your head one too many times or something?" I have to admit it's pretty funny, even the second time around. Even when I feel like I'm crazy; even when I feel like I could scream.

But even weirder are the little blips and wrinkles, the things that have shifted around. Sarah Grundel, for example. On my way to second period I see her standing against a bank of lockers, twirling her goggles around her index finger and talking to Hillary Hale. As I walk by I catch just a bit of their conversation.

". . . so excited. I mean, Coach says my time could still go down by a half second—"

"We have two weeks before the semis. You can totally do it."

I stop dead when I hear this. Sarah sees me staring at her and gets really uncomfortable. She smoothes her hair and tugs on her skirt, which is riding up on her waist.

Then she waves.

"Hey, Sam," she says. She pulls on her skirt again.

"Were you—" I take a deep breath to keep from stuttering

like an idiot. "Were you just talking about semifinals? For swim team?"

"Yeah." Sarah's face lights up. "Are you going to come?"

Even though I'm freaking out, it still occurs to me that this is a *really* stupid question. I've never gone to a swim meet in my life, and the idea of sitting on a slimy tile floor and watching Sarah Grundel splash around in a bathing suit is about as appealing as the chow mein from Hunan Kitchen. To be honest, the only sporting event I ever go to is homecoming, and after four years I still don't understand any of the rules. Lindsay usually brings a flask of something for the four of us to share, so that could have something to do with it.

"I thought you weren't competing." I try hard to act casual. "I heard some rumor . . . like maybe you were late and the coach freaked out. . . ."

"You heard a rumor? About me?" Sarah's eyes go wide and she looks like I just handed her a winning lotto ticket. I guess she's of the "no press is bad press" philosophy.

"I guess I was wrong." I think of seeing her car in the third-to-last spot and feel heat flood my face. Of course she wasn't late today. Of course she's still competing. She didn't have to walk from Upper Lot today. She was late *yesterday*.

My head starts pounding and suddenly I just want to get out of there.

Hillary's looking at me strangely. "Are you okay? You look really pale."

94

"Yeah. Fine. Bad sushi last night." I put one hand on the lockers to steady myself. Sarah starts babbling about the time she got food poisoning from the mall, but I'm already walking away, feeling like the hallway is rolling and buckling underneath me.

Déjà vu. It's the only explanation.

If you repeat something enough, you can almost make yourself believe it.

I'm feeling so shaken up I almost forget that Ally's waiting for me in the bathroom by the science wing. I go into the stall and flip the lid of a toilet down and just sit there, only half listening while she babbles. I remember something Mrs. Harbor once said on one of her crazy tangents in English: that Plato believed that the whole world—everything we can see—was just like shadows on a cave wall. We can't actually see the real thing, the thing that's casting the shadow in the first place. I have that feeling now, of being surrounded by shadows, like I'm seeing the impression of the thing before the thing itself.

"Hello? Are you even listening to me?"

Ally rattles the door and I look up, startled. I notice *AC=WT* scrawled on the inside of the door. Below it a smaller note reads: *Go back to the trailer, ho.*

"You said pretty soon you'd have to shop for bras in the maternity section," I say automatically. Of course I wasn't really listening. Not this time, anyway.

I'm wondering, vaguely, why Lindsay came all the way down

here to write on the bathroom wall—why it was important to her, I mean. She'd already written it a dozen times in the stalls across from the cafeteria, and that's the bathroom everyone uses. I'm not even sure why she dislikes Anna, and it reminds me that I still don't know when she started hating Juliet Sykes so much either. It's weird how much you can know about someone without knowing everything. You'd think someday you'd come to the end of it.

I stand up and swing the door open, pointing to the graffiti. "When did Lindsay do this?"

Ally rolls her eyes. "She didn't. Copycat artist."

"Really?"

"Uh-huh. There's one in the girls' locker room too. Copycat." She whips her hair into a ponytail and starts pinching her lips to make them swell up. "It's so lame. We can't do anything in this school without everyone doing the same thing."

"Lame." I run my fingers over the words. They're thick and black, like worms, drawn in permanent marker. I wonder, briefly, whether Anna uses this bathroom.

"We should sue for copyright infringement. Can you imagine? Twenty bucks for every time somebody bites our style. We'd be rolling in it." She giggles. "Mint?"

Ally holds out an Altoids tin. Even though she's still a virgin—and will be, for the foreseeable future (or at least until she goes to college), since she's completely obsessed with Matt Wilde—she insists on taking birth control pills, which she

96

keeps crumpled up in their foil pack right there alongside her mints. She claims it's so her dad won't find them, but everyone knows she likes to flash them during class so that people will think she's having sex. Not that anybody's fooled. Thomas Jefferson is small: you know these things.

One time Elody told Ally she had "pregnancy breath" and we all died over it. It was junior year in May and we were all lying out on Ally's trampoline. It was the Saturday morning after she'd had one of her best parties yet. We were all just a little hungover, our brains fuzzy, stuffed on all the pancakes and bacon we'd put down at the diner, totally happy. I lay there while the trampoline dipped and swayed, closing my eyes against the sun, wishing that the day would never end.

The bell rings and Ally squeals, "Ooh! We're gonna be late."

Again that pit opens in my stomach. A part of me is tempted to hide all day in the bathroom, but I can't.

I know you know what happens next. That I get to chem late. That I take the last seat next to Lauren Lornet. That Mr. Tierney passes out a quiz with three questions on it.

The worst part of it? I've seen the quiz before and I *still* don't know the answers.

I ask to borrow a pen. Lauren starts whispering to me; she wants to know if it's working okay. Mr. Tierney's book comes down with a bang.

Everyone jumps but me.

Class. Bell. Class. Bell.

Crazy. I'm going crazy.

By the time the roses get delivered in math class my hands are shaking. I take a deep breath before I open the little laminated card attached to the rose Rob sent me. I imagine it will say something incredible, something surprising, something that will make everything better.

You're beautiful, Sam.

I'm so happy to be with you.

Sam, I love you.

I lift the corner of the card gently and peek inside.

Luv y—

I close the card quickly and put it in my bag.

"Wow. It's beautiful."

I look up. The girl dressed like an angel is standing there, staring at the rose she's just laid on my desk: pink and cream petals swirled together like ice cream. She still has her hand outstretched and tiny blue veins crisscross her skin like a web.

"Take a picture. It'll last longer," I snap at her. She blushes as red as the roses she's holding and stammers out an apology.

I don't bother reading the note that's attached to this one, and for the rest of class I keep my eyes glued to the blackboard to avoid any sign from Kent. I'm concentrating so hard on not looking at him I almost miss it when Mr. Daimler winks at me and smiles.

Almost.

After class Kent catches up with me, holding the pink-and-cream rose, which I'd deliberately left on my desk.

"You forgot this," he says. As always his hair is flopping over one eye. "It's okay, you can say it: I'm amazing."

"I didn't forget it." I'm struggling not to look at him. "I didn't want it."

I sneak a glance at him and see his smile fade for a second. Then it's back on full-force, like a friggin' laser beam.

"What do you mean?" He tries to pass it to me. "Didn't anybody ever tell you that the more roses you get on Cupid Day, the more popular you are?"

"I don't think I need any help in that department. Especially from you."

His smile definitely drops then. Part of me hates what I'm doing, but all I can think of is the memory—or dream—or whatever it is—when he leans in and I think he's going to kiss me, I'm sure of it, but instead he whispers, *I see right through you.*

You don't know me. You don't know anything about me. Thank God.

I dig my nails into my palms.

"I never said the rose was from me," he says. His voice is so low and serious it startles me. I meet his eyes; they're bright green. I remember when I was little my mom used to say that God mixed the grass and Kent's eyes from the same color.

"Yeah, well. It's pretty obvious." I just want him to stop looking at me like that.

He takes a deep breath. "Look. I'm having a party tonight—"

That's when I see Rob loping into the cafeteria. Normally I would wait for him to notice me, but today I can't.

"Rob!" I yell out.

He turns and sees me, gives me half a wave, and starts to turn around again.

"Rob! Wait!" I take off down the hallway. I'm not exactly running—Lindsay, Ally, Elody, and I made a pact years ago never to run on school grounds, not even in gym class (let's face it: sweating and huffing aren't exactly attractive)—but it's a close call.

"Whoa, Slamster. Where's the fire?"

Rob puts his arms around me and I bury my nose in his fleece. It smells a little like old pizza—not the best smell, especially when it's mixed with lemon balm—but I don't care. My legs are shaking so badly I'm afraid they'll give out. I just want to stand there forever, holding on to him.

"I missed you," I say into his chest.

For a second his arms tense around me. But when he tilts my face up toward his, he's smiling.

"Did you get my Valogram?" he asks.

I nod. "Thanks." My throat is tight and I'm worried I'll start to cry. It feels so good to have his arms around me, like he's the only thing holding me up. "Listen, Rob. About tonight—"

I'm not even sure what I'm going to say, but he cuts me off.

"Okay. What is it now?"

I pull back just a little bit so I can look at him. "I—I want to . . . I'm just—things are all crazy today. I think I might be sick or—or something else."

He laughs and pinches my nose with two fingers. "Oh, no. You're not getting out of this one." He puts his forehead to mine and whispers, "I've been looking forward to this for a long time."

"I know, me too. . . ." I've imagined it so many times: the way the moon will be dipping past the trees and coming through the windows and lighting up triangles and squares on the walls; the way his fleece blanket will feel against my bare skin when I take my clothes off.

And then I've imagined the moment afterward, after Rob has kissed me and told me he loved me and fallen asleep with his mouth just parted and I sneak off to the bathroom and text Elody and Lindsay and Ally.

I did it.

It's the middle part that's harder to picture.

I feel my phone buzz in my back pocket: a new text. My stomach flips. I already know what it will say.

"You're right," I say to Rob, squeezing my arms around him. "Maybe I should come over right after school. We can hang out all afternoon, all night."

"You're cute." Rob pulls away, adjusts his hat and his back-pack. "My parents don't clear out until dinnertime, though."

"I don't care. We can watch a movie or someth—"

"Besides." Rob's looking over my shoulder now. "I heard about some party at what's-his-name's—dude with the bowler hat. Ken?"

"Kent," I say automatically. Rob knows his name, obvi-ously—everyone knows everyone here—but it's a power thing. I remember telling Kent, *I shouldn't even know your name,* and feel queasy. Voices are swelling through the hall, and people start passing Rob and me. I can feel them staring. They're probably hoping for a fight.

"Yeah, Kent. I might stop by for a while. We can meet up there?"

"You really want to go?" I'm trying to squash the panic well-ing up inside me. I lower my head and look up at him the way I've seen Lindsay do with Patrick when she's really desperate for something. "It'll just mean less time with me."

"We'll have plenty of time." Rob kisses his fingers and taps them, twice, against my cheek. "Trust me. Have I ever let you down?"

You'll let me down tonight. The thought comes to me before I can stop it.

"No," I say too loudly. Rob's not listening, though. Adam Marshall and Jeremy Forker have just joined us, and they're all doing the greeting thing where they jump on one another and wrestle. Sometimes I think Lindsay's right and guys are just like animals.

I pull out my phone to check my text, though I don't really need to.

Party @ Kent McFreaky's 2nite. In?

My fingers are numb as I text back, *Obv.* Then I go into lunch, feeling like the sound of three hundred voices has weight, like it's a solid wind that will carry me up, up, and away.

BEFORE I WAKE

"So? You nervous?" Lindsay lifts one leg in the air and swivels it back and forth, admiring the shoes she's just stolen from Ally's closet.

Music thumps from the living room. Ally and Elody are out there singing their heads off to "Like a Prayer." Ally's not even close to on key. Lindsay and I are lying on our backs on Ally's mongo bed. Everything in Ally's house is 25 percent bigger than in a normal person's: the fridge, the leather chairs, the televisions—even the magnums of champagne her dad keeps in the wine cellar (strictly hands-off). Lindsay once said it made her feel like Alice in Wonderland.

I settle my head against an enormous pillow that says THE BITCH IS IN. I've had four shots already, thinking it would calm me down, and above me the lights are winking and blurring. We've cracked all the windows open, but I'm still feeling feverish.

"Don't forget to breathe," Lindsay's saying. "Don't freak out if it hurts a little—especially at first. Don't tense up. You'll make it worse."

I'm feeling pretty nauseous and Lindsay's not making it better. I couldn't eat all day, so by the time we got to Ally's house, I was starving and scarfed about twenty-five of the toast-pesto-goat-cheese snacks that Ally whipped up. I'm not sure how well the goat cheese is mixing with the vodka. On top of it, Lindsay made me eat about seven Listerine breath strips because the pesto had garlic in it, and she said Rob would feel like he was losing his virginity to an Italian line cook.

I'm not even that nervous about Rob—I mean, I can't focus on being nervous about him. The party, the drive, the possibility of what will happen there: that's what's really giving me stomach cramps. At least the vodka's helped me breathe, and I'm not feeling shaky anymore.

Of course, I can't tell Lindsay any of this, so instead I say, "I'm not going to freak. I mean, everybody does it, right? If Anna Cartullo can do it . . ."

Lindsay pulls a face. "Ew. Whatever you're doing, it's not what Anna Cartullo does. You and Rob are 'making love.'" She puts quotes in the air with her fingers and giggles, but I can tell she means it.

"You think?"

"Of course." She tilts her head to look at me. "You don't?"

I want to ask, *How do you know the difference?*

In movies you can always tell when people are supposed to be together because music swells up behind them—dumb, but true. Lindsay's always saying she couldn't live without Patrick and I'm not sure if that's how you're supposed to feel or not.

Sometimes when I'm standing in the middle of a crowded place with Rob, and he puts his arm around my shoulders and pulls me close—like he doesn't want me to get bumped or spilled on or whatever—I feel a kind of heat in my stomach like I've just had a glass of wine, and I'm completely happy, just for that second. I'm pretty sure that's what love is.

So I say to Lindsay, "Of course I do."

Lindsay giggles again and nudges me. "So? Did he bite the bullet and just say it?"

"Say what?"

She rolls her eyes. "That he *loves* you."

I pause for just a second too long, thinking of his note: *Luv ya.* The kind of thing you pencil in somebody's yearbook when you don't know what else to say.

Lindsay rushes on. "He will. Guys are idiots. Bet you he says it tonight. Just after you . . ." She trails off and starts humping her hips up and down.

I smack her with a pillow. "You're a dog, you know that?"

She growls at me and bares her teeth. We laugh and then lie in silence for a minute, listening to Elody's and Ally's howls from the other room. They're on to "Total Eclipse of the Heart" now. It feels nice to be lying there: nice and normal. I think of all the times we must've laid in exactly this spot, waiting for Elody and Ally to finish getting ready, waiting to go out, waiting for something to happen—time ticking and then falling away, lost forever—and I suddenly wish I could remember each one singularly, like somehow if I could remember them all, I could have them back.

"Were you nervous? The first time, I mean." I'm kind of embarrassed to ask so I say it quietly.

I think the question catches Lindsay off guard. She blushes and starts picking at the braiding on Ally's bedspread, and for a moment there's an awkward silence. I'm pretty sure I know what she's thinking, though I would never say it out loud. Lindsay, Ally, Elody, and I are as close as you can be, but there are still some things we never talk about. For example, even though Lindsay says Patrick is her first and only, this isn't technically true. Technically, her first was a guy she met at a party when she was visiting her stepbrother at NYU. They smoked pot, split a six-pack, and had sex, and he never knew she hadn't done it before.

We don't talk about that. We don't talk about the fact that we can never hang out at Elody's house after five o'clock because her mother will be home, and drunk. We don't talk about the fact that Ally never eats more than a quarter of what's on her plate, even though she's obsessed with cooking and watches the Food Network for hours on end.

We don't talk about the joke that for years trailed me down

hallways, into classrooms, and on the bus, that wove its way into my dreams: "What's red and white and weird all over? Sam Kingston!" And we definitely don't talk about the fact that Lindsay was the one who made it up.

A good friend keeps your secrets for you. A best friend helps you keep your own secrets.

Lindsay rolls over on her side and props herself on one elbow. I wonder if she's finally going to mention the guy at NYU. (I don't even know his name, and the few times she's ever made reference to him she called him the Unmentionable.)

"I wasn't nervous," she says quietly. Then she sucks in a deep breath and her face splits into a grin. "I was horny, baby. *Randy*." She says it in a fake British accent and then jumps on top of me and starts making a humping motion.

"You're impossible," I say, pushing her off me. She rolls all the way off the bed, cackling.

"You love me." Lindsay gets up on her knees and blows the bangs out of her face. She leans forward and rests her elbows on the bed. She suddenly gets serious.

"Sam?" Her eyes are wide and she drops her voice. I have to sit up to hear her over the music. "Can I tell you a secret?"

"Of course." My heart starts fluttering. She knows what's happening to me. It's happening to her, too.

"You have to promise not to tell. You have to swear not to freak out."

She knows; she knows. It's not just me. My head clears and

107

everything sharpens around me. I feel totally sober. "I swear." The words barely come out.

She leans forward until her mouth is only an inch from my ear. "I . . ."

Then she turns her head and burps, loudly, in my face.

"Jesus, Lindz!" I fan the air with my hand. She sinks onto her back again, kicking her legs into the air and laughing hysterically. "What is wrong with you?"

"You should have seen your face."

"Are you *ever* serious?" I say it jokingly, but my whole body feels heavy with disappointment. She doesn't know. She doesn't understand. Whatever is happening, it's happening only to me. A feeling of complete aloneness overwhelms me, like a fog.

Lindsay dabs the corners of her eyes with a thumb and jumps to her feet. "I'll be serious when I'm dead."

That word sends a shock straight through me. Dead. So final, so ugly, so short. The warm feeling I've had since taking the shots drains out of me, and I lean over to shut Ally's window, shivering.

The black mouth of the woods, yawning open. Vicky Hallinan's face . . .

I try to decide what will happen to me if it turns out I really have gone bat-shit insane. Just before eighth period I stood ten feet away from the main office—home to the principal, Ms. Winters, and the school psychiatrist—willing myself to go in and say the words: *I think I'm going crazy.* But then there was a bang and Lauren Lornet shot into the hall, sniffling, probably crying over some boy drama or fight with her parents or something *normal*. In that second all of the work I'd done to fit in vanished. Everything is different now. *I'm* different.

"So are we going or what?" Elody bursts into the room in front of Ally. They're both breathless.

"Let's do it." Lindsay picks up her bag and swings it over one shoulder.

Ally starts to giggle. "It's only nine thirty," she says, "and Sam already looks like she could barf."

I stand up and wait for a second while the ground steadies underneath me. "I'll be fine. I'm fine."

"Liar," Lindsay says, and smiles.

THE PARTY, TAKE TWO

"This is how a horror movie starts," Ally says. "Are you sure he's number forty-two?"

"I'm sure." My voice sounds like it's coming from a distance. The huge crush of fear has returned. I can feel it pressing on me from all directions, squeezing the breath out of me.

"This better not screw with my paint job," Lindsay says as a branch scrapes along the passenger door with the sound of a nail dragging against a chalkboard.

The woods fall away, and Kent's house comes looming out of the darkness, white and sparkling, like it's made of ice. The way it just emerges there, surrounded on all sides by black, reminds me of the scene in *Titanic* when the iceberg rises out of the water and guts the ship open. We're all silent for a second. Tiny pellets of rain ping against the windshield and the roof, and Lindsay switches off her iPod. An old song pipes quietly from the radio. I can just make out the lyrics: *Feel it now like you felt it then. . . . Touch me now and around again. . . .*

"It's almost as big as your house, Al," Lindsay says.

"Almost," Ally says. I feel a tremendous wave of affection for her at that moment. Ally, who likes big houses and expensive cars and Tiffany jewelry and platform wedges and body glitter. Ally, who's not that smart and knows it, and obsesses over boys who aren't good enough for her. Ally, who's secretly an amazing cook. I know her. I get her. I know all of them.

In the house Dujeous roars through the speakers: *All MCs in the house tonight, if your lyrics sound tight then rock the mic.* The stairs roll underneath me. When we get upstairs Lindsay takes the bottle of vodka away from me, laughing.

"Slow down, Slam-a-Lot. You've got business to take care of."

"Business?" I start laughing a little, little gasps of it. It's so smoky I can hardly breathe. "I thought it was making love."

"The business of making love." She leans in and her face swells like a moon. "No more vodka for a while, okay?"

I feel myself nodding and her face recedes. She scans the room. "I've gotta find Patrick. You gonna be okay?"

"Perfect," I say, trying to smile. I can't manage it: it's like the muscles in my face won't respond. She starts to turn away and I grab her wrist. "Lindz?"

"Yeah?"

"I'm gonna come with you, okay?"

She shrugs. "Yeah, sure. Whatever. He's in the back somewhere—he just texted me."

We start pushing past people. Lindsay yells back to me, "It's like a maze up here." Things are going past me in a blur—snippets of conversation and laughter, the feel of coats brushing against my skin, the smell of beer and perfume and shower gel and sweat—all of it whirling and spinning together.

Everyone looks the way they do in dreams, familiar but not too clear, like they could morph into someone else at any second. *I'm dreaming*, I think. This is all a dream: this whole day has been a dream, and when I wake up I'll tell Lindsay how the dream felt real and hours long, and she'll roll her eyes and tell me that dreams never last longer than thirty seconds.

It's funny to think about telling Lindsay—who's tugging on my hand and tossing her hair impatiently in front of me—that I'm only *dreaming* of her, that she's not really here, and I giggle, starting to relax. It's all a dream; I can do whatever I want. I can kiss anybody I want to, and as we walk past groups of guys I check them off in my head—Adam Marshall, Rassan Lucas, and Andrew Roberts—I could kiss each and every one if I wanted to. I see Kent standing in the corner talking to Phoebe Rifer and I think, *I could walk up and kiss the heart-shaped mole under his eye, and it wouldn't make a difference.* I don't know where the idea comes from. I would never kiss Kent, not even in a dream. But I could if I wanted to. Somewhere I'm lying stretched out under a warm blanket on a big bed surrounded by pillows, my hands folded under my head, sleeping.

I lean forward to tell Lindsay this—that I'm dreaming of yesterday and maybe yesterday was its own dream too—when I see Bridget McGuire standing in a corner with her arm around Alex Liment's waist. She's laughing and he's bending down to nuzzle her neck. She looks up at that moment and sees me watching them. Then she takes his hand and drags him over to me, pushing other people out of the way.

"*She'll* know," she's saying over her shoulder to him, and then she turns her smile on me. Her teeth are so white they're glowing. "Did Mrs. Harbor give out the essay assignments today?"

"What?" I'm so confused it takes me a second to realize she's talking about English class.

"The essay assignments. For *Macbeth*?"

She nudges Alex and he says, "I missed seventh period." He meets my eyes and then looks away, taking a swig of beer.

I don't say anything. I don't know what to say.

"So did she give them out?" Bridget looks like she always does: like a puppy just waiting for a treat. "Alex *had* to skip. Doctor's appointment. His mom made him get some shot to, like, prevent meningitis. How lame is that? I mean, four people died of it last year. You have more of a chance of being hit by a car—"

"He should get a shot to prevent herpes," Lindsay says, snickering, but so quietly I only hear because I'm standing right next to her. "It's probably too late, though."

"I don't know," I say to Bridget. "I cut."

I'm staring at Alex, watching his reaction. I'm not sure whether he noticed Lindsay and me standing outside of Hunan Kitchen today, peering inside. It doesn't seem like it.

He and Anna had been huddled over some grayish meat congealing in a plastic bowl, just like I'd expected them to be. Lindsay had wanted to go in and mess with them, but I'd threatened to puke on her new Steve Madden boots if we even caught a whiff of the nasty meat-and-onion smell inside.

By the time we left The Country's Best Yogurt, they were gone, and we only saw them again briefly at the Smokers' Lounge. They were leaving just as Lindsay was lighting up. Alex gave Anna a quick kiss on the cheek, and we saw them walk off in two different directions: Alex toward the cafeteria, Anna toward the arts building.

They were long gone by the time Lindsay and I passed the Nic Nazi on her daily patrol. They weren't busted today.

And Bridget doesn't know where he *really* was during seventh.

All of a sudden things start clicking into place—all the fears I've been holding back—one right after another like dominoes falling. I can't deny it anymore. Sarah Grundel got the parking space because we were late. That's why she's still in the semi-finals. Anna and Alex didn't have a fight because I convinced Lindsay to keep walking. That's why they weren't caught out at the Smokers' Lounge, and that's why Bridget is hanging off Alex instead of crying in a bathroom.

This isn't a dream. And it's not déjà vu.

It's really happening. It's happening *again*.

It feels like my whole body goes to ice in that second. Bridget's babbling about having never cut a class, and Lindsay's nodding and looking bored, and Alex is drinking his beer, and then I really can't breathe—fear is clamping down on me like a vise, and I feel like I might shatter into a million pieces right then and there. I want to sit down and put my head between my knees, but I'm worried that if I move, or close my eyes, or do anything, I'll just start to unravel—head coming away from neck coming away from shoulder—all of me floating away into nothing.

The head bone disconnected from the neck bone, the neck bone disconnected from the backbone . . .

I feel arms wrap around me from behind and Rob's mouth is on my neck. But even he can't warm me up. I'm shivering uncontrollably.

"Sexy Sammy," he singsongs, turning me around to him. "Where've you been all my life?"

"Rob." I'm surprised I can still speak, surprised I can still think. "I really need to talk to you."

"What's up, babe?" His eyes are bleary and red. Maybe it's because I'm terrified, but certain things seem sharper to me than they ever have, clearer. I notice for the first time that the crescent-shaped scar under his nose makes him look kind of like a bull.

"We can't do it here. We need to . . . we need to go somewhere. A room or something. Somewhere private."

He grins and leans into me, breathing alcohol on my face while he tries to kiss me. "I get it. It's *that* kind of conversation."

"I'm serious, Rob. I'm feeling—" I shake my head. "I'm not feeling right."

"You're never feeling right." He pulls away, frowning at me. "There's always something, you know?"

"What are you talking about?"

He sways a little bit on his feet and imitates. *"I'm tired tonight. My parents are upstairs. Your parents will hear."* He shakes his head. "I've been waiting months for this, Sam."

The tears are coming. My head throbs with the effort of keeping them back. "This has nothing to do with that. I swear, I—"

"Then what *does* it have to do with?" He crosses his arms.

"I just really need you right now." I barely get the words out. I'm surprised he even hears me.

He sighs and rubs his forehead. "All right, all right. I'm sorry." He puts one hand on the top of my head.

I nod. Tears start coming and he wipes two of them away with his thumb.

"Let's talk, okay? We'll go somewhere quiet." He rattles his empty beer cup at me. "But can I at least get a topper first?"

"Yeah, sure," I say, even though I want to beg him to stay with me, to put his arms around me and never let go.

"You're the best," he says, ducking down to kiss my cheek. "No crying—we're at a party, remember? It's supposed to be fun." He starts backing away and holds up his hand, fingers extended. "Five minutes."

I press myself against the wall and wait. I don't know what else to do. People are going past me, and I keep my hair down and in my face so no one will be able to tell the tears are still coming. The party is loud, but somehow it seems remote. Words are distorted and music sounds the way it does at a carnival, like all the notes are off balance and just colliding with one another.

Five minutes pass, then seven. Ten minutes pass, and I tell myself I'll wait five more minutes and then go look for him, even though the idea of moving seems impossible. After twelve minutes I text, *Where r u?* but then remember that yesterday he told me he'd set his phone down somewhere.

Yesterday. Today.

And this time, when I imagine myself lying somewhere, I'm not sleeping. This time I imagine myself stretched out on a cold stone slab, skin as white as milk, lips blue, and hands folded across my chest like they've been placed there. . . .

I take a deep breath and force myself to focus on other

things. I count the Christmas lights framing the *E.T.* movie poster over a couch, and then I count the bright red glowing cigarette butts weaving around through the half darkness like fireflies. I'm not a math geek or anything, but I've always liked numbers. I like how you can just keep stacking them up, one on top of the other, until they fill any space, any moment. I told my friends this one day, and Lindsay said I was going to be the kind of old woman who memorizes phone books and keeps flattened cereal boxes and newspapers piled from floor to ceiling in her house, looking for messages from space in the bar codes.

But a few months later I was sleeping over, and she confessed that sometimes when she's upset about something she recites this Catholic bedtime prayer she memorized when she was little, even though she's half Jewish and doesn't even believe in God anyway.

> *Now I lay me down to sleep,*
> *I pray thee, Lord, my soul to keep.*
> *If I should die before I wake,*
> *I pray thee, Lord, my soul to take.*

She'd seen it embroidered on a pillow in her piano teacher's house, and we laughed about how lame embroidered pillows were. But until I fell asleep that night I couldn't get the prayer out of my head. That one line kept replaying over and over in my mind: *If I should die before I wake.*

I'm just about to force myself away from the wall when I

hear Rob's name. Two sophomores have stumbled into the room, giggling, and I strain to hear what they're saying.

". . . his second in two hours."

"No, Matt Kessler did the first one."

"They both did."

"Did you see how Aaron Stern is, like, holding him above the keg? *Completely* upside down."

"That's what a keg stand *is*, duh."

"Rob Cokran is *so* hot."

"Shhh. Oh my God."

One of the girls elbows the other one when she notices me. Her face goes white. She's probably terrified: she's been talking about my boyfriend (misdemeanor), but, more specifically, she's been talking about how hot he is (felony). If Lindsay were here, she would freak out, call the girls whores, and get them booted from the party. If she were here she would expect *me* to freak out. Lindsay thinks that underclassmen—specifically sophomore girls—need to be put in their place. Otherwise they'll overrun the universe like cockroaches, protected from nuclear attack by an armor of Tiffany jewelry and shiny lipgloss shells.

I don't have the energy to give these girls attitude, though, and I'm glad Lindsay's not with me so she can't give me crap about it. I should have known Rob wouldn't come back. I think about today, when he told me to trust him, when he said that he'd never let me down. I should have told him he was full of it.

I need to get out. I need to be away from the smoke and the music. I need a place to think. I'm still freezing, and I'm sure I look awful, though I don't feel like I'm going to cry anymore. We once watched this health video about the symptoms of shock, and I'm pretty much the poster child for all of them. Difficulty breathing. Cold, clammy hands. Dizziness. Knowing this makes me feel even worse.

Which just goes to show you should never pay attention in health class.

The line for both bathrooms is four deep and all of the rooms are packed. It's eleven o'clock and everyone who has planned on showing is here. A couple of people say my name, and Tara Flute gets in my face and says, "Oh my God. I love your earrings. Did you get them at—"

"Not now." I cut her off and keep going, desperate to find somewhere dark and quiet. To my left is a closed door, the one with all of the bumper stickers plastered to it. I grip the doorknob and shake it. It doesn't open, of course.

"That's the VIP room."

I turn around and Kent is standing behind me, smiling.

"You've got to be on the list." He leans against the wall. "Or slip the bouncer a twenty. Whichever."

"I—I was looking for the bathroom."

Kent tilts his head toward the other side of the hall, where Ronica Masters, obviously drunk, is hammering on a door with her fist.

"Come on, Kristen!" she's yelling. "I really have to pee."

Kent turns back to me and raises his eyebrows.

"My bad," I say, and try to push past him.

"Are you okay?" Kent doesn't exactly touch me, but he holds his hand up like he's thinking about it. "You look—"

"I'm fine." The last thing in the world I need right now is pity from Kent McFuller, and I shove back into the hallway.

I've just decided to go outside and call Lindsay from the porch—I'll tell her I need to leave ASAP, I *have* to leave—when Elody barrels into the hall, throwing her arms around me.

"Where the hell have you been?" she screeches, kissing me. She's sweating, and I think of Izzy climbing into my bed and putting her arms around me, tugging on my necklace. I should never have gotten out of bed today.

"Let me guess, let me guess." Elody leaves her arms around me and starts bumping her hips like we're grinding on a dance floor. She rolls her eyes to the ceiling and starts moaning, "Oh, Rob, oh, Rob. Yeah. Just like that."

"You're a pervert." I push her off me. "You're worse than Shaw."

She laughs and grabs my hand, starts dragging me toward the back room. "Come on. Everyone's in here."

"I have to go," I say. The music back here is louder and I'm yelling. "I don't feel good."

"What?"

"I don't feel good!"

She points to her ear like, *I can't hear you*. I'm not sure if it's true or not. Her palms are wet and I try to pull away, but at that second Lindsay and Ally spot me, and they start squealing, jumping all over me.

"I was looking for you for ages," Lindsay says, waving her cigarette.

"In Patrick's mouth, maybe." Ally snorts.

"She was with Rob." Elody points at me, swaying on her feet. "Look at her. She *looks* guilty."

"Hussy!" Lindsay screeches. Ally pipes in with, "Trollop!" and Elody yells out, "Harlot!" This is an old joke of ours: Lindsay decided *slut* was too boring last year.

"I'm going home," I say. "You don't have to drive me. I'll figure it out."

Lindsay must think I'm kidding. "Go home? We only got here, like, an hour ago." She leans forward and whispers, "Besides, I thought you and Rob were going to . . . *you know*." As though she didn't just scream out in front of everybody that I already had.

"I changed my mind." I do my best to sound like I don't care, and the effort it takes is exhausting. I'm angry at Lindsay without knowing why—for not ditching the party with me, I guess. I'm angry at Elody for dragging me back here and at Ally for always being so clueless. I'm angry at Rob for not caring how upset I am, and I'm angry at Kent *for* caring. I'm angry at everyone and everything, and in that second I fantasize about the cigarette Lindsay's waving catching on the curtains, about fire racing over the room and consuming everyone. Then, immediately, I feel guilty. The last thing I need is to morph into one of those people who's always wearing black and doodling guns and bombs on her notebook.

Lindsay's gaping at me like she can see what I'm thinking. Then I realize she's looking over my shoulder. Elody turns pink. Ally's mouth starts opening and closing like a fish's. There's a dip in the noise of the party, like someone has just hit pause on a soundtrack.

Juliet Sykes. I know it will be her before I turn around, but I'm still surprised when I see her, still struck with that same sense of wonder.

She's pretty.

Today when I saw her drifting through the cafeteria she looked like she always did, hair hanging in her face, baggy clothing, shrunken into herself like she could be anyone, anywhere, a phantom or a shadow.

But now she's standing straight and her hair is pulled back and her eyes are glittering.

She walks across the room toward us. My mouth goes dry. I want to say no, but she's standing in front of Lindsay before I can get the word out. I see her mouth moving, but what she says takes a second to understand, like I'm hearing it from underwater.

"You're a bitch."

Everyone is whispering, staring at our little huddle: me, Lindsay, Elody, Ally, and Juliet Sykes. I feel my cheeks burning. The sound of voices begins to swell.

"What did you say?" Lindsay is gritting her teeth.

"A bitch. A mean girl. A bad person." Juliet turns to Elody. "You're a bitch." To Ally. "You're a bitch." Finally her eyes click on mine. They're exactly the color of sky.

"You're a bitch."

The voices are a roar now, people laughing and screaming out, "Psycho."

"You don't know me," I croak out at last, finding my voice, but Lindsay has already stepped forward and drowns me out.

"I'd rather be a bitch than a psycho," she snarls, and puts two hands on Juliet's shoulders and shoves. Juliet stumbles backward, pinwheeling her arms, and it's all so horrible and familiar. It's happening again; it's *actually* happening. I close my eyes. I want to pray, but all I can think is, *Why, why, why, why.*

When I open my eyes Juliet is coming toward me, drenched, arms outstretched. She looks up at me, and I swear to God it's like she knows, like she can see straight into me, like this is somehow *my* fault. I feel like I've been punched in the stomach and the air goes out of me and I lunge at her without thinking, push her and send her backward. She collapses into a bookshelf and then spins off of it, grabbing the doorframe to steady herself. Then she ducks out into the hallway.

"Can you believe it?" someone is screeching behind me.

"Juliet Sykes is packing some *cojones*."

"Cuckoo for Cocoa Puffs, man."

People are laughing, and Lindsay leans over to Elody and says, "Freak." The empty bottle of vodka is dangling from her hand. She must have dumped the rest on Juliet.

I start shoving my way out of the room. It seems as though even more people have come in and it's almost impossible to move. I'm really pushing, using my elbows when I have to, and everyone's giving me weird looks. I don't care. I need out.

I finally make it to the door and there's Kent, staring at me with his mouth set in a line. He shifts like he's about to block me.

I hold up my hand. "Don't even think about it." The words come out as a growl.

Without a sound he moves so I can squeeze past him. When I'm halfway down the hall I hear him shout out, "Why?"

"Because," I yell back. But really I'm thinking the same thing.

Why is this happening to me?

Why, why, why?

"How come *Sam* always gets shotgun?"

"Because you're always too drunk to call it."

"I can't *believe* you bailed on Rob like that," Ally says. She's got her coat hunched up around her ears. Lindsay's car is so cold our breaths are all solid white vapor. "You're going to be in so much trouble tomorrow."

If there is a tomorrow, I almost say. I left the party without saying good-bye to Rob, who was stretched out on a sofa, his eyes half shut. I'd been locked in an empty bathroom on the first floor for a half hour before that, sitting on the cold, hard rim of a bathtub, listening to the music pulsing through the walls and ceiling. Lindsay had insisted I wear bright red lipstick, and when I checked my face in the mirror, I saw that it had begun to bleed away from my lips, like a clown's. I took it off slowly with balled-up tissues, which I left floating in the toilet bowl, little blooming flowers of pink.

At a certain point your brain stops trying to rationalize things. At a certain point it gives up, shuts off, shuts down. Still, as Lindsay turns the car around—driving up on Kent's lawn to do it, tires spinning in the mud—I'm afraid.

Trees, as white and frail as bone, are dancing wildly in the wind. The rain is hammering the roof of the car, and sheets of water on the windows make the world look like it's disintegrating. The clock on the dashboard is glowing: 12:38.

I'm gripping my seat as Lindsay speeds down the driveway, branches whipping past us on either side.

"What about the paint job?" I say, my heart hammering in my chest. I try to tell myself I'm okay, I'm fine, that nothing's going to happen. But it doesn't do any good.

"Screw it," she says. "Car's busted anyway. Have you seen the bumper?"

"Maybe if you stopped hitting parked cars," Elody says with a snort.

"Maybe if you *had* a car." Lindsay takes one hand off the wheel and leans over, reaching for her bag at my feet. As she tips she jerks the steering wheel, and the car runs up a little into the woods. Ally slides across the backseat and collapses into Elody, and they both start laughing.

I reach over and try to grab the wheel. "Jesus, Lindz."

Lindsay straightens up and elbows me off. She shoots me a look and then starts fumbling with a pack of cigarettes. "What's up with you?"

"Nothing. I—" I look out the window, biting back tears that are suddenly threatening to come. "I just want you to pay attention, that's all."

"Yeah? Well, I want you to keep off the wheel."

"Come on, guys. No fighting," Ally says.

"Give me a smoke, Lindz." Elody's half reclining on the backseat, and she flails her arm wildly.

"Only if you light one for me," Lindsay says, tossing her pack into the backseat. Elody lights two cigarettes and passes one to Lindsay. Lindsay cracks a window and exhales a plume of smoke. Ally screeches.

"Please, please, no windows. I'm about to drop dead from pneumonia."

"You're about to drop dead when I kill you," Elody says.

"If you were gonna die," I blurt out, "how would you want it to be?"

"Never," Lindsay says.

"I'm serious." My palms are damp with sweat and I wipe them on the seat cushion.

"In my sleep," Ally says.

"Eating my grandma's lasagna," Elody says, and then pauses and adds, "or having sex," which makes Ally shriek with laughter.

"On an airplane," Lindsay says. "If I'm going down, I want everyone to go down with me." She makes a diving motion with her hand.

"Do you think you'll know, though?" It's suddenly important for me to talk about this. "I mean, do you think you'll have an idea of it . . . like, *before*?"

Ally straightens up and leans forward, hooking her arms over the back of our seats. "One day my grandfather woke up, and he swore he saw this guy all in black at the foot of his bed—big hood, no face. He was holding this sword or whatever that thingy is called. It was Death, you know? And then later that day he went to the doctor and they diagnosed him with pancreatic cancer. *The same day.*"

Elody rolls her eyes. "He didn't die, though."

"He could have died."

"That story doesn't make any sense."

"Can we change the subject?" Lindsay brakes for just a second before yanking the car out onto the wet road. "This is so morbid."

Ally giggles. "SAT word alert."

Lindsay cranes her neck back and tries to blow smoke in Ally's face. "Not all of us have the vocabulary of a twelve-year-old."

Lindsay turns onto Route 9, which stretches in front of us, a giant silver tongue. A hummingbird is beating its wings in my chest—rising, rising, fluttering into my throat.

I want to go back to what I was saying—I want to say, *You would know, right? You would know before it happened*—but Elody bumps Ally out of the way and leans forward, the cigarette dangling from her mouth, trumpeting, "Music!" She grabs for the iPod.

"Are you wearing your seat belt?" I say. I can't help it. The terror is everywhere now, pressing down on me, squeezing the breath from me, and I think: *if you don't breathe, you'll die.* The clock ticks forward. 12:39.

Elody doesn't even answer, just starts scrolling through the iPod. She finds "Splinter," and Ally slaps her and says it should be her turn to pick the music, anyway. Lindsay tells them to stop fighting, and she tries to grab the iPod from Elody, taking both hands off the wheel, steadying it with one knee. I grab for it again and she shouts, "Get off!" She's laughing.

Elody knocks the cigarette out of Lindsay's hand and it lands between Lindsay's thighs. The tires slide a little on the wet road, and the car is full of the smell of burning.

If you don't breathe . . .

Then all of a sudden there's a flash of white in front of the car. Lindsay yells something—words I can't make out, something like *sit* or *shit* or *sight*—and suddenly—

Well.

You know what happens next.

THREE

In my dream I am falling forever through darkness.

Falling, falling, falling.

Is it still falling if it has no end?

And then a shriek. Something ripping through the sound-lessness, an awful, high wailing, like an animal or an alarm—

Beepbeepbeepbeepbeepbeep.

I wake up stifling a scream.

I shut off the alarm, trembling, and lie back against my pillows. My throat is burning and I'm covered in sweat. I take long, slow breaths and watch my room lighten as the sun inches its way over the horizon, things beginning to emerge: the Victoria's Secret sweatshirt on my floor, the collage Lindsay made me years ago with quotes from our favorite bands and cut-up magazines. I listen to the sounds from downstairs, so familiar and constant it's like they belong to the architecture, like they've been built up out of the ground with the walls: the clanking of my father in the kitchen, shelving dishes; the frantic scrabbling sound of our pug, Pickle, trying to get out the back door, probably to pee and run around in circles; a low murmur that means my mom's watching the morning news.

When I'm ready, I suck in a deep breath and reach for my phone. I flip it open.

The date flashes up at me.

Friday, February 12.

Cupid Day.

"Get up, Sammy." Izzy pokes her head in the door. "Mommy says you're going to be late."

"Tell Mom I'm sick." Izzy's blond bob disappears again.

Here's what I remember: I remember being in the car. I remember Elody and Ally fighting over the iPod. I remember the wild spinning of the wheel and seeing Lindsay's face as the car sailed toward the woods, her mouth open and her eyebrows raised in surprise, as though she'd just run into someone she knew in an unexpected place. But after that? Nothing.

After that, only the dream.

This is the first time I really think it—the first time I allow myself to think it.

That maybe the accidents—both of them—were real.

And maybe I didn't make it.

Maybe when you die time folds in on you, and you bounce around inside this little bubble forever. Like the after-death equivalent of the movie *Groundhog Day*. It's not what I imagined death would be like—not what I imagined would come afterward—but then again it's not like there's anyone around to tell you about it.

Be honest: are you surprised that I didn't realize sooner? Are you surprised that it took me so long to even think *the word—* death? Dying? Dead?

Do you think I was being stupid? Naive?

Try not to judge. Remember that we're the same, you and me.

I thought I would live forever too.

"Sam?" My mom pushes open the door and leans against the frame. "Izzy said you felt sick?"

"I . . . I think I have the flu or something." I know I look like crap so it should be believable.

My mom sighs like I'm being difficult on purpose. "Lindsay will be here any second."

"I don't think I can go in today." The idea of school makes me want to curl up in a ball and sleep forever.

"On Cupid Day?" My mom raises her eyebrows. She glances at the fur-trimmed tank top that's laid out neatly over my desk chair—the only item of clothing that isn't lying on the floor or hanging from a bedpost or a doorknob. "Did something happen?"

"No, Mom." I try to swallow the lump in my throat. The worst is knowing I can't tell anybody what's happening—or what's happened—to me. Not even my mom. I guess it's been years since I talked to her about important stuff, but I start wishing for the days when I believed she could fix anything. It's funny, isn't it? When you're young you just want to be older, and then later you wish you could go back to being a kid.

My mom's searching my face really intensely. I feel like at any second I could break down and blurt out something crazy so I roll away from her, facing the wall.

"You love Cupid Day," my mom prods. "Are you sure nothing happened? You didn't fight with your friends?"

"No. Of course not."

She hesitates. "Did you fight with Rob?"

That makes me want to laugh. I think about the fact that he left me waiting upstairs at Kent's party and I almost say, *Not yet.* "No, Mom. God."

"Don't use that tone of voice. I'm just trying to help."

"Yeah, well, you're not." I bury deeper under the covers, keeping my back turned to her. I hear rustling and think she'll come and sit next to me. She doesn't, though. Freshman year after a big fight I drew a line in red nail polish just inside my door, and I told her if she ever came past the line I'd never speak to her again. Most of the nail polish has chipped off by now, but in places you can still see it spotted over the wood like blood.

I meant it at the time, but I'd expected her to forget after a while. But since that day she's never once stepped foot in my room. It's a bummer in some ways, since she never surprises me by making up my sheets anymore, or leaving folded laundry or a new sundress on my bed like she did when I was in middle school. But at least I know she's not rooting through my drawers while I'm at school, looking for drugs or sex toys or whatever.

"If you want to come out here, I'll get the thermometer," she says.

"I don't think I have a fever." There's a chip in the wall in the exact shape of an insect, and I push my thumb against the wall, squishing it.

I can practically feel my mom put her hands on her hips. "Listen, Sam. I know it's second semester. And I know you think that gives you the right to slack off—"

"Mom, that is not it." I bury my head under the pillow, feeling like I could scream. "I told you, I don't feel good." I'm half afraid she'll ask me what's wrong and half hoping she will.

She only says, "All right. I'll tell Lindsay you're thinking of going in late. Maybe you'll feel better after a little more sleep."

I doubt it. "Maybe," I say, and a second later I hear the door click shut behind her.

I close my eyes and reach back into those final moments, the last memories—Lindsay's look of surprise and the trees lit up like teeth in the headlights, the wild roar of the engine— searching for a light, a thread that will connect this moment to that one, a way to sew together the days so that they make sense.

But all I get is blackness.

I can't hold back my tears anymore. They come all at once, and before I know it I'm sobbing and snotting all over my best Ethan Allen pillows. A little later I hear scratching against my door. Pickle has always had a dog sense for when I'm crying, and in sixth grade after Rob Cokran said I was too big of a dork for him to go out with—right in the middle of the cafeteria, in front of everybody—Pickle sat on my bed and licked the tears off one after another.

I don't know why that's the example that pops into my head, but thinking about that moment makes a new rush of anger and frustration swell up inside of me. It's strange how much the memory affects me. I've never mentioned that day to Rob—I doubt he remembers—but I've always liked to think about it when we're walking down the hallway, our fingers interlaced, or when we're all hanging out in Tara Flute's basement, and Rob looks over at me and winks. I like to think how funny life is: how so much changes. How *people* change.

But now I just wonder when, exactly, I became cool enough for Rob Cokran.

After a while the scratching on my door stops. Pickle has finally realized he's not getting in, and I hear his paws ticking against the floor as he trots off. I don't think I've ever felt so alone in my life.

I cry until it seems amazing that one person could have so many tears. It seems like they must be coming from the very tips of my toes.

Then I sleep without dreaming.

ESCAPE TACTICS

I wake up thinking about a movie I once saw. The main character dies somehow—I forget how—but he's only half dead. One part of him is lying there in a coma, and one part of him is wandering the world, kind of in limbo. The point is, so long as he's not completely 100 percent dead, a piece of him is trapped in this in-between place.

This gives me hope for the first time in two days. The idea that I might be lying somewhere in a coma, my family bending over me and everyone worrying and filling my hospital room with flowers, actually makes me feel *good*.

Because if I'm not dead—at least not *yet*—there may be a way to stop it.

My mom drops me off in Upper Lot just before third period starts (.22 miles or not, I will not be seen getting out of my mom's maroon 2003 Accord, which she won't trade in because she says it's "fuel efficient"). Now I can't wait to get to school. I have a gut feeling I'll find the answers there. I don't know how or why I'm stuck in this time loop, but the more I think about it, the more convinced I am that there's a reason for it.

"See you later," I say, and start to pop out of the car.

But something stops me. It's the idea that's been bugging me for the past twenty-four hours, what I was trying to talk to my friends about in the Tank: how you might not ever really know. How you might be walking down the street one day and—*bam!*

Blackness.

"It's cold, Sam." My mom leans over the passenger seat and gestures for me to shut the door.

I turn around and stoop down to look at her. It takes me a second to work the words out of my mouth, but I mumble, "Iloveyou."

I feel so weird saying it, it comes out more like *olivejuice*. I'm not even sure if she understands me. I slam the door quickly before she can respond. It's probably been years since I've said "I love you" to either of my parents, except on Christmas or birthdays or when they say it first and it's pretty much expected. It leaves me with a weird feeling in my stomach, part relief and part embarrassment and part regret.

As I'm walking toward school I make a vow: there's not going to be an accident tonight.

And whatever it is—this bubble or hiccup in time—I'm busting out.

Here's another thing to remember: hope keeps you alive. Even when you're dead, it's the only thing that keeps you alive.

137

· · ·

The bell has already rung for third period, so I book it to chem. I get there just in time to take a seat—big surprise—next to Lauren Lornet. The quiz goes off, same as yesterday and the day before—except by now I can answer the first question myself.

Pen. Ink. Working? Mr. Tierney. Book. Slam. Jump.

"Keep it," Lauren whispers to me, practically batting her eyelashes at me. "You're going to need a pen." I start to try to pass it back, as usual, but something in her expression sparks a memory. I remember coming home after Tara Flute's pool party in seventh grade and seeing my face in the mirror lit up exactly like that, like somebody had handed me a winning lottery ticket and told me my life was about to change.

"Thanks." I stuff the pen into my bag. She's still making that face—I can see it out of the corner of my eye—and after a minute I whip around and say, "You shouldn't be so nice to me."

"What?" Now she looks completely stunned. Definitely an improvement.

I have to whisper because Tierney's started his lesson again. Chemical reactions, blah, blah, blah. Transfiguration. Put two liquids together and they form a solid. Two plus two does not equal four.

"Nice to me. You shouldn't be."

"Why not?" She squinches up her forehead so her eyes nearly disappear.

"Because I'm not nice to you." The words are surprisingly hard to get out.

"You're nice," Lauren says, looking at her hands, but she obviously doesn't mean it. She looks up and tries again. "You don't . . ."

She trails off, but I know what she's going to say. *You don't have to be nice to me.*

"Exactly," I say.

"Girls!" Mr. Tierney bellows, slamming his fist down on his lab station. I swear he goes practically neon.

Lauren and I don't talk for the rest of class, but I leave chem feeling good, like I've done the right thing.

"That's what I like to see." Mr. Daimler drums his fingers on my desk as he walks the aisles at the end of class collecting homework. "A big smile. It's a beautiful day—"

"It's supposed to rain later," Mike Heffner interjects, and everyone laughs. He's an idiot.

Mr. Daimler doesn't skip a beat. "—and it's Cupid Day. Love is in the air." He looks straight at me and my heart stops for a second. "*Everyone* should be smiling."

"Just for you, Mr. Daimler," I say, making my voice extra sweet. More giggles and one loud snort from the back. I turn around and see Kent, head down, scribbling furiously on the cover of his notebook.

Mr. Daimler laughs and says, "And here I thought I'd gotten

139

you excited about differential equations."

"You got her excited about *something*," Mike mutters. More laughter from the class. I'm not sure if Mr. Daimler hears—he doesn't seem to—but the tips of his ears turn red.

The whole class has been like this. I'm in a good mood, certain everything will be okay. I've got it all figured out. I'm going to get a second chance. Plus Mr. Daimler's been paying me extra attention. After the Cupids came in he took a look at my four roses, raised his eyebrows, and said I must have secret admirers everywhere.

"Not so secret," I said, and he winked at me.

After class I gather up my stuff and go out into the hall, pausing for just a second to check over my shoulder. Sure enough, Kent's bounding along after me, shirt untucked, messenger bag half open and slapping against his thigh. What a mess. I start walking toward the cafeteria. Today I looked more carefully at his note: the tree is sketched in black ink, each dip and shadow in the bark shaded perfectly. The leaves are tiny and diamond shaped. The whole thing must have taken him hours. I stuck it between two pages of my math book so it wouldn't get crushed.

"Hey," he says, catching up with me. "Did you get my note?"

I almost say to him, *It's really good*, but something stops me. "'Don't drink and love?' Is that some kind of a catchphrase I don't know about?"

"I consider it my civic duty to spread the word." Kent puts his hand over his heart.

A thought flashes—*you wouldn't be talking to me if you could remember*—but I push it aside. This is Kent McFuller. He's lucky I'm talking to him at all. Besides, I don't plan on being at the party tonight: no party, no Juliet Sykes, no reason for Kent to wig out on me. Most important, no accident.

"More like spread the weirdness," I say.

"I take that as a compliment." Kent suddenly looks serious. He scrunches up his face so that all the light freckles on his nose come together like a constellation. "Why do you flirt with Mr. Daimler? He's a perv, you know."

I'm so surprised by the question it takes me a second to answer. "Mr. Daimler is *not* a perv."

"Trust me, he is."

"Jealous?"

"Hardly."

"I don't *flirt* with him, anyway."

Kent rolls his eyes. "Sure."

I shrug my shoulders. "Why so interested?"

Kent goes red and drops his eyes to the floor. "No reason," he mumbles.

My stomach dips a little bit, and I realize a part of me was hoping his answer would be different—more personal. Of course, if Kent *did* confess his undying love for me right there, in the hallway, it would be disastrous. Despite his weirdness

I have no desire to publicly humiliate him—he's nice and we were childhood friends and all that—but I could never, ever, ever date him, not in a million lifetimes. Not in *my* lifetime, anyway: the one I want back, where yesterdays are followed by todays and then tomorrows. The bowler hat alone makes it impossible.

"Listen." Kent shoots me a look out of the corner of his eye. "My parents are going away this weekend, and I'm having some people over tonight. . . ."

"Uh-huh." Up ahead I see Rob loping toward the cafeteria. At any second he'll spot me. I can't handle seeing him right now. My stomach clenches and I leap in front of Kent, turning my back to the cafeteria. "Um . . . where's your house again?"

Kent looks at me strangely. I did basically just set myself up like a human barricade. "Off Route Nine. You don't remember?" I don't respond and he looks away, shrugging. "I guess you wouldn't, really. You were only there a few times. We moved just before middle school. From Terrace Place. You remember my old house on Terrace Place, right?" The smile is back. It's true: his eyes are exactly the color of grass. "You used to hang out in the kitchen and steal all the good cookies. And I chased you around these huge maple trees in the front yard. Remember?"

As soon as he mentions the maple trees a memory rises up, expanding, like something breaking the surface of water and rippling outward. We were sitting in this little space in between two enormous roots that curved out of the ground like animal spines. I remember that he split two maple-wing seeds and stuck one on his nose and one on mine, telling me that this way everyone would know we were in love. I was probably only five or six.

"I—I . . ." The last thing I need is for him to remind me of the good old days, when I was all knees and nose and glasses, and he was the only boy who would come near me. "Maybe. Trees kinda all look the same to me, you know?"

He laughs even though I wasn't trying to be funny. "So you think you'll come tonight? To my party?"

This brings me back to reality. The party. I shake my head and start backing away. "No. I don't think so."

His smile falters a little. "It'll be fun. Big. Senior memories. Best time of our lives and all that crap."

"Right," I say sarcastically. "High school heaven."

I turn around and start walking away from him. The cafeteria is packed, and as I approach the double doors—one of which is propped open with an old tennis shoe—the noise of the students greets me with a roar.

"You'll come," he calls after me. "I know you will."

"Don't hold your breath," I call back, and I almost add, *It's better this way.*

THE RULES OF SURVIVAL

"What do you mean you *can't* go out?"

Ally's looking at me like I just said I wanted to go to prom with Ben Farsky (or Fart-sky, as we've been calling him since fourth grade).

I sigh. "I just don't feel like it, okay?" I switch tactics and try again. "We go out every weekend. I just—I don't know. I want to stay in, like we used to."

"We used to stay in because we couldn't get into any senior parties," Ally says.

"Speak for yourself," Lindsay says.

This is harder than I thought it would be.

I flash on my mom asking if I'd had a fight with Rob and before I can think too much about it I blurt out, "It's Rob, okay? We . . . we're having issues."

I flip open my phone, checking for texts for the millionth time. When I first came into the cafeteria Rob was standing behind the registers, loading his fries with ketchup and barbecue sauce (his favorite). I couldn't bring myself to go up to him, so instead I hurried to our table in the senior section and sent him a text: *We have 2 talk*.

He texted back right away. *Bout?*

2nite, I wrote back, and since then my phone's been silent. Across the cafeteria, Rob is leaning against the vending machines talking to Adam Marshall. He has his hat twisted sideways on his head. He thinks it makes him look older.

I used to love collecting all these little facts about him, storing them together and holding them close inside of me, like if I gathered up all the details and remembered them—the fact that he likes barbecue sauce but not mustard, that his favorite team is the Yankees even though he prefers basketball to baseball, that once when he was little he broke his leg trying to jump over a car—I would totally understand him. I used to think that's what love was: knowing someone so well he was like a part of you.

But more and more I'm feeling like I *don't* know Rob.

Ally's jaw actually drops. "But you're supposed to—*you know.*"

She kind of looks like a mounted fish with her mouth open like that, so I turn away, fighting the urge to laugh. "We were supposed to, but . . ." I've never been a good liar and my brain goes totally blank.

"But?" Lindsay prompts.

I reach into my bag and pull out the note he sent me, which is now crumpled and has a piece of gum, half unwrapped, sticking to it. I push it across the table. "But this."

Lindsay wrinkles her nose and flips open the card with the very tips of her fingernails. Ally and Elody lean over and they both read. They're all silent for a second afterward.

Finally Lindsay closes the card and pushes it back to me. "It's not that bad," she says.

"It's not that good, either." I was only trying to fake an excuse to keep us away from the party tonight, but as soon as I start talking about Rob, I get really worked up. "*Luv ya?* What kind of crap is that? We've been going out since October."

"He's probably just waiting to say it," Elody says. She pushes the bangs out of her eyes. "Steve doesn't say it to me."

"That's different. You don't expect him to say it."

Elody looks away quickly, and it occurs to me that maybe, despite everything, she does.

There's an awkward pause, and Lindsay jumps in. "I don't see what the trauma is. You know Rob likes you. It's not like it would be a one-night stand or anything."

"He *likes* me, but . . ." I'm about to confess that I'm not sure that we're good together, but at the last second I can't. They would think I was insane. I don't even understand it myself, really. It's like the idea of him is better than the *him* of him. "Look. I'm not going to have sex with him just so he'll say that he loves me, you know?"

I don't even mean for the words to come out, and for a second I'm so startled by them, I can't say anything else. That isn't why I was planning to have sex with Rob—to hear the words, I mean. I just wanted to get it over with. I think. Actually, I'm not sure why it seemed so important.

"Speak of the devil," Ally mutters.

Then I smell lemon balm and Rob's planting a wet kiss on my cheek.

"Hi, ladies." He reaches over to take a fry from Elody, and she moves her tray just out of reach. He laughs. "Hey, Slammer. Did you get my note?"

"I got it." I look down at the table. I feel like if I meet his eyes I'll forget everything, forget the note and how he left me alone and how when he kisses me he keeps his eyes open.

At the same time, I don't *really* want anything to change.

"So? What'd I miss?" Rob leans forward and puts his hands on the table—a little too hard, I think. Lindsay's Diet Coke jumps.

"The party at Kent's and how Sam doesn't want to go," Ally blurts out. Elody elbows her in the side and Ally yelps.

Rob swivels his head and looks at me. His face is completely expressionless. "Is that what you wanted to talk about?"

"No—well, kind of." I wasn't expecting him to mention the text, and it flusters me that I can't tell what he's thinking. His eyes look extra dark, almost cloudy. I try to smile at him, but I feel like my cheeks are all stuffed with cotton. I can't help but picture him swaying on his feet and holding up his hand and saying, "Five minutes."

"Well?" He straightens up and shrugs. "What, then?"

Lindsay, Ally, and Elody are all staring at me. I can feel their eyes like they're emitting heat. "I can't talk about it here. I mean, not now." I tip my head in their direction.

Rob laughs: a short, harsh sound. And now I can tell he's mad and just hiding it.

"Of course not." He backs away, both hands raised like he's warding something off. "How 'bout this? You let me know when you're *ready* to talk. I'll *wait* to hear from you. I would never want to, you know, *pressure* you." He elongates some of the words, and I can hear the sarcasm in his voice—just barely, but it's there.

It's obvious—to me, at least—that he's talking about way more than our having a talk, but before I can respond he gives a flourish with his hand, a kind of bow, and then turns around and walks away.

"Jeez." Ally pushes around the turkey sandwich on her plate. "What was that about?"

"You're not really fighting, are you, Sam?" Elody asks, eyes wide.

Before I have to answer Lindsay makes a kind of hissing noise and juts her chin up, gesturing behind me. "Psychopath alert. Lock up the knives and babies."

Juliet Sykes has just walked into the cafeteria. I've been so focused on today—on fixing it, on the idea that I can fix it—I've totally forgotten about Juliet. But now I whip around, more curious about her than I've ever been. I watch her drifting through the cafeteria. Her hair is down and concealing her face: fuzzy, soft hair, so white it reminds me of snow. That's what she looks like, actually—like a snowflake being buffeted around in the wind, twisting and turning on currents of air. She doesn't even glance up in our direction, and I wonder if even now she's planning it, planning to follow us tonight and embarrass us in front of everybody. It doesn't seem like she would have it in her.

I'm so focused on watching her that it takes me a second

to realize Ally and Elody have just finished a round of *Psycho killer, qu'est-ce que c'est* and are now laughing hysterically. Lindsay's holding up her fingers, crossed, like she's warding off a curse, and she keeps repeating, "Oh, Lord, keep the darkness away."

"Why do you hate Juliet?" I ask Lindsay. It's strange to me that I've never thought of asking until recently. I always just accepted it.

Elody snorts and almost coughs up her Diet Coke. "Are you serious?"

Lindsay's clearly not prepared for the question. She opens her mouth, closes it, and then tosses her hair and rolls her eyes like she can't believe I'm even asking. "I don't *hate* her."

"Yes, you do." It was Lindsay who found out that Juliet wasn't sent a single rose freshman year, and Lindsay's idea to send her a Valogram. It was Lindsay who nicknamed her Psycho, and who, all those years ago, spread the story of Juliet peeing on the Girl Scout camping trip.

Lindsay stares at me like I've lost my mind. "Sorry," she says, shrugging. "No breaks for mental-health patients."

"Don't tell me you feel bad for her or something," Elody says. "You know she should be locked up."

"Bellevue." Ally giggles.

"I was just wondering," I say, stiffening when Ally says the B-word. There's still always the possibility that I've gone totally, clinically cuckoo. But somehow I don't think so anymore. An article I once read said that crazy people don't worry about being crazy—that's the whole problem.

"So are we *really* staying in tonight?" Ally says, pouting. "The *whole* night?"

I suck in my breath and look at Lindsay. Ally and Elody look at her too. She has final say on all of our major decisions. If she's hell-bent on going to Kent's, I'll have a hard time getting out of it.

Lindsay leans back in her chair and stares at me. I see something flicker in her eyes, and my heart stops, thinking that she'll tell me to suck it up, that a party will do me good.

But instead she cracks a smile and winks at me. "It's just a party," she says. "It'll probably be lame anyways."

"We can rent a scary movie," Elody pipes up. "You know, like we used to."

"It's up to Sam," Lindsay says. "Whatever she wants."

I could kiss her right then.

I cut English with Lindsay again. We pass Alex and Anna in Hunan Kitchen, but today Lindsay doesn't even pause, probably because she's trying extra hard to be nice to me and she knows I hate confrontations.

I hesitate, though. I think of Bridget putting her arms around Alex and looking at him like he's the only guy on earth. She's annoying, okay, but she deserves way better than him. It's too bad.

"Hello? Stalk much?" Lindsay says.

I realize I'm just standing there staring past the ripped-up flyers advertising five-dollar lunch specials and local theater groups and hair salons. Alex Liment has spotted me through the window. He's staring straight back at me.

"I'm coming." It is too bad, but really, what can you do? Live and let live.

In The Country's Best Yogurt, Lindsay and I both get heaping cups of double chocolate with crushed peanut butter cups, and I add sprinkles and Cap'n Crunch cereal. I have my appetite back, that's for sure. Everything is working out the way I planned it. There won't be any party tonight, at least not for us; there won't be any driving or cars. I'm sure that this will fix everything—that the kink in time will be ironed out, that I'll wake up from whatever nightmare I've been living. Maybe I'll sit up, gasping, in a hospital bed somewhere, surrounded by friends and family. I can picture the scene perfectly: my mom and dad tearful, Izzy crying while she hangs on my neck, Lindsay and Ally and Elody and—

An image of Kent flashes through my head and I push it away quickly.

—And Rob. Of course Rob.

But this is the key, I'm sure of it. Live the day out. Follow the rules. Stay away from Kent's party. Simple.

"Careful." Lindsay grins, shoveling a huge spoonful of yogurt into her mouth. "You don't want to be fat *and* a virgin."

"Better than fat with gonorrhea," I say, flicking a chocolate chip at her.

She flicks one back. "Are you kidding? I'm so clean you could eat off me."

"The Lindsay buffet. Does Patrick know you're giving it up like that?"

"Gross."

Lindsay is wrestling with her jumbo cup, trying to dig out the perfect bite. But we're both laughing, and she ends up lobbing a full spoonful of yogurt at me. It hits me right above the left eye.

She gasps and claps one hand over her mouth. The yogurt slides down my face and lands with a plop right on the fur covering my left boob.

"I am so, so sorry," Lindsay says, her voice muffled by her hand. Her eyes are wide, and it's obvious she's trying not to laugh. "Do you think your shirt is ruined?"

"Not yet," I say, and dig out a big scoop of yogurt and flick it at her. It hits her in the side of her head, right in her hair.

She shrieks, "Bitch!" and then we're ducking around the TCBY hiding behind chairs and tables, digging big scoops of double chocolate and using our spoons like catapults to peg each other.

YOU CAN'T JUDGE A GYM TEACHER BY HIS HANDLEBAR MUSTACHE

Lindsay and I can't stop cracking up on the way back to school. It's hard to explain, but I'm feeling happier than I have in years, like I'm noticing everything for the first time: the sharp smell of winter, the light strange and slanted, the way the clouds are drawing over the sky slowly. The fur of our tank tops is completely matted and gross, and we have water stains everywhere. Cars keep honking at us, and we wave and blow them all kisses. A black Mercedes rolls by, and Lindsay bends over, smacks her butt, and screams, "Ten dollar! Ten dollar!"

I punch her in the arm. "That could be my dad."

"Sorry to break it to you, but your dad does *not* drive a Mercedes." Lindsay pushes her hair out of her face. It's stringy and wet. We had to wash off in the bathroom as the woman at TCBY screamed at us and threatened to call the police if we ever stepped foot in the store again.

"You're impossible," I say.

"You know you love me," she says, grabbing my arm and huddling up next to me. We're both freezing.

"I do love you," I say, and I really mean it. I love her, I love the ugly mustard yellow bricks of Thomas Jefferson and the magenta-tinted halls. I love Ridgeview for being small and boring, and I love everyone and everything in it. I love my life. I want my life.

"Love you too, babes."

When we get back to school Lindsay wants to have a cigarette, even though the bell for eighth is going to ring any second.

"Two drags," Lindsay says, widening her eyes, and I laugh

and let her pull me along because she knows I can never say no to her when she makes that face. The Lounge is empty. We stand right next to the tennis courts, huddled together, while Lindsay tries to get a match lit.

Finally she does, and she takes a long drag, letting a plume of smoke out of her mouth.

A second later we hear a shout from across the parking lot: "Hey! You! With the cigarette!"

We both freeze. Ms. Winters. Nic Nazi.

"Run!" Lindsay screams after a split second, dropping her cigarette. She takes off behind the tennis courts even though I yell, "Over here!" I see the big blond pouf of Ms. Winters's hair bobbing over the cars—I'm not sure if she's seen us or just heard us laughing. I duck behind a Range Rover and cut across Senior Alley to one of the back doors in the gym as Ms. Winters keeps screaming, "Hey! *Hey!*"

I grab the handle and rattle it, but the door sticks. For a second my heart stops, and I'm sure it's locked, but then I slam up against it and it opens into a storage closet. I jump inside and close the door behind me, heart thumping in my chest. A minute later I hear feet pound past the door. Then I hear Ms. Winters mutter, "Shit," and the footsteps start retreating backward.

The whole thing—the day, the fight in The Country's Best Yogurt, the almost-bust, the idea of Lindsay crouching somewhere in the woods in her skirt and new Steve Madden boots—strikes me as so funny I have to clap my hand over my mouth to keep from laughing. The room I'm standing in smells like soccer cleats and jerseys and mud, and with the stack of orange cones and bag full of basketballs piled in the corner, there's barely enough room for me to stand. One side of the room is windowed and it looks into an office: Shaw's, probably, since he basically lives in the gym. I've never actually seen his office. His desk is piled with papers, and there's a computer flashing a screen saver that looks like it's a cheesy picture of a beach. I inch closer to the window, thinking how hilarious it would be if I could bust him with something dirty, like some underwear peeking out of a desk drawer or a porn mag or something, when the door of his office swings open and there he is.

Instantly I drop to the ground. I have to scrunch up in a ball, and even then I'm paranoid that my ponytail might be peeking up over the windowsill. It sounds stupid considering everything that's been happening, but all I can think in that moment is, *If he sees me, I'm* really *dead. Good-bye, Ally's house; hello, detention.*

My face is sandwiched up next to a half-open duffel bag that looks like it's full of old basketball jerseys. I don't know if they've never been washed or what, but the smell makes me want to gag.

I hear Shaw moving around his desk, and I'm praying— *praying*—that he doesn't come close enough to the desk to see me bellying up to a bunch of old sports equipment. I can already hear the rumors: Samantha Kingston found humping driver's ed cones.

There's a minute or two of shuffling, and my legs start cramping. The first bell has already rung for eighth—less than three minutes to class—but there's no way for me to sneak out. The door is noisy, and besides, I have no way to know which direction he's facing. He could be staring at the door.

My only hope is that Shaw has class eighth, but it doesn't sound like he's in a hustle to be anywhere. I imagine being trapped here until school ends. The stink alone will finish me off.

I hear Shaw's door creak open again, and I perk up, thinking he's leaving after all. But then a second voice says, "Damn. I missed them."

I would recognize that nasal whine anywhere. Ms. Winters.

"Smokers?" Shaw says. His voice is almost as high-pitched as hers. I had no idea they even knew each other. The only times I've ever seen them in the same room are at all-school assemblies, when Ms. Winters sits next to Principal Beneter looking like someone just set off a stink bomb directly under her chair, and Shaw sits with the special ed teachers and the health instructor and the driver's ed specialist and all the other weirdos who are on faculty but aren't real teachers.

"Do you know that the students call that little area the 'Smokers' Lounge'?" I can almost hear Ms. Winters pinching her nose.

"Did you get a look at them?" Shaw asks, and my muscles tense.

"Not a good one. I could hear them and I smelled the smoke."

Lindsay's right: Ms. Winters is definitely half greyhound.

"Next time," Shaw says.

"There must be two thousand cigarette butts out there," Ms. Winters says. "You'd think with all the health videos we show them—"

"They're teenagers. They do the opposite of what you say. That's part of the deal. Pimples, pubic hair, and bad attitude."

I almost lose it when Shaw says *pubic hair*, and I think Ms. Winters will lecture him, but she only says, "Sometimes I don't know why I bother."

"It's been one of those days, huh?" Shaw says, and there's the sound of someone bumping against a desk, and a book thudding to the ground. Ms. Winters actually *giggles*.

And then, I swear to God, I hear them *kissing*. Not little bird pecks either. Open-mouthed, slurpy, moaning kind of kissing.

Oh, shit. I literally have to bite my own hand to keep from screaming, or crying, or bursting out laughing, or getting sick—or all of the above. *This. Cannot. Be. Happening.* I'm desperate to take out my phone and text the girls, but I don't want to move. Now I really don't want to get caught, since Shaw and the Nazi will think I've been spying on their little sex party. Barf.

Just when I feel like I can't stand one more second squeezed up next to the sweaty jerseys, listening to Shaw and Winters suck face like they're in some bad porno, the second bell rings. I am now officially late to eighth period.

"Oh, God. I'm supposed to be meeting with Beanie," Ms. Winters says. Beanie's the students' name for Mr. Beneter, the principal. Of all the shocking things that I've heard in the past two minutes, the most shocking is that she knows the nickname—and uses it.

"Get out of here," Mr. Shaw says, and then I swear—I *swear*—I hear him smack her butt.

Oh. My. God. This is better than the time Marcie Harris got caught masturbating in the science lab (with a test tube up her you-know-what, if you believe the rumors). This is better than the time Bryce Hanley got suspended for briefly running an online porn site. This is better than any scandal that's hit Thomas Jefferson so far.

"Do you have class?" Ms. Winters says, practically cooing.

"I'm done for the day," Shaw says. My heart sinks—there's no way I'll be able to stay here for another forty-five minutes. Never mind the cramp snaking up my hamstrings and thighs: I've got amazing gossip to spread. "But I have to set up for soccer tryouts."

"Okay, babe." *Babe?* "I'll see you tonight."

"Eight o'clock."

I hear the door open and I know Ms. Winters has left. Thank

God. From the way they were pillow talking I was worried I was about to be treated to the symphony of another make-out session. I'm not sure my hamstrings or my psyche could take it.

After a few seconds of moving around and tapping some things on the keyboard, I hear Shaw go to the door. The room next to me goes dark. Then the door opens and closes, and I know I'm in the clear.

I say a silent hallelujah and stand up. The pins and needles in my legs are so bad I nearly topple over, but I toddle over to the door and lean into it. When I make it outside I stand there stamping my feet and taking long, deep breaths of clean air. Finally I let it out: I throw my head back and laugh hysterically, cackling and snorting and not even caring if I look deranged.

Ms. Winters and Mr.-effing-Shaw. Who would have guessed it in a million, trillion years?

As I head up from the gym it strikes me how strange people are. You can see them every day—you can think you know them—and then you find out you hardly know them at all. I feel exhilarated, kind of like I'm being spun around a whirlpool, circling closer and closer around the same people and the same events but seeing things from different angles.

I'm still giggling when I get to Main, even though Mr. Kummer will freak that I'm late, and I still have to stop by my locker and pick up my Spanish textbook (he told us on the first day that we should treat our textbooks like children. Obviously, he doesn't have any). I'm pressing Send on a text to Elody, Ally, and Lindsay—*u ll nvr believe what jst happnd*—when, *bam!* I run smack into Lauren Lornet.

Both of us stumble backward, and my phone flies out of my hand and skitters across the hall.

"Shit!" We collide so hard it takes me a second to recover my breath. "Watch where you're going."

I start toward my phone, wondering if I can ask her to pay if the screen's cracked or something, when she grabs my arm. Hard. "What the . . . ?"

"Tell them," she says wildly, pushing her face up to mine. "You've got to tell them."

"What are you talking about?" I try to pull away, but she grabs my other arm too, like she wants to shake me. Her face is red and splotchy and she has an all-over sticky look. It's obvious she's been crying.

"Tell them I didn't do anything wrong." She jerks her head back over her shoulder. We're standing directly in front of the main office, and I see her in that moment the way she was yesterday, hair hanging over her face, tearing down the hall.

"I really don't know what you're talking about," I say, as gently as possible, because she's freaking me out. She probably has biweekly visits with the school psychologist to control her paranoia, or OCD, or whatever her issue is.

She takes a deep breath. Her voice is shaky. "They think I

cheated off you in chem. Beanie called me in. . . . But I didn't. I swear to God I didn't. I've been studying. . . ."

I jerk back, but she keeps her grip on my arms. The feeling of being caught in a whirlpool returns, but this time it's horrible: I'm being pulled down, down, down, like there's a weight on me.

"You cheated off me?" My words feel like they're coming from a distance. I don't even sound like myself.

"I didn't, I swear to God I—" Lauren gives a shuddering sob. "He'll fail me. He said he would fail me if my grades didn't get better, and I got a tutor and now they think I—he said he'd call Penn State. I'll never go to college and I—you don't understand. My dad will kill me. He'll kill me." She really does shake me then. Her eyes are full of panic. "You have to tell them."

I finally manage to wrench away. I feel hot and sick. I don't want to know this, don't want to know any of it.

"I can't help you," I say, backing away, still feeling like I'm not actually saying the words, just hearing them spoken aloud from somewhere.

Lauren looks like I've just slapped her. "What? What do you mean you can't help? Just tell them—"

My hands are shaking as I go to pick up my phone. It slips out of my grasp twice and lands back on the floor both times with a clatter. It's not supposed to be like this. I feel like someone's pressed the Reverse button on a vacuum cleaner and all of the junk I've done is spewing back onto the carpet for me to see.

"You're lucky you didn't break my phone," I say, feeling numb. "This cost me two hundred dollars."

"Were you even *listening* to me?" Lauren's voice is rising hysterically. I can't bring myself to meet her eyes. "I'm screwed, I'm finished—"

"I can't help you," I say again. It's like I can't remember any other words.

Lauren lets out something that's halfway between a scream and a sob. "You said I shouldn't be nice to you today. You know what? You were right. You're awful, you're a bitch, you're—"

Suddenly it's like she remembers where we are: who she is, and who I am. She claps her hand over her mouth so quickly it makes a hollow, echoing sound in the hallway.

"Oh, God." Now her voice comes out as a whisper. "I'm so sorry. I didn't mean it."

I don't even answer. Those words—*you're a bitch*—make my whole body go cold.

"I'm sorry. I—please don't be mad."

I can't stand it—can't stand to hear her apologize to me. And before I know it I'm running—full-out running down the hall, my heart pounding, feeling like I need to scream or cry or smash my fist into something. She calls after me, but I don't know what it is, I don't care, I can't know, and when I push into the girls' bathroom, I throw my back against the door and sink down against it until my knees are pressed into my chest, my throat squeezed up so tight it hurts to breathe. My phone keeps buzzing, and once I've calmed down a bit, I flip it open and find texts from Lindsay, Ally, and Elody: *What? Dish. Spill. Did u make up w Rob?*

I throw my phone into my bag and rest my head in my hands, waiting for my pulse to return to normal. All of the happiness I felt earlier is gone. Even the Shaw and Winters situation doesn't seem funny anymore. Bridget and Alex and Anna and Sarah Grundel and her stupid parking space and Lauren Lornet and the chem test—it feels like I've been caught up in some enormous web and every way I turn I see that I'm stuck to someone else, all of us wriggling around in the same net. And I don't want to know any of it. It's not my problem. I don't care.

You're a bitch.

I don't care. I have bigger things to worry about.

Finally I stand up. I've given up on going to Spanish. Instead I splash cold water on my face and then reapply my makeup. My face is so pale under the harsh fluorescent lights, I hardly recognize it.

ONLY THE DREAM

"Come on, cheer up." Lindsay whacks me on the head with a pillow. We're sitting on the couch in Ally's den.

Elody pops the last spicy tuna roll into her mouth, which I'm not sure is such a great idea, as it's now been perched on an

163

ottoman for the past three hours. "Don't worry, Sammy. Rob'll get over it."

All of them think Rob's the reason I'm quiet. But of course, it isn't. I'm quiet because as soon as the clock inched its way past twelve, the fear crept back in. It's been filling me slowly, like sand running through an hourglass. With every second I'm getting closer and closer to the Moment. Ground zero. This morning I was certain that it was simple—that all I had to do was stay away from the party, stay away from the car. That time would lurch back on track. That I would be saved.

But now my heart feels like it's being squashed between my ribs, and it gets harder and harder to breathe. I'm terrified that in one second—in the space between a breath—everything will evaporate into darkness, and I'll once again find myself alone in my bedroom at home, waking up to the screaming of the alarm. I don't know what I'll do if that happens. I think my heart will break. I think my heart will stop.

Ally switches off the television and throws down the remote. "What should we do now?"

"Let me consult the spirits." Elody slides off the couch and onto the floor, where earlier we'd set up a dusty Ouija board for old time's sake. We tried to play, but everyone was obviously pushing, and the indicator kept zipping onto words like *penis* and *choad*, until Lindsay started screaming "Perv spirits! Child molesters!" into the air.

Elody shoves the indicator with two fingers. It spins once

before settling over the word YES.

"Look, Ma." She holds up her hands. "No hands."

"It wasn't a *yes* or *no* question, doofus." Lindsay rolls her eyes and takes a big sip of the Châteauneuf-du-Pape we swiped from the wine cellar.

"This town sucks," Ally says. "Nothing ever happens."

Twelve thirty-three. Twelve thirty-four. I've never seen seconds and minutes rush by so fast, tumble over one another. Twelve thirty-five. Twelve thirty-six.

"We need music or something," Lindsay says, jumping up. "We can't just sit around here like bums."

"Definitely music," Elody says. She and Lindsay run into the next room, where the Bose sound dock is.

"No music." I groan, but it's too late. Beyoncé is already blasting. The vases begin to rattle on the bookshelves. My head feels like it's going to explode, and chills are running up and down my body. Twelve thirty-seven. I nestle deeper into the couch, drawing a blanket up over my knees, and cover my ears.

Lindsay and Elody march back into the room. We're all in old boxer shorts and tank tops. Lindsay's obviously just raided Ally's mudroom because she and Elody are now also decked out in ski goggles and fleece hats. Elody's hobbling along with one foot jammed in a child's snowshoe.

"Oh my God!" Ally screams. She holds her stomach and doubles over, laughing.

Lindsay gyrates with a ski pole between her legs, rocking back and forth. "Oh, Patrick! Patrick!"

The music is so loud I can barely hear her, even when I take my hands off my ears. Twelve thirty-eight. One minute.

"Come on!" Elody shouts, extending her hand to me. I'm so full of fear I can't move, can't even shake my head, and she leans forward and yells, "Live a little!"

So many thoughts and words are tumbling through my head. I want to yell, *No, stop* or *Yes, live,* but all I can do is squeeze my eyes shut and picture seconds running like water into an infinite pool, and I imagine all of us hurtling through time and I think, *Now, now, it's going to happen now—*

And then everything goes silent.

I'm afraid to open my eyes. A deep emptiness opens up inside me. I feel nothing. This is what it's like to be dead.

Then a voice: "Too loud. You'll blow out your eardrums before you're twenty."

I snap open my eyes. Mrs. Harris, Ally's mom, is standing in the doorway in a glistening raincoat, smoothing down her hair. And Lindsay's standing there in her ski goggles and hat, and Elody's awkwardly trying to pry her foot out of the snowshoe.

I made it. It worked. Relief and joy flood me with so much force I almost cry out.

But instead, I laugh. I burst out laughing in the silence, and

Ally gives me a dirty look, like, Now *you decide it's funny?*

"Are you girls drunk?" Ally's mother stares at each of us in turn and then frowns at the nearly empty bottle of wine on the floor.

"Hardly." Ally throws herself on the couch. "You killed the buzz."

Lindsay flips the goggles onto her head. "We were having a dance party, Mrs. Harris," she says brightly, as if dancing around half naked and decked out in winter sports equipment was a Girl Scouts–mandated activity.

Mrs. Harris sighs. "Not anymore. It's been a long day. I'm going to bed."

"Moooom," Ally whines.

Mrs. Harris shoots her a look. "No more music."

Elody finally wrenches her foot free and stumbles backward, collapsing against one of the bookshelves. *Martha Stewart's Homekeeping Handbook* comes flying out and lands at her feet. "Oops." She turns bright red and looks at Mrs. Harris like she expects to be spanked any minute.

I can't help it. I start giggling again.

Mrs. Harris rolls her eyes to the ceiling and shakes her head. "Good night, girls."

"Nice going." Ally leans over and pinches my thigh. "Retard."

Elody starts giggling and imitates Lindsay's voice. "We were having a dance party, Mrs. Harris."

"At least I didn't fall into a bookshelf." Lindsay bends over and wiggles her butt at us. "Kiss it."

"Maybe I will." Elody dives for her, pretending like she's going to. Lindsay shrieks and dodges her. Ally hisses, *"Shhhh!"* right as we hear Mrs. Harris yell, *"Girls!"* from upstairs. Pretty soon they're all laughing. It feels great to laugh with them.

I'm back.

An hour later Lindsay, Elody, and I are settled on the L-shaped couch. Elody has the top bit, and Lindsay and I are lying end-to-end. My feet are pressed against Lindsay's, and she keeps wiggling her toes to annoy me. But nothing can annoy me right now. Ally has dragged in her air mattress and her blankets from upstairs (she insists she can't sleep without her Society comforter). It's just like freshman year. We've put the television on low because Elody likes the sound, and in the dark room the glow of the screen reminds me of summers spent breaking into the pool club to go night-swimming, of the way the light shines up through all that black water, of stillness and feeling like you're the only person alive in the whole world.

"You guys?" I whisper. I'm not sure who's still awake.

"Mmmf," Lindsay grunts.

I close my eyes, letting the feeling of peace sweep over me, fill me from head to toe. "If you had to relive one day over and over, which one would you pick?"

Nobody answers me, and in a little while I hear Ally start

snoring into her pillow. They're all asleep. I'm not tired yet. I'm still too exhilarated to be here, to be safe, to have broken out of whatever bubble of time and space has been confining me. But I close my eyes anyway and try to imagine what kind of day I would choose. Memories speed by—dozens and dozens of parties, shopping trips with Lindsay, pigging out at sleepovers and crying over *The Notebook* with Elody, and even before that, family vacations and my eighth birthday party and the first time I ever dove off the high board at the pool and the water fizzed up my nose and left me dizzy—but all of them seem imperfect somehow, spotted and shadowy.

On a perfect day there wouldn't be any school, that's for sure. And there would be pancakes for breakfast—my mom's pancakes. And my dad would make his famous fried eggs, and Izzy would set the table like she sometimes does at holidays, with different mismatched plates and fruit and flowers that she gathers from around the house and dumps in the middle of the table and calls a "thenterpeeth."

I close my eyes and feel myself letting go, like tipping over the edge of an abyss, darkness rising up to carry me away. . . .

Bringbringbring.

I'm pulled back from the edge of sleep and for one horrible second I think: *it's my alarm, I'm home, it's happening again.* I strike out, a spasm, and Lindsay yelps, "Ow!"

The sound of that one word makes my heart go still and my breathing return to normal.

Bringbringbring. Now that I'm fully alert I realize it's not my alarm. It's the telephone, ringing shrilly in various rooms, creating a weird echo effect. I check the clock. One fifty-two.

Elody groans. Ally rolls over and murmurs, "Turn it off." The telephone stops ringing and then starts again, and all of a sudden Ally sits up, straight as a rod, totally awake.

She says, "Shit. Shit. My mom's gonna kill me."

"Make it stop, Al," Lindsay says, from underneath her pillow.

Ally tries to untangle herself from her sheets, still muttering, "Shit. Where's the freaking *phone*?" She trips and ends up stumbling out of bed and hitting the ground with her shoulder. Elody moans again, this time louder.

Lindsay says, "I'm trying to sleep, people."

"I need the phone," Ally hisses back.

It's too late, anyway. I hear footsteps moving upstairs. Mrs. Harris has obviously woken up. A second later the phone stops ringing.

"Thank God." Lindsay rustles around, burrowing farther under her covers.

"It's almost two." Ally stands up—I can see the vague outline of her form hobbling back over to the bed. "Who the hell calls at two in the morning?"

"Maybe it's Matt Wilde, confessing his love," Lindsay says.

"Very funny," Ally says. She settles back in bed and we all get quiet. I can just hear the low murmur of Mrs. Harris's voice above us, the creaking of her footsteps as she paces. Then I very distinctly hear her say: "Oh, no. Oh my God."

"Ally—" I start.

But she's heard it too. She gets up and turns on the light, then switches off the television, which is still on low. The sudden brightness makes me wince. Lindsay curses and pulls the covers over her head.

"Something's wrong." Ally hugs herself, blinking rapidly. Elody reaches for her glasses, then props herself up on two elbows. Eventually Lindsay realizes the light's not going off and she emerges from under her cocoon.

"What's the problem?" She balls her hands into fists, rubbing her eyes.

No one answers. We all have a growing sense of it now: something is *very* wrong. Ally's just standing there in the middle of the room. In her oversized T-shirt and baggy shorts she looks much younger than she is.

At a certain point the voice upstairs stops, and the footsteps move diagonally across the floor, in the direction of the stairs. Ally moves back to the air mattress, folding her legs underneath her and biting her nails.

Mrs. Harris doesn't seem surprised to find us sitting up, waiting for her. She's wearing a long silk nightgown and has an eye mask perched on top of her head. I've never seen Mrs. Harris looking less than perfect and it makes fear yawn open in my stomach.

171

"What?" Ally's voice is semihysterical. "What happened? Is it Dad?"

Mrs. Harris blinks and seems to focus on us like she's just been called out of a dream. "No, no. It's not your father." She takes a breath, then blows it out loudly. "Listen, girls. What I'm about to tell you is very upsetting. I'm only telling you in the first place because you'll find out soon enough."

"Just tell us, Mom."

Mrs. Harris nods slowly. "You all know Juliet Sykes."

This is a shock: we all look at one another, completely bewildered. Of all the words that Mrs. Harris could have said at this moment, I'm pretty sure "You all know Juliet Sykes" ranks pretty high on our list of the unexpected.

"Yeah. So?" Ally shrugs.

"Well, she—" Mrs. Harris breaks off, smoothing down her nightgown with her hands, and starts again. "That was Mindy Sachs on the phone."

Lindsay raises her eyebrows, and Ally gives a knowing sigh. We all know Mindy Sachs too. She's fifty and divorced but still dresses and acts like a sophomore. She's more gossip-obsessed than anybody at our school. Whenever I see Ms. Sachs I'm reminded of the game we used to play when we were kids, where one person whispers a secret and the next person repeats it and so on and so on, except in Ridgeview Ms. Sachs is the only one doing the whispering. She and Mrs. Harris sit on the school board together, so Mrs. Harris always knows about divorces and who just lost all their money and who's having an affair.

"Mindy lives just next to the Sykes'," Mrs. Harris continues. "Apparently their street has been swarming with ambulances for the past half hour."

"I don't get it," Ally says, and maybe it's the hour or the stress of the past few days, but I'm not getting it either.

Mrs. Harris has her arms folded across her chest and she hugs herself a little, like she's cold. "Juliet Sykes is dead. She killed herself tonight."

Silence. Total silence. Ally stops chewing on her nails, and Lindsay sits as still as I've ever seen her. I really think for several seconds my heart stops beating. I feel a strange tunneling sensation, like I've been parachuted out of my body and am now just looking at it from far away, like for a few moments we're all just pictures of ourselves.

I'm suddenly reminded of a story my parents once told me: back when Thomas Jefferson was called Suicide High, some guy hanged himself inside his own closet, right there among the mothball-smelling sweaters and old sneakers and everything. He was a loser and played in the band and had bad skin and next to no friends. So nobody thought anything of it when he died. I mean, people were sad and everything, but they *got* it.

But the next year—the next year to the day—one of the most popular guys in school killed himself in the *exact same way*. Everything was the same: method, time, place. Except this guy was captain of the swim team and the soccer team, and apparently when the police went into the closet, there were so many old athletic trophies on the shelves it looked like he'd been entombed in a gold vault. He left only a one-line note: *We are all Hangmen.*

"How?" Elody asks, barely a whisper.

Mrs. Harris shakes her head, and for a second I think she might cry. "Mindy heard the gunshot. She thought it was a firecracker. She thought it was a prank."

"She shot herself?" Ally says it quietly, almost reverentially, and I know we're all thinking the same thing: that's the worst way of any.

"How are they . . ." Elody adjusts her glasses and licks her lips. "Do they know why?"

"There was no note," Mrs. Harris says, and I swear I can hear something go around the room: a tiny exhalation. A breath of relief. "I just thought you should know." She goes to Ally and bends over, kissing her forehead. Ally pulls away, maybe in surprise. I've never seen Mrs. Harris kiss Ally before. I've never seen Mrs. Harris look so much like a *mother* before.

After Mrs. Harris leaves we all sit there while the silence stretches out and expands in huge rings around us. I feel like we're all waiting for something, but I'm not sure what. Finally Elody speaks.

"Do you think . . ." Elody swallows, looking back and forth

from one to the other of us. "Do you think it's because of our rose?"

"Don't be stupid," Lindsay snaps. I can tell she's upset, though. Her face is pale, and she twists and untwists the edge of her blanket. "It's not like it was the first time."

"That makes it even worse," Ally says.

"At least we knew who she was." Lindsay catches me staring at her hands, and she places them firmly in her lap. "Most people just acted like she was invisible."

Ally bites her lip.

"Still, on her last day . . ." Elody trails off.

"She's better off this way," Lindsay says. This is low, even for her, and we all stare.

"What?" She lifts her chin and stares back at us defiantly. "You know you're all thinking it. She was miserable. She escaped. Done."

"But—I mean, things could have gotten better," I say.

"They wouldn't have," Lindsay says.

Ally shakes her head and draws her knees to her chest. "God, Lindsay."

I'm in shock. The weirdest part of it all is the gun. It seems so harsh, so loud, so physical a way to do it. Blood and brains and searing heat. If she had to do it—to die—she should have drowned, should have just walked into the water until it folded over her head. Or she should have jumped. I picture Juliet floating this way and that, like she's being supported by currents of air. I can imagine her spreading her arms and leaping off a bridge or a canyon somewhere, but in my head she starts soaring upward on the wind as soon as her feet leave the ground.

Not a gun. Guns are for cop dramas and 7-Eleven holdups and crack addicts and gang fights. Not for Juliet Sykes.

"Maybe we should have been nicer to her," Elody says. She looks down like she's embarrassed to say it.

"Please." Lindsay's voice is loud and hard in comparison. "You can't be mean to someone forever and then feel bad when she dies."

Elody lifts her head and stares at Lindsay. "But I *do* feel bad." Her voice is getting stronger.

"Then you're a hypocrite," Lindsay says. "And that's worse than anything."

She gets up and shuts off the light. I hear her climb back on the couch and rustle around in the blankets, settling in.

"If you'll excuse me," she says, "I have sleep to catch up on."

There's total silence for a while. I'm not sure if Ally's lying down or not, but as my eyes adjust to the darkness I see that she isn't: she's still sitting there with her knees drawn up to her chest, staring straight ahead.

After a minute she says, "I'm going to sleep upstairs." She gathers up her sheets and blankets, making extra noise, probably to get back at Lindsay.

A moment later Elody says, "I'm going with her. The couch

is too lumpy." She's obviously upset too. We've been sleeping on this couch for years.

After she leaves I sit for a while listening to Lindsay breathe. I wonder if she's sleeping. I don't see how she could be. I feel as awake as I've ever been. Then again, Lindsay's always been different from most people, less sensitive, more black-and-white. My team, your team. This side of the line, that side of the line. Fearless, and careless. I've always admired her for that—we all have.

I feel restless, like I need to know the answers to questions I'm not sure how to ask. I ease off the couch slowly, trying not to wake Lindsay, but it turns out she's not sleeping after all. She rolls over, and in the dark I can just make out her pale skin and the deep hollows of her eyes.

"You're not going upstairs, are you?" she whispers.

"Bathroom," I whisper back.

I feel my way out into the hallway and pause there. Somewhere a clock is ticking, but other than that it's totally silent. Everything is dark and the stone floor is cold under my feet. I run one hand along the wall to orient myself. The sound of the rain has stopped. When I look outside I see the rain has turned to snow, thousands of snowflakes melting down the latticed windows and making the moonlight that comes through the panes look watery and full of movement, shadows twisting and blurring on the floor, alive. There's a bathroom here, but that's not where I'm headed. I ease open the door that leads to

Ally's basement and grope my way down the stairs, holding on to both banisters.

As soon as my feet hit the carpet at the bottom of the stairs, I fumble on the wall to my left, eventually finding the light switch. The basement is suddenly revealed, big and stark and normal-looking: beige leather couches, an old Ping-Pong table, another flat-screen TV, and a circular area with a treadmill, an elliptical machine, and a three-sided mirror at its center. It's cooler here and smells like chemicals and new paint.

Just beyond the exercise area is another door, which leads into the room we've always referred to as the Altar of Allison Harris. The room is papered with Ally's old drawings, none of them good, most dating back to elementary school. The bookshelves are crowded with pictures of her: Ally dressed up like an octopus for Halloween in first grade, Ally wearing a green velvet dress and smiling in front of an enormous Christmas tree absolutely collapsing with ornaments, Ally squinting in a bikini, Ally laughing, Ally frowning, Ally looking pensive. And on the lowest shelf, every single one of Ally's old yearbooks, from kindergarten on. Ally once showed us how Mrs. Harris had gone through all the books, one by one, placing colored sticky tabs on each one of Ally's friends from year to year. ("So you can remember how popular you always were," Mrs. Harris had told her.)

I drop to my knees. I'm not sure exactly what I'm looking for, but there's an idea taking shape in my head, some old memory that disappears whenever I will it to take form, like those Magic Eye games where you can only see the hidden shape when your eyes aren't in focus.

I start with the first-grade yearbook. I open it directly to Mr. Christensen's class—just my luck—and there I am, standing a little ways apart from the group. The flash reflected in my glasses makes it impossible to see my eyes. My smile is closer to a wince, as though the effort hurts. I flip past the picture quickly. I hate looking through old yearbooks; they don't exactly bring back a flood of positive memories. Mine are stashed somewhere in the attic, with all the other crap my mom insists I keep "because you might want it later," like my old dolls and a ratty stuffed lamb I used to carry with me everywhere.

Two pages later I find what I'm looking for: Mrs. Novak's first-grade class. And there Lindsay is, front and center as always, beaming a big smile at the camera. Next to her is a thin, pretty girl with a shy smile and hair so blond it could be white. She and Lindsay are standing so close together their arms are touching all the way from their elbows to their fingertips.

Juliet Sykes.

In the second-grade yearbook, Lindsay is kneeling in the front row of her class. Again, Juliet Sykes is next to her.

In the third-grade yearbook, Juliet and Lindsay are separated by several pages. Lindsay was in Ms. Derner's class (with me—that was the year she invented the joke: "What's red and white and weird all over?"). Juliet was in Dr. Kuzma's class.

Different pages, different classes, different poses—Lindsay has her hands clasped in front of her; Juliet is standing with her body angled slightly to the side—and yet they look exactly the same, wearing identical powder blue Petit Bateau T-shirts and matching white capri pants, which cut off just below the knee; their hair, blond and shining, parted neatly down the middle; the glint of a small silver chain around both of their necks. That was the year it was cool to dress up like your friends—your best friends.

I pick up the fourth-grade yearbook next, my fingers heavy and numb, cold running through me. There's a big Technicolor portrait of the school on its cover, all neon pinks and reds, probably painted by an art teacher. It takes me a while to find Lindsay's class, but as soon as I do my heart starts racing. There she is with that same huge smile, like she's daring the camera to catch her looking less-than-perfect. And next to her is Juliet Sykes. Pretty, happy Juliet Sykes, smiling like she has a secret. I squint, focusing on a tiny blurred spot between them, and think I can just make out that their index fingers are linked together loosely.

Fifth grade. I find Lindsay easily, standing front and center in Mrs. Krakow's classroom, smiling so widely it looks like she's baring her teeth. It takes me longer to find Juliet. I go through all the photographs looking for her and have to start over from the beginning before I spot her, far up in the right-hand corner, sandwiched between Lauren Lornet and Eileen Cho, shrinking backward like she wants to suck herself out of the frame altogether. Her hair hangs in front of her face like a curtain. Next to her, both Lauren and Eileen are angled slightly away, as though they don't want to be associated with her, as though she has some contagious disease.

Fifth grade: the year of the Girl Scout trip, when she peed in her sleeping bag and Lindsay nicknamed her Mellow Yellow.

I put the yearbooks back carefully, making sure to order them correctly. My heart is thumping wildly, an out-of-control drum rhythm. I suddenly want to get out of the basement as quickly as possible. I shut off the lights and feel my way up the stairs blindly. The darkness seems to swirl with shapes and shadows, and terror rises in my throat. I'm sure that if I turn around I'll see her, all in white, stumbling with her hands outstretched, reaching for me, face bloody and broken apart.

And then I'm upstairs and there she is: a vision, a nightmare. Her face is completely in shadow—a hole—but I can tell she's staring at me. The room tilts; I grab on to the wall to keep myself steady.

"What's your problem?" Lindsay steps farther into the hall, the moonlight falling differently so that her features emerge. "Why are you looking at me like that?"

"Jesus." I bring my hand to my chest, trying to press my heart back to its normal rhythm. "You scared me."

"What were you doing down there?" Her hair is messed up, and in her white boxers and tank top she could be a ghost.

"You were friends with her," I say. It pops out like an accusation. "You were friends with her for years."

I'm not sure what answer I'm expecting, but she looks away and then looks back at me.

"It's not our fault," she says, like she's daring me to contradict her. "She's totally wacked. You know that."

"I know," I say. But I get the feeling she's not even talking to me.

"And I heard her dad's, like, an alcoholic," Lindsay presses on, her voice suddenly quick, urgent. "Her whole *family's* wacked."

"Yeah," I say. For a minute we just stand there in silence. My body feels heavy, useless, the way it sometimes does in nightmares when you have to run but you can't. After a while something occurs to me and I say, "Was."

Even though we've been standing in silence, Lindsay inhales sharply, as though I've interrupted her in the middle of a long speech. "What?"

"She *was* wacked," I say. "She's not anything anymore."

Lindsay doesn't respond. I go past her into the dark hallway and find my way to the couch. I settle in under the blankets, and a little while later she comes in and joins me.

Lying there, convinced I won't be able to sleep, I remember the time in the middle of junior year when Lindsay and I snuck out on a random weeknight—a Tuesday or a Thursday—and drove around because there was nothing else to do. At some point she pulled over abruptly on Fallow Ridge Road and cut the headlights, waiting until another car began to squeeze its way toward us on the single-lane road. Then she roared the engine and blazed the lights to life and began careening straight toward it. I was screaming at the top of my lungs, the headlights growing huge as suns, certain we were going to die, and she was gripping the steering wheel and calling out over my screams, "Don't worry—they always swerve first." She was right, too. At the last second the other car jerked abruptly into the ditch.

That's what I remember just before the dream pulls me under.

In my dream I am falling through darkness.

In my dream I fall forever.

FOUR

Even before I'm awake, the alarm clock is in my hand, and I break from sleep completely at the same moment I hurl the clock against the wall. It lets out a final wail before shattering.

"Whoa," Lindsay says, when I slide into the car fifteen minutes later. "Is there a job opening in the red-light district I don't know about?"

"Just drive." I can barely look at her. Anger is seething through me like liquid. She's a fraud: the whole world is a fraud, one bright, shiny scam. And somehow *I'm* the one paying for it. I'm the one who died. I'm the one who's trapped.

Here's the thing: it shouldn't be me. Lindsay's the one who drives like she's in the real-life version of Grand Theft Auto. Lindsay's the one who's always thinking of ways to punk people or humiliate them, who's always criticizing everybody. Lindsay's the one who lied about being friends with Juliet Sykes and then tortured her all those years. I didn't do anything; I just followed along.

"You're gonna freeze, you know." Lindsay chucks her cigarette and rolls up the window.

"Thanks, Mom." I flip down the mirror to make sure that my lipstick hasn't smeared. I've folded my skirt over a couple of times so it barely covers my ass when I sit down, and I'm wearing five-inch platforms that I bought with Ally as a joke at a store that we're pretty sure only caters to strippers. I've kept the fur-trimmed tank top, but I've added a rhinestone necklace, again purchased as a joke one Halloween when we all dressed up as Naughty Nurses. It says SLUT in big, sparkly script.

I don't care. I'm in the mood to get looked at. I feel like I could do anything right now: punch somebody in the face, rob a bank, get drunk and do something stupid. That's the only benefit to being dead. No consequences.

Lindsay misses my sarcasm, or ignores it. "I'm surprised your parents even let you out of the house like that."

"They didn't." Another thing making my mood foul is the ten-minute screaming match I had with my mother before storming out of the house. Even when Izzy went to hide in her room and my father threatened to ground me for life (*Ha!*), the words kept coming. It felt so good to scream, like when you pick a scab and the blood starts flowing again.

You are not walking out that door unless you go upstairs and put on some more clothing. That's what my mom said. *You'll catch pneumonia. More important, I don't want people in school getting the wrong impression about you.*

And suddenly it had all snapped inside of me, broken and snapped. "You care *now*?" She jerked back at the sound of my voice like I'd reached out and slapped her. "You want to help *now*? You want to protect me *now*?"

What I really wanted to say was, *Where were you four days ago? Where were you when my car was spinning off the edge of a road in the middle of the night? Why weren't you thinking of me? Why weren't you* there? I hate both of my parents right now: for sitting quietly in our house, while out in the darkness my heart was beating away all of the seconds of my life, ticking them off one by one until my time was up; for letting the thread between us stretch so far and so thin that the moment it was severed for good they didn't even feel it.

At the same time I know that it's not really their fault, at least not completely. I did my part too. I did it on a hundred different days and in a thousand different ways, and I know it. But this makes the anger worse, not better.

Your parents are supposed to keep you safe.

"Jesus, what's your problem?" Lindsay looks at me hard for a second. "You wake up on the wrong side of the bed or something?"

"For a few days now, yeah."

I'm getting really sick of this low half-light, the sky a pale and sickly blue—not even a real blue—and the sun a wet mess on the horizon. I read once that starving people start fantasizing about food, just lying there dreaming for hours about hot mashed potatoes and creamy blobs of butter and steak running red blood over their plates. Now I get it. I'm starved for different light, a different sun, different sky. I've never really thought about it before, but it's a miracle how many kinds of light there are in the world, how many skies: the pale brightness of spring, when it feels like the whole world is blushing; the lush, bright boldness of a July noon; purple storm skies and a green queasiness just before lightning strikes and crazy multicolored sunsets that look like someone's acid trip.

I should have enjoyed them more, should have memorized them all. I should have died on a day with a beautiful sunset. I should have died on summer vacation or winter break. I should have died on any other day. Leaning my forehead against the window, I fantasize about sending my fist up through the glass, all the way into the sky, and watching it shatter like a mirror.

I think about what I'll do to survive all of the millions and millions of days that will be exactly like this one, two face-to-face mirrors multiplying a reflection into infinity. I start formulating a plan: I'll stop coming to school, and I'll jack somebody's car and drive as far as I can in a different direction every day. East, west, north, south. I allow myself to fantasize about going so far and so fast that I lift off like an airplane, zooming straight up and out to a place where time falls away like sand being blown off a surface by the wind.

Remember what I said about hope?

• • •

"Happy Cupid Day!" Elody singsongs when she gets into the Tank.

Lindsay stares from Elody back to me. "What is this? Some kind of competition for Least Dressed?"

"If you got it, flaunt it." Elody eyes my skirt as she leans forward to grab her coffee. "Forget your pants, Sam?"

Lindsay snickers. I say, "Jealous much?" without turning away from the window.

"What's wrong with her?" Elody leans back.

"Someone forgot to take her happy pills this morning."

Out of the corner of my eye I see Lindsay look back at Elody and make a face like, *Leave it.* Like I'm a kid who needs to be handled. I think of those old photos where she's standing pressed arm-to-arm with Juliet Sykes, and then I think of Juliet's head blown open and splattered on some basement wall. Again the fury returns, and it's all I can do to keep from turning to her and screaming that she's a fake, a liar, that I can see right through her.

I see right through you. . . . My heart flips when I remember Kent's words.

"I know something that'll cheer you up." Elody starts rummaging around in her bag, looking pleased with herself.

"I swear to God, Elody, if you're about to give me a condom right now . . ." I press my fingers to my temples.

Elody freezes and frowns, holding up a condom between

188

two fingers. "But . . . it's your present." She looks at Lindsay for support.

Lindsay shrugs. "Up to you," she says. She's not looking at me, but I can tell my attitude is really starting to piss her off, and to be honest, I'm happy about it. "If you want to be a walking STD farm."

"You would know all about that." I don't even mean for it to slip out; it just does.

Lindsay whips around to face me. "What did you say?"

"Nothing."

"Did you say—"

"I didn't say anything." I lean my head against the glass.

Elody's still sitting there with the condom dangling between her fingers. "C'mon, Sam. No glove, no love, right?"

Losing my virginity seems absurd to me now, the plot point of a different movie, a different character, a different lifetime. I try to reach back and remember what I love about Rob—what I loved about him—but all I get is a random collection of images in no particular order: Rob passing out on Kent's couch, grabbing my arm and accusing me of cheating; Rob laying his head on my shoulder in his basement, whispering that he wants to fall asleep next to me; Rob turning his back on me in sixth grade; Rob holding up his hand and saying, *Five minutes*; Rob taking my hand for the first time ever when we were walking through the hall, a feeling of pride and strength going through me. They seem like the memories of somebody else.

That's when it really hits me: none of it matters anymore. Nothing matters anymore.

I twist around in my seat, reaching back to grab the condom from Elody.

"No glove, no love," I say, giving her a tight smile.

Elody cheers. "That's my girl."

I'm turning around again when Lindsay slams on the brakes at a red light. I jet forward and have to reach out one hand to keep from hitting the dash and then, as the car stops moving, slam back against the headrest. The coffee in the cup holder jumps its lip and splashes my thigh.

"Oops." Lindsay giggles. "So sorry."

"You really are a hazard." Elody laughs and reaches around to buckle her seat belt.

The anger I've felt all morning pours out in a rush. "What the hell is wrong with you?"

Lindsay's smile freezes on her face. "Excuse me?"

"I said, *What the hell is wrong with you?*" I grab some napkins from inside the glove compartment and start wiping off my leg. The coffee's not even that hot—Lindsay had the lid off to cool it—but it leaves a splotchy red mark on my thigh, and I feel like crying. "It's not that hard. Red light: stop. Green light: go. I know that yellow might be a little harder for you to grasp, but you'd think with a little practice you could come to terms with it."

Lindsay and Elody are both staring at me in stunned silence, but I don't stop, I can't stop, this is all Lindsay's fault, Lindsay and her stupid driving. "They could train monkeys to drive better than you. So what? What is it? You need to prove you don't give a shit? That you don't care about anything? You don't care about anybody? Tap a fender here, swipe a mirror there, oops, thank God we have our airbags, that's what bumpers are for, just keep going, keep driving, no one will ever know. Guess what, Lindsay? You don't have to prove anything. We already know you don't give a shit about anybody but yourself. We've *always* known."

I run out of air then, and for a second after I stop speaking, there's total silence. Lindsay's not even looking at me. She's staring straight ahead, both hands on the wheel, knuckles white from clutching it so tightly. The light turns green and she presses her foot on the accelerator, hard. The engine roars, sounding like distant thunder.

It takes Lindsay a while to speak and when she does her voice is low and strangled-sounding. "Where the hell do you get off . . . ?"

"Guys." Elody pipes up nervously from the back. "Don't fight, okay? Just drop it."

The anger is still running through me, an electrical current. It makes me feel sharper and more alert than I have in years. I whirl around to face Elody.

"How come you never stand up for yourself?" I say. She shrinks back a little, her eyes darting between Lindsay and me. "You know it's true. She's a bitch. Go ahead, say it."

"Leave her out of it," Lindsay hisses.

Elody opens her mouth and then gives a minute shake of her head.

"I knew it," I say, feeling triumphant and sick at the same time. "You're scared of her. I knew it."

"I told you to leave her alone." Lindsay finally raises her voice.

"*I'm* supposed to leave her alone?" The sharpness, the sense of clarity is disappearing. Instead everything feels like it's spinning out of my control. "You're the one who treats her like shit all the time. It's *you. Elody's so pathetic. Look at Elody climbing all over Steve—he doesn't even like her. Look, Elody's trashed again. Hope she doesn't puke in my car, don't want the leather to smell like alcoholic.*"

Elody draws in a sharp breath on the last word. I know I've gone too far. The second I say it I want to take it back. My mirror is still flipped down, and I can see Elody staring out the window, mouth quivering like she's trying not to cry. Number one rule of best friends: there are certain things that you never, ever say.

All of a sudden Lindsay slams on the brakes. We're in the middle of Route 120, about a half mile from school, but there's a line of traffic behind us. A car has to swerve into the other lane to avoid hitting us. Thankfully there's no oncoming traffic. Even Elody cries out.

"Jesus." My heart is racing. The car passes us, honking furiously. The passenger rolls down his window and yells something, but I can't hear it; I just see the flash of a baseball hat and angry eyes. "What are you doing?"

The people in the cars in line behind us start leaning on their horns too, but Lindsay throws the car in park and doesn't move.

"Lindsay," Elody says anxiously, "Sam's right. It's not funny."

Lindsay lunges for me, and I think she's going to hit me. Instead she leans over and shoves open the door.

"Out," she says quietly, her voice full of rage.

"What?" The cold air rushes into the car like a punch to the stomach, leaving me deflated. The last of my anger and fearlessness goes with it, and I just feel tired.

"Lindz." Elody tries to laugh, but the sound comes out high-pitched and hysterical. "You can't make her walk. It's freezing."

"Out," Lindsay repeats. Cars are starting to pull around us now, everyone honking and rolling down their windows to yell at us. All of their words get lost in the roar of the engines and the bleating of the horns, but it's still humiliating. The idea of getting out now, of being forced to walk in the gutter while all of those dozens of cars roll by me, with all those people *watching*, makes me shrink back against my seat. I look to Elody for more support, but she looks away.

Lindsay leans over. "I. Said. Get. Out," she whispers, and

her mouth is so close to my ear if you couldn't hear her you'd think she was telling me a secret.

I grab my bag and step into the cold. The freezing air on my legs almost paralyzes me. The second I'm out of the car Lindsay guns it, peeling away with the door still swinging open.

I start walking in the leaf-and-trash-filled ditch that runs next to the road. My fingers and toes go numb almost instantly, and I stomp my feet on the frost-covered leaves to keep the blood flowing. It takes a minute for the long line of traffic to begin to unwind, and horns are still honking away, the sound like the fading wail of a passing train.

A blue Toyota pulls up next to me. A woman leans out—gray-haired, probably in her sixties—and shakes her head.

"Crazy girl," she says, frowning at me.

For a moment I just stand there, but as the car starts to pull away, I remember that it doesn't matter, none of it matters, so I throw up my middle finger, hoping she sees.

All the way to school I repeat it again—it doesn't matter, none of it matters—until the words themselves lose meaning.

Here's one of the things I learned that morning: if you cross a line and nothing happens, the line loses meaning. It's like that old riddle about a tree falling in a forest, and whether it makes a sound if there's no one around to hear it.

You keep drawing a line farther and farther away, crossing it every time. That's how people end up stepping off the edge of the earth. You'd be surprised at how easy it is to bust out of orbit, to spin out to a place where no one can touch you. To lose yourself—to get lost.

Or maybe you wouldn't be surprised. Maybe some of you already know.

To those people I can only say: I'm sorry.

I skip my first four periods just because I can, and spend a couple of hours walking the halls with no real goal or destination. I almost hope someone will stop me—a teacher or Ms. Winters or a teacher's aide or *someone*—and ask what I'm doing, even accuse me point-blank of cutting and send me to the principal's office. Fighting with Lindsay left me unsatisfied, and I still feel a vague but pressing desire to *do* something.

Most of the teachers just nod or smile, though, or give me a half wave. They have no way of knowing my schedule, no way of knowing whether I have a free period or whether class was canceled, and I'm disappointed by how easy it is to break the rules.

When I walk into Mr. Daimler's class I deliberately don't look at him, but I can feel his eyes on me, and after I slide into my desk, he comes straight over.

"It's a little early in the season for beach clothes, don't you think?" He grins.

Normally whenever he looks at me for longer than a few seconds, I get nervous, but today I force myself to keep my eyes on his. Warmth spreads over my whole body; it reminds me of standing under the heat lamps in my grandmother's house when I was no older than five. It's amazing that eyes can do that, that they can transform light into heat. I've never felt that way with Rob.

"If you got it, flaunt it," I say, making my voice soft and steady. I see something flicker in his eyes. I've surprised him.

"I guess so," he murmurs, so quietly I'm sure I'm the only one who hears. Then he blushes bright red like he can't believe himself. He nods at my desk, which is empty except for a pen and the small square notebook Lindsay and I use to pass back and forth between classes, writing notes to each other. "No roses today? Or did your bouquet get too heavy to carry around?"

I haven't been to any of my classes so I haven't collected any Valograms. I don't even care. In the past I would rather have died than be seen in the halls of Thomas Jefferson on Cupid Day without a single rose. In the past I would have considered it a fate *worse* than death.

Of course, that was before I actually knew.

I toss my head, shrugging. "I'm kind of over it." It's as though confidence is flowing into me from someone else, someone older and beautiful, like I'm only playing a part.

He smiles at me, and again I see something moving in his eyes. Then he goes back to his desk and claps his hands, gesturing for everybody to take their seats. As always the dirty hemp necklace is peeking out from under his collar, and I let myself think about looping my fingers through it, pulling him toward me, and kissing him. His lips are thick—but not too thick—and shaped exactly how a guy's mouth should be shaped, like if he just parted his lips at all, your mouth would fit directly on top of it. I think of the picture from his high school yearbook, when he's standing with his arm around his prom date. She was thin, long brown hair, even smile. Like me.

"All right, everyone," he's saying as people shuffle and scrape into their desks, giggling and ruffling their bouquets. "I know it's Cupid Day and love is in the air, but guess what? So are derivatives."

A couple of people groan. Kent bangs in the door, almost late, his bag flapping open and papers literally scattering behind him, like he's Hansel or Gretel and he has to make sure someone can follow his trail of half-completed sketches and notes to math class. His black-and-white checkered sneakers peek out under his oversized khakis.

"Sorry," he mutters breathlessly to Mr. Daimler. "Emergency at the *Tribulation*. Printer problems. Malignant paper tumor in tray two. Had to operate immediately or risk losing it." As soon as he makes it halfway up the aisle to his seat, his math textbook—which was riding higher and higher on a wave of crumpled paper inside his open bag—pops out and slams to the floor, and everybody laughs. I feel a surge of irritation. Why is he always such a mess? How hard is it to zip up a bag?

He catches me looking at him, and I guess he mistakes my facial expression for concern, because he grins at me and mouths, *Walking disaster.* As though he's proud of it.

I turn my attention back to Mr. Daimler. He's standing at the front of the room with his arms crossed, his expression fake-serious. That's another thing I like about him: he's never really mad.

"Glad the printer pulled through," he says, raising his eyebrows. His sleeves are rolled up and his arms are tan. Or maybe that's just the color of his skin: like burnt honey. "As I was saying, I know there's a lot of excitement on Cupid Day, but that doesn't mean we can just ignore the regular—"

"Cupids!" someone squeals, and the class dissolves into giggles. Sure enough, there they are: the devil, the cat, and the pale white angel with her big eyes.

Mr. Daimler throws up his hands and leans against his desk. "I give up," he says. Then he turns his smile to me for just a second—just a second, but long enough for my whole body to light up like a Christmas display.

The angel delivers three of my roses—the ones from Rob, Tara Flute, and Elody—and then keeps sorting methodically through her bouquet, flipping each card over and checking for my name. There's something careful and sincere about her movements, like she's super focused on doing everything correctly. As she reads off the addressee she mouths the name quietly to herself, wonderingly, as though she can't believe there are so many people in the school, so many roses to deliver, so many friends. It's painful to watch and I stand up abruptly, grabbing the cream-and-pink rose from her hands. She jumps back, startled.

"It's mine," I say. "I recognize it."

She nods at me, wide-eyed. I doubt a senior has ever spoken to her in her life. She begins to open her mouth.

I lean in so that no one else can hear me. "Don't say it," I say, and her eyes go even wider. I can't stand to hear her say it's beautiful. I can't stand it when the rose—and everything else—is all garbage now, meaningless. "It's just going in the trash."

I mean it too. As soon as Mr. Daimler ushers the Cupids out the door—everyone in class still giggling and showing off the notes their friends have written them and trying to predict how many roses they can expect by the end of the day—I scoop up my roses and sail to the front of the classroom, dumping them in the big trash can right next to Mr. Daimler's desk.

Instantly, the giggling stops. Two people gasp and Chrissy Walker actually makes the sign of the cross, like I've just crapped on a Bible or something. That's how big of a deal the roses are. Becca Roth half rises from her seat, like she wants to dive in after the roses and rescue them from the fate of being crushed under paper and pencil shavings, failed quizzes, and empty soda cans. I don't even look in Kent's direction. I don't want to see his face.

Becca blurts, "You can't just throw out your roses, Sam. Someone sent those to you."

"Yeah," Chrissy pipes up. "It's so not done."

I shrug. "You can have them if you want." I gesture to the trash can, and Becca casts a wistful look in that direction. She's probably trying to decide whether the social boost she would get from having four extra roses is worth the ego hit she would take for Dumpster-diving to get them.

Mr. Daimler smiles, winks at me. "You sure you want to do that, Sam?" He raises upturned hands. "You're breaking people's hearts right and left."

"Oh, yeah?" All of this will be gone, vanished, erased tomorrow, and tomorrow will be erased the next day, and the next day will be erased after that, all of it wiped clean and spotless. "What about yours?"

It goes dead silent in the room; somebody coughs. I can tell Mr. Daimler doesn't know whether I'm deliberately baiting him or not.

He licks his lips nervously and runs a hand through his hair. "What?"

"Your heart." I pull myself up so I'm sitting on the corner of his desk, my skirt riding up almost to my underwear. My heart is beating so fast it's a hum. I feel like I'm skimming above the air. "Am I breaking it?"

"Okay." He looks down, fiddles with one of his sleeves. "Take a seat, Sam. It's time to get started."

"I thought you were enjoying the view." I lean back a little and stretch my arms above my head. There's a kind of electricity in the air, a zipping, singing tension running in all directions; it feels like the moment right before a thunderstorm, like every particle of air is extracharged and vibrating. A student in the back of the class laughs and another one mutters, "Jesus." Maybe it's my imagination, but I think I recognize Kent's voice.

Mr. Daimler looks at me, his face dark. "Sit."

"If you insist." I swivel off the edge of the desk and move around to his chair, then sit down and cross my legs slowly, folding my hands in my lap. Little giggles and gasps erupt around the classroom, bursts of sound. I don't know where this is coming from, this feeling of complete and total control. Up until a few months ago, I still turned to Jell-O whenever a guy talked to me, including Rob. But this feels easy, natural, like I've slipped into the skin that belongs to me for the first time in my life.

"In your *own* chair." Mr. Daimler's practically growling and his face is dark red, almost purple. I've made him lose it—probably a first in Thomas Jefferson history. I know that in whatever game we're playing I've just won a point. The idea makes my stomach drop a little—not in a bad way, more like at the moment right before you reach the highest part of the roller coaster, when you know that at any second you'll be at the very top of the park, looking down over everything, pausing there for a fraction of a second, about to have the ride of your life. It's the dip in your stomach right before everything goes flying apart in a blast of wind, and screaming, right before you let go completely. The laughter in the room grows to a roar. If you were standing outside, you might mistake it for applause.

For the rest of the class I keep quiet, even though people keep whispering and breaking out into giggles, and I get three notes sent my way. One of them is from Becca and says, *You are awesome*; one of them is from Hanna Gordon and says, *He's soooo hot.* Another one lands in my lap, all balled up like trash, before I can see who threw it in my direction. It says, *Whore.* For a moment I feel a hot flush of embarrassment, like nausea or vertigo. But it passes quickly. None of this is real anymore. *I'm* not even real anymore.

A fourth note arrives just before class ends. It's in the form of a miniature airplane, and it literally sails to me, landing with a whisper on my desk just as Mr. Daimler turns back from writing an equation on the board. It's so perfect I hate to touch it, but I unfold its wings, and there's a message written in neat block letters.

You are too good for that.

Even though there's no signature, I know it's from Kent, and for a second something sharp and deep goes through me, something I can't understand or describe, a blade running up under my ribs and making me almost gasp for breath. I shouldn't be dead. It shouldn't be me.

I take the note very carefully and tear it in half, then I tear it in half again.

We've been restless all class and Mr. Daimler gives up two minutes before the bell rings.

"Don't forget: test on Monday. Limits and asymptotes." He goes to his desk and leans on it, looking tired. There's a mass exhalation, a collective sigh of coats rustling and chairs scraping against the linoleum. "Samantha Kingston, please see me after class."

He's not even looking at me, but the tone of his voice makes me nervous. For the first time it occurs to me that I could really be in trouble. Not that it matters, but if Mr. Daimler makes me sit through a lecture about responsibility I'll die of embarrassment. I'll die *again*.

Good luck, Becca mouths to me on her way out. We're not even friends—Lindsay calls her the TurkeyJerk, because she eats turkey sandwiches every single day—but the fact that she says it makes the knot ease up in my stomach.

Mr. Daimler waits until the last student files out of the classroom—I see Kent hovering at the doorway out of the corner of my eye—and then walks slowly to the door and closes it. Something about the way the door clicks—so final, so quick—makes my heart skip a beat. I close my eyes for a second, feeling like I'm back in the car with Lindsay on Fallow Ridge Road with the misty headlights of a second car bearing down on us in the darkness, an accusation. They always swerve first, she'd said, but at that second I understand with total and perfect clarity that that's not why she did it—why she does it. She does it for that one thrilling moment when you don't know, when you come up against someone who doesn't swerve and instead find yourself plummeting off the road into the darkness.

When I open my eyes Mr. Daimler has his hands on his hips. He's staring at me.

"What the hell were you thinking?"

The harshness in his voice startles me. I've never been cursed at by a teacher.

"I . . . I don't know what you're talking about." My voice comes out sounding thinner, younger, than I wanted it to.

"The shit back there—right there, in front of everybody. What were you thinking?"

I stand up so I'm not just sitting there looking up at him like a little kid. My legs are wobbly, and I have to steady myself with one hand against the desk. I take a deep breath, trying to pull it together. It doesn't matter: all of it will be erased, cleaned away.

"I'm sorry," I say, feeling a little bit stronger. "I really don't know what you're talking about. Did I do something wrong?"

He looks toward the door and a muscle twitches in his jaw. Just that, that little twitch, returns all my confidence. I want to reach out and touch him, put my fingers in his hair.

"You could get in a lot of trouble, you know," he says, not looking at me. "You could get *me* in a lot of trouble."

The first bell rings: class is officially over now. The singing feeling returns to my blood, to the air. I step carefully around my desk and walk straight to the front of the classroom. I stop when we're only a few feet away from each other. He doesn't back away. Instead he finally looks at me. His eyes are so deep and full of something it almost frightens me off. But it doesn't.

I lean casually against Becca's desk, tipping backward and resting on my elbows so I'm totally laid out in front of him, chest, legs, everything. My head feels like it has floated away from my body; my body feels like it has floated away from my blood, like I'm just dissolving into energy and vibration.

"I don't mind trouble," I say in my sexiest voice.

Mr. Daimler is staring into my eyes, not looking at the rest of me, but somehow I know that it's an effort. "What are you doing?"

My skirt is riding so high I know my underwear is showing. It's a pink lace thong, one of the first I've ever owned. Thongs always make me feel like there is a rubber band up my butt, but last year Lindsay and I bought the same pair at Victoria's Secret and swore to wear them.

The words come to me from a script, from a movie: "I can stop if you want." My voice comes out breathy but not because I'm trying. I am no longer breathing—everything, the whole world, freezes in that moment while I wait for his response.

But when he speaks he sounds tired, annoyed—not at all what I was expecting. "What do you *want*, Samantha?"

The tone of his voice startles me, and for a second my mind spins blankly. He's staring at me with a look of impatience now, as if I've just asked him to change my grade. The second bell rings. I feel like at any moment he'll dismiss me, remind me about the quiz on Monday. I've somehow lost control of the situation and I don't know how to fix it. The vibration in the air is still there, but now it feels ominous, like the air is full of sharp things getting ready to drop.

"I . . . I want you." I don't mean for it to come out so uncertain. This *is* what I want. This is what I've been wanting: Mr. Daimler. My mind keeps spinning in a blind panic, and I can't remember his first name, and I feel like laughing hysterically; I'm stretched out half naked in front of my math teacher and I don't know his name. Then it comes to me. Evan. "I want you, Evan," I say, a little more boldly. It's the first time I've ever used his first name.

He stares at me for a long time. I start to get nervous. I want to look away or pull down my skirt or cross my arms, but I force myself to stay still.

"What are you thinking about?" I finally ask, but instead of answering he just walks straight to me and puts his arms on my shoulders, pushing me backward so I tip over onto Becca's desk. Then he's bending over me, kissing me and licking my neck and ear and making little grunting noises that remind me of Pickle when he has to pee. Pressed against him I feel tiny; his arms are strong, groping all over my shoulders and arms.

He slides one hand up my shirt and squeezes my boobs one after the other, so hard I almost cry out. His tongue is big and fat. I think, *I'm kissing Mr. Daimler, I'm kissing Mr. Daimler, Lindsay will never believe it,* but it doesn't feel anything like I've imagined. His five o'clock shadow is rough on my skin, and I have this horrible thought that this is what my mom feels when she kisses my dad.

When I open my eyes I see the plain speckled ceiling tiles of the classroom—the ceiling tiles I've spent hours and hours staring at this semester—and my mind starts circling around them, counting, like I'm a fly buzzing somewhere outside my body. I think, *How can the same ceiling still be here while this is happening? Why isn't the ceiling coming down?* All of a sudden it's not fun anymore: all those sharp glittery things drop out of the air at once, and at the same time something drops deep inside of me. I feel like I'm sobering up after drinking all night.

I put my hands on his chest and try to push him off, but he's too heavy, too strong. I can feel his muscles under my fingertips—he used to play lacrosse in high school, Lindsay and I found out—and above that, a fine layer of fat. He's leaning on me with his full weight and I can't breathe. I'm crushed underneath him, my legs split apart on either side of his hips, his stomach warm and fat and heavy on mine. I wrestle my mouth away from his. "We—we can't do this here."

The words just pop out without my meaning them to. What I

wanted to say was, *We can't do this. Not here. Not anywhere.*

What I wanted to say was, *Stop.*

He's breathing hard, still staring at my mouth. There's a tiny bead of sweat at his hairline, and I watch it trace its way across his forehead and down to the tip of his nose. Finally he pulls away from me, rubs his hand over his jaw, and nods.

The moment he's off me I scrabble up to my feet and tug down my skirt, not wanting him to see that my hands are shaking.

"You're right," he says slowly. He gives a quick shake of his head, as though trying to rouse himself from sleep. "You're right."

He takes a few steps backward and turns his back to me. For a second we just stand there, not speaking. My brain is all static. He's only a few feet away from me, but he looks hopelessly, impossibly far, like someone you can just make out distantly, a silhouette in the middle of a blizzard.

"Samantha?" Finally he turns back to me, rubbing both eyes and sighing, like I've exhausted him. "Listen, what happened here . . . I don't think I need to tell you that this has to stay strictly between you and me."

He's smiling at me, but it's not his normal, easy smile. There's no humor in it. "This is important, Samantha. Do you understand?" He sighs again. "Everyone makes mistakes. . . ." He trails off, watching me.

"Mistakes," I repeat, the word pinging around in my head.

I'm not sure whether he thinks he made a mistake, or I did. Mistake, mistake, mistake. A strange word: stinging, somehow.

Mr. Daimler's mouth, eyes, nose—his whole face seems to be rearranging itself into unfamiliar patterns, like a Picasso painting. "I need to know that I can count on you."

"Of course you can," I hear myself say, and he looks at me, relieved, like if he could, he would pat me on the head and say, *Good girl.*

After that I just stand there for a bit. I'm not sure if he's going to come around and kiss me or give me a hug—it seems insane just to *leave*, to pick up my stuff and go as though nothing's happened. But after he blinks at me for a bit, he finally says, "You're late for lunch," and now I know I really am being dismissed. So I grab my bag and go.

As soon as I'm out in the hall I lean up against a wall, grateful for the feeling of the stone against my back. Something bubbles up inside me, and I don't know whether I should jump up and down or laugh or scream. Fortunately the halls are empty. Everybody's already at lunch.

I take out my phone to text Lindsay, but then I remember that we're in a fight. There's no text from her asking if I want to go to Kent's party. She must still be mad. I'm not sure whether I'm fighting with Elody, too. Remembering what I said in the car makes me feel horrible.

I think about texting Ally—I'm pretty sure she's not mad

at me, at least—and I spend a long time trying to figure out how to word it. It feels weird to write *I kissed Mr. Daimler*, but if I write *Evan* she won't know who I'm talking about. *Evan Daimler* feels wrong too, and besides, we did more than just kiss. He was on *top* of me.

In the end I drop my phone back into my bag without writing anything. I figure I'll just wait until I've made up with Lindsay and Elody and tell them in person. It'll be easier that way, easier to make it sound better than it was, and I'll get to see their faces. The thought of how jealous Lindsay will be makes the whole thing more than worth it. I put some concealer on my chin to cover the red spots where Mr. Daimler's face gave me an exfoliation I didn't need, and then I head to lunch.

YOU CAN'T JUDGE A BOOK BY ITS STEEL-TOED COMBAT BOOTS

When I march into the cafeteria ten minutes late, our usual table is empty, and I know that I have been officially and deliberately ditched.

For a fraction of a second I can feel everyone's eyes lift in my direction, staring. I bring my hand up to my face without meaning to, suddenly terrified that everyone will see the rawness on my chin and know what I've been doing.

I duck out into the hall again. I need to be alone, need to pull it together. I head for the bathrooms, but as I get close, two sophomores (Lindsay calls them s'mores because they're always stuck together and more than two will get you sick) come bursting out of the door, giggling, arm-in-arm. Lunch is prime bathroom traffic time—everyone needs to reapply lip gloss, complain about feeling fat, threaten to upchuck in one of the stalls—and the last thing I need right now is a steady stream of stupid.

I head to the old bathroom at the far end of the science wing. Hardly anyone uses it since a newer bathroom—with toilets that don't clog 24/7—was installed last year between the labs. The farther I get from the cafeteria, the more the roar of voices drops away, until they sound just like the ocean from far away. I get calmer with every step. My heels beat a steady rhythm on the tile floor.

The science wing is empty, as expected, and smells, as always, like chemical cleaners and sulfur. Today there's something else, though: the smell of smoke and something earthier, more pungent. I push against the bathroom door and for a second nothing happens. I push harder and there's a grating sound; I jam my shoulder against the door, and finally it swings open, carrying me inside with it. Instantly I hit my knee on a chair that has been propped up against the doorknob and pain shoots up my leg. The smell in the bathroom is much stronger.

I drop my bag and lean over, clutching my knee. "Shit."

"What the hell?"

The voice makes me jump. I didn't realize there was anyone

else in the bathroom. I look up and Anna Cartullo's standing there, holding a cigarette in one hand.

"Jesus," I say. "You scared me."

"*I* scared *you?*" She leans up against the counter and taps her ashes in the sink. "You, like, *forced* your way in. Don't you know how to knock?" Like I've just broken into her house.

"Sorry I ruined your party." I make a halfhearted move for the door.

"Wait." She holds up a hand, looking nervous. "Are you going to tell?"

"Tell what?"

"About this." She inhales and blows a cloud of smoke. The cigarette she's smoking is extra thin and it looks like she rolled it herself. Then it hits me: it's a joint. The weed must be mixed with *a lot* of tobacco because I didn't recognize the smell immediately, and I come home with my clothes reeking of it after every party. Elody once said it was lucky my mom never came into my room, or she would think I was dealing pot out of my dirty laundry hamper.

"So what? You just come in here and smoke your lunch?" I'm not saying it to be mean, but it comes out that way. Her eyes dart to the floor for a second, and then I notice an empty sandwich bag and a half-eaten bag of chips sitting on the tiles. It occurs to me I've never once seen her in the cafeteria. She must eat her lunch here every day.

"Yeah. I like the décor." She sees me looking at the sandwich bag, stubs out the joint, and crosses her arms. "What are you doing here, anyway? Don't you have . . . ?" She stops herself, but I know what she's about to say. *Don't you have friends?*

"I had to pee," I say. This is obviously a lie since I've made zero effort to use the toilet, but I'm too tired to come up with a different excuse, and she doesn't ask me for one.

We stand there in awkward silence for a bit. I've never spoken a word to Anna Cartullo in my life, at least in the life I had before the car crash—beyond one time when I said, "Don't call her an evil wench," after she called Lindsay an evil wench. But I'd rather stay here with her than go out into the hall. Finally I think, *Screw it,* and I sit down in the chair and prop my leg up on one of the sinks. Anna's eyes are slightly unfocused now, and she's more relaxed, slouching up against one of the walls. She nods at my knee. "Looks swollen."

"Yeah, well, somebody stuck a chair right inside the door."

She starts giggling. She's definitely stoned. "Nice shoes." She raises her eyebrows at my feet, which are dangling over one of the circular sinks. I can't tell if she's being sarcastic. "Hard to walk in, huh?"

"I can walk," I say, too quickly. Then I shrug. "Short distances, anyway."

She snorts and then covers her mouth.

"I bought them as a joke." I don't know why I feel the need to defend myself to Anna Cartullo, but I guess nothing is the way it's supposed to be today. All the rules have pretty much gone out the window. Anna's relaxing, too. She acts like it's not weird that we're hanging out in a bathroom the size of a prison cell when we should be at lunch.

She hops up on the counter and wiggles her feet in my direction. Unsurprisingly, she's not wearing anything Cupid Day–related. She has on a couple of layered black tank tops and an open hoodie. Her jeans are fraying at the hem and have a safety pin through the fly where they're missing a button. She's wearing enormous wedge round-toe boots that kind of look like Doc Martens on crack.

"You need a pair of these." She clicks her heels together, a punked-out Dorothy trying to get home from Oz. "Most comfortable shoes I ever owned."

I look at her like, *Yeah, right.* She shrugs. "Don't knock 'em till you try 'em."

"Okay, then, pass them over."

Anna looks at me for a long second, like she's not sure if I'm serious.

"Look." I kick my shoes off. They hit the ground with a clatter. "We'll trade."

Anna bends over wordlessly, unzips her boots, and wiggles out of them. Her socks are rainbow-striped, which surprises me. I would have expected skulls or something. She peels these off next and balls them up in one hand, starting to pass them to me.

"Ew." I wrinkle my nose. "No, thank you. I'd rather go commando."

She shrugs, laughing. "Whatever."

When I zip into her boots I realize she's right. They are super comfortable, even without socks. The leather is cool and very soft. I admire them on my feet.

"I feel like I should be terrorizing children." I knock the bulging steel-tipped toes together, which make a satisfying clicking sound.

"I feel like I should be turning tricks." Anna has maneuvered her way into my heels and is now teetering experimentally around the bathroom, arms out like she's on a tightrope.

"Same size feet," I point out, though it's obvious.

"Eight and a half. Pretty common." She glances over her shoulder at me, like she's considering saying something else, then reaches under the sink and pulls out her bag, a beat-up patchwork hobo thing that looks like she made it herself. She extracts a small Altoids tin. Inside there's a dime bag of weed—I guess Alex Liment is good for something—rolling papers, and a few cigarettes.

She starts rolling another spliff, carefully balancing her life studies packet on her lap to use as a tray. (Side note: so far I've seen the life studies packet used as (1) an umbrella, (2) a makeshift towel, (3) a pillow, and now this. I have never actually seen anyone study with it, which either means that everyone who graduates from Thomas Jefferson will be totally unprepared for life or that certain things can't be learned in bullet-point format.) Her fingers are thin and move quickly.

She's obviously had practice. I wonder if that's what she and Alex do together after they've had sex, just lie there side by side, smoking. I wonder if she ever thinks about Bridget when they're doing it. I'm tempted to ask.

"Stop staring at me," she says without looking up.

"I'm not." I tilt my head back and stare at the vomit-colored ceiling, am reminded of Mr. Daimler, and look back at her. "There aren't too many other options."

"No one asked you to come in here." Some of the edge returns to her voice.

"Public property." There's a split second when her face goes dark and I'm sure she's going to freak out and this will be the end of our shiny, happy time together. I rush on, "It's seriously not that bad in here. For a bathroom, you know."

She looks at me suspiciously, like she's sure I'm only baiting her so I can make fun of her afterward.

"You could get some pillows for the floor." I look around. "Decorate a bit or something."

She ducks her head, concentrating on her fingers. "There's this artist I've always liked—the guy who does all the stairs going up and down at the same time—"

"M. C. Escher?"

She glances up, obviously surprised I know who she's talking about. "Yeah, him." A smile flits across her face. "I was thinking of, I don't know, hanging one of his prints in here. Just taping it up, you know, for something to look at."

"I have, like, ten of his books in my house," I blurt out, glad she's not going to stay mad and kick me out of the bathroom. "My dad's an architect. He's into that stuff."

Anna rolls up the joint, licks the seam, and finishes it off with a few twists of her fingers. She nods at the chair. "If you're going to sit in that you can at least block the door. That way it's *private* property."

The chair grates against the tile floor as I scoot backward against the door, and both of us wince, catch ourselves wincing, and laugh. Anna pulls out a purple lighter with flowers on it—not the lighter I expected of her—and tries to spark the joint. The lighter sputters a few times and she throws it down, cursing. The next time she rummages through her bag she pulls out a lighter in the shape of a naked female torso. She presses on the head and little blue flames come shooting out the nipples. Now *that* is the kind of lighter I would expect Anna Cartullo to have.

Anna's face gets serious, and she takes a long pull of the joint, then stares at me through the cloud of blue smoke.

"So," she says, "why do you guys hate me?"

Of all the things I expect her to say, it's not this. Even more unexpected, she holds the spliff out in my direction, offering me some.

I hesitate for only a second. Hey, just because I'm dead doesn't mean I'm a saint.

"We don't hate you." It doesn't come out convincingly. The

truth is I'm not sure. I don't hate Anna, really; Lindsay's always said she does, but it's hard to know what Lindsay's reasons are for anything. I take a hit off the joint. I've only smoked weed once before, but I've seen it done a hundred times. I inhale and my lungs are full of smoke: a heavy taste like chewing on moss. I try to hold my breath, the way you're supposed to, but the smoke tickles the back of my throat. I start coughing and hand the joint back.

"Then what's the reason?" She doesn't say, *For all the shitty things you've done.* For the bathroom graffiti. For the fake email blast sophomore year: *Anna Cartullo has chlamydia.* She doesn't have to. She passes the joint back to me.

I take another hit. Already things are warping, certain objects blurring and others sharpening, like someone's messing with the focus on a camera. No wonder people still talk to Alex, even though he's a douche. He deals good stuff. "I don't know." Because it's easy. "I guess you need to take things out on somebody."

The words are out of my mouth before I realize they're true. I take another hit and pass the joint back to Anna. I feel like everything's been amplified, like I can feel the heaviness of my arms and legs and hear my heart pumping and blood tumbling through my veins. And at the end of the day it will all be silenced, at least until time skips back on its wheel and starts again.

The bell rings. Lunch is over. Anna says, "Shit, shit, I have to *be* somewhere," and begins trying to gather up her stuff. She accidentally knocks over the Altoids tin. The bag of weed goes flying under the sink, and the papers flit and flutter everywhere. "Shit."

"I'll help," I say. We both get down on our hands and knees. My fingers feel numb and bloated, and I'm having trouble peeling the papers off the ground. This strikes me as hilarious, and Anna and I both start laughing, leaning on each other, gasping for breath. She keeps saying "Shit" at intervals.

"Better hurry," I say. All of the anger and pain from the past few days is lifting, leaving me feeling free and careless and happy. "Alex will be pissed."

She freezes. Our foreheads are so close we're almost touching.

"How did you know I was meeting Alex?" she says. Her voice is clear and low.

I realize too late that I've screwed up. "Seen you sneaking back through Smokers' Lounge after seventh once or twice," I say vaguely, and she relaxes.

"You're not going to tell anyone, are you?" she asks, biting her lower lip. "I wouldn't want—" She stops herself and I wonder if she's going to say something about Bridget. But she just shakes her head and continues gathering up the papers, working quickly now.

The idea of telling on Anna Cartullo for sleeping with Alex after what I've just done—after Mr. Daimler—is hilarious.

I've got no right to say anything to anybody. I'm smoking weed in a bathroom, I have no friends, my math teacher stuck his tongue down my throat, my boyfriend hates me because I won't sleep with him. I'm dead, but I can't stop living. The absurdity of everything really hits me in that second and I start laughing again. Anna's gotten serious. Her eyes are big bright marbles.

"What?" she says. "Are you laughing at me?"

I shake my head, but I can't respond right away. I'm laughing too hard to breathe. I've been kind of squatting next to her, but I'm shaking so hard, the laughter heaving through me, that I tumble backward, landing on my butt with a loud thump. Anna cracks a smile again.

"You're crazy," she says, giggling.

I take a few gasping breaths. "Least I don't barricade myself in bathrooms."

"Least I don't get stoned off half a joint."

"Least I don't sleep with Alex Liment."

"Least I don't have bitchy friends."

"Least I have friends."

We're going back and forth, laughing harder and harder. Anna cracks up so hard she bends to the side and supports herself on one elbow. Then she rolls over all the way so she's just lying there on the bathroom floor making these hilarious yelping noises that remind me of a poodle. Every so often she snorts, which just makes me go off again.

"Let me tell you something," I say, as soon as I can get the words out.

"Hear, hear." Anna pretends to pound a gavel and then snorts into her palm.

I love the feeling of thickness around me. I'm swimming in murk. The green walls are water. "I kissed Mr. Daimler." As soon as I say it I die laughing again. Those must be the four most ridiculous words in the English language.

Anna heaves herself up on one elbow. "You did *what*?"

"*Shhhh.*" I bob my head up and down. "We kissed. He put his hand up my shirt. He put his hand . . ." I gesture between my legs.

She shakes her head from side to side. Her hair whips around her face, reminding me of a tornado. "No way. No way. No way."

"I swear to God."

She leans forward, so close I can smell her breath on my face. She's been sucking on an Altoid. "That is sick. You know that, right?"

"I know."

"Sick, sick, sick. He went to high school here, like, ten years ago."

"Eight. We checked."

She lets out a loud howl of laughter, and for a second she lays her head down on my shoulder. "They're all perverts," she says, the words quiet and directed straight into my ear.

Then she pulls away and says, "Shit! I'm so dead."

She stands up, steadying herself with one hand on the wall. She teeters for a moment as she stands in front of the mirror, smoothing down her hair. She takes a small bottle from her back pocket and squeezes a couple of drops into each eye. I'm still on the floor, staring up at her from below. She seems to be miles and miles away.

I blurt out, "You're too good for Alex."

She's already stepped over me on her way to the door. I see her back stiffen and I think she's going to be angry. She pauses, one hand resting on the chair.

But when she turns around she's smiling. "You're too good for Mr. Daimler," she says, and we both crack up again. Then she shoves the chair out of the way and tugs the door open, slipping into the hall.

After she's gone I sit with my head back, enjoying the way the room feels like it's doing loops. *This is what it's like to be the sun,* I think, and then I think how stoned I am, and then I think how funny it is to know that you're stoned but not be able to stop thinking stoned thoughts.

I see something white peeking out from underneath the sink: a cigarette. I lean down and find another one. Anna forgot to pick them up. Just then there's a sharp knock on the door, and I snatch both cigarettes up and get to my feet. As soon as I stand the circling and the feeling of being under-water gets worse. It seems to take me forever to push the chair out of the way. Everything is so heavy.

"You forgot these," I say, holding the cigarettes up between two fingers as I open the door.

It's not Anna, though. It's Ms. Winters, standing in the hallway with her arms crossed and her face pinched up so tightly it looks like her nose is a black hole and the rest of her face is getting slowly sucked into it.

"Smoking on school property is forbidden," she says, pronouncing each word carefully. Then she smiles, showing all of her teeth.

THE PUGS

In the Thomas Jefferson High School *R & R (Rules and Regulations Handbook)*, it says that *any student caught smoking on school property is subject to three days' suspension.* (I know this by heart because all the smokers like to tear this page out of the handbook and burn it at the Lounge, sometimes crouching and sticking their cigarettes in the flames to catch a light, as the words on the page curl and blacken and smoke into nothing.)

But I get off with only a warning. I guess the administration makes exceptions for students who have dirt on a certain vice principal and a certain gym teacher/soccer coach/mustache fan. Ms. Winters looked like she was going to have a massive coronary when I'd started going off about *role models* and *my poor impressionable mind*—I love that expression, as though everyone under the age of twenty-one has all the brain power of dental plaster—and *the administration's responsibility to set an example*, especially when I'd reminded her about page sixty-nine in the *R & R: it is forbidden to engage in lewd or sexually inappropriate acts in or around school property*. (That one I know because the page has been torn out and hung up about a thousand times in various bathrooms on campus, the margins decorated with drawings of a decidedly lewd and sexually inappropriate nature. The administration was totally asking for it, though. Who puts a rule like that on page sixty-nine?)

At least the hour and a half I spent with Ms. Winters has sobered me up. The last bell has just rung, and all around me students are sweeping out of classrooms, making way more noise than is necessary—shrieking, laughing, slamming lockers, dropping binders, shoving one another—a jittery, mindless, restless noise unique to Friday afternoons. I'm feeling good, and powerful, and I'm thinking, *I have to find Lindsay*. She won't believe it. She'll die laughing. Then she'll put her arm around my shoulder and say, "You're a rock star, Samantha Kingston," and everything will be fine. I'm keeping an eye out for Anna Cartullo, too—while I was sitting in Ms. Winters's office it occurred to me that we never switched shoes again. I'm still wearing her monster black boots.

I swing out of Main. The cold makes my eyes sting, and a sharp pain shoots up my chest. February really is the worst month. A half dozen buses are idling in a line next to the cafeteria, engines choking and coughing, letting up a thick black wall of exhaust. Through the dirt-filmed windows the pale faces of a handful of underclassmen—all slouched in their seats, hoping not to be seen—are featureless and interchangeable. I start cutting across the faculty lot toward Senior Alley, but I'm only halfway there when I see a big-ass silver Range Rover—its walls thudding with the bass of "No More Drama"—tear out of the alley and start gunning it toward Upper Lot. I stop, all of the good buzzy feeling draining out of me quickly and at once. Of course, I didn't really expect Lindsay to be waiting for me, but deep down I guess I was hoping for it. Then it hits me: I have no ride, nowhere to go. The last place I want to be is at home. Even though I'm freezing, I feel prickles of heat rising up from my fingers, crawling up my spine.

It's the weirdest thing. I'm popular—really popular—but I don't have that many friends. What's even weirder is that it's the first time I've noticed.

"Sam!"

I turn around and see Tara Flute, Bethany Harps, and Courtney Walker coming toward me. They always travel in a pack, and even though we're kinda-friends with all of them, Lindsay calls them the Pugs: pretty from far away, ugly up close.

"What are you doing?" Tara always has a perma-smile, like she's constantly auditioning for an ad for Crest toothpaste, and she turns it on me now. "It's, like, a thousand degrees below zero."

I toss my hair over one shoulder, trying to look nonchalant. The last thing I need is for the Pugs to know I've been ditched. "I had to tell Lindsay something." I gesture vaguely in the direction of Senior Alley. "She and the girls had to jet out without me—some community-service thing they do once a month. Lame."

"So lame," Bethany says, nodding vigorously. As far as I can tell, her only role in life is to agree with whatever has just been said.

"Come with us." Tara slips her arm in mine and squeezes. "We're headed to La Villa to shop. Then we thought we'd hit up Kent's party. Sound good?"

I briefly run through my other options: home is obviously out. I won't be welcome at Ally's. Lindsay has made that clear. Then there's Rob's . . . sitting on the couch while he plays Guitar Hero, making out a little bit, pretending not to notice when he tears another bra because he can't figure out the clasp. Making conversation and waving while his parents pack up the car for the weekend. Pizza and lukewarm beer from the garage stash as soon as they're gone. Then more making out. No, thank you.

I scan the parking lot once more, looking for Anna. I feel kind of bad about taking off with her boots—but then again, it's not exactly like *she's* made an effort to find *me*. Besides,

Lindsay always said a new pair of shoes could change your life. And if I was ever in need of a serious life change—or afterlife change, whatever—it's now.

"Sounds perfect," I say, and if possible Tara's smile gets a little wider, teeth so white they look like bone.

As we leave school I tell the Pugs—I can't help but think of them that way—about my trip to the office, and how Ms. Winters has been getting her freak on with Mr. Shaw, and how I got off without a detention, because I promised her I would destroy a camera-phone pic of one of her love sessions in Shaw's office (fabricated, obviously—there's no way I'd ever hang on to evidence of their coupling, much less in high-digital format). Tara is gasping she's laughing so hard, and Courtney's looking at me like I've just cured cancer or developed a pill that makes you grow a cup size, and Bethany covers her mouth and says, "Holy mother of Lord Cocoa Puffs." I'm not exactly sure what that means, but it's definitely the most original thing I've ever heard her say. It all makes me feel good and confident again, and I remind myself that this is my day: I can do whatever I want.

"Tara?" I squinch forward. Tara's car is a tiny two-door Civic, and Bethany and I are crushed in the backseat. "Can we stop at my house for a second before we hit the mall?"

"Sure." There's her smile again, reflected in the rearview like a piece of sky. "Need to drop something?"

"Need to *get* something," I correct her, shooting her my biggest smile back.

It's almost three o'clock, so I figure my mom should be back from yoga, and sure enough her car is in the driveway when we pull up to the house. Tara starts to pull in behind the Accord, but I tap her shoulder and gesture for her to keep going. She inches her car along the road until we're hidden behind a cluster of evergreens my mom had the landscaper plant years ago, after she discovered that our then-neighbor, Mr. Horferly, liked to take midnight strolls on his property totally in the buff. This is pretty much the answer to every problem you encounter in suburbia: plant a tree, and hope you don't see anyone's privates.

I hop out of the car and loop around the side of the house, praying my mom isn't looking out one of the windows in the den or my dad's study. I'm banking on the fact that she's in the bathroom, taking one of her infamously long showers before going to pick up Izzy at gymnastics. Sure enough, when I slide my key in the back door and slip into the kitchen, I hear the patter of water upstairs and a few high, warbling notes: my mom is singing. I hesitate for a split second, long enough to place the tune—Frank Sinatra, "New York, New York"—and say a prayer of thanks that the Pugs aren't witness to my mom's impromptu performance. Then I tiptoe into the mudroom, where, as usual, my mom has deposited her enormous purse. It is sagging on its side. Several coins and a roll of breath mints have spilled out onto the washing machine, and a corner of her green Ralph Lauren wallet is just peeking out from under the thick leather loop of a shoulder strap. I remove the wallet carefully, listening, all the while, to the rhythm of the water upstairs, ready to cut and run if it stops flowing. My mom's wallet is a mess, too, crammed with photos—Izzy, me, me and Izzy, Pickle wearing a Santa's costume—receipts, business cards. And credit cards.

Especially credit cards.

I fish out the Amex carefully. My parents only use it for major purchases so there's no way my mom will notice it's missing. My palms are prickly with sweat and my heart is beating so hard it's painful. I carefully close up the wallet and slip it back into the purse, making sure it's in the exact same position as before.

Above me, there's a final rush of water, a screeching sound as the pipes shudder dry, and then silence. My mom's Sinatra rendition drops off. Shower over. For a second I'm so terrified I can't get my feet to move. She'll hear me. She'll catch me. She'll see me with the Amex in hand. Then the phone starts ringing, and I hear her footsteps heading out of the bathroom, crossing the hallway, hear her singsonging, "Coming, coming."

In that second I'm gone, slipping out of the mudroom, crossing the kitchen, out the back door—and running, running, running around the side of the house, the frost-coated grass biting my calves, trying to keep from laughing, clutching the cold plastic Amex so hard that when I open my palm later, I see it's left a mark.

Normally at the mall I have a very strict spending limit: twice a year my parents give me five hundred dollars for new clothes, and on top of that I can spend whatever I make babysitting for Izzy or doing other servant-type things my parents ask me to do, like wrap presents for our neighbors at Christmastime or rake the leaves in November or help my dad unclog the storm drains. I know five hundred dollars sounds like a lot, but you have to keep in mind that Ally's Burberry galoshes cost almost that—and she wears those in the rain. *On her feet.* So I've never been that big into shopping. It's just not that fun, particularly when you're best friends with Ally Endless-Limit-Credit-Card Harris and Lindsay My-Stepdad-Tries-to-Buy-My-Affection Edgecombe.

Today, that problem is solved.

First stop is Bebe, where I pick up a gorgeous spaghetti-strap dress that's so tight I have to suck all the way in just to squeeze into it. Even then Tara has to duck into the dressing room and help me zip up the last half inch. I kind of like how Anna's boots look with the dress, actually, sexy and tough, like I'm a video-game assassin or an action hero. I make *Charlie's Angels* poses at the mirror for a bit, shaping my fingers into a gun, pointing at my reflection, and mouthing, *Sorry.* Pulling the trigger, and imagining an explosion.

Courtney nearly loses it when I hand over my credit card without even looking at the total. Not that I don't catch a glimpse. It's pretty hard to miss the big green *$302.10* flashing on the register, blinking up at me like it's accusing me of something. My stomach gives a little hula performance as the saleswoman slides over the receipt for me to sign, but I guess all those years of forging my own doctor's notes and tardy excuses pays off because I give a perfect, looping imitation of my mom's script, and the saleswoman smiles and says, "Thank you, Ms. Kingston," like *I've* just done *her* a favor. And just like that I walk out with the world's most perfect black dress nestled in tissue paper at the bottom of a crisp white shopping bag. *Now* I understand why Ally and Lindsay love shopping. It's much better when you can have whatever you want.

"You are so lucky your parents give you a credit card," Courtney says, trotting after me as we leave the store. "I've been begging mine for years. They say I have to wait until I'm in college."

"They didn't exactly give it to me," I say, raising one eyebrow at her. Her mouth falls open.

"No way." Courtney shakes her head so fast her brown hair whips back and forth in a blur. "No way. You did not—are you saying you *stole*—?"

"Shhhh." La Villa Mall is supposed to be Italian-themed, all big, marble fountains and flagstone walkways. The sound gets bounced and zipped and mixed around so it's impossible to make out what people are saying unless they're standing right next to you, but still. No point in pushing it now that I'm on a roll. "I prefer to think of it as borrowing, anyway."

"My parents would strangle me." Courtney's eyes are so wide I'm worried her eyeballs will pop out. "They would kill me until I was dead."

"Totally," Bethany says.

We hit the MAC store next, and I get a full-on makeover from a guy named Stanley who's skinnier than I am, while the Pugs try on different shades of eyeliner and get yelled at for breaking into the unopened lip glosses. I buy everything Stanley uses on me: foundation, concealer, bronzing powder, eye shadow prep, three shades of eye shadow, two shades of eyeliner (one white for under the eye), mascara, lip liner, lip gloss, four different brushes, one eyelash curler. It's so worth it. I leave looking like I'm a famous model, and I can feel people staring at me as we walk through La Villa. We pass a group of guys who must be in college at least, and one of them mutters, "Hot." Tara and Courtney are flanking me and Bethany trails behind. I think: *This is how Lindsay must feel all the time.*

Next is Neiman Marcus: a store I never go into unless Ally drags me, since everything costs a billion dollars. Courtney tries on weird old-lady hats, and Bethany takes pictures of her and threatens to post them online. I pick up this amazing forest green faux-fur shrug that makes me look like I should be partying on a private jet somewhere, and a pair of silver-and-garnet chandelier earrings.

The only snag comes when the woman at the cashier—*Irma*, according to her name tag—asks to see my ID.

"ID?" I blink at her innocently. "I *so* never keep it on me. Last year my identity was stolen."

She stares at me for a long time like she's thinking about letting it slide, then pops her gum and gives me a tight smile. She pushes the shrug and the earrings back across the counter. "Sorry, *Ellen*. ID required for all purchases over two hundred and fifty dollars."

"I prefer Ms. Kingston, actually." I give her a tight smile right back. Bitch. That gum-popping trick? *Lindsay* invented it.

Then again, I'd be a bitch too if my parents had named me Irma.

Suddenly inspired, I root around in my purse until I fish out my membership card to Hilldebridge Swim and Tennis, my mom's gym. I swear, security there is tighter than an airport—like obesity in America is somehow a terrorist plot, and the next big thing to go will be the nation's elliptical machines—and the card features a tiny picture of me, a membership ID number, and my last name and initials: KINGSTON, S. E.

Irma screws up her face. "What does the S stand for?"

My mind does that thing where it hiccups and then goes totally blank. "Um—Severus."

She stares at me. "Like in *Harry Potter*?"

"It's German, actually." I should *never* have offered to read those stupid books to Izzy. "You can see why I go by my middle name."

Irma's still hesitating, biting the corner of her lip. Tara's standing right next to me, running her fingers over my Amex like some of the credit line will rub off on her. She leans forward and giggles.

"I'm sure *you* understand." Tara squints a little, like she's trying hard to make out the name tag from a distance of six inches. "It's Irma, isn't it?"

Courtney comes up behind us, wearing a wide-brimmed hat with a gigantic feathered robin sprouting out of its side. "Did people ever call you *Worma* when you were little? Or *Squirma*?"

Irma folds her mouth into a thin white line, reaches for my card, and swipes.

"*Guten Tag*," I say as we leave: the only German I know.

Tara and Co. are still laughing about Irma as we pull out of the parking lot of La Villa. "I can't believe it," Courtney keeps repeating, leaning forward to look at me, like I'm suddenly going to disappear. This time they've given me shotgun automatically. I didn't even have to call it. "I can't freaking believe it."

I allow myself a small smile as I turn to the window, and am momentarily startled by the reflection I see there: huge dark eyes, smoke and shadow, full red lips. Then I remember the makeup. For a second I didn't recognize myself.

"You're so awesome," Tara says, then palms the steering wheel and curses as we just miss the light.

"Please." I wave the air vaguely. I'm feeling pretty good. I'm almost glad Lindsay and I got into a fight this morning.

"Oh, shit, no way." Courtney beats on my shoulder as a huge Chevy Tahoe, vibrating with bass, pulls up next to us. Even though it's freezing, all the windows are down: it's the college guys from La Villa, the ones who checked us out earlier. Who checked *me* out. They're laughing and fighting over something in the car—one of them yells, "Mike, you're a pussy"—pretending not to see us, the way guys do when they're just dying to look.

"They are so hot," Tara says, leaning over me to get a clearer view, then ducking quickly back to the wheel.

"You should get their number."

"Hello? There are four of them."

"Their *numbers*, then."

"Totally."

"I'm gonna flash them," I say, and am suddenly thrilled with the perfect, pure simplicity of it: I'm going to do it. So much easier and cleaner than *Maybe I should* or *Won't we get in trouble?* or *Oh my God, I could never.* Yes. Three letters. I twist around to Courtney. "Do you dare me?"

Her eyes are doing that bug thing again. Tara and Bethany stare at me like I've sprouted tentacles.

"You wouldn't," Courtney says.

"You can't," Tara says.

"I can, I would, and I'm going to." I roll down the window, and the cold slams me, blots out everything, numbs my whole body so I just feel myself in bits and pieces, an elbow bobbing here, a thigh cramping, fingers tingling. The music pumping from the boys' car is so loud it makes my ears hurt, but I can't hear any words or melody, just the rhythm, throbbing, throbbing—so loud it's not even sound anymore, just vibration, feeling.

"Hey." At first I can only croak the word out, so I clear my throat and try again. "Hey. Guys."

The driver swivels his head in my direction. I can hardly focus I'm so keyed up, but in that second I see he's not that cute, actually—he has kind of crooked teeth and a rhinestone stud in one ear, like he's a rapper or something—but then he says, "Hey, cutie," and I see his three friends lean over toward the window to look, one, two, three heads popping up like jacks-in-the-box, like the Whack-a-Mole game at Dave & Buster's, *one, two, three*, and I'm lifting my shirt, and there's a roar and a rushing, singing sound in my ears—laughter? screaming?—and Courtney's yelling, "Go, go, go." Then our tires screech, and the car lurches forward, sliding a bit, the wind biting my face, and the smell of scorched rubber and gasoline stinking up the air. My heart sinks slowly back from my throat to my chest, and the warmth and feeling comes back to my body. I roll up the window. I can't explain the feelings going through me, a rush like you get from laughing too hard or spinning too long in a circle. It's not exactly happiness, but I'll take it.

"Priceless! *Legendary!*" Courtney's thumping the back of my seat, and Bethany's just shaking her head and reaching forward to touch me, eyes wide, amazed, like I'm a saint and she's trying to cure herself of a disease. Tara's screaming with laughter. She can barely watch the road, her eyes are tearing up so badly. She chokes out, "Did you see their *faces*? Did you *see*?" and I realize I didn't see. I couldn't see anything, couldn't feel anything but the roaring around me, heavy and loud, and it occurs to me that I'm not sure whether this is what it's like to be really, truly alive or this is what it's like to be dead, and it strikes me as hilarious. Courtney thumps me one more time, and I see her face rising behind me in the rearview mirror, red as a sun, and I start laughing too, and the four of us laugh all the way back to Ridgeview—over eighteen miles—while the world streaks past us in a smear of blacks and grays, like a bad painting of itself.

We stop at Tara's house so everyone can change. Tara helps get me into my dress again, and after I slip on the fur shrug and the earrings and let my hair down—which is all wavy from being twisted up in a half-knot all day—I turn to the mirror and my heart actually reindeer-prances in my chest. I look at least twenty-five. I look like somebody else. I close my eyes, remember standing in the bathroom when I was little as the steam from my shower retreated from the mirrors, praying for a transformation. I remember the sick taste of disappointment every time my face reemerged, as plain as it ever was. But this time when I open my eyes it works. There I am: different and gorgeous and not myself.

Dinner's on me, of course. We go to Le Jardin du Roi, this super expensive French restaurant where all the waiters are hot and French. We pick the most expensive bottle of wine on the menu, and nobody asks to see our IDs, so we order a round of champagne. It's so good, we ask for another round even before the appetizers come. Bethany gets drunk right away and starts flirting with the waiters in bad French, just because last year she spent the summer in Provence. We must order half the menu: tiny melt-in-your-mouth cheese puffs, thick slabs of pâté that probably have more calories than you're supposed to eat in a day, goat cheese salad and mussels in white wine and steak béarnaise and a whole sea bass with its head still attached and crème brûlée and mousse au chocolat. I think it's the best food I've ever tasted, and I eat until I can hardly breathe, and if I take one more bite I really will bust my dress. Then, as I'm signing the check, one of the waiters (the cutest one) brings over four miniature glasses of sweet pink liquor *for the digestion*, except, of course, he says it *for ze deejestee-on*.

I don't realize how much I've had to drink until I stand up and the world swings wildly for a second, like it's struggling to find its balance, and I think maybe the *world's* drunk, not me, and start to giggle. We step out into the freezing air and it helps sober me up a little.

I check my phone and see that I have a text from Rob. *What's up w u? We had a plan 4 2nite.*

"Come on, Sam," Courtney calls. She and Bethany have climbed into the backseat of the Civic. They're waiting for me to take shotgun again. "Party time."

I quickly write a text back to Rob. *We're on. C u soon.*

Then I get in the car, and we head to the party.

The party's just getting started when we arrive, and I beeline for the kitchen. Since it's still early and pretty clear of people I notice a ton of details in the rooms I haven't seen before. The place is so stocked with little carved wood statues and funky oil paintings and old books it could be a museum.

The kitchen is brightly lit and everything here looks sharp and separate. There are two kegs lined up directly inside the doorway, and most of the people are gathered here. It's basically guys at this point, plus some sophomores. They're huddled in clumps, gripping their plastic cups like they contain their whole life force, and their smiles are so forced I can tell their cheeks are hurting.

"Sam." Rob sees me and does a double take as soon as I

come in. He shoulders his way toward me, then backs me up against the wall, leaning a hand on either side of my head so I'm penned in. "I didn't think you were gonna show."

"I told you I was coming." I put my hands on his chest, feeling his heartbeat skip under my fingers. It makes me sad for some reason. "Did you get my text?"

He shrugs. "You were acting weird all day. I thought maybe you didn't like my rose."

Luv ya. I'd forgotten about that; forgotten about how upset I was. None of that matters now. They're just words, anyway. "The rose was fine."

Rob smiles and puts one hand on my head, like I'm a pet. "You look hot, babe," he says. "You want a beer?"

I nod. The wine I had at the restaurant is already wearing off. I feel way too sober, too aware of my whole body, my arms hanging there like dead weights. Rob has started to turn away when he suddenly stops, staring down at my shoes. He looks up at me, half amused, half puzzled. "What are those?" He points at Anna's boots.

"Shoes." I point one of my toes and the leather doesn't even budge. This pleases me for some reason. "You like them?"

Rob makes a face. "They look like army boots or something."

"Well, *I* like them."

He shakes his head. "They don't look like you, babe."

I think of all the things I've done today that would shock

Rob: cutting all my classes, kissing Mr. Daimler, smoking pot with Anna Cartullo, stealing my mom's credit card. Things that aren't *like me*. I'm not even sure what that means; I'm not sure how you know. I mentally try to add up all the things I've done in my life, but no clear picture emerges, nothing that will tell me what kind of person I am—just a lot of haziness and blurred edges, indistinct memories of laughing and driving around. I feel like I'm trying to take a picture into the sun: all of the people in my memories are coming back featureless and interchangeable.

"You don't know everything about me," I say.

He gives a half laugh. "I know you look cute when you're mad." He taps a finger between my eyes. "Don't frown so much. You'll get wrinkles."

"How about that beer?" I say, grateful when Rob turns away. I was hoping that seeing him would relax me, but instead it's making me jumpy.

When Rob comes back with my beer, I take my cup and go upstairs.

At the top of the stairs I almost collide with Kent. He takes a quick step backward when he sees me.

"Sorry," we both say at the same time, and I can feel myself blushing.

"You came," he says. His eyes look greener than ever. There's a weird expression on his face—his mouth is all twisted like he's chewing on something sour.

"Seems like it's the place to be." I look away, wishing he would stop staring at me. Somehow I know he's going to say something awful. He's going to say that he can see through me again. And I get this crazy urge to ask him what he sees—like he can help *me* figure out *me*. But I'm afraid of his answer.

He looks at his feet. "Sam, I wanted to say . . ."

"Don't." I hold up a hand. Then it hits me: he knows what happened with Mr. Daimler. He can tell. I know I'm being paranoid, but the certainty is so strong it makes my head spin, and I have to reach out and grab on to the banister. "If this is about what happened in math, I don't want to hear it."

He looks up at me again, his mouth set in a line. "What *did* happen?"

"Nothing." Once again I feel Mr. Daimler's weight pressing into me, the heat of his mouth clamped over mine. "It's none of your business."

"Daimler's a dirtbag, you know. You should stay away from him." He looks at me sideways. "You're too good for that."

I think of the note that sailed onto my desk earlier. I *knew* it was from him. The thought of Kent McFuller feeling sorry for me, looking down on me, makes something break inside.

My words come out in a rush. "I don't have to explain anything to you. We're not even friends. We're—we're nothing."

Kent takes a step back, lets out a noise that's halfway between a snort and a laugh. "You're really unbelievable, you know that?" He shakes his head, looking disgusted or sad, or maybe both. "Maybe everyone's right about you. Maybe you are just a shallow—" He stops.

"What? A shallow *what*?" I feel like slapping him to get him to look at me, but he keeps his eyes turned toward the wall. "A shallow bitch, right? Is that what you think?"

His eyes click back on mine, clear and dull and hard, like rock. Now I wish he hadn't looked at me at all. "Maybe. Maybe it's like you said. We're not friends. We're not anything."

"Yeah? Well, at least I don't walk around pretending to be better than everybody else." It explodes out of me before I can stop it. "You're not perfect, you know. I'm sure you've done bad things. I'm sure you do bad things." As soon as I say it, though, I get the feeling it's not true. I just know it somehow. Kent McFuller doesn't do bad things. At least, he doesn't do bad things to other people.

Now Kent *does* laugh. "*I'm* the one who pretends to be better than everybody?" He narrows his eyes. "That's really funny, Sam. Anyone ever tell you how funny you are?"

"I'm not kidding." I'm balling my fists up against my thighs. I don't know why I'm so angry at him, but I could shake him, or cry. He knows about Mr. Daimler. He knows all about me, and he hates me for it. "You shouldn't make people feel bad just because they're not, like, perfect or whatever."

His mouth falls open. "I never said—"

"It's not my fault I can't be like you, okay? I don't get up in the morning thinking the world is one big shiny, happy place,

okay? That's just not how I work. I don't think I can be fixed."
I mean to say, *I don't think "it" can be fixed*, but it comes out
wrong, and suddenly I'm on the verge of crying. I have to take
big gulping breaths to try to keep the tears down. I turn away
from Kent so he won't see.

There's a moment of silence that seems to last forever. Then
Kent rests his hand on my elbow just for a second, his touch
like the wings of something brushing me. Just that one little
touch gives me the chills.

"I was going to tell you that you look beautiful with your hair
down. That's all I was going to say." Kent's voice is steady and
low. He moves around me to the head of the stairs, pausing just
at the top. When he turns back to me he looks sad, even though
he's smiling the tiniest bit.

"You don't need to be fixed, Sam." He says the words, but
it's like I don't even hear them; it's like they go through my
whole body at the same time, like I'm absorbing them from
the air. He must know it's untrue. I open my mouth to tell him
so, but he's already disappearing down the stairs, melting into
the crowd of people flowing into the house. I'm a nonperson,
a shadow, a ghost. Even *before* the accident I'm not sure that
I was a whole person—that's what I'm realizing now. And I'm
not sure where the damage begins.

I take a big swig of beer, wishing I could just go blotto. I
want the world to drop away. I take another big gulp. The beer
is cold, at least, but tastes like moldy water.

"Sam!" Tara's coming up the stairs, her smile like the beam of a flashlight. "We've been looking for you." When she gets to the top she pants a little, putting her right hand on her stomach and bending over. In her left hand she's holding a cigarette, half smoked. "Courtney did recon. She found the good stuff."

"Good stuff?"

"Whiskey, vodka, gin, cassis, the works. Booze. The good stuff."

She grabs my hand and we go back down the stairs, which are slowly getting clogged with people. Everyone's moving in the same direction: from the entrance to the beer and then up the stairs. In the kitchen we push through the clot of people gathered by the keg. On the opposite side of the kitchen there's a door with a handwritten sign on it. I recognize Kent's handwriting.

It says: PLEASE DO NOT ENTER.

There's a footnote written in tiny letters along the bottom of the page: SERIOUSLY, GUYS. I'M HOSTING THE PARTY AND IT'S THE ONE THING I ASK. LOOK! THERE'S A KEG BEHIND YOU!

"Maybe we shouldn't—" I start to say, but Tara has already slipped through the door so I follow her.

It's dark on the other side of the door, and cold. The only light comes from two enormous bay windows that face out onto the backyard.

I hear giggling from somewhere deeper in the house, then

the sound of someone bumping into something. "Careful," someone hisses, and then I hear Courtney say, "*You* try to pour in the dark."

"This way," Tara whispers. It's weird how people's voices get softer in the dark, like they can't help it.

We're in the dining room. There's a chandelier drooping from the ceiling like an exotic flower, and heavy curtains pooling at either side of the windows. Tara and I skirt around the dining room table—my mom would have a coronary from excitement, it must seat at least twelve—and out into a kind of alcove. This is where the bar is. Beyond the alcove is another dark room: from the sofas and bookshelves I can just make out, it looks like a library or a living room. I wonder how many rooms there are. The house seems to extend forever. It's even darker here, but Courtney and Bethany are rooting around in some cabinets.

"There must be fifty bottles in here," Courtney says. It's too dark to read labels, so she opens each bottle and sniffs it, guessing at the contents. "This is rum, I think."

"Freaky house, huh?" Bethany says.

"I don't mind it," I say quickly, not sure why I feel defensive. I bet it's beautiful during the day: room after room of light. I bet Kent's house is always quiet, or there's always classical music playing or something.

Glass shatters next to me and something wet splatters on my leg. I jump as Courtney whispers, "What did you do?"

"It's not me," I say as Tara says, "I didn't mean to."

"Was that a vase?"

"Ew. Some of it got on my shoe."

"Let's just take the bottle and get out of here."

We slip back into the kitchen just as RJ Ravner yells, "Fire in the hole!" Matt Dorfman takes a cup of beer and starts chugging it. Everyone laughs and Abby McGail claps when he's drained the cup. Someone turns up the music, and Dujeous comes on and everyone starts singing along. *All MCs in the house tonight, if your lyrics sound tight then rock the mic. . . .*

I hear high-pitched laughter. Then a voice from the front hallway: "God, I guess we came at the right time."

My stomach jumps into my throat. Lindsay's here.

THERE ARE CERTAIN THINGS YOU NEVER SAY

Here's Lindsay's big secret: when she came back from visiting her stepbrother at NYU our junior year, she was awful for days—snapping at everybody, making fun of Ally for having weird food issues, making fun of Elody for being such a lush and a pushover, making fun of me for always being the last to do things, from picking up on trends to going to third base (which I didn't do until late sophomore year). Elody, Ally, and I knew something must have happened in New York, but Lindsay wouldn't tell us when we asked her, and we didn't push it. You don't push things with Lindsay.

Then one night toward the end of the school year, we were

all at Rosalita's, this crappy Mexican restaurant one town over where they don't card, having margaritas and waiting for our dinners to come. Lindsay wasn't really eating—hadn't really been eating since returning from New York. She wouldn't touch the free chips, saying she wasn't hungry, and instead kept dipping a finger into the salt that was rimming her margarita glass and eating the crystals one by one.

I don't remember what we were talking about, but all of a sudden Lindsay blurted out, "I had sex." Just like that. We all stared at her in silence, and she leaned forward and told us in a breathless rush how she'd been drunk and how because her stepbrother wasn't ready to leave the party the guy—the Unmentionable—offered to walk her back to the dorm where she was staying with her stepbrother. They'd had sex on her stepbrother's twin long bed with Lindsay fading in and out, and the guy—the Unmentionable—was gone even before Lindsay's brother got back from the party.

"It was only, like, three minutes," she said at the end, and I knew then she was already filing it away under Things We'll Never Talk About, tucking it back in some far corner of her mind and building other, alternate stories on top of it, better stories: I went to New York and had a great time. I'm totally going to move there one day. I kissed a guy, and he wanted to come home with me, but I wouldn't let him.

Right after that our food came. Lindsay was hugely relieved after telling us—even though she swore us on pain of death to absolute secrecy—and her whole mood changed instantly. She sent back the salad she'd ordered ("Like I want to choke down that rabbit crap") and ordered cheese-and-mushroom quesadillas, pork-stuffed burritos with extra sour cream and guacamole, an order of chimichangas for the table to split, and another round of margaritas. It was like a weight had been lifted, and we had the best dinner we'd had in years. All of us were stuffing our faces, even Ally, and drinking margarita after margarita in different flavors—mango, raspberry, orange— and laughing so loudly at least one table asked to be moved to a different part of the restaurant. I don't remember what we were even talking about, but at one point Ally took a picture of Elody wearing a flour tortilla on her head and holding up a bottle of hot sauce. In the corner of the frame, you can see a third of Lindsay's profile. She's doubling over, cracking up, her face a bright purple. One hand is clutching her stomach.

After dinner Lindsay threw down her mom's credit card to pay for the whole thing. She's only supposed to use it for emergencies, but she leaned forward over the table and made us all grab hands like we were praying. "This, my friends, was an emergency," she said, and we all laughed because she was being melodramatic as usual. The plan was to go off to a party in the arboretum: a tradition on the first warm weekend of the year. We had the whole night ahead of us. Everyone was in a good mood. Lindsay was being normal again.

Lindsay went to the bathroom to fix her makeup, and five

seconds after she left the table, all those margaritas and all that laughing hit me at once: I'd never had to pee so bad in my life. I sprinted to the bathroom, still laughing, while Elody and Ally pegged me with half-eaten chips and crumpled napkins and yelled, "Send us a postcard from the Niagara Falls" and "If it's yellow, keep it mellow!" so that yet another table asked to be moved.

The bathroom was single-person, and I leaned up against the door, calling for Lindsay to let me in, rattling the handle at the same time. I guess she'd been in a rush to get in there because she hadn't locked the door correctly and it opened as I was leaning against it. I tumbled into the bathroom, still laughing, expecting to find Lindsay standing in front of the mirror with her lips puckered, applying two coats of MAC Vixen lip gloss.

Instead she was kneeling on the floor in front of the toilet, and the remains of the quesadillas and the pork-stuffed burrito were floating on the surface of the water. She flushed but not quickly enough. I saw two whole undigested tomato pieces swirl down the toilet bowl.

All the laughter left me instantly. "What are you doing?" I asked, even though it was obvious.

"Shut the door," she hissed.

I closed it quickly, the noise of the restaurant vacuumed away, leaving silence.

Lindsay got up from her knees slowly. "Well?" she said,

looking at me like she was already preparing her arguments—like she expected me to accuse her of something.

"I had to pee," I said. It's so lame, but I couldn't think of anything else. There was a tiny piece of food clinging to a strand of hair and seeing it made me feel like bursting into tears. She was Lindsay Edgecombe: she was our armor.

"Pee then," she said, looking relieved, though I thought I saw a flicker of something else—maybe sadness.

I did. I peed while Lindsay bent over the sink, cupping her hands and sipping water from them, rolling it around in her mouth and gargling. That's a funny thing: you think, when awful things happen, everything else just stops, like you would forget to pee and eat and get thirsty, but it's not really true. It's like you and your body are two separate things, like your body is betraying you, chugging on, idiotic and animal, craving water and sandwiches and bathroom breaks while your world falls apart.

I watched Lindsay fish out a Listerine strip and place one in her mouth, grimacing slightly. Then she went to work with her makeup, touching up her mascara and reapplying her lip gloss. The bathroom was small, but she seemed very far away.

Finally she said, "It's not a habit or anything. I think I just ate too quickly."

"Okay," I said, and forever afterward I didn't know if she was telling the truth.

"Don't tell Al or Elody, okay? I don't want them freaking out over nothing."

"Obviously," I said.

She paused, pressed her lips together, puckered them at the mirror. Then she turned toward me. "You guys are my family. You know that, right?"

She said it casually, as though she were complimenting my jeans, but I knew that it was one of the most sincere things she'd ever said to me. I knew that she really *meant* it.

We went to the party in the arboretum as planned. Elody and Ally had a great time, but I got a stomachache and had to double up on the hood of Ally's car. I'm not sure if it was the food or what, but it felt like something was trying to claw its way out of my stomach.

Lindsay had a great night: that night she kissed Patrick for the first time. Three months later, at the tail end of the summer, they had sex. When she told us about losing her virginity to her boyfriend—the candles, the blanket on the floor, the flowers, the whole nine yards—and how great it was that her first time was so romantic, none of us even batted an eyelash. We all rushed in and congratulated her, asked her for details, told her we were jealous. We did it for Lindsay, to make her happy. She would have done it for us.

That's the thing about best friends. That's what they do. They keep you from spinning off the edge.

Lindsay, Elody, and Ally must head upstairs as soon as they arrive—considering they're packing their own vodka, it's a safe bet—because I don't see them again until an hour or so later. I've had three shots of rum and it all hits me at once: the room is a spinning, blurring world of color and sound. Courtney has just finished off the bottle of rum so I get a beer. I have to concentrate on every step, and when I get to the keg I stand there for a second, forgetting what I've come for.

"Beer?" Matt Dorfman fills a cup and holds it out to me.

"Beer," I say, pleased the word comes out so clear, pleased that I remembered that this is what I wanted.

I make my way upstairs. Things register in short bursts, a movie reel that's been chopped up: the feel of the rough wood banister; Emma McElroy leaning back against a wall, her mouth open and gasping—maybe laughing?—like a fish on a hook; Christmas lights winking, blurred light. I'm not sure where I'm going or who I'm looking for, but all of a sudden there's Lindsay across the room and I realize I've made it all the way to the back of the house, the cigarette room. Lindsay and I look at each other for a second and I'm hoping she'll smile at me, but she just looks away. Ally's standing next to her. She bends forward and whispers something to Lindsay, then makes her way over to me.

"Hey, Sam."

"Did you have to ask permission to talk to me?" These words

don't come out so clearly.

"Don't be a bitch." Ally rolls her eyes. "Lindsay's really upset about what you said."

"Is Elody mad?" Elody's in the corner with Steve Dough, swaying against him while he talks to Liz Hummer like she's not even there. I want to go over and hug her.

Ally hesitates, looks at me from under the fringe of her bangs. "She's not mad. You know Elody."

I can tell Ally's lying, but I'm too drunk to pursue it.

"You didn't call me today." I hate that I've said it. It makes me feel like an outsider again, like someone trying to break into the group. It's only been a day, but I *miss* them: my only real friends.

Ally takes a sip of the vodka she's holding, then winces. "Lindsay was freaking out. I told you, she was really upset."

"It's true though, isn't it? What I said."

"It doesn't matter if it's true." Ally shakes her head at me. "She's Lindsay. She's ours. We're each other's, you know?"

I've never really thought of Ally as smart, but this is probably the smartest thing I've heard in a long time.

"You should say you're sorry," Ally says.

"But I'm *not* sorry." I'm definitely slurring now. My tongue is thick and weighty in my mouth. I can't make it do what I want it to. I want to tell Ally everything—about Mr. Daimler and Anna Cartullo and Ms. Winters and the Pugs—but I can't even think of the words.

"Just say it, Sam." Ally's eyes have started to roam around the party. Then suddenly she takes a quick step backward. Her mouth goes slack and she brings a hand to her mouth.

"Oh my God," she says, staring over my shoulder. Her mouth's curving up into a smile. "I don't believe it."

It feels like time freezes as I turn around. I read once that at the edge of a black hole, time stops completely, so if you ever sailed into it, you'd just be stuck there at the lip forever, forever being torn apart, forever dying. That's what it feels like in that second. The crush of people circled around me, an endless lip, more and more people.

And there she is standing in the doorway. Juliet Sykes. Juliet Sykes—who yesterday blew her brains out with her parents' handgun.

Her hair is tied up in a ponytail and I can't help it; I picture it knotted and clotted with blood, a big gaping hole directly underneath her little flip of hair. I'm terrified of her: a ghost in the door, the kind of stuff you have nightmares about when you're a kid, the kind of thing they make horror movies about.

A phrase comes back from a news show I had to watch about the convicts on death row for my ethics and issues elective: dead man walking. I thought it was awful when I first heard it, but now I really *understand* it. Juliet Sykes is a dead man walking. I guess I am too, in a way.

"No," I say, without meaning to say it out loud. I take a step backward, and Harlowe Rosen squeals and says, "That's my *foot.*"

"I don't believe it," Ally says again, but it sounds far away. She's already turning away from me, calling out to Lindsay over the music. "Lindsay, did you see who it is?"

Juliet sways in the doorway. She looks calm, but her hands are balled into fists.

I throw myself forward, but everyone chooses that moment to press even closer around me. I can't watch it again. I don't want to see what happens next. I'm not very steady on my feet, and I keep getting knocked back and forth, rocketing between people like a pinball, trying desperately to get out of the room. I know I'm stepping on people and throwing elbows in their backs, but I don't care. I need out.

Finally I break through the knot of people. Juliet is blocking the doorway. She's not even looking at me. She's standing as still as a statue, her eyes locked some distance over my shoulder. She's looking at Lindsay. I understand then that it's Lindsay she really wants—it's Lindsay she hates the most—but it doesn't make me feel any better.

Just as I'm about to push past her, a tremor runs through her body and she locks eyes with me.

"Wait," she says to me, and puts a hand on my wrist. It's as cold as ice.

"No." I pull away from her and keep going, stumbling forward, nearly choking on my fear. Jumbled images of Juliet keep flashing in my mind: Juliet doubled over, hands outstretched, drenched in beer and stumbling; Juliet lying on a cold floor in a pool of blood. I'm not thinking clearly, and in my head the two images merge and I see her roving around the room while everyone laughs, her hair soaked, dripping, drenched in blood.

I'm so distracted I don't see Rob in the hallway until I've run straight into him.

"Hey." Rob is drunk now. He has an unlit cigarette dangling from his lips. "Hey, you."

"Rob . . ." I press myself against him. The world is spinning. "Let's get out of here, okay? We'll go to your house. I'm ready now, just me and you."

"Whoa, cowgirl." One half of Rob's mouth ticks slowly upward, but the other doesn't quite manage to join it. "After the cigarette." He starts moving toward the back of the house. "Then we'll go."

"No!" I nearly scream it.

He turns back to me, swaying, and before he can react, I've already plucked the cigarette out of his mouth and I'm kissing him, my hands cupped on either side of his face, shoving my body into his. It takes him a second to realize what's happening, but then he starts pawing me over my dress, rolling his tongue around in circles, groaning a little bit.

We're both staggering back and forth in the hallway, almost like we're dancing. I feel the floor buckle and roll, and Rob accidentally pushes me hard against the wall and I gasp.

"Sorry, babe." His eyes cross, uncross.

"We need a room." From the back of the house I can just hear the chanting starting. *Psycho, Psycho.* "We need a room *now*."

I take Rob's hand and we stumble down the hall, forcing our way against the tide of people moving in the other direction. They're all going to see what the noise is about.

"In here." Rob slams as hard as he can against the first closed door he comes to, the one with all the bumper stickers. There's a popping sound and we both tumble inside. I kiss him again and try to lose myself in the feeling of the closeness of our bodies and his warmth, try to block out the rising howls of laughter from the back room. I pretend I'm just a body with a mind as blank and fuzzy as a TV full of snow. I try to shrink myself down, center myself in my skin, like the only feeling that exists is in Rob's fingers.

Once the door is shut it's pitch-black. The darkness around us hasn't let up at all—either there are no windows here or they're curtained off. It's so dark it's almost *heavy*-looking, and I get a sudden hysterical fear that we're stuck in a box. Rob's lurching on his feet so much by this point, his arms locked around me, it makes me dizzy. I feel a wave of nausea, and I push him backward until we encounter something soft: a bed. He tips over and I climb on top of him.

"Wait," he mumbles.

"Isn't this what you wanted?" I whisper. Even now I can hear the sounds of laughter and the screaming—*Psycho, Psycho*—piping thinly over the music. I kiss Rob harder and he wrestles with the zipper of my dress. I hear fabric ripping but I don't care. I slide the dress down to my waist, and Rob starts his attack on my bra.

"Are you shure about this?" Rob slurs in my ear.

"Just kiss me." *Psycho, Psycho.* The voices are echoing down the hall. I slide my hands under Rob's fleece and wrestle it over his head, then start kissing his neck and underneath the collar of his polo shirt. His skin tastes like sweat and salt and cigarettes, but I keep kissing while his hands move over my back and down toward my butt. An image of Mr. Daimler on top of me—and the speckled ceiling—rises out of the darkness, but I push it away.

I take Rob's shirt off so now we're pressed chest-to-chest. Our skin keeps making these weird, slurpy, suction sounds as our stomachs come together and then pop apart. At a certain point his hands fall away. I'm still kissing him, moving down his chest, feeling the fuzz of hair scattered there. Chest hair has always grossed me out; it's another thing I don't think about tonight.

Rob's gotten quiet. He's probably shocked. I've never even done this much with him before. Normally when we hook up he's the one who takes charge. I've always been afraid I'll do something wrong. It feels so awkward to act like you know what you're doing. I've never even been totally naked with him.

"Rob?" I whisper, and he moans quietly. My arms are shaking from holding my weight up for so long so I stand up. "Do you want me to take my dress off?"

Silence. My heart is beating fast, and even though the room is cold, sweat is tickling my underarms. "Rob?" I repeat.

All of a sudden he lets out an enormous, honking snore and rolls over. The snores continue, long waves of them.

For a while I just stand there and listen to it. When Rob snores it's always reminded me of when I was little and used to sit on the front porch and watch my dad make narrow circles on the back of his six-year-old Sears ride-on mower, which growled so badly I had to cover my ears. I never went inside, though. I loved to watch the neat little compact tracks of green my dad left in his wake, hundreds of tiny blades of grass spinning through the air like ballerinas.

It's so dark in the room it takes me forever to find my bra and stupid fur thing; I have to grope on my hands and knees for them. I'm not upset. I'm not feeling much of anything, not really thinking, just ticking off things I have to do. Find the bra. Hitch up the dress. Get out the door.

I slip into the hallway. The music's pumping at a normal volume, and people are flowing in and out of the back room. Juliet Sykes is gone.

A couple of people give me weird looks. I'm sure I'm a mess but don't have the energy to care. It's amazing how well I'm holding it together, actually, and even though my brain is foggy I think that very clearly: *It's amazing how well you're holding it together.* I think, *Lindsay would be proud.*

"Your dress isn't zipped." Carly Jablonski giggles at me.

Behind her someone says, "What were you doing in there?"

I ignore them. I just keep moving—floating, really, without really knowing where I'm headed—drifting down the stairs and out onto the wraparound porch and, when the cold hits me like a punch, back into the house and into the kitchen. Suddenly the idea of the dark, quiet house lying peacefully beyond the DO NOT ENTER sign, full of moonlit squares and the quiet tickings of old clocks, seems appealing. So I go that way, beyond the door, through the dining room, through the alcove where Tara spilled the vase, my boots crunching on the glass, into the living room.

One wall is almost all windows. It faces out onto the front lawn. Outside, the night looks silvery and frosted, all the trees wrapped in a shroud of ice, like they've been built out of plaster. I begin to wonder if everything in this world, the world I'm stuck in, is just a replica, a cheap imitation of the real thing. Then I sit down on the carpet—in the exact center of a perfect square of moonlight—and I begin to cry. The first sob is almost a scream.

I don't know how long I'm there—at least fifteen minutes, since I manage to pretty much cry myself out. In the process I snot all over myself and completely ruin my fur shrug with mascara and face gunk. But at a certain point I become aware that there's someone else in the room.

I get very still. Parts of the room are lost in shadow, but I can sense something moving at its periphery. A checkered sneaker flickers in and out of view.

"How long have you been standing there?" I ask, wiping my nose for the fortieth time on the back of my arm.

"Not long." Kent's voice is very quiet. I can tell he's lying, but I don't mind. It actually makes me feel better to know I wasn't alone this whole time.

"Are you okay?" He takes a few steps into the room so the moonlight hits him and turns him silver. "I mean, you're obviously not okay, but I just wanted to know if, you know, there's anything I could do or something you want to talk about or—"

"Kent?" I interrupt him. He always did have a habit of launching into tangents, even when we were little.

He stops. "Yeah?"

"Do you—could I maybe have a glass of water?"

"Yeah. Give me a sec." He sounds relieved to do something, and I hear the whisper of his sneakers on the carpet. He's back in under a minute with a tall glass of water. It has just the right amount of ice cubes.

After I take a few long gulps I say, "Sorry for being back here. The sign and everything."

"That's okay." Kent sits cross-legged on the carpet next to

me, not so close that we're touching but close enough that I can feel him sitting there. "I mean, the sign was pretty much for other people. You know, to keep people from breaking my parents' shit or whatever. I've never really had a party before."

"Why did you have one now?" I say, just to keep him talking.

He gives a half laugh. "I thought if I had a party, you would come."

I feel a rush of embarrassment, heat spreading up from my toes. His comment is so unexpected I don't know what to say. He doesn't seem embarrassed though. He just sits there looking at me. So typical Kent. He never understood that you can't just say something like that.

The silence has lasted a couple beats too long. I grasp for something to say. "This room must get a lot of light during the day."

Kent laughs. "It's like being in the middle of the sun."

Silence again. We can still hear the music, but it's muffled, like it has to travel miles before it reaches us. I like that.

"Listen." Just trying to say what I want to say makes a lump swell up in my throat. "I'm sorry about earlier. I really—thanks for making me feel better. I'm sorry I've always been . . ." At the last second I can't say it after all. *I'm sorry I've always been awful. I'm sorry there's something wrong with me.*

"I meant what I said earlier," Kent says quietly. "About your hair."

263

He shifts slightly—a fraction of an inch, moving closer—and it hits me then that I'm sitting in the middle of a moonlit room with Kent McFuller.

"I should go." I stand up. I'm still not very steady on my feet, and the room tilts with me.

"Whoa." Kent gets up, reaching out a hand to steady me. "You sure you're okay?"

"I—" It occurs to me I don't know where to go and I have nobody to get me there, anyway. I can't stand the thought of Tara grinning at me, and Lindsay's obviously out. At this point it's so awful it's funny, and I let out a short laugh. "I don't want to go home."

Kent doesn't ask why. I'm grateful for that. He just shoves his hands in his pockets. The outlines of his face are touched with light, like he's glowing.

"You could . . ." He swallows. "You could always stay here."

I stare at him. Thank God it's dark. I have no idea what my face looks like.

He quickly stutters, "Not, like, *stay* with me. Obviously not. I just meant—well, we have a couple guest rooms, with sheets already on the beds and stuff. *Clean* sheets, obviously, it's not like we leave them on after people—"

"Okay."

"—use them, that would be gross. We actually have a house-keeper who comes twice a week and—"

"Kent? I said okay. I mean, I'd like to stay. If you don't mind."

He stands there for a second with his mouth hanging open as though he's sure he's misheard me. Then he takes his hands out of his pockets, curls them and uncurls them, lifts them and drops them against his thighs. "Sure, yeah, no, that's fine."

But for another minute he doesn't move. He just stares at me. The hotness returns, only this time it's moving into my head, making everything seem cloudy and remote. My eyes are suddenly heavy.

"You're tired," he says, and his voice is soft again.

"It's been a long day," I say.

"Come on." He reaches out his hand and without thinking I take it. It's warm and dry, and as he leads me deeper into the house, away from the music, into the shadows, I close my eyes and remember how he used to slip his hand in mine and whisper, *Don't listen to them. Just keep walking. Keep your head up.* It almost feels like no time has passed. It doesn't feel crazy that I'm holding hands with Kent McFuller and I'm letting him lead me somewhere—it feels normal.

The music fades away altogether. Everything is so quiet. Our feet barely make a sound on the carpets, and each room is a web of shadow and moonlight. The house smells like polished wood and rain and just a little bit like chimney smoke, like someone's recently had a fire. I think, *This would be a perfect house to get snowed into.*

"This way," Kent says. He pushes open a door—it creaks on

its hinges—and I hear him fumbling for a light switch on the wall.

"No," I say.

He hesitates. "No light?"

"No light."

Very slowly he guides me inside the room. Here it's almost completely dark. I can barely make out the outline of his shoulders.

"The bed's over here."

I let him pull me over to him. We're only inches away, and it's like I can *feel* his impression in the darkness, like it's taking on a form around him. We're still holding hands, but now we're face-to-face. I never realized how tall he was: at least four inches taller than I am. There's the strangest amount of warmth coming off him. It's everywhere, radiating outward, making my fingers tingle.

"Your skin," I say, barely a whisper. "It's hot."

"It's always this way," he says. Something rustles in the dark and I know he has moved his arm. His fingers hover half an inch from my face, and it's like I can *see* them, burning hot and white. He drops his arm, taking the warmth with him.

And it's the weirdest thing, but standing there with Kent McFuller in a room so pitch-black it could be buried somewhere, I feel the tiniest of tiny things spark inside me, a little flame at the very bottom of my stomach that makes me unafraid.

"There are extra blankets in the closet," he says. His lips are right by my cheek.

"Thank you," I whisper back.

He stays until I've gotten into bed, and then he draws up the blankets around my shoulders like it's normal, like he's been putting me to bed every night of my whole life. Typical Kent McFuller.

FIVE

You see, I was still looking for answers then. I still wanted to know why. As though somebody was going to answer that for me, as though any answer would be satisfying.

Not then, but afterward, I started to think about time, and how it keeps moving and draining and flowing forever forward, seconds into minutes into days into years, all of it leading to the same place, a current running forever in one direction. And we're all going and swimming as fast as we can, helping it along.

My point is: maybe you can afford to wait. Maybe for you there's a tomorrow. Maybe for you there's one thousand tomorrows, or three thousand, or ten, so much time you can bathe in it, roll around in it, let it slide like coins through your fingers. So much time you can waste it.

But for some of us there's only today. And the truth is, you never really know.

I wake up gasping, the alarm bringing me out of darkness, as if it has brought me up from the depths of a lake. It is the fifth time I've woken up on February 12, but today I'm relieved. I switch off the alarm and lie in bed, watching the milky white light steal slowly over the walls, waiting for my heartbeat to go back to normal. A swath of sunlight ticks upward over the collage Lindsay made for me. In the bottom she's written in pink glittery ink, *Love you 4ever.* Today Lindsay and I are friends again. Today no one's angry at me. Today I didn't kiss Mr. Daimler or sit bawling my eyes out alone at a party.

Well, not totally alone. I imagine the sun filling Kent's house slowly, frothing upward like champagne.

As I lie there I start making a mental list of all the things I'd like to do in my life, as though they're still possible. Most of them are just plain crazy, but I don't think about that, just go on listing and listing like it's as easy as writing up what you need from the grocery store. Fly in a private jet. Eat a fresh-baked croissant from a bakery in Paris. Ride a horse all the way from Connecticut to California but stay in only the best hotel rooms along the way. Some of them are simpler: take Izzy to Goose Point, a place I discovered the first and only time I'd ever tried to run away. Order the Fat Feast at the diner—a bacon cheeseburger, a milk shake, and an entire plate of cheese fries—and eat it without stressing, like I used to do on my birthday every single year. Run around in the rain. Have scrambled eggs in bed.

By the time Izzy slinks into my room and hops up into bed with me, I'm actually feeling calm.

"Mommy says you have to go to school," Izzy says, head-butting my shoulder.

"I'm not going to school."

That's it: that's how it starts. One of the best—and worst—days of my life starts with those five words.

I grab Izzy's stomach and tickle her. She still insists on wearing her old *Dora the Explorer* T-shirt, but it's so small it leaves the big pink stripe of her belly—the only fat on her body—exposed. She squeals with laughter, rolling away from me.

"Stop it, Sam. I said, *Stop it!*"

Izzy is shrieking and laughing and thrashing around when my mom comes to the door.

"It's six forty-five." She stands in the doorway, keeping both of her feet neatly aligned just behind the flaking red line from all those years ago. "Lindsay will be here any minute."

Izzy slaps my hands away and sits up, her eyes shining. I've never noticed it before, but she really does look like my mom. It makes me sad for a minute. I wish she looked more like me. "Sam was tickling."

"Sam's going to be late. You too, Izzy."

"Sam's not going to school. And I'm not either." Izzy puffs out her chest like she's prepared to do battle over it. Maybe she'll look like me when she's older. Maybe when time starts marching forward again—even if I get swept out with it, like litter on a tide—her cheekbones will get high and she'll have a growth spurt and her hair will turn darker. I like to think it's true. I like to think that later on people will say, *Izzy looks just like her sister, Sam.*

They'll say, *You remember Sam? She was pretty.* I'm not really sure what else they *could* say: *She was nice. People liked her. She was missed.* Maybe none of those things.

I push the thought out of my mind and return to my mental list. A kiss that makes my whole head feel like it's exploding. A slow dance in the middle of an empty room to really great music. A swim in the ocean at midnight, with no clothes on.

My mom rubs her forehead. "Izzy, go get your breakfast. I'm sure it's ready by now."

Izzy scrambles over me. I squeeze the chub of her stomach and get one last squeal out of her before she jumps off the bed and dashes out the door. The one thing that can get Izzy moving that quickly is a toasted cinnamon raisin bagel with peanut butter, and I imagine being able to give her a cinnamon raisin bagel with peanut butter every single day for the rest of her life, filling a whole house with them.

When Izzy's gone my mom looks at me, hard. "What's this about, Sam? You feel sick?"

"Not exactly." One thing that is not on my wish list is to spend even one second in a doctor's office.

"What, then? There must be something. I thought Cupid Day was one of your favorites."

"It is. Or, I mean, it was." I sit up on my elbows. "I don't know, it's kind of stupid, if you think about it."

She raises her eyebrows.

I start rattling on, not really thinking about what I want to say before I say it, but afterward I realize it's true. "The whole point is just to show other people how many friends you have. But everybody *knows* how many friends everybody else has. And it's not like you actually *get* more friends this way or, I don't know, get closer to the friends you do have."

My mom smiles a tiny bit, one side of her mouth cocking upward. "Well, you're lucky to have very good friends, and to know it. I'm sure the roses are very meaningful to some people."

"I'm just saying, the whole thing is kind of sleazy."

"This doesn't sound like the Samantha Kingston I know."

"Yeah, well, maybe I'm changing." I don't mean those words either, until I hear them. Then I think that they might be true, and I feel a flicker of hope. Maybe there's still a chance for me, after all. Maybe I *have* to change.

My mom stares at me with this expression on her face like I'm a recipe she can't quite master. "Did something happen, Sam? Something with your friends?"

Today I'm not so annoyed at her for asking. Today it strikes me as kind of funny, actually. I so wish that the only thing bothering me was a fight with Lindsay, or something dumb Ally said.

272

"It's not my friends." I grasp for something that'll make her cave. "It's . . . it's Rob."

My mom wrinkles her brow. "Did you have a fight?"

I slump a little farther down into the bed, hoping it makes me look depressed. "He . . . he dumped me." In some ways it's not a lie. Not like he broke up with me, exactly, but like maybe we weren't ever *serious* serious in the way I believed for so long. Is it even possible to go out with someone seriously who doesn't really know you?

It works even better than I expected. My mom brings her hand up to her chest. "Oh, sweetie. What happened?"

"We just wanted different things, I guess." I fiddle with the edge of my comforter, thinking of all those nights alone with him in the basement, bathed in blue light, feeling sheltered from the whole world. It's not so much of a stretch to look upset when I think about that, and my bottom lip starts to tremble. "I don't think he ever really liked me. Not *really really*." This is the most honest thing I've said to my mother in years, and I suddenly feel very exposed. I have a flashback then of standing in front of her when I was five or six and having to strip naked while she checked me all over for deer ticks. I shove down farther into the covers, balling up my fists until my nails dig into my palms.

Then the craziest thing in the world happens. My mom steps straight over the flaking red line and strides over to the bed, like it's no big deal. I'm so surprised I don't even protest as she bends over me and plants a kiss on my forehead.

"I'm so sorry, Sam." She smoothes my forehead with her thumb. "Of course you can stay home."

I expected more of an argument and I'm left speechless.

"Do you want me to stay home with you?" she asks.

"No." I try to give her a smile. "I'll be fine. Really."

"I want to stay home with Sam!" Izzy has come to the door again, this time halfway dressed for school. She's in a yellow-and-pink phase—not a flattering combination, but it's kind of hard to explain color palettes to an eight-year-old—and has pulled on a mustard yellow dress over a pair of pink tights. She's also wearing big, scrunchie yellow socks. She looks like some kind of tropical flower. A part of me is tempted to freak out at my mom for letting Izzy wear whatever she wants. The other kids *must* make fun of her.

Then again, I guess Izzy doesn't care. That's another thing that strikes me as funny: that my eight-year-old sister is braver than I am. She's probably braver than most of the people at Thomas Jefferson. I wonder if that will ever change, if it will get beaten out of her.

Izzy's eyes are enormous and she clasps her hands together like she's praying. "Please?"

My mom sighs, exasperated. "Absolutely not, Izzy. There's nothing wrong with you."

"I'm feeling sick," Izzy says. This is made slightly unbelievable by the fact that she's hopping and pirouetting from foot to foot as she says it, but Izzy's never been a great liar.

"Did you eat your breakfast yet?" My mom crosses her arms and makes her "strict parent" face.

Izzy bobs her head. "I think I have food poisoning." She doubles over, grabs her stomach, then immediately straightens up and begins hopping again. I can't help it; a little giggle escapes.

"Come on, Mom," I say. "Let her stay home."

"Sam, please don't encourage her." My mom turns to me, shaking her head, but I can tell she's wavering.

"She's in third grade," I say. "It's not like they actually learn anything."

"Yes we do!" Izzy crows, then claps her hand over her mouth when I give her a look. My little sister: apparently not a champion negotiator, either. She shakes her head and quickly stutters. "I mean, we don't do that much."

My mom lowers her voice. "You know she'll be bugging you all day, right? Wouldn't you rather be alone?"

I know she's expecting me to say yes. For years that's been the buzzword of the house: Sam just wants to be left *alone*. Want some dinner? *I'll bring it up to my room.* Where you headed? *Just want to be alone.* Can I come in? *Just leave me alone. Stay out of my room. Don't talk to me when I'm on the phone. Don't talk to me when I'm listening to music. Alone, alone, alone.*

Things change after you die, though—I guess because dying

is about the loneliest thing you can do.

"I don't mind," I say, and I mean it. My mom throws up her hands and says, "Whatever," but even before it's out of her mouth, Izzy's charging through my room and has belly flopped on top of me, throwing her arms around my neck and screeching, "Can we watch TV? Can we make mac and cheese?" She smells like coconut as usual, and I remember when she was so small we could fit her in the sink to give her a bath, and she would sit there laughing and smiling and splashing like the best place in the world to be was in a 12" × 18" square of porcelain, like the sink was the biggest ocean in the world.

My mom gives me a look that says, *You asked for it.*

I smile over Izzy's shoulder and shrug.

And it's as easy as that.

INTO THE WOODS

It's weird how much people change. For example, when I was a kid I loved all of these things—like horses and the Fat Feast and Goose Point—and over time all of them just fell away, one after another, replaced by friends and IMing and cell phones and boys and clothes. It's kind of sad, if you think about it. Like there's no continuity in people at all. Like something ruptures when you hit twelve, or thirteen, or whatever the age is when you're no longer a kid but a "young adult," and after that you're a totally different person. Maybe even a less happy person. Maybe even a worse one.

Here's how I first discovered Goose Point: one time before Izzy was born my parents refused to buy me this little purple bike with a pink flowered basket on it and a bell. I don't remember why—maybe I already had a bike—but I flipped out and decided to run away. Here are the basic two rules of running away successfully:

1. Go somewhere you know.
2. Go somewhere nobody else knows.

I didn't know these two rules then, obviously, and I think my goal was the opposite: to go somewhere I didn't know and then be discovered by my parents, who would feel so bad they'd agree to buy me whatever I wanted, including the bike (and maybe a pony).

It was May, and warm. Every day the light lasted longer and longer. One afternoon I packed my favorite duffel bag and snuck out the back door. (I remember thinking I was smart for avoiding the front yard, where my father was doing yard work.) I also remember exactly what I packed: a flashlight; a sweatshirt; a bathing suit; an entire package of Oreos; a copy of my favorite book, *Matilda*; and an enormous fake pearl-and-gold necklace my mom had given me to wear on Halloween that year. I didn't know where I was going, so I just went straight, over the deck and down the stairs and across the backyard, into the woods that separated our property from our neighbor's. I followed the woods for a while, feeling really sorry for myself and half hoping that some hugely rich person would spot me and take pity on me and adopt me and buy me a whole garage full of purple bicycles.

But then after a while, I got kind of into it, the way kids do. The sun was hazy and gold. All the leaves looked like they were haloed in light, and there were tiny birds darting everywhere, and layers and layers of velvet-green moss under my feet. All of the houses dropped away. I was *deep* in the woods, and imagined I was the only person who'd ever come this far. I imagined I would live there forever, sleeping on a bed of moss, wearing flowers in my hair and living in harmony with the bears and foxes and unicorns. I came to a stream and had to cross it. I climbed an enormous, high hill, as big as a mountain.

At the top of the hill was the biggest rock I'd ever seen. It curved upward and out from the hillside like the potbellied hull of a ship, but it had a top as flat as a table. I don't remember much about that first trip other than eating Oreos, one after another, and feeling like I owned that whole portion of the woods. I also remember that when I came home, my stomach cramping from all the cookies, I was disappointed my parents hadn't been more worried about me. I was positive I'd stayed away for hours and hours and hours, but the clock showed I'd been gone less than forty minutes. I decided then that the rock was special: that time didn't move there.

I went there a lot that summer, whenever I needed to escape, and the summer after that. One time I was lying stretched out on top of the rock, staring at the sky all pink and purple like the stretch taffy at carnivals, and I saw hundreds of geese migrating, a perfect V. A single feather floated down through the air and landed directly next to my hand. I christened the place Goose Point, and for years kept the feather in a small, decorative box wedged into one of the stone ridges running along its underbelly. Then one day the box was gone. I figured it had been blown away during a storm, and searched through the leaves and undergrowth for hours and, when I couldn't find it, cried.

Even after I quit horseback riding, I climbed up to Goose Point sometimes, though I went less and less. I went there one time in sixth grade after all the boys in gym class rated my butt as "too square." I went there when I wasn't invited to Lexa Hill's sleepover birthday party, even though we'd been part-ners in science class and spent four months giggling over how cute Jon Lippincott was. Each time I came back home, less time had passed than I expected. Each time, I still told myself, though I knew it was stupid, that Goose Point was special.

Then one day Lindsay Edgecombe came into Tara Flute's kitchen when I was standing there and put her face to mine and whispered, "Do you want to see something?" and in that moment my life changed forever. Since that day I'd never once been back.

Maybe that's why I decide to take Izzy there, even though it's absolutely freezing outside. I want to see if it's still the same at all, or if I am. It's important to me, for some reason. And besides, of all the things on my mental checklist, it's the easiest. It's not like a private jet's just going to park itself outside my house. And skinny-dipping now will get me arrested or give me pneumonia or both.

So I guess this is the next best thing. And I guess that's when it starts to hit me: the whole point is, you do what you can.

"Are you sure this is the right way?" Izzy's bobbing next to me, wrapped in so many layers she looks like the abominable snowman. As usual she has insisted on accessorizing, and is wearing pink-and-black leopard-spotted earmuffs and two different scarves.

"This is the right way," I say, even though at first I was positive we were in the wrong place. Everything is so *small*. The stream—a thin, frozen black trickle of water, and cobwebbed all over with ice—is no wider than a single step. The hill beyond it slopes gently upward, even though in my memory it's always been a mountain.

But the worst part is the new construction. Someone bought the land back here, and there are two houses in different stages of completion. One of them is just a skeleton, rising out of the ground, all bleached wood and splinters and spikes, like a shipwreck washed up onto land. The other one is nearly finished. It's enormous and blank-looking, like Ally's house, and it squats there on the hill like it's staring at us. It takes me a while to realize why: there are no blinds on any of the windows yet.

I feel heavy with disappointment. Coming here was obviously a bad idea, and I'm reminded of something my English teacher, Mrs. Harbor, once said during one of her random tangents. She said that the reason you can never go home again—we were studying a list of famous quotes and discussing their meaning, and that was one of them, by Thomas Wolfe, "You can't go home again"—isn't necessarily that *places* change, but that *people* do. So nothing ever looks the same.

I'm about to suggest we turn around, but Izzy has already leaped across the stream and is scampering up the hill.

"Come on!" she yells back over her shoulder. And then, when she's only another fifty feet from the top, "I'll race you!"

At least Goose Point is as big as I remember it. Izzy hoists herself up onto the flat top, and I climb up after her, my fingers already numb in my gloves. The surface of the rock is covered with brittle, frozen leaves and a layer of frost. There's enough room for both of us to stretch out, but Izzy and I huddle close together so we'll stay warm.

"So what do you think?" I say. "You think it's a good hiding place?"

"The best." Izzy tilts her head back to look at me. "You really think time goes slower here?"

I shrug. "I used to think that when I was little." I look around. I hate how you can see houses from here now. It used to feel so remote, so secret. "It used to be a lot different. A lot better. There weren't any houses, for one. So you really felt like you were in the middle of nowhere."

"But this way if you have to pee, you can go and knock on someone's door and just ask." She lisps all of her *s*'s: *thith, thomeone, jutht, athk.*

I laugh. "Yeah, I guess so." We sit for a second in silence. "Izzy?"

"Yeah?"

"Do—do the other kids ever make fun of you? For how you talk?"

I feel her stiffen underneath her layers and layers. "Sometimes."

"So why don't you do something about it?" I say. "You could learn to talk differently, you know."

"But this is my *voice*." She says it quietly but with insistence. "How would you be able to tell when I was talking?"

This is such a weird Izzy-answer I can't think of a response to it, so I just reach forward and squeeze her. There are so many things I want to tell her, so many things she doesn't know: like how I remember when she first came home from the hospital, a big pink blob with a perma-smile, and she used to fall asleep while grabbing on to my pointer finger; how I used to give her piggyback rides up and down the beach on Cape Cod, and she would tug on my ponytail to direct me one way or the other; how soft and furry her head was when she was first born; that the first time you kiss someone you'll be nervous, and it will be weird, and it won't be as good as you want it to be, and that's okay; how you should only fall in love with people who will fall in love with you back. But before I can get any of it out, she's scrambling away from me on her hands and knees, squealing.

"Look, Sam!" She slides up close to the edge and pries at something wedged in a fissure of rock. She turns around on her knees, holding it out triumphantly: a feather, pale white, edged with gray, damp with frost.

I feel like my heart is breaking in that second because I know I'll never be able to tell her any of the things I need to. I don't even know where to begin. Instead I take the feather from her and zip it into one of the pockets of my North Face jacket. "I'll keep it safe," I say. Then I lie back on the freezing stone and stare up at the sky, which is just beginning to darken as the storm moves in. "We should go home soon, Izzy. It's going to rain."

"Soon." She lies down next to me, putting her head in the crook of my shoulder.

"Are you warm enough?"

"I'm okay."

It's actually not so cold once we're huddled next to each other, and I unzip my jacket a little at the neck. Izzy rolls over on one elbow and reaches out, tugging on my gold bird necklace.

"How come Grandma didn't give me anything?" she says. This is an old routine.

"You weren't alive yet, birdbrain."

Izzy keeps on tugging. "It's pretty."

"It's mine."

"Was Grandma nice?" This is also part of the routine.

"Yeah, she was nice." I don't remember much about her either, actually—she died when I was seven—except the motion of her hands through my hair when she brushed it, and the way she always sang show tunes, no matter what she was doing. She used to bake enormous orange-chocolate muffins, too, and she always made mine the biggest. "You would have liked her."

Izzy blows air out between her lips. "I wish nobody ever died," she says.

I feel an ache in my throat, but I manage to smile. Two conflicting desires go through me at the same time, each as sharp as a razorblade: *I want to see you grow up* and *Don't ever change.* I put my hand on the top of her head. "It would get pretty crowded, Fizz," I say.

"I'd move into the ocean," Izzy says matter-of-factly.

"I used to lie here like this all summer long," I tell her. "I'd come up here and just stare at the sky."

She rolls over on her back so she's staring up as well. "Bet this view hasn't changed much, has it?"

What she says is so simple I almost laugh. She's right, of course. "No. This looks exactly the same."

I suppose that's the secret, if you're ever wishing for things to go back to the way they were. You just have to look up.

I check my phone when I get home: three new text messages. Lindsay, Elody, and Ally have each texted me the exact same thing: *Cupid Day <3 U*. They were probably together when they sent it. That's a thing we sometimes do, type up and send the exact same messages at exactly the same time. It's stupid, but it makes me smile. I don't reply, though. In the morning I sent Lindsay a text letting her know she should go to school without me, but even though we're not fighting today, I felt weird tacking our usual "xxo" at the end. Somewhere—in some alternate time or place or life or something—I'm still mad at her and she's mad at me.

It amazes me how easy it is for things to change, how easy it is to start off down the same road you always take and wind up somewhere new. Just one false step, one pause, one detour, and you end up with new friends or a bad reputation or a boyfriend or a breakup. It's never occurred to me before; I've never been able to see it. And it makes me feel, weirdly, like maybe all of these different possibilities exist at the same time, like each moment we live has a thousand other moments layered underneath it that look different.

Maybe Lindsay and I are best friends and we hate each other, both. Maybe I'm only one math class away from being a slut like Anna Cartullo. Maybe I am like her, deep down. Maybe we all are: just one lunch period away from eating alone in the bathroom. I wonder if it's ever really possible to know the truth about someone else, or if the best we can do is just stumble into each other, heads down, hoping to avoid collision. I think of Lindsay in the bathroom of Rosalita's, and wonder how many people are clutching secrets like little fists, like rocks sitting in the pits of their stomachs. All of them, maybe.

The fourth text is from Rob and it just says, *R u sick?* I delete it and then shut off my phone.

Izzy and I spend the rest of the afternoon watching old DVDs, mostly old Disney and Pixar movies we both love, like *The Little Mermaid* and *Finding Nemo*. We make popcorn with extra butter and Tabasco sauce, the way my dad always makes it, and hunker down in the den with all the lights off while the sky outside grows darker and the trees start to whip around in the wind. When my mom comes home we petition her for a Formaggio Friday—we used to go to the same Italian restaurant every Friday night and that's what we called it, because the restaurant (which had checked red-and-white plastic tablecloths and an accordion player and fake plastic roses on the tables) was so cheesy—and she says she'll think about it, which means we're going.

It's been forever since I've been at home on a weekend night, and when my dad comes home and sees Izzy and me piled on the couch, he staggers through the door, clutching at his heart like he's having a heart attack.

"Is it a hallucination?" he says, setting down his briefcase. "Could it be? Samantha Kingston? Home? On a Friday?"

I roll my eyes. "I don't know. Did you do a lot of acid in the sixties? Could be a flashback."

"I was two years old in 1960. I came too late for the party." He leans down and pecks me on the head. I pull away out of habit. "And I'm not even going to *ask* how you know about acid flashbacks."

"What's an acid flashback?" Izzy crows.

"Nothing," my dad and I say at the same time, and he smiles at me.

We do end up going to Formaggio's (official name: Luigi's Italian Home Kitchen), which actually isn't Formaggio's (or Luigi's) anymore and hasn't been for years. Five years ago a sushi restaurant moved in and replaced all of the fake art-deco tiles and glass lanterns with sleek metal tables and a long oak bar. It doesn't matter, though. It will always be Formaggio's to me.

The restaurant is super crowded, but we get one of the best tables, right next to the big tanks of exotic fish that sit next to the windows. As usual my dad makes a bad joke about how much he loves *see*-food restaurants, and my mother tells him to stick to architecture and leave comedy to the professionals. At dinner my mom's extra nice to me because she thinks I'm going through breakup trauma, and Izzy and I order half the menu and wind up full on edamame and shrimp shumai and tempura and seaweed salad before the meal even comes. My dad has two beers and gets tipsy and entertains us with stories about crazy clients, and my mom keeps telling me to order whatever I want, and Izzy puts a napkin over her head and pretends to be a pilgrim tasting California rolls for the first time.

Up until then it's a good day—one of the best. Close to perfect, really, even though nothing special happened at all. I guess I've probably had a lot of days like this, but somehow they're never the ones you remember. That seems wrong to me now. I think of lying in Ally's house in the dark and wondering whether I've ever had a day worth reliving. It seems to me like living this one again and again wouldn't be so bad, and I imagine that's what I'll do—just go on like this, over and over, until time winds completely down, until the universe stops.

Just before we get our dessert, a big group of freshmen and sophomores I recognize from Jefferson come filing in. A few of them are still wearing JV swim jackets. They must have had a late meet. They seem so young, hair scraped away from their faces, ponytails, no makeup—totally different from the way they look when they show up to our parties, when it looks like they've just spent an hour and a half getting freebies at the MAC counter. A couple of them catch me staring and drop their eyes.

"Green tea and red bean ice cream." The waitress sets down a big bowl and four spoons in front of us. Izzy goes to town on the red bean.

My dad groans and puts a hand on his stomach. "I don't know how you can still be hungry."

"Growing girl." Izzy opens her mouth, showing off the ice cream mushed on her tongue.

"Gross, Izzy." I pick up my spoon and scoop a little bit from the green-tea side.

"Sykes! Hey! Sykes!"

I whip around at the sound of her name. One of the swim-team girls is half standing out of her chair, waving. I scan the restaurant, looking for Juliet, but there's only one person at the door. She's thin and pale and very blond, and she's standing and shaking her shoulders to get the rain off her jacket. It takes me a second to recognize her, but as she turns a complete circle, looking for her friends, I do: the Cupid from math class—the angel who delivered my roses.

When she sees the rest of her teammates, she raises her hand briefly and gives a quick flutter of her fingers. Then she starts threading her way over to them, and as she moves past our table, I catch a glimpse of her neon-blue-and-orange swim jacket and it's like the whole room goes still and only those five letters remain, lit up like signs.

SYKES.

Juliet's little sister.

"Earth to Sammy." Izzy is poking me with the butt end of her spoon. "Your ice cream's getting melty."

"Not hungry anymore." I put my spoon down and push away from the table.

"Where are you going?" Mom reaches out and puts her hand

on my wrist, but I barely feel it.

"Five minutes." And then I'm walking over to the swim-team table, the whole time staring at the pale girl and her heart-shaped face. I can't believe I didn't see the resemblance before. They've got the same wide-spaced blue eyes, the same translucent skin and pale lips. Then again, until recently I've never really looked at Juliet, even though I must have seen her ten thousand times.

The swim-team girls have gotten their menus, and they're laughing and swatting each other. I distinctly hear one of them say Rob's name—probably saying how cute he looks in his lacrosse jersey (I should know; I used to say it all the time). I've never cared less about anything. When I'm about four feet away from the table one of them spots me and instantly the whole table goes silent. The girl who was talking about Rob goes the color of the menu she's holding.

Little Sykes is squeezed in at the very end of the table. I walk directly up to her.

"Hey." Now that I'm standing here I'm not exactly sure why I came over. The funniest part about it is that *I'm* the one who's nervous. "What's your name?"

"Um . . . did I do something?" Her voice is actually trembling. The rest of the girls aren't helping. They're looking at me like they expect at any second I'm going to lunge forward and swallow her head or something.

"No, no. I just . . ." I give her a small smile. Now that I see it, the resemblance between her and Juliet unnerves me. "You have an older sister, right?"

Her mouth tightens into a thin line, and her eyes go cloudy, like she's putting up a wall. I don't blame her. She probably thinks I'm going to pick on her for having a freak for a big sister. It must happen a lot.

But she tilts up her chin and stares at me straight in the eye. It kind of reminds me of something Izzy would do. *Sam's not going to school, and I'm not going either.* "Yeah. Juliet Sykes." Then she waits patiently, waits for me to start laughing.

Her eyes are so steady I look down. "Yeah. I, um, know Juliet."

"You do?" She raises her eyebrows.

"Well, kind of." All the girls are staring at me now. I have a feeling they're having a hard time keeping their jaws from dropping open. "She's—she's kind of my lab partner."

I figure this is a safe bet. Science is mandatory, and everybody gets assigned lab partners.

Juliet's sister's face relaxes a little bit. "Juliet's really good at bio. I mean, she's really good at school." She lets herself smile. "I'm Marian."

"Hey." Marian is a good name for her: a pure name, somehow. My palms are sweating. I wipe them on my jeans. "I'm Sam."

Marian drops her eyes and says shyly, "I know who you are."

Two arms circle around my waist. Izzy has come up behind me. The point of her chin pokes me in the side.

"Ice cream's almost gone," she says. "You sure you don't want any?"

Marian smiles at Izzy. "What's your name?"

"Elizabeth," Izzy says proudly, then sags a little. "But everybody calls me Izzy."

"When I was little everybody called me Mary." Marian makes a face. "But now everybody calls me Marian."

"I don't mind Izzy that much," Izzy says, chewing on her lip like she's just decided it.

Marian looks up at me. "You have a little sister too, huh?"

Suddenly I can't stand to look at her. I can't stand to think about what will happen later. I *know*: the stillness of the house, the gunshot.

And then . . . what? Will she be the first one down the stairs? Will that final image of her sister be the one that lasts, that wipes out whatever other memories she's stored up over the years?

I go into a panic, trying to think what kind of memories Izzy has of me—will have of me.

"Come on, Izzy. Let's let the girls eat." My voice is trembling, but I don't think anyone notices. I pat Izzy on the head and she gallops back toward our table.

The girls at the table are getting more confident now. Smiles are sprouting up, and they're all looking at me in awe, like they can't believe how nice I'm being, like I've given them a present. I hate it. They should hate me. If they knew what kind of person I was, they would hate me, I'm sure of it.

I don't know why Kent pops into my head right then, but he does. He would hate me too if he knew everything. The realization makes me strangely upset.

"Tell Juliet not to do it," I blurt out, and then can't believe I've said it.

Marian wrinkles her forehead. "Do what?"

"Science-project thing," I say quickly, and then add, "she'll know what I'm talking about."

"Okay." Marian's beaming at me. I start to turn away, but she calls me back. "Sam!"

I turn around, and she claps her hand over her mouth and giggles, like she can't believe she had the courage to say my name.

"I'll have to tell her tomorrow," she says. "Juliet's going out tonight." She says it like she's saying, *Juliet's going to be valedictorian*. I can just picture the scene. Mom and dad and sister downstairs, Juliet locked in her bedroom as usual, blasting music, alone. And then—miracle of miracles—she descends, hair swept back, confident, cool, announcing she is headed to a party. They must have been so happy, so proud. Their lonely little girl making good at the end of senior year.

To Kent's party. To find Lindsay—to find me. To be pushed and tripped and soaked with beer.

The sushi's not sitting so well with me all of a sudden. If they had any idea . . .

"I'll definitely tell her tomorrow, though." Marian beams at me, a headlight bearing down at me through the dark.

All the way home I'm trying to forget Marian Sykes. When my dad wishes me good night—he's always ready to pass out after a beer, and tonight he had (gasp!) two—I'm trying to forget Marian Sykes. When Izzy comes in half an hour later, showered and clean-smelling in her ratty Dora pj's, and plants a sloppy wet kiss on my cheek, I'm trying to forget her; and an hour after that, when my mother stands at my door and says, "I'm proud of you, Sam," I'm still thinking of her.

My mother goes to bed. Silence fills the house. Somewhere in the deep darkness a clock is ticking, and when I close my eyes I picture Juliet Sykes coming toward me calmly, her shoes tapping against a wood floor, blood flowing from her eyes. . . .

I sit up in bed, heart pounding. Then I get up, find my North Face in the dark.

This morning I swore that there was nothing in the world that could make me go back to Kent's party, but here I am, tiptoeing down the stairs, edging along in the dark hallways, sneaking my mom's keys off the shelf in the mudroom. She's been amazingly human today, but the last thing I need to deal with is some big conversation of the what-makes-me-think-I-can-cut-school-and-then-go-out variety.

I try to tell myself that Juliet Sykes isn't really my problem, but I keep imagining how horrible it would be if this were her day. If she had to live it over and over again. I think pretty much everybody—even Juliet Sykes—deserves to die on a better day than that.

The hinges on the back and front door squawk so loudly they might as well be alarm clocks (sometimes I think my parents have engineered this deliberately). In the kitchen I carefully spill some olive oil on a paper towel, and I rub this onto the hinges on the back door. Lindsay taught me this trick. She's always developing new, better ways to sneak out, even though she has no curfew, and it doesn't matter one way or the other when she leaves and when she comes home. I think she misses that, actually. I think that's why she's always meticulous about the details—she likes to pretend that she has to be.

The door with its Italian-seasoned hinges swings open with barely a whisper, and I'm out.

I haven't really thought through why I'm heading to Kent's, or what I'm going to do once I'm there, and instead of driving there directly, I find myself turning on random streets and dead-end cul-de-sacs, circling up and down. The houses are mostly set back from the street, and lit windows appear magically in the dark like hanging lanterns. It's amazing how different everything looks at night—almost unrecognizable, especially in the rain. Houses sit hulking back on their lawns, brooding and alive. It looks so different from the Ridgeview of the day, when everything is clean and polished and trimmed neatly, when everything unfolds in an orderly way, husbands heading to their cars with coffee mugs, wives following soon after, dressed in pilates gear, tiny girls in Baby Gap dresses and car seats and Lexus SUVs and Starbucks cups and *normalcy*. I wonder which one is the true version.

There are hardly any cars on the road. I keep crawling along at fifteen miles per hour. I'm looking for something, but I don't know what. I pass Elody's street and keep going. Each street-lamp casts a neat funnel of light downward, illuminating the inside of the car briefly, before I'm left again in darkness.

My headlights sweep over a crooked green street sign fifty feet ahead: Serenity Place. I suddenly remember sitting in Ally's kitchen freshman year while her mom chattered on the phone endlessly, pacing back and forth on the deck in bare feet and yoga pants. "She's getting her daily dose of gossip," Ally had said, rolling her eyes. "Mindy Sachs is better than *Us Weekly*." And Lindsay had put in how ironic it was that Mrs. Sachs lived on Serenity Place—*like she doesn't bring the noise with her*— and it was the first time I really understood the meaning of the word ironic.

I yank my wheel at the last second and brake, rolling down Serenity Place. It's not a long street—there are no more than two dozen houses on it—and like many streets in Ridgeview, ends in a cul-de-sac. My heart leaps when I see a silver Saab parked neatly in one of the driveways. The license plate reads: MOM OF4. That's Mrs. Sachs's car. I must be close.

The next house down is number fifty-nine. It is marked with a tin mailbox in the shape of a rooster, which stretches up from a flowerbed that is at this point in the year no more than a long patch of black dirt. SYKES is printed along the rooster's wing, in letters so small you have to be looking before you can see them.

I can't really explain it, but I feel like I would have known the house anyway. There's nothing *wrong* with it—it's no different from any other house, not the biggest, not the smallest, decently taken care of, white paint, dark shutters, a single light burning downstairs. But there's something else, some quality I can't really identify that makes it look like the house is too big for itself, like something inside is straining to get out, like the whole place is about to bust its seams. It's a desperate house, somehow.

I turn into the driveway. I have no business being here, I know that, but I can't help it. It's like something's tugging me inside. The rain is coming down hard, and I grab an old sweatshirt from the backseat—Izzy's, probably—and use it to shield my head as I sprint from the car to the front porch, my breath clouding in front of me. Before I can think too much about what I'm doing, I ring the doorbell.

It takes a long time for someone to answer the door, and I do a little jog, my breath steaming out in front of me, trying to stay warm. Finally there's a shuffling sound from inside, and then a scraping of hinges. The door swings open, and a woman stands there, blinking at me confusedly: Juliet's mother. She is wearing a bathrobe, which she holds closed with one hand. She is as thin as Juliet and has the same clear blue eyes and pale skin as both of her daughters. Looking at her, I am reminded of a wisp of smoke curling up into the dark.

"Can I help you?" Her voice is very soft.

I'm kind of thrown. For some reason I expected Marian would be the one to come to the door. "My name is Sam— Samantha Kingston. I'm looking for Juliet." Because it worked the first time I add, "She's my lab partner."

From inside, a man—Juliet's father, I guess—shouts, "Who is it?" The voice is barking and loud, and so different from Mrs. Sykes's voice I unconsciously shuffle backward.

Mrs. Sykes jumps a little, and turns her head quickly, inadvertently swinging the door open an extra couple of inches. The hallway behind her is dark. Swampy blue and green shadows dance up one wall, images projected from a television in a room I can't see. "It's no one," she says quickly, her voice directed into the darkness behind her. "It's for Juliet."

"Juliet? Someone's here for Juliet?" He sounds exactly like a dog. *Bark, bark, bark, bark.* I fight a wild, nervous urge to laugh.

"I'll take care of it." Mrs. Sykes turns back to me. Again, the door swings closed with her movement, as though she is leaning on it for support. Her smile doesn't quite reach her eyes. "Juliet's not home right now. Is there something I can help you with?"

"I, um, missed school today. We had this big assignment. . . ." I trail off helplessly, starting to regret having come. Despite my North Face, I'm shivering like a maniac. I must *look* like a maniac too, hopping from foot to foot, holding a sweatshirt over my head for an umbrella.

Mrs. Sykes seems to notice, finally, that I'm standing in the rain. "Why don't you come in," she says, and steps backward into the hall. I follow her inside.

An open door to the left leads directly off the hall: that's where the television is. I can just make out an armchair and the silhouette of someone sitting there, the edge of an enormous jaw touched with blue from the screen. I remember what Lindsay said then, about Juliet's dad being an alcoholic. I vaguely remember hearing that same rumor, and something else too—that there'd been an accident, something about semi-paralysis or pills or something. I wish I'd paid more attention.

Mrs. Sykes catches me looking and walks quickly over to the door, pulling it shut. It is now so dark I can barely see, and I realize I'm still cold. If the heat is on in the house, I can't feel it. From the TV room I hear the sounds of a horror-film scream, and the steady syncopated rhythm of machine gun fire.

Now I'm *definitely* regretting coming. For a second I have this wild fantasy that Juliet comes from a whole family of crazy serial killers, and that at any second Mrs. Sykes is going to go *Silence of the Lambs* on me. *The whole family's wacked*, that's what Lindsay had said. The darkness is pressing all around me, stifling, and I almost cry out with gratitude when Mrs. Sykes switches on a light and the hall appears lit up and normal, and not full of dead human trophies or something. There's a dried flower arrangement on a side table decorated with lace, next to a framed family photo. I wish I could look at it more closely.

"Was it important, this assignment?" Mrs. Sykes asks, almost in a whisper. She shoots a nervous glance in the direction of the TV room, and I wonder if she thinks she's being too loud.

"I just . . . I kind of promised Juliet I would pick up some stuff for our makeup presentation on Monday." I try to lower my voice, but she still winces. "I thought Juliet said she would be home tonight."

"Juliet went out," she says, and then, as if she's unused to saying the words and is testing them on her tongue, repeats, "She went out. But maybe she left it for you?"

"I could look for it," I say. I want to see her room, I realize: that's why I'm here. I need to see it. "She probably just dumped it on her bed or something." I try to sound casual, like Juliet and I are on really good terms with each other—like it's not weird for me to waltz into her house at ten thirty on a Friday night and try to weasel my way into her bedroom.

Mrs. Sykes hesitates. "Maybe I can call her cell phone," she says, and then adds apologetically, "Juliet hates to have anyone in her room."

"You don't have to call her," I say quickly. Juliet will probably tell her mom to sic the cops on me. "It's not that important. I'll pick it up tomorrow."

"No, no. I'll call her. It will just take a second." Juliet's mom is already disappearing into the kitchen. It's amazing how quickly and soundlessly she moves, like an animal slipping in and out of the shadows.

I consider jetting out while she's in the kitchen. I think about going home, crawling into bed, watching old movies on my computer. Maybe I'll make a pot of coffee and sit up all night long. If I never go to sleep, maybe today will *have* to turn into tomorrow. I wonder idly how long I can go without sleep before I flip my shit and start running down the street in my underwear, hallucinating purple spiders.

But instead I just stand there, waiting. There's nothing else to do, so I take a few steps forward and bend down to look at the photograph on the table. For a second I'm confused: it's a picture of an unfamiliar woman, probably twenty-five or thirty, with her arms wrapped around a good-looking guy in a flannel shirt. The colors are all saturated and Technicolor-bright, and the couple looks perfect, sparkling, all white teeth and dazzling smiles and beautiful brown hair. Then I see the words printed in the lower bottom corner of the picture—ShadowCast Images, Inc.—and realize that this isn't even a real family photo. It's one of the generic pictures that gets sold along with the picture frame, a shiny, happy advertisement for all the shiny, happy moments you can capture forever inside the *5" × 7" sterling silver frame with butterfly detail*. No one has bothered to replace it.

Or maybe the Sykes family doesn't have too many shiny, happy moments to remember.

I pull away quickly, wishing I hadn't looked. Even though it's just a picture of two models, I feel, weirdly, like I've seen something way *too* personal, like I've accidentally caught a glimpse of someone's inner thigh or nose hairs or something.

Mrs. Sykes still isn't back so I wander out of the hall into the living room on the right. It is mostly dark, and it's all plaids and lace and dried flowers. It looks as though it hasn't been redecorated since the fifties.

There's a single, dull light shining near the window, casting a circular reflection on the black pane of glass, a version of the room appearing in miniature there.

And a face.

A screaming face pressed up against the window.

I let out a squeak of fear before I realize that this, too, is a reflection. There's a mask mounted on a table just in front of the window, facing outward. I go over to it and lift it carefully from its perch. It's a woman's face crafted from newspaper and red stitching, which is crisscrossed over the skin like horrible scars. Words run up the bridge of the nose and across the forehead, certain headlines visible or halfway visible, like BEAUTY REMEDY and TRAGEDY STRIKES, and little scraps of paper are unfurling from various places on her face, like she's molting. The mouth and the eyes are cut completely away, and when I lift the mask to my face, it fits well. The reflection in the window is awful; I look like something diseased, or a monster from a horror movie. I can't look away.

"Juliet made that."

The voice behind me makes me jump. Mrs. Sykes has reappeared and is leaning against the door, frowning at me.

I pop the mask off, return it quickly to its perch. "I'm so sorry. I saw it and . . . I just wanted to try it on," I finish lamely.

Mrs. Sykes comes over and rearranges the mask, straightening it, making sure it's aligned correctly. "When Juliet was younger she was always drawing, always sketching or painting something or sewing her own dresses." Mrs. Sykes shrugs, flutters a hand. "I don't think she's very interested in that stuff now."

"Did you talk to Juliet?" I ask nervously, waiting for her to kick me out.

Mrs. Sykes blinks at me several times, as though trying to squeeze me into focus. "Juliet . . ." she repeats, and then shakes her head. "I called her phone a couple of times. She didn't answer. She doesn't usually go out on the weekends. . . ." Mrs. Sykes looks at me helplessly.

"I'm sure she's fine," I say as cheerfully as I can, feeling like each word is a knife going down into my stomach. "She probably didn't hear her phone."

Suddenly the thing I want most of all is to get out of there. I can't stand to lie to Mrs. Sykes. She looks so sad, standing in her nightgown, ready for bed—as though she's already asleep, sort of. That's what the whole house feels like, as though it's wrapped up in a heavy sleep, the kind that stifles you, won't let you wake, drags you back into the sheets, drowning, even when you fight it.

I imagine Juliet sneaking up to her room in the dark, and the silence, through the atmosphere of sleep so thick it feels solid, the lullaby of creaking floorboards and quietly hissing radiators, the slow revolutions of people orbiting wordlessly around one another. . . . And then . . .

Bang.

Mrs. Sykes walks me back to the front hall. "You can come by tomorrow," she says. "I'm sure Juliet will have everything ready by then. She's usually very responsible. A good girl."

"Sure. Tomorrow." I don't even like to say the word, and I wave a quick good-bye before dashing once again through the dark to my car.

It's even colder than it was earlier. The rain, half ice, pings off the hood of my car as I sit there waiting for the engine to warm up, blowing on my hands and shivering, grateful to be out of there. As soon as I'm out of the house, a weight eases up off my chest, like the atmosphere and pressure inside is different, heavier. My first impression was right: it really is a desperate house. I see Juliet's mom silhouetted by the window. I wonder if she's waiting for me to leave or for her daughter to come home.

That's when I make a decision. I know what I'll do. I'll go to Kent's house and I'll catch Juliet, and if I have to, I *will* hit her in the face. I'll make her see how stupid the whole death idea is. (It's certainly no picnic for me.) If it comes down to it, I'll tie her up in the back of my car so she *can't* get her hands on the gun.

I realize I've never *really* done something good for someone else, at least not for a while. I volunteer sometimes for Meals on Wheels, but that's because colleges like that kind of thing; BU especially mentioned charity on the application portion of their website. And obviously I'm nice to my friends, and I give *great* birthday gifts (I once spent a month and a half collecting cow-shaped saltshakers to give to Ally, because she loves cows and salt). But I don't usually do good things just for the hell of it. This will be my good thing.

Then I have a glimmer of an idea. I remember when we were studying Dante in English, and Ben Gowan kept asking if the souls in purgatory ever got cast down into hell (Ben Gowan once got suspended for three days for drawing a picture of a bomb blowing up our cafeteria and all of these decapitated heads flying everywhere, so for him the question was normal), and Mrs. Harbor went off on one of her tangents and said that no, that wasn't possible, but that some modern Christian thinkers believed you could go *up* from purgatory into heaven once you'd done enough time there. I've never really believed in heaven. It always sounded like a crazy idea: everybody happy and reunited, Fred Astaire and Einstein doing a tango on the clouds, that kind of stuff.

But then again, I never really believed I'd have to relive one day forever, either. It's no crazier than what's already happened to me. Maybe the whole point is I have to prove that I'm a good person. Maybe I have to prove that I deserve to move on.

Maybe Juliet Sykes is the only thing between me and an eternity of chocolate fountains and perfect love and guys who always call when they say they will and banana sundaes that actually help you burn calories.

Maybe she's my ticket out.

UNFASHIONABLY LATE

I don't even bother pulling into Kent's driveway. I'm not planning on being here long, and I don't want to get blocked in. Besides, something about tramping through the woods in the rain appeals to me. It's a trial, another way I can sacrifice myself. And from my very limited memories of Sunday school (my mom gave up the fight after I threw a tremendous tantrum when I was seven and threatened to convert to voodoo, even though I wasn't sure exactly what that was), I know that that's how it works: you have to sacrifice something.

I pull over onto the shoulder of Route 9, grabbing Izzy's sweatshirt again, which is now soaking wet. Still, it's better than nothing. I drape it over my head and get out of the car, pausing for just a second. The road is empty, stretches of black interspersed with weak pools of yellow light from the street-lamps. I try to locate the exact spot where Lindsay's car went spiraling off the road that first night, but it all looks the same. It could have been anywhere. I reach back once more for some memory of life beyond the collision, beyond the blackness, but I get nothing.

I grab a flashlight from the trunk and set off through the woods.

It's a longer walk than I would have thought, and the ground alternates between a thin coat of hard ice and slurpy gloop that sucks at my purple New Balances like quicksand. After a few minutes I can hear the faint throb of music from the party, pulsing through the darkness like it belongs there, like its rhythm is part of the night. It's another ten minutes before I see the faint twinkle of lights flashing sporadically beyond the trees—thank God, since I was beginning to think I was walking in circles—and another five before the woods thin out and I can see the house, a big pile of ice-cream cake sitting on that lawn, shimmering in and out as the rain bends and splits the lights from the porch. I'm totally freezing, and 100 per-cent regretting my decision to come on foot. That's the whole problem with sacrifice. It's a pain, literally.

As soon as I walk through the door, two girls giggle and a whole group of juniors goes totally gape-jawed. I don't blame them. I know I must look like shit. Before leaving the house, I didn't even bother to change out of my lounge pants—a pair of way oversized velour sweats my mom gave me back when they were still in.

I don't waste any time on the juniors, though. I'm already worried I may have arrived too late.

Tara is coming down the stairs as I'm pushing my way up, and I grab her, leaning into her ear. "Juliet Sykes!" I have to yell it.

"What?" she yells back, smiling.

"Juliet Sykes! Is she here?"

Tara taps her ear to show she can't hear me. "You're looking for Lindsay?"

Courtney is behind Tara and leans forward, flopping her chin on Tara's shoulder. "We found the secret stash—rum and stuff. Tara broke a vase." She giggles. "You want some?"

I shake my head. I've never been this sober around people this wasted, and I say a brief prayer that I'm not half as annoying as they are when I'm drunk. I continue up the stairs as Tara yells, "Lindsay's in the back."

Before I'm totally out of earshot I hear Courtney shriek, "Did you see what she's wearing?"

I take a deep breath and tell myself it doesn't matter. What matters is finding Juliet. I can at least do that one thing.

But with every step I'm losing hope. The upstairs hallway is totally packed, and unless she hasn't come to the party at all—which seems like too much to hope—it seems unlikely that she hasn't already left.

Still, I push on, finally making it to the very back room. Lindsay catapults on me as soon as I get into the room—she actually leaps over five people—and for a second I'm so grateful to see her, happy and drunk and my best friend, and to get treated to one of her famous super-squish hugs, that I forget why I'm here.

"Bad girl." She slaps my hand as she pulls away. "You cut school but come out to party? Naughty, naughty."

"I'm looking for someone," I say. I scan the room: Juliet's not here. Not that I expected her to be, I don't know, sitting on the couch and chatting it up with Jake Somers, but it's instinct—and wishful thinking—to look.

"Rob's downstairs." Lindsay steps back and holds up her hand, framing me in the angle between her thumb and forefinger. "You look like the homeless man who stole Wal-Mart. Are you trying *not* to get laid or something?"

Irritation flares up again. Lindsay, who always has something to say.

"Have you seen Juliet Sykes?" I ask.

Lindsay stares at me for a split second and then bursts out laughing. "Are you serious?"

A feeling of enormous relief washes over me. Maybe she never showed. Maybe she had car trouble, or lost her nerve, or—

"She called me a bitch." In that moment Lindsay shatters me. She did come. "Can you believe it?" Lindsay's still cracking up. She loops one arm around my shoulder and calls out, "Elody! Ally! Sammy's here! And she's looking for her best friend, Juliet!"

Elody doesn't even turn around; she's too busy with Steve Dough. But Ally swings in my direction, smiles, yells, "Hi, sweetie!" and then holds up the empty bottle of vodka.

"If you see Juliet," she calls out, "ask her what she did with the rest of my drink!" She and Lindsay think this is hilarious, and Lindsay calls back, "Psychotini!"

I *am* too late. The realization makes me feel sick, and my anger at Lindsay comes rushing back.

"My best friend?" I repeat. "That's funny. I thought *you* were the one who was buddy-buddy with Juliet."

"What are you talking about?" Lindsay's face gets serious.

"Childhood friends. Best friends. Rug rats. Sand bunnies." Lindsay looks like she's about to say something again, but I cut her off. "I saw the pictures. So what happened? Did she catch you farting or something? See you blow a snot rocket? Discover that the famous Lindsay Edgecombe isn't perfect after all? What did she do that was so bad?"

Lindsay opens her mouth and then closes it. "She's a freak," she whispers fiercely, but I see something in her eyes I've never seen before, an expression I can't quite identify.

"Whatever." I *have* to find Juliet Sykes.

I fight my way back downstairs, ignoring the people calling my name, tapping my shoulder, and whispering about the fact that I've shown up in public looking like I'm about to go to sleep—which is, of course, exactly what happened. I figure if I'm quick enough I can catch Juliet on the way out. She must have parked somewhere. She's probably blocked in. It will take an hour to get people to move their cars (if she can even convince anybody to help at all, which is doubtful) and even longer if she decides to hoof it home.

Thankfully I make it downstairs without a run-in with Rob. The last thing I need is to explain myself to him. There's a group of sophomores standing near the entryway, looking terrified and more or less sober, so I take my shot with them.

"Have you seen Juliet Sykes?"

They stare at me blankly.

I sigh, swallowing my frustration. "Blond hair, blue eyes, tall." They're still looking at me vacantly, and I realize I'm not exactly sure how to describe her. *Loser*, I almost say—I would have said three days ago. But now I can't get it out. "Pretty," I say, testing the word. When that doesn't work I squeeze my fists into my palms. "Probably soaking wet."

Finally the girls' faces light up with recognition. "Bathroom," one of them says, pointing to a little alcove just before the kitchen. There's a line of people gathered in front of a closed door. One of them is crossing her legs and hopping up and down. One of them keeps rapping on the door. One of them points to her watch and says something I can't hear, but she looks pissed.

"She's been in there for, like, twenty minutes," a sophomore says. My stomach drops to my feet and I almost get sick right there.

Bathrooms have pills. Bathrooms have razors. People lock themselves in bathrooms when they want to do bad things, like have sex or throw up. Or kill themselves.

It's not supposed to go this way. I'm supposed to save you. I elbow over to the bathroom, shoving through the line of people crowded there.

"Move," I say to Joanne Polerno, and she drops her hand immediately and steps aside.

I press my ear to the door, listening for sounds of crying or retching or anything. Nothing. My stomach does another dip. Then again, it's almost impossible to hear, with the music pounding so loudly.

I knock softly and call out, "Juliet? Are you okay?"

"Maybe she's sleeping," Chrissy Walker says. I shoot her a look that I hope will communicate how stupidly unhelpful that comment is.

I knock again, mashing my face against the door. It's hard to tell whether I hear a faint moan from inside—at that second the music shrieks even louder, drowning out everything else. But I can imagine her there, fading, just beyond the door, wrists hacked up and blood everywhere. . . .

"Get Kent," I say, sucking in a long breath.

"Who?" Joanne says.

"I have to pee," Rachel says, hopping up and down.

"Kent McFuller. Now. Do it," I bark at Joanne, and she looks startled but scurries off into the hallway. Every second feels like an eternity. It's the first time I really understand what Einstein said about relativity, how time bends around and stretches out like a gummy bear.

"What do you care, anyway?" Rachel says, grumbling just loud enough so I can hear.

I don't answer. The truth is I have no answer, really. I have to save Juliet—I feel that. It's my good thing. I have to save *myself*.

I'm suddenly not sure if that makes me better or worse than someone who does nothing, so I push the thought out of my mind.

Joanne comes back with Kent in tow. He looks worried, his forehead crinkly underneath the shaggy brown hair that's falling down over his eyes. My stomach does a flip. Yesterday we were in a dark room no more than two inches apart, so close I could feel the amazing heat of his skin.

"Sam," he says, and leans forward to grab my wrist, staring deep in my eyes. "Are you okay?"

I'm so surprised by the sudden touch I pull away just a

fraction, and Kent takes back his hand. I don't know how to explain the way this makes my insides go hollow.

"I'm fine," I say, totally aware in that moment of how ridiculous I must look to him: the messed up hair, the sweatpants. He, by comparison, looks actually kind of put together. There's something scruffy-cute about his checkered sneakers and loose, low-belted khakis, and the sleeves of his oxford are rolled up, showing off a tan he got God-knows-where. Certainly not in Ridgeview in the past six months.

He looks confused. "Joanne said you needed me."

"I do need you." It comes out weird and intense-sounding, and I feel a furious fit of blushing coming on. "I mean, I don't need you. I just need—" I take a deep breath. I think I see a momentary spark in Kent's eyes and it distracts me. "I'm worried Juliet Sykes is locked in the bathroom." Just after I say it, I wince. I sound ridiculous. He'll probably tell me I'm being insane. After all, he doesn't know what I know.

The spark dies and his face gets serious. He steps beyond me and tries the door, then he pauses for a second, thinking. He doesn't tell me I'm crazy or paranoid or anything. He simply says, "There's no key. I could try to pick the lock. We can always break it open if we have to."

"I'm going to pee upstairs," Rachel announces, then turns on her heel and wobbles off.

Kent reaches in his back pocket and pulls out a handful of safety pins. "Don't ask," he says when I raise my eyebrows. I hold up my hands and don't push the issue. I'm grateful he's taking charge without asking questions.

He squats down, bends the safety pin backward, and uses it to jimmy the lock. He's keeping his ear pressed to the door like he's listening for a click. Finally my curiosity gets the better of me.

"Do you have an after-school job robbing banks or something?"

He grimaces, tries the door, slips the safety pin back in his pocket, and selects a credit card from his wallet. "Hardly." He wedges the credit card in the crevice between the frame and the door and wiggles. "My mom used to keep the junk food locked behind our pantry door."

He straightens up and twists the handle. The door opens an inch, and my heart flies up into my throat. Part of me is hoping that Juliet's face will appear, furious, or that the door will be slammed closed again from inside. That's what I would do if someone tried to open the bathroom door when I was inside. That is, if I was still awake—alive—to close it.

But the door just sits there, open that little inch. Kent and I just look at each other at first. I think we're both scared to open it any farther.

Then Kent nudges the door with his toe, calling "Juliet?" as the door swings open—again, time stretches; it seems to take forever—and in that second, or half second, I somehow have the time to conjure up every horrible possibility, to imagine her body crumpled on the ground.

And then the door finishes swinging, and the bathroom is there: perfectly clean, perfectly normal, and perfectly empty. The lights are on, and there's a damp hand towel draped over the sink. The only thing slightly out of the ordinary is the window. It's wide open, and rain has been battering in onto the tiles below.

"She went out the window," Kent says at the same time I'm thinking it. I can't quite place his tone. It's half sad, half admiring.

"Shit." Of course. After a humiliation like that, she would have looked for the easiest escape possible, the one that would attract the least attention. The window looks out onto a sloping side lawn and, of course, the woods. She must have made a dash for it, planning to loop around back toward the driveway.

I hurtle out of the bathroom. Kent calls, "Wait!" but I'm already down the hall and out the door, pushing onto the porch.

I grab my flashlight and the sweatshirt from behind a planter where I'd left them and head out across the lawn. The rain isn't so bad just at the moment, more of a freezing mist falling in solid layers from above, but it's the kind of cold that goes right through you. I keep my flashlight trained on the ground as I sweep around to the side of the house. I'm not exactly a master tracker, but I've read enough old mysteries to know that you should always look for footprints. Unfortunately, the mud is so gross and damp that everything looks churned up. Still, at the base of the bathroom I find a deep indent, where she must have landed, and a series of scuffly-looking marks going, as I suspected, straight to the woods.

I wrap my sweatshirt more tightly around me and plunge in after her. I can't see anything but a few feet of light extending in a bouncing circle in front of me. I've never been scared of the dark exactly, but the endless scrapings and groanings of the trees and the constant patter of rain through the branches make it sound like the woods are alive and babbling away, like one of those crazy people you see in New York City who are always pushing grocery carts filled with empty bags.

There's no point in trying to follow Juliet's footprints. They're totally invisible in the soggy paste of decaying leaves, mud, and rotting bark. Instead I strike out in what I hope is the general direction of the road, hoping to catch her on her walk home. I'm pretty sure this is what she intends to do. If you're so desperate to ditch a party—and the people in it—that you climb out a window, it's hardly likely that you'll stroll back minutes later and ask people to move their Hondas.

The rain starts coming down harder, rattling through the icy branches, the sound of bone on bone. My chest aches from the cold, and even though I'm moving as fast as I can, my fingers feel numb and I'm having trouble holding on to the flashlight. I can't wait to get to my car and turn the heat on full blast. Then

I'll drive the streets looking for her. If worse comes to worse I'll intercept her at her house. If only I make it out of these freaking woods.

I push myself forward even faster, half jogging now, trying to stay warm. Every few moments I call out "Juliet!" but I don't expect to get an answer. The patter of the rain is getting heavier and more constant, big fat drops of it splashing on the back of my neck and making me gasp.

"Juliet! Juliet!"

The patter turns into a rush. Daggers of icy water slice into me. I keep up the jog, the flashlight like lead in my hand. I can't feel my toes anymore; I don't even know if I'm going in the right direction. I could be running around in circles, for all I know.

"Juliet!"

I start to get scared. I turn a full circle, sweeping my flashlight through the darkness: nothing but dense trees pressing in on either side of me. It didn't take me this long to walk through the woods on the way to Kent's, I'm sure of it. My fingers feel like they're twice the size they should be, and as I'm spinning, the flashlight flies out of my hand. There's a crash and the sound of splintering. The light sputters and dies, and I'm left totally in darkness.

"Shit. Shit, shit, shit." Cursing out loud makes me feel better.

I take a few hesitant steps in the direction of the flashlight, keeping my arms out in front of me so I don't collide with anything. After a few shuffling steps I drop to my knees, instantly destroying my house pants as wetness seeps through the fabric. I rake my hands in the sludge in front of me, trying hard not to think too much about what I'm touching. Rain is driving into my eyes. My fleece is clinging to my skin, and it smells like wet dog. I'm shivering uncontrollably. This is what happens when you try to help people. You get screwed. I feel a lump building in my throat.

In order to keep from a total meltdown, I think about what Lindsay would say if she were stuck with me in the middle of the night in the middle of woods that extend who knows how many miles in the middle of a monsoon, if she saw me tearing at the ground like a deranged mole, completely covered in mud.

"Samantha Kingston," she would say, smiling, "I always knew deep down you were a very dirty girl."

The thought only cheers me up for a second. Lindsay's not here with me. Lindsay's probably making out with Patrick in a toasty warm and very dry room right now, or passing a joint back and forth and wondering out loud to Ally why I've been acting so freak-tastic. I'm completely lost, completely miserable, and completely alone. The ache in my throat intensifies until I feel like there's an animal trying to claw its way out of my throat.

And I'm suddenly angry at Juliet—so angry I could punch her. I don't see how she can be so selfish. No matter what—no matter how bad things are—she has a *choice*. Not all of us are so lucky.

That's when I hear the most beautiful sound I've ever heard in the entirety of my seventeen years of life (plus five days of life-after-death).

I hear honking.

The sound is far away, and it fades almost as soon as it begins—a low wail through the night as someone speeding by leans on the horn. I'm closer to the road than I thought.

I scramble to my feet and go as quickly as I can toward the source of the sound, keeping my arms outstretched like a mummy, slapping away branches and the slick touch of the evergreens. My heart is pounding with excitement, and I strain for a noise—any other noise—to guide me. After a minute or so I hear another honk, this one closer. I could sob with relief. Another minute and I hear the thudding bass of a stereo system, tuning in and then out again as a car speeds away. Another minute and I can see, faintly through the trees, the glimmer of the light from the streetlamps. I've found the road.

As the lights get closer and the trees thin, I can see a little better, and I start booking it. I'm so busy fantasizing about piles and piles of blankets—I'll take every single one I can find in the house—and hot chocolate and warm slippers and *showers* that I don't see Juliet Sykes until the last minute, when I nearly trip over her.

She's huddled seven or eight feet from the road, her arms wrapped around her knees. Water has turned her white top totally transparent, and I can see her bra—striped—and all the bones of her spine. I'm so surprised to come across her like that, I forget, momentarily, that she's the whole reason I'm out here in the first place.

"What are you doing?" I say, loudly over the rain.

She looks up at me. The streetlamps light up her face. Her eyes are dull. "What are you doing?" she parrots back at me.

"I'm, um, looking for you actually." Her face doesn't register any emotion—no surprise, no shock, no anger, nothing. It throws me. "Aren't you cold?"

She shakes her head, just barely, and keeps staring at me with those dull, tired eyes. This isn't nearly how I pictured it would be. I thought she would be happy that I've come to look for her—grateful, even. Or maybe she would be mad. In any case, I thought she would be *something*.

"Listen, Juliet—" I can hardly talk, my teeth are chattering so badly. "It's, like, almost one o'clock in the morning, and it's freezing out here. Do you maybe want to come over to my house for a bit? And talk? I know what happened in there"—I nod back in the direction of Kent's house—"and I feel really bad about it." I just want her to get in the damn car, but it's true; I *do* feel bad.

Juliet stares at me for a long, hard second, the rain blurring the few feet between us. She starts to stand, and I feel sure that's done it, but instead she turns away and takes several steps toward the road.

"Sorry," she says. Her voice isn't apologetic, though. It's flat.

I reach out and grab her wrist. It feels impossibly tiny in my hand, like this one time I found a baby bird near Goose Point, and I picked it up and it died there, taking its final, gasping, fluttering breaths in my palm. Juliet doesn't pull away, but she stares at my hand like it's a snake about to bite her.

"Listen," I try again. "Listen. I know this is going to sound crazy, but . . ." The wind rushes through the trees and releases a new volley of rain. "I have a feeling that we have something in common, you and me. If we could just go somewhere and talk about it . . ."

"I'm not going anywhere," Juliet says. She stares out at the road, and I think I see a small, sad smile playing on her lips. Then it's gone.

I've been outside too long. My mind is grinding to a halt. Nothing's making sense anymore. Weird images keep flashing through my head, a bizarre fantasy reel of warm things. A pool filled with steaming hot chocolate. A stack of blankets piled all the way to the roof of my house. And part of me just thinks, *Screw it*. Let her do what she's going to do. Tomorrow there will be a big rewind anyway.

But there's a bigger part of me—my inner bull, my mom used to call it—that says she *owes* me this. I'm covered in mud;

I'm absolutely freezing; and half the population of Thomas Jefferson thinks I'm a pajama-wearing freak.

"How about we go to your house?" I figure she'll have to go back there eventually. She gives me a strange look, and for a second I feel like she's staring straight through me.

"Why are you doing this?" she says.

I have to yell even louder than before. Cars are starting to pull out of Kent's driveway, zooming by us on the wet road. "I—I want to help you."

She shakes her head, an infinitesimal gesture. "You hate me."

She's edging closer and closer to the road, and it's making me extremely nervous. A car roars by us, bass pumping. It glitters when it passes under the streetlamp, and I can just make out the silhouette of someone laughing. Somewhere to my right I think I hear my name, but it's hard to tell over the pounding rain.

"I don't hate you. I don't *know* you. But I'd like to change that. Start over." I'm almost screaming now. I'm not sure if she can still hear me.

She says something I don't hear. Another car goes flashing by, a silver bullet.

"What?"

Juliet turns her head a fraction of an inch and says, louder, "You're right. You don't know me."

Another car. Laughter rings out as it passes. Someone

throws a beer bottle into the woods and it shatters. Then I'm sure I hear someone calling my name, though I can't tell exactly which direction it comes from. The wind shrieks, and I suddenly realize that Juliet's only a half inch from the road, teetering on the thin line where the pavement begins, like she's balancing on a tightrope.

"Maybe you should come away from the road," I say, but all the time in the back of my head, there's an idea growing and swelling, a horrible, sickening realization, massing up and taking shape like clouds on the horizon. Someone calls my name again. And then, still in the distance, I hear the throaty wail of "Splinter" by Fallacy pumping from someone's car.

"Sam! Sam!" I recognize it as Kent's voice now.

Last night for the last time . . . you said you would be mine again . . .

Juliet turns to face me then. She's smiling, but it's the saddest smile I've ever seen.

"Maybe next time," she says. "But probably not."

"Juliet," I try to say, but the name catches in my throat. I feel like fear has turned me to stone. I want to say something, to move, to reach out and grab her, but time goes so quickly, and then the realization bursts and explodes as the music from the speakers gets louder and a silver Range Rover rockets out of the darkness. Like a bird or an angel—like she's throwing herself off a cliff—Juliet lifts her arms and hurtles onto the road, and there's a scream piercing the air and a sickening crunch, and it's not until Juliet's body flies sideways off the hood of Lindsay's car and lands crumpled facedown in the road, and the Range Rover sails into the woods and crashes, splintering, crumpling against a tree, and long ribbons of smoke and flame begin licking the air, that I realize I'm the one screaming.

BEFORE I WAKE

Kent catches up to me then. "Sam," he says breathlessly, eyes searching my face. "Are you okay?"

"Lindsay," I whisper. It's the only thing that I can think to say. "Lindsay and Elody and Ally are in that car."

He turns to the road. Black pillars of smoke are rising out of the woods. From where we're standing we can just see the battered metal bumper, rising like a finger over the dip of the earth.

"Wait here," he says. It's a miracle, but he sounds calm. He runs into the road, whipping his phone out, and I hear him yelling directions to someone on the other end. *There's been an accident. Fire. Route nine, just past Devon Drive.* He kneels by Juliet's body. *At least one person hurt.*

Other cars are squealing to a halt now. People climb out of their cars uncertainly, everyone suddenly sober, everyone speaking in whispers, staring at the tiny crumpled body in the road, at the smoke and fire licking up from the woods. Emma McElroy pulls over and gets out with her hands cupped over her mouth, eyes bugging out of her head, leaving the door to her Mini hanging open and the radio blasting. Jay-Z's "99 Problems" booms through the night, and the *normalcy* of it is the most horrible thing of all. Someone shrieks, "For God's sake, Emma, shut that off." Emma scrambles back to her car, and then there's silence except for the pounding of the rain, and the sounds of someone sobbing loudly.

I feel like I'm in a dream. I keep trying to move, but I can't. I don't even feel the rain anymore. I don't feel my body.

There's only one thought revolving around and around and around in my head: the flash of white just before we pinwheeled into the yawning mouth of the woods, Lindsay yelling something I couldn't quite make out.

Not *sit* or *shit* or *sight*.

Sykes.

Then a long, piercing wail comes from the other side of the woods, and Lindsay stumbles up to the road, her mouth open and tears streaming down her face. Kent is there, supporting Ally, who's limping and coughing but looks okay.

Lindsay's screaming, "Help! Help! Elody's still in there! Somebody help her! Please!" She's so hysterical her words swell together, transforming into an animal howl. She sinks down on the pavement and sobs, her head in her hands. Then another wailing joins in: sirens in the distance.

Nobody moves. Everything starts happening in short, choppy bursts—at least, that's what it seems like to me—like I'm watching a movie while a strobe light goes on and off.

More and more students massing in the rain, standing as still and silent as statues. The police sirens turning, lighting the scene up red, then white, then red, then white. Figures in uniform—an ambulance—a stretcher—two stretchers. Juliet's body laid out neatly, tiny and fragile, just like the bird all those years ago. Lindsay throwing up as the second stretcher bears a body up from the totaled car, and Kent rubbing her back. Ally sobbing with her mouth open, which is weird, because I don't hear a sound. At some point I lift my eyes to the sky and see that the rain has transformed into snow—fat, white flakes swirling out of the darkness as if by magic. I have no idea how long I've been standing there. I'm surprised to see that when I look back at the road there's hardly anyone left there at all, just a few stragglers and a solitary police car and Kent, jumping up and down to keep warm, talking to an officer. The ambulances are gone. Lindsay's gone. Ally's gone.

Then Kent's standing in front of me though I didn't see him move. *How did you do that?* I try to say, but nothing comes out.

"Sam." Kent's speaking to me, and I get the feeling he's said my name more than once. I feel a squeezing sensation and it takes me a second to realize he has his hands on my arms. It takes me a second to realize I still *have* arms, and in that moment it's like I slam back into my body, and the force of everything I've seen hits me and my legs buckle and I slump forward. Kent catches me, holds me up.

"What happened?" I whisper, dazed. "Is Elody . . . ? Is Juliet . . . ?"

"*Shhh.*" His lips are close to my ear. "You're freezing."

"I have to go find Lindsay."

"You've been out here for over an hour. Your hands are like ice." He shrugs out of the heavy sweater he's wearing and drapes it over me. There are white snowflakes caught in his lashes. He places his hands gently under my elbows and steers me back toward the driveway. "Come on. Let's get you warm."

I don't have the strength to argue. I let him lead me to the house. His hands never leave me, and even though he's barely grazing my back, I feel like without him I would fall.

It seems like we're back at Kent's house without even moving. Then we're in the kitchen, and he's pulling out a chair and putting me in it. His lips are moving and his tone is comforting, but I can't understand what he's saying. Then there's a thick blanket over my shoulders and a shooting pain in my fingers and toes as the feeling comes back to them, as though someone's sticking hot, sharp needles in me. Still, I can't stop shivering. My teeth are clacking together with a noise like dice rattling in a cup.

The kegs are still in the corner, and there are half-empty cups everywhere, and cigarette butts swimming in them, but the music's off and the house feels totally different without any people in it. My mind is focusing on a bunch of tiny details, ricocheting from one to the other like a Ping-Pong ball: the embroidered sign above the sink that says MARTHA STEWART DOES NOT LIVE HERE; the snapshots posted on the refrigerator, of Kent and his family on the beach somewhere, of relatives I don't know, of old postcards from Paris, Morocco, San Francisco; rows of mugs displayed behind the glass cabinets, with slogans on them like CAFFEINE OR BUST and IT'S TEA TIME.

"One marshmallow or two?" Kent is saying.

"What?" My voice comes out croaky and weird. All my other senses come online in a rush: I hear the hissing of milk heating in a pot; Kent's face comes into focus, sweet and concerned, bits of snow melting out of his shaggy brown hair. The blanket around my shoulders smells like lavender.

"I'll just put in a couple," Kent says, turning back to the stove. In a minute there's an oversized mug (This one says HOME IS WHERE THE CHOCOLATE IS) steaming in front of me, filled with foamy hot chocolate—the real kind, not the kind you get from a package—and big, bobbing marshmallows. I don't know whether I've asked for this out loud or whether he's just read my mind.

Kent sits across from me at the table and watches me take a sip. It's delicious, just sweet enough and full of cinnamon and something else I can't identify, and I put the mug down with slightly steadier hands.

"Where's Lindsay?" I say as the scene comes back to me: Lindsay on her knees in front of everyone, throwing up. She must have been out of her mind—Lindsay would never do something like that in public. "Is she okay?"

Kent nods, his eyes fixed on my face. "Lindsay's fine. She had to go to the hospital to be checked out for shock and stuff. But she's going to be okay."

"She—Juliet came so fast." I close my eyes, envisioning the white blur, and when I open them, Kent looks like his insides are getting torn out. "Is she . . . I mean, is Juliet . . . ?"

He shakes his head once. "There was nothing they could do," he says, so quietly if I didn't know what he was going to say I would never have heard him.

"I saw her . . ." I start to speak and find I can't. "I could have grabbed her. She was so close."

"It was an accident." Kent looks down. I'm not sure whether he really believes it.

No, it wasn't, I want to say. I think of her strange half smile as she said, *Maybe next time, but probably not*, and close my eyes, willing the memory away.

"What about Ally? Is she okay?"

"Ally's fine. Not even a scratch." Kent's voice gets stronger, but there's a pleading sound to it, and I understand he's trying to get me to stop talking—he doesn't want me to ask what I'm about to ask.

"Elody?" My voice comes out in a whisper.

Kent looks away. A muscle works in his jaw.

"She was sitting in the front seat," he says finally, as though each and every word hurts, and I think of Elody leaning forward and whining, *Why does Sam always get shotgun?* "The passenger side took most of the impact."

I wonder if that's how they would have explained it to my parents at the hospital—collision, passenger side, impact. "Is she . . . ?" I can't say the word.

He looks at me like he's about to cry. He looks older than I've ever seen him, his eyes dark and full and sad. "I'm so sorry, Sam," he says quietly.

"What are you telling me?" I ball my fists up so tightly I can feel my nails dig into my skin. "Are you saying she's—that she's—" I break off, still unable to say it. Saying it will make it real.

Kent looks like each word is something sharp he has to bring up from his stomach. "It was—it would have been instant. Painless."

"Painless?" I repeat, my voice shaking. "Painless? You don't know that. You *can't* know that." There's a fist in my throat. "Is that what they said? They said it was *painless*? Like it was peaceful? Like it was *okay*?"

Kent reaches for my hand across the table. "Sam . . ."

"No." I scrape my chair back from the table and stand up. My whole body is vibrating with rage. "No. Don't tell me it's going to be okay. Don't tell me it didn't hurt her. You don't

331

know—you have no idea—none of you have any idea how much it hurts. It hurts—"

I'm not even sure whether I'm talking about Elody or myself. Kent stands up and wraps his arms around me. I find myself with my head buried in his shoulder, sobbing. He keeps me pressed tightly to him, and he's making little noises into my hair, and before I totally let go of everything and succumb to the blackness washing through me, I have the strangest, dumbest thought—that my head fits perfectly in Kent's shoulder.

Then the thought of Elody and Juliet becomes too much, and a heavy veil drops down over my mind, and I cry. It's the second night in a row I've totally lost it in front of Kent, though, of course, he couldn't know that. I should be grateful he doesn't remember that only last night we sat together in a dark room with our knees almost touching, but instead it makes me feel even more alone. I'm lost in a fog, in a mist, and at some point when I start to come back to myself I realize that Kent is literally holding me up. My feet are barely skimming the ground.

His mouth is buried in my hair and I feel his breath close to my ear. A zip of electricity goes through me, which makes me feel awful and more confused than ever. I pull away, putting a little bit of space between us. He keeps his arms on either side of mine, though, bracing me, and I'm glad. He's solid and warm.

"You're still freezing," he says. He puts the back of his hand against my cheek for one millisecond, but when he pulls away

I can feel the outline of his hand, like it's scalded me. "Your clothes are soaking."

"Underwear," I blurt out.

He wrinkles his forehead. "What?"

"My . . . um, underwear. I mean, my pants and fleece and underwear . . . it's all full of snow. Well, mostly melted water now. It's really cold." I'm too exhausted to care about being embarrassed. Kent just bites his lip and nods.

"Stay here," he says. "And drink up." He nods to the hot chocolate.

He guides me back into the chair and disappears. I'm still shivering, but at least I can hold the mug without slopping it all over the table. I don't think about anything but the motion of the mug to my lips and the taste of the cocoa, the ticking of a cat-tailed clock, and the drifting white outside the windows. In a few seconds Kent's back with an enormous fleece, faded sweatpants, and folded striped boxers.

"They're mine," he says, and then turns bright red. "I mean, not mine. I didn't wear them yet or anything. My mom bought them for me—" He catches himself and swallows. "I mean, I bought them for myself, like, Tuesday. Tags still on and everything."

"Kent?" I interrupt him.

He sucks in a breath. "Yeah?"

"I'm really sorry, but . . . do you mind being quiet?" I gesture to my head. "My brain is full of fuzz."

333

"I'm sorry." He exhales. "I don't know what to do. I wish . . . I wish that there was more."

"Thanks," I say. I know he's making an effort and I manage a weak smile.

He lays the clothes down on the table, along with a big, fluffy white towel. "I didn't know . . . I thought if you were still cold you could take a shower." He blushes at the word *shower*.

I shake my head. "I really just want to sleep." I've forgotten about sleep, and I feel a huge lift when I say it: all I have to do is sleep.

As soon as I fall asleep this nightmare will be over.

Still, a twittering feeling of anxiety rises up inside me. What if the day doesn't rewind this time? What if this is it? I think of Elody and feel the hot chocolate coming back up in my throat.

Kent must see the expression on my face because he crouches down so we're at eye level. "Can I do anything? Can I get you anything?"

I shake my head, trying not to cry again. "I'll be okay. It's just . . . the shock." I swallow hard. "I just want to . . . I want to rewind, you know?"

He nods once, and puts his hand over mine. I don't pull it away. "If I could make it better I would," he says.

In some ways it's a stupid, obvious thing to say, but the *way* he says it, so honest and simple like it's the truest thing there is, makes tears prick in my eyes. I take the clothes and the towel and go out into the hall to the bathroom we broke into to find Juliet. I go in and shut the door. The window's still open and flurries of snow whirl in from outside. I shut the window. It makes me feel better already, like I'm already starting the process of erasing everything that's happened tonight. Elody will be fine.

After all, *I* was the one who was supposed to be in the front seat.

I hang the hand towel Juliet left by the sink and strip out of my clothes, shaking. The shower is too hard to resist after all, and I turn the water on as high and as hot as it can go and get in. It's one of those rain-forest showers where the water pours on you straight from above in a long, heavy stream. When it hits the marble tiles under my feet, it lets up big clouds of steam. I stay in the shower so long my skin gets pruny.

I put on Kent's fleece, which is supersoft and smells like laundry detergent and, for some reason, freshly mowed grass. Then I snap the tags off the boxers and slip my legs into them. They're too big on me, obviously, but I like how clean and crisp they feel on my skin. The only other boxers I've seen are Rob's, usually crumpled up on his floor or shoved under his bed and stained with things I have no desire to identify. Last, I put on the sweatpants, which pool over my feet. Kent has given me socks, too, the big fluffy kind. I ball up all of my clothes and leave them just outside the bathroom door.

When I go back in the kitchen, Kent's standing there, exactly as I left him. Something flickers in his eyes when I come in, but I'm not sure what it is.

"Your hair's wet," he says softly, but he says it like he's actually saying something else.

I look down. "I showered, after all."

Silence stretches between us for a few beats. Then he says, "You're tired. I'll drive you home."

"No." I say it more forcefully than I meant to, and Kent looks startled.

"No—I mean, I can't. I don't want to go home right now."

"Your parents . . ." Kent trails off.

"Please." I don't know which would be worse: if my parents have already heard and are sitting there, waiting for me, waiting to grill me and ask me questions and talk about hospitals in the morning and therapists to help me deal—or if they haven't heard yet and I come home to a dark house.

"There's a guest room here," Kent says. His hair is finally drying into little wisps and waves.

"No guest rooms." I shake my head resolutely. "I want to be in a *room* room. A lived-in room."

Kent stares at me for a second and then says, "Come with me." He reaches for my hand as he passes and I let him take it. We go up the stairs and down the hall and to the bedroom with all the bumper stickers on it. I should have known it was his. He fiddles with the door—"It sticks," he explains—and finally pops it open. I inhale sharply. The smell is just the same as it was last night when I was here with Rob, but everything is different—the darkness looks softer, somehow.

"Give me a second." Kent squeezes my hand and pulls away. I hear the rustling of the curtains and I gasp: suddenly three enormous windows, stretching from floor to ceiling and taking up one entire wall, are revealed. He hasn't turned on a light, but he may as well have. The moon is huge and luminous and bounces through all the dazzling white snow, growing brighter. The whole room is bathed in a beautiful, silver light.

"It's amazing," I say. I breathe out; I didn't even realize I was holding my breath.

Kent smiles quickly. His face is silhouetted in moonlight. "It's great at night. Not so great at sunrise, though." He starts to draw the curtains closed.

"Leave them open," I cry out, and then add, "please." I suddenly feel shy.

Kent's room is enormous, and smells like that same incredible mixture of Downy laundry detergent and grass shavings. It's the freshest smell in the world, the smell of open windows and crisp sheets. Last night I couldn't make out anything but the bed. Now I see the room is lined completely with bookshelves. There's a desk in the corner, stacked with a computer and more books. There are pictures framed on the walls, blurred figures moving, but I can't make out the details. A monster beanbag chair squats in one corner and Kent catches me staring at it.

"I've had it since seventh grade," he says. He sounds embarrassed.

"I used to have one like that," I say. I don't add why I chucked it: because Lindsay said it looked like a lumpy boob. I can't think about Lindsay now, or Ally. I definitely can't think about Elody.

Kent draws the blankets down on his bed and then stands back, turning away so I have some privacy. I climb into the bed and lie down, my limbs heavy and achingly stiff, feeling a little self-conscious, but so numb with exhaustion I don't care. There's a curved wooden headboard and a matching footboard, and as soon as I'm stretched out, I'm reminded of being in a sleigh. I tilt my head so I can see the snow drifting down, and then close my eyes, imagining that I'm flying through a forest on my way to somewhere good: a trim little white house in the distance, candles burning in its windows.

"Good night," Kent whispers. He's so quiet I'd forgotten he was standing there.

I snap my eyes open and sit up on one elbow. "Kent?"

"Yeah?"

"Can you maybe stay with me a bit?"

He nods, and rolls the desk chair over to the side of the bed without speaking. He tucks his knees up to his chin and looks at me. The moonlight coming in through the windows turns his hair a soft silver.

"Kent?"

"Yeah?"

"Do you think it's weird that I'm here with you?" I close my eyes when I say it so I don't have to look at his face.

"I'm the editor in chief of the *Tribulation*," he says. "And I once went three hundred and sixty-five days wearing Crocs. I don't think anything's weird."

"I forgot about the Crocs phase," I say. I'm finally warm under the covers, and I feel sleep creeping up on me, like I'm standing on a hot beach with a gentle tide pulling at my toes. "Kent?"

"Yeah?"

"Why are you being so nice to me?"

There's quiet for so long I begin to think he won't answer. I imagine I can hear the snow drifting to earth, covering over the day, erasing it clean. I'm too frightened to open my eyes, terrified that I'll break the spell, terrified he'll look angry or hurt.

"Remember the time in second grade right after my grandfather died?" he says finally, speaking in a low, quiet voice. "I burst into tears in the lunchroom and Phil Howell called me a faggot. That only made me cry harder, even though I didn't know what a faggot was." He laughs softly.

I keep my eyes squeezed shut, coasting on his voice. Last year Phil Howell was found half naked with Sean Trebor in the back of his dad's BMW. It's funny how things turn out.

"Anyway, when I told him to leave me alone he smacked

my tray, and food went flying everywhere. I'll never forget: we were having mashed potatoes and turkey burgers. And you went up and scooped the potatoes off the floor with your hands and shoved them straight into Phil's face. And then you picked up the turkey burger and crumbled it down Phil's T-shirt. You said, *You're worse than the hot lunch*." He laughs again. "That was a big insult in second grade. And Phil was so surprised, and he looked so ridiculous standing there with mashed potato and chives smeared all over him, that I just started laughing and laughing, and it was the first time I'd laughed since I'd heard the news about—about my grandfather." He pauses. "Do you remember what I said to you that day?"

The memory is there, a balloon swelling from somewhere so far inside me I thought it was lost, the whole scene clear and perfect now.

"You're my hero," we both say at the same time. I don't hear Kent move, but all of a sudden his voice is closer, and he's found my hands in the dark, and he's cupping them in his.

"I vowed after that day that I would be your hero too, no matter how long it took," he whispers.

We stay like that for what feels like hours, and all the time sleep is dragging at me, pulling me away from him, but my heart is fluttering like a moth, beating back the dreams and the darkness and the fog crowding my brain. Once I sleep, I lose him. I lose this moment forever.

"Kent?" I say, and my voice seems to have to rise from inside the fog, taking forever to get from my brain to my mouth.

"Yeah?"

"Promise you'll stay here with me?" I say.

"I promise," he whispers.

And then, just at that moment, when I'm no longer sure if I'm dreaming or awake or walking some valley in between where everything you wish for comes true, I feel the flutter of his lips on mine, but it's too late, I'm slipping, I'm gone, he's gone, and the moment curls away and back on itself like a flower folding up for the night.

SIX

This time, when I dream, there is sound. As I fall through the darkness there's a tinkly, jangly song playing, like the kind of music you hear in doctors' offices and elevators, and without knowing how I know, I realize that the music is piping all the way from the guidance counselor's office at Thomas Jefferson.

As soon as I realize this, little bright spots start exploding through the darkness, a zooming gallery of all the annoying inspirational posters my guidance counselor, Mrs. Gardner, keeps on her walls, except in my dream they're all blown up by about a hundred times, each the size of a house. In one, Einstein is pictured over the words GRAVITY IS NOT RESPONSIBLE FOR FALLING IN LOVE. There's a poster with Thomas Edison's quote: GENIUS IS 1 PERCENT INSPIRATION AND 99 PERCENT PERSPIRATION. I'm thinking of trying to grab one of them and worrying about whether it will hold my weight when I spin past a picture of a striped cat hanging off the branch of a tree by its nails. It says HANG IN THERE.

And it's the funniest thing: as soon as I see it, the whistling in my ears stops and the feeling of terror drains away, and I realize this whole time I haven't been falling at all. I've been floating.

The alarm that wakes me is the sweetest sound I've ever heard. I sit up, a bubble of laughter rising inside me. I have the urge to touch everything in my room—the walls, the window, the collage, the photos cluttering my desk, the Tahari jeans strewn across my floor and my bio textbook and even the dull light just creeping over the windowsill. If I could cup it in my hands and kiss it, I would.

"Someone's in a good mood," my mom says when I come downstairs. Izzy's at the table in front of her peanut butter bagel, taking slow, careful bites, as usual.

"Happy Cupid Day," my father says. He's standing at the stove burning eggs for my mom's breakfast.

"My favorite," I say, scooting in to steal a bite from Izzy's bagel. Izzy squeals and slaps at my hand. I plant a big, sloppy kiss on her forehead.

"Stop slobbering on me," she says.

"See you later, Fizzy Lizard," I say.

"Don't call me Lizard." Izzy sticks a peanut butter–coated tongue out at me.

"You look like a lizard when you do that."

"Do you want any breakfast, Sam?" my mom asks. I never eat breakfast at home, but my mom still asks me every day—when she catches me before I duck out, anyway—and in that moment I realize how much I love the little everyday routines of my life: the fact that she always asks, the fact that I always say no because there's a sesame bagel waiting for me in Lindsay's car, the fact that we always listen to "No More Drama" as we pull into the parking lot. The fact that my mom always cooks spaghetti and meatballs on Sunday, and the fact that once a month my dad takes over the kitchen and makes his "special stew," which is just hot-dog pieces and baked beans and lots of extra ketchup and molasses, and I would never admit to liking it, but it's actually one of my favorite meals. The details that are my life's special pattern, like how in handwoven rugs what really makes them unique are the tiny flaws in the stitching, little gaps and jumps and stutters that can never be reproduced.

So many things become beautiful when you really look.

"No breakfast. Thanks, though." I go to my mom and wrap my arms around her. She yelps, surprised. I guess it has been a couple of years since we've hugged, except the mandatory two-second squeeze on birthdays. "Love you."

When I pull away she stares at me as though I've just announced I'm quitting school to become a contortionist in the circus.

"What?" my dad says, dumping a pan in the sink and wiping

344

his hands on the dishtowel. "No love for your old man?"

I roll my eyes. I hate it when my dad tries to "teen-speak," as he calls it, but I don't call him out on it. Nothing can get me down today.

"Bye, Dad." I let him wrap me in one of his infamous bear hugs. I'm filled with love from the top of my head to the bottom of my toes, a bubbly feeling like someone's shaken my insides up like a Coke bottle. Everything—the dishes in the sink, Izzy's bagel, my mom's smile—looks sharp, like it's made out of glass or like I'm seeing it for the first time. It's dazzling, and again I have the desire to go around and touch it all, make sure that it's real. If I had time I would, too. I would put my hands around the half-eaten grapefruit on the counter and smell it. I would run my fingers through Izzy's hair.

But I don't have time. It's Cupid Day, and Lindsay's outside, and I have business to take care of. Today I'm going to save two lives: Juliet Sykes's, and mine.

LET THERE BE LIGHT

"Beep, beep!" Lindsay shouts out her window as I scurry down the icy walkway, sucking the cold air into my lungs, loving the way it burns, loving even the bitter stink of Lindsay's cigarette and the exhaust that's clotting the air. "Hot mama! How much?"

"If you have to ask," I say, sliding into the passenger seat, "you can't afford it."

She grins and hands me my coffee before I can reach for it. "Happy Cupid Day."

"Happy Cupid Day," I say, and we clink Styrofoam cups.

She too looks clearer to me than ever before. Lindsay, with her angel's face and messy, dirty blond hair and chipped black nail polish and battered leather Dooney & Bourke bag that always has a film of tobacco and half-unwrapped Trident Original at the bottom. Lindsay, who hates being bored, always moving, always running. Lindsay, who once said—"It's the world against us, babes"—drunk and looping her arms around our shoulders when we were out in the arboretum and really meaning it. Lindsay, mean and funny and ferocious and loyal and mine.

I lean over impulsively and kiss her cheek.

"Whoa, lesboing out much?" Lindsay shrugs a shoulder up to her cheek and wipes off my lip gloss. "Or just practicing for tonight?"

"Maybe both," I say, and she laughs long and loud.

I take a sip of my coffee. It's scalding and has to be the best coffee in all of Ridgeview, in all the world. God bless Dunkin' Donuts.

Lindsay chatters about how many roses she expects to get and whether Marcy Posner will, as usual, break down and cry in the bathroom during fifth period because Justin Streamer dumped her three years ago on Cupid Day, thus permanently sealing her fate as only medium-popular, and I look out the window and watch Ridgeview go by in a blur of gray. I try to imagine how, in only a few months, the trees will shoot their tiny stems into the sky, the barest spray of flowers and green breathed over everything like a mist. And then, a few months after that, the whole town will be an explosion of green: so many trees and so much grass it will look like a painting still dripping wet. I can imagine it waiting under the surface of the world, like the slides just have to be flipped in the projector and summer will be here.

And there's Elody, teetering down the lawn in her shoes with no jacket on and her arms wrapped around her chest. When I see her, radiant and alive, the relief is so huge I let out a tremendous shriek of laughter. Lindsay raises her eyebrows at me.

"She'll freeze," I gasp, by way of explanation.

Lindsay twirls her finger by her ear. "She's totally cuckoo for Cocoa Puffs."

"Did someone say Cocoa Puffs?" Elody says, getting into the car. "I'm starving."

I twist around to look at her. It's all I can do to keep from climbing into the backseat and jumping on her. I feel an overwhelming urge to touch her, make sure she's really real and here and *alive*. In some ways she's the bravest and most delicate of all of us. I wish I could somehow tell her this.

"What?" Elody scrunches up her nose at me, and I realize I'm staring. "What's wrong? Do I have toothpaste on my face or something?"

"No," I say, and again the laughter bubbles out of me, a surge of happiness and relief. I think; I could stay forever in this one moment. "You look beautiful."

Lindsay giggles, checks Elody out in the rearview. "There are some bagels under your butt, *beautiful*."

"*Mmm*, butt bagels." Elody reaches into the bag and pulls out a bagel, half squashed, then makes a big deal of taking an enormous bite out of it. "Tastes like Victoria's Secret."

"Tastes like thong floss," I say.

"Tastes like crack," Lindsay says.

"Tastes like fart," Elody says, and Lindsay spits coffee on the dashboard, and I start laughing and can't stop, and all the way to school we're thinking of flavors for butt bagels, and I'm thinking that this—my life, my friends—might be weird or screwy or imperfect or damaged or whatever, but it's never seemed better to me.

As we're pulling into the school's parking lot, I scream for Lindsay to brake. She slams to a stop and Elody curses as coffee slops all over her.

"What the hell?" Lindsay puts a hand on her chest. "You scared me to death."

"Oh—um. Sorry. I thought I saw Rob." Up ahead I'm watching Sarah Grundel's Chevrolet turn into Senior Alley fifteen seconds ahead of us. The parking space is a small thing, a detail, but today I'm not going to do *anything* wrong. I don't want to take any chances. It's like the game we used to play when we were little, where we had to avoid all the cracks in the sidewalk or else it meant we'd kill off our mothers. Even if you didn't believe in it, you made sure you were stepping correctly, just in case. "Sorry. My bad."

Lindsay rolls her eyes and steps on the gas again. "Please tell me you're not going psycho stalker."

"Leave her alone." Elody leans forward and pats my shoulder. "She's just nervous about tonight."

I bite my lip to keep from giggling. If Lindsay and Elody had any clue at all about what was *actually* running through my head, they would probably have me committed. All morning, whenever I close my eyes, I keep imagining the feeling of Kent McFuller's lips brushing against mine, as light as butterfly wings; of the crown of light surrounding his head and the way his arms felt when he was keeping me on my feet. I lean my head against the window. My smile is reflected back at me, growing wider and wider as Lindsay drives up and down Senior Alley, cursing because Sarah Grundel took the very last parking space.

Instead of following Elody and Lindsay into Main, I break off and head toward Building A, where the nurses' office is, muttering an excuse about a headache. That's where the roses are stored on Cupid Day, and I have some adjustments to make. Okay, so maybe lying isn't 100 percent kosher on the Good Deeds Scale (especially lying to your best friends), but it's for a very, very good cause.

The nurses' office is long and narrow. Normally a double row of cots runs its length, but the cots have been cleared out and replaced by huge folding tables. The heavy curtains that usually keep the place movie theater–dark have all been drawn back, and the room is literally sparkling with light. Light bounces off the metal wall fixtures and zigzags crazily over the bright white walls. There are roses everywhere—overflowing their trays, stashed in corners, a few of them even scattered across the ground, petals trampled—and if you didn't know that there was actually an organizing principle to all of it, and a purpose, you would just think that someone had set off some kind of a rose bomb.

Ms. Devane, who usually oversees Cupid Day, isn't around, but there are three Cupids standing over one of the bins, giggling. They jump and scoot backward when I come in. They've been reading the notes, obviously. It's strange to think about—those little scraps of paper, snippets of words, half compliments and backhanded compliments and broken promises and semi-wishes and almost expressions of what you really want to say: they never tell the full story, or even half of it. A room full of words that are nearly the truth but not quite, each note fluttering off the stem of its rose like a broken butterfly wing. None of the girls talks to me as I start walking the aisle, scanning the labels on the trays, looking for the S's. I doubt that anybody else has ever barged in on the Rose Room, especially not a senior. Finally I find the tray labeled: *St–Ta*. There are five or six roses for Tamara Stugen and another half dozen for Andrew Svork and three for a Burt Swortney, who has the most unfortunate name I've heard of in a long time. And there it is: the single rose for Juliet Sykes with a note looped delicately around its stem. MAYBE NEXT YEAR, BUT PROBABLY NOT. *Maybe next time, but probably not.*

"Um . . . can I help you with something?" One of the girls inches forward a couple of feet. She's twisting her hands together and looks absolutely petrified.

Juliet's rose is thin and young, delicately tinged with pink. All of its petals are closed. It hasn't bloomed yet.

"I need roses," I say. "Lots of them."

CORRECTIONS AND ADJUSTMENTS

I leave the Rose Room feeling keyed up and energetic, like I've just had three mocha lattes from Caffeine Rush in the mall. I replaced Juliet's single rose with an enormous bouquet—I shelled out forty bucks for two dozen—and a note printed in block letters that says FROM YOUR SECRET ADMIRER. I only wish I could be around when she receives them. I'm positive it's going to make her day. More than that: I'm positive it's going to make things right. She'll have even more roses than Lindsay Edgecombe. I start thinking about Lindsay's eyes bugging out of her head when she sees that Juliet Sykes has beaten her for the title of Most Valograms this year, and I let out a huge snort of laughter right in the middle of AP American

History. Everyone whips around and stares at me, but I don't care. This must be what it's like to do drugs: the feeling of coasting over everything, of everything looking new and fresh and lit up from inside. Except without the next-day guilt and the hangover. And possible prison sentence.

When Mr. Tierney distributes his pop quiz, I spend the whole twenty minutes drawing hearts and balloons around the questions, and when he comes around to collect the papers I give him a smile so bright he actually winces, like he's not used to people looking happy.

Between classes I scour the hallways, looking for Kent. I'm not even sure what I'll say to him when I see him. I *can't* really say anything. He doesn't know that we've spent the past two nights together, that both nights we were so close that if one of us had breathed we would have ended up kissing, that last night I think we might have. But I have this incredible urge just to be around him, to see him doing those familiar, Kent-like things: flipping his hair out of his eyes, smiling his lopsided smile, shuffling his ridiculous checkered sneakers, and tucking his hands into the over-long cuffs of his button-downs. My heart shoots into my throat every time I think I see his loping walk, or catch sight of some floppy brown hair on a boy—but it's never him, and each time it isn't, my heart does a reverse trajectory down into the very pit of my stomach.

I'm guaranteed to see him in calc, at least. After life skills, I stop in the bathroom, and spend the three minutes before bell primping in front of the mirror, ignoring the s'mores chattering on either side of me, and trying hard not to focus on the fact that I'll come face-to-face with Mr. Daimler in less than five minutes. My stomach's been performing its roller-coaster move so often—a combination of waiting for Juliet to get the roses, hoping to see Kent, and being disappointed—I'm not sure it can withstand forty-five minutes of having to watch Mr. Daimler smirk and wink and grin at the class. I will away the memory of his tongue inside my mouth, wet and sloppy.

"*Such* a slut." One of the sophomores is coming out of a bathroom stall, shaking her head.

For one paranoid second I'm sure she's talking about me— that somehow she has just read my mind—but then her friends explode with laughter, and one of them says, "I know. I hear she had sex with, like, three people on the basketball team," and I realize they're talking about Anna Cartullo. The stall door is swinging open and Lindsay's scrawl is obvious. *AC=WT.* And underneath it: *Go back to the trailer, ho.*

"You shouldn't believe everything you hear," I blurt out, and all three girls instantly shut their mouths and stare at me.

"It's true," I say, feeling bolder now that I have such a captive audience. "You know how most rumors start?"

The girls shake their heads. They're standing so close I think for a second their skulls are going to knock together.

"Because somebody feels like it."

The bell rings then, and the sophomores scurry for the door like they've been let out of class. I stand there, willing my feet out the door and down the hall and down a flight of stairs and to the right and into calc, but nothing happens. Instead I'm fixated by the writing on the stall door, how Ally laughed and pointed to the copycat artists elsewhere. *AC=WT.* I'm pretty sure Lindsay wrote it on a whim—four measly letters, stupid, meaningless—probably to test out a new marker and see how much ink it had. It would have been better, almost, if she'd meant it. It would be better if she really hated Anna. Because it matters. It *has* mattered.

Without thinking about the fact that at this point I'm going to be late to calc, I dampen a strip of paper towel, just as an experiment, and begin scrubbing at the writing on the stall door. It doesn't budge. But then, because I've started, I can't stop. I look under the sink and find a dried-out Brillo pad and a can of Comet. I have to brace the door with one arm and lean hard with the other, scrubbing furiously, but after a little while the graffiti on the door has lightened, and after a little while longer you can hardly see the letters at all. I feel so good once I've gotten them off that first door, I go down the row and scrub the remaining two, even though my arm is aching and cramping and I've actually started to sweat a little bit in my tank top, mentally cursing Lindsay the whole time for her whims, for using permanent marker.

When all three stalls are finished I turn the doors out and

look at their reflections in the mirror: blank, clean, featureless, the way stall doors should be. And for some reason it fills me with such pride and happiness I do a little dance right there, tapping my heels on the tile floor. It feels like I've reached back in time and corrected something. I haven't felt so alive, so capable of *doing* things, in I don't know how long.

By now I really have ruined my makeup. Little pricks of sweat are beading across my forehead and the bridge of my nose. I splash cold water on my face and dry off with a scratchy paper towel, starting all over again with the mascara and cream blush in Rose Petal that Lindsay and I both use religiously. My heart is looping crazily in my chest, partly from exhilaration, partly from nerves. Next period is lunch, and lunchtime is showtime.

"Will you stop doing that?" Elody leans forward and presses my fingers—which have been tapping—flat against the table. "You're driving me crazy."

"You're not turning rexi, are you, Sam?" Lindsay gestures to my sandwich, which I've only nibbled around the edges. *Rexi* is her word for anorexic, although I've always thought it sounded like something you would name a dog.

"That's what you get for ordering the mystery meat." Ally makes a face at my roast beef, which I've ordered despite the fact that it's borderline unacceptable. Things That Don't Matter When You've Lived the Same Day Six Times and Died on at

Least Two of Them: lunch meats and their relative coolness.

To my surprise Lindsay sticks up for me. "It's all mystery meat, Al. The turkey tastes like shoe bottoms."

"Nasty," Elody agrees.

"I've always hated the turkey here," Ally admits, and we all look at one another and burst out laughing.

It feels good to laugh, and the knot in my shoulders relaxes. Still, my fingers start up their involuntary drumming again, moving all on their own. I'm scanning every single person who enters the cafeteria, looking alternately for Kent—it's like, what, he doesn't *eat* now?—and Juliet's shock of white blond hair. So far, nada.

". . . to Juliet?"

I've been totally zoning out, *thinking* about Juliet, that for a second when I hear her name I think I've only imagined it—or worse, said it aloud myself. But then I see that Lindsay's looking at Ally, a strange smile curling on her lips, and I know she must have just asked about whether Juliet got our rose. I totally forgot that Ally and Juliet have biology together, and I'm suddenly breathless. The room seems to tilt as I wait for Ally to respond. *Oh my God, you guys, it was the weirdest thing . . . she got the biggest bouquet of flowers . . . she actually* smiled.

Ally claps a hand over her mouth, her eyes bugging out. "Oh my God, you guys. I totally forgot to tell you—"

Hands clamp down over my eyes and I'm so wound up I let out a little squeal. The hands smell like grease and—of course—lemon balm. Lindsay, Ally, and Elody crack up as Rob pulls his hands off my eyes. When I look up at him he's smiling, but there's a tightness around his eyes and I can tell he's unhappy.

"You avoiding me now?" he says, snapping the strap of my tank top like he's five.

"Not exactly," I say, trying to sound pleasant. "What do you mean?"

He jerks his head back toward the soda machine. "I've been standing over there for, like, fifteen minutes." His voice is low; he's clearly not happy to be having this conversation in front of my friends. "You haven't looked over or come over or anything."

You made me wait longer than that, I want to say, but obviously he wouldn't get it. Besides, as I watch him shuffling his scuffed-up New Balance sneakers, I realize he's not really so horrible. Yeah, he's selfish and not-so-smart and drinks too much and flirts with other girls and can't take off a bra for the life of him, not to mention what comes afterward, but someday he'll grow up a little and make a girl really happy.

"I'm not ignoring you, Rob, it's just . . ." I blow air out of my cheeks, stalling. I've never broken up with anybody before, and all the clichés keep running through my head. *It's not you, it's me.* (No—it is him. *And* me.) *We're better off friends.* (We were never friends.) "Things between us have been . . ."

He squints at me like he's trying to read in a different

357

language. "You got my rose, right? Fifth period? You read the note?"

Like this will make it better. "Actually," I say, trying to keep the impatience out of my voice, "I didn't get your rose. I cut fifth."

"Miss Kingston." Across the table, Elody puts her hand to her chest and pretends to be shocked. "I am very disappointed in you." More giggling.

I shoot her a look and turn back to Rob. "But that's not the point. The point is—"

"I didn't get a rose from you," Rob says, and I can see him very slowly starting to put it together: something is wrong. When Rob thinks, you can almost see gears shifting together in his brain.

This morning I made one other change in the Rose Room. I stopped by the C's and carefully rifled through Rob's roses—skipping over the rose from Gabby Haynes, his ex-girlfriend, which said, *When are we going to hang out like you promised, sexy?*—and removed the one from me, with the little note I spent hours agonizing over.

Lindsay slaps at Rob's arm, still thinking this is all a joke. "Be patient, Rob," she says, winking at him. "Your rose is coming."

"Patient?" Rob scowls as though the word tastes bad in his mouth. He crosses his arms and stares at me. "I get it. There is no rose, right? Did you forget or something?"

Something in his voice makes my friends finally get it. They go silent, staring back and forth from Rob to me, me to Rob.

Let me rephrase: someday he'll make a *sorority* girl really happy, a blonde named Becky with D boobs who doesn't mind getting man-handled like meat in a marinade.

"I didn't *forget*—" I start to say, but he cuts me off.

His voice is calm, very low, but I can hear the anger running underneath it—hard and cold and cutting. "You make such a huge deal about Cupid Day. And then you don't keep up your end of the bargain. Typical."

Inside, my stomach is working like it's trying to digest a whole cow, but I lift my chin, staring at him. "Typical? What's that supposed to mean?"

"I think you know." Rob passes a hand over his eyes and looks suddenly mean, reminding me of this trick my dad used to do where he would bring his hand down over his face, changing all of his features from happy to sad, then from sad back to happy, in an instant. "You don't exactly have a perfect history of keeping your promises—"

"Psycho alert," Lindsay shouts out, probably hoping to diffuse the tension.

It works, kind of. I stand up so quickly I knock over my chair. Rob looks at me, disgusted, then taps the chair with his toe—not hard, but enough so that it's loud—and says, "Find me later."

He stalks off into the cafeteria, but I'm not watching him anymore. I'm watching Juliet float, drift, skim into the room.

Like she's already dead and we're just seeing her flickering back to life in patches, imperfectly.

She's not carrying anything, either, not a single stem, just a lumpy brown paper bag as always. My disappointment is so heavy and real I can *taste* it, a bitter lump in the back of my throat.

". . . And then one of the Cupids came in, and I swear, she had, like, three dozen flowers, all for Juliet."

I whip around. "What did you say?"

Ally frowns a little at my tone of voice, but she repeats, "She just got, like, this huge bouquet of roses delivered to her. I've never seen so many roses." She starts to giggle. "Maybe Psycho has a stalker."

"I just don't understand what happened to *our* rose," Lindsay says, pouting. "I specifically told them third period, bio."

"What did she do with them?" I interject.

Ally, Elody, and Lindsay stare at me. "Do with what?" Ally says.

"The roses. Did she—did she throw them out?"

"Why do you care?" Lindsay wrinkles her nose.

"I just—I *don't* care. It's just . . ." They're all staring at me blankly. Elody has her mouth open and I can see mushed-up french fries in it. "I think it's nice, okay? If someone sent her all those roses . . . I don't know. I just think it's nice."

"She probably sent them herself," Elody says, starting to giggle again.

I finally lose my temper. "Why? Why would you say that?"

Elody jerks back like I've hit her. "I'm just—it's *Juliet*."

"Yeah, exactly. It's *Juliet*. So what's the point? Nobody gives a shit about her. Nobody pays any attention." I lean forward, pressing both hands on the table, my head pounding from anger and frustration. "What's. The. Point?"

Alley frowns at me. "Is this because you're upset about Rob?"

"Yeah." Lindsay folds her arms. "What's up with that anyway? Are you guys okay?"

"This isn't about Rob," I say, squeezing the words out through gritted teeth.

Elody jumps in. "It was a joke, Sam. Yesterday you said you were scared Juliet would bite you if you went too close. You said she probably had rabies."

That's what really breaks me—right then, when Elody says that. Or rather, when she reminds me that I said that: yesterday, six days ago, a whole different *world* ago. How is it possible, I think, to change so much and not be able to change anything at all? That's the very worst thing about all of this, a feeling of desperate hopelessness, and I realize my question to Elody is the question that's been tearing me up all along. What's the point? If I'm dead—if I can't change anything, if I can't fix it—*what's the point?*

"Sam's right." Lindsay winks at me, still not getting it. "It's

Cupid Day, you know? A time of love and forgiveness, even for the psychos of the world." She raises a rose like it's a glass of champagne. "To Juliet."

Ally and Elody lift their roses, giggling. "To Juliet," they say in unison.

"Sam?" Lindsay raises an eyebrow. "Care to toast with us?"

I spin around and head to the back of the senior section, to the door that leads directly to the parking lot. Lindsay shouts something, and Ally calls, "She didn't throw them out, okay?"

I keep going anyway, threading past tables piled with food and roses and bags, everyone talking and laughing, oblivious. I get a pang in my stomach that feels like regret. Everything looks so stupidly, happily normal: everyone just wasting time because they have so much of it to waste, minutes slipping by on *who's with who* and *did you hear*.

On the horizon is the black line of clouds, just sitting there, a curtain about to be closed. I scan the parking lot, looking for Juliet, bouncing up and down on my toes to keep warm. Music blares from a car in Senior Alley and I recognize Krista Murphy's silver Taurus gun up toward the exit. Otherwise the parking lot is still. Juliet has melted away somewhere into the landscape of metal and pavement.

I take a breath and exhale a cloud, enjoying the sharp sting of the air on my throat. I'm almost relieved that Juliet is gone. I'm not sure exactly what I would have said to her. And she didn't throw out the flowers, after all. That's a good sign. I stand there for a second more, bouncing on my toes, thinking, *Tonight's the night I'm going to get free of this thing.* Thinking of all the things I'm going to do more of in my life. Go up to Goose Point with Izzy, until she's too old to stand it. Hang out with Elody one-on-one. Drive into New York and go to a Yankees game with Lindsay, and stuff my face with hot dogs and catcall all the players.

Kiss Kent. Really kiss him, slow and long, somewhere outside—maybe while it's snowing. Maybe standing in the woods. He'll lean forward and he'll have little snowflakes on his eyelashes again and he'll brush the hair away from my face and put a warm hand behind my neck, so warm it's almost burning—

"Hey, Sam." Kent's voice.

I spin around with a squeak, tripping on my own feet. Just like with Juliet Sykes, I'm so lost in fantasy about Kent that his actual appearance seems like a dream or wishful thinking. He's wearing an old corduroy blazer with patches sewn onto the elbows like a deranged—and adorable—English teacher. The corduroy looks soft and I get the urge to reach out and touch it, an urge that has nothing to do with my general sense of today and the preciousness of things.

Kent's hands are buried in his pockets, and his shoulders are shrugged toward his ears like he's trying to stay warm. "No calculus today?"

"Um . . . no." I've been waiting to run into him all day, but now my mind is a blank.

"That's too bad." Kent grins at me, jogging on his feet. "You missed some roses." He whips his bag over one shoulder and unzips it, pulling out the cream-and-pink-swirled rose with a gold note card fluttering from one end. "A few of them went back to the office, I think. But I—uh, I wanted to bring this one to you myself. It's a little crushed. Sorry."

"It's not crushed," I say quickly. "It's beautiful."

He bites the edge of his lip—the cutest thing I've ever seen. I think he might be nervous. His eyes are flitting over my face and then away, and each time they land on me it feels like the world is falling away and it's just the two of us in the middle of a bright, green field.

"You didn't miss anything in math," he says, and I recognize a Kent McFuller babble coming on. "I mean, we went over some of the stuff from Wednesday's homework because some people were, like, freaking out about the quiz on Monday. But mostly everyone was a little bit antsy, I think because of Cupid Day, and Daimler didn't really care that—"

"Kent?"

He blinks and shuts up. "Yeah?"

"Did you send me this?" I hold up the rose. "I mean, is it from you?"

His smile gets so big it's like a huge beam of sunshine. "I'll never tell," he says, winking.

I've unconsciously taken several steps toward him, so I can feel the heat coming off his body. I wonder what he would do if I pulled him to me right now, brushed my lips against his the way he did—the way I hope he did—last night. But even the idea sends a flurry of butterflies upward from my stomach, my whole body feeling quivery and uncertain.

At that moment I remember what Ally said to us on the first day, the day it all started: that if a group of butterflies takes off in Thailand it can cause rainstorms in New York. And I think of all the thousands of billions of steps and missteps and chances and coincidences that have brought me here, facing Kent, holding a pink-and-cream-swirled rose, and it feels like the biggest miracle in the world.

"Thank you," I blurt out, and quickly add, "you know . . . for bringing me this."

He ducks his head, looking pleased and embarrassed. "No problem."

"I, um, hear you're having a party tonight?" I'm mentally kicking myself for sounding so lame. In my head, this played out so much easier. In my head, he would lean down and do the thing with his lips again, the soft fluttery thing. I'm desperate to make it all go right again, desperate to get back to that feeling I had last night—*we* had last night, he *must* have felt it—but I'm afraid that anything I say could screw it up. A temporary sadness for what I've lost overwhelms me. Somewhere in the endless spinning of eternity that one, tiny, fraction of a second where our lips met is lost forever.

"Yeah." His face lights up. "Parents out of town, you know. Are you coming?"

"Definitely," I say, so forcefully he looks kind of startled. "I mean," I continue at a normal volume, "it's going to be the place to be, right?"

"Let's hope so." Kent's voice is slow and warm, like syrup, and I wish I could close my eyes and just listen to it. "I got two kegs." He twirls his finger in the air like, *whoop-dee-doo*.

"I would come anyway." I mentally kick myself: what does that even *mean*?

Kent looks like he gets it, though, because he blushes. "Thanks," he says. "I was hoping you would. I mean, I figured you would because you're always at parties, you know, out and stuff, but I didn't know if there was another party or something, or maybe you and your friends do something different on Fridays—"

"Kent?"

He does that adorable quick stop of his mouth. "Yeah?"

I lick my lips, unsure of how to say what I want to, squeezing my hands into fists.

"I—I have something to tell you."

He puckers his forehead. Adorable—how did I not realize how adorable he is?—and not making it any easier.

Deep breaths, in and out. "It's going to sound completely insane, but—"

"Yeah?" He leans even closer, until our lips are less than four inches apart. I can smell peppermint candy on his breath, and my head starts spinning wildly like it's been turned into a gigantic merry-go-round.

"I, um, I—"

"Sam!"

Kent and I both instinctively take one step back as Lindsay shoulders her way out of the cafeteria door, my messenger bag and hers slung over one arm. I'm actually grateful for the interruption, since I was either about to confess that I died a few days ago or that I was falling for him.

Lindsay lumbers over, being really melodramatic about the fact that she's carrying two bags, like they're both made out of iron. "So are we going?"

"What?"

Her eyes flit momentarily over Kent, but other than that she doesn't even acknowledge him. She plants herself almost directly in front of him like he's not even there, like he's not worth her time, and when Kent looks away and pretends not to notice I feel sick. I want to convey, somehow, that she isn't me—that I know he's worth my time. He's better than my time.

"Are we going to The Country's Best Yogurt or what?" She puts a hand on her stomach and makes a face. "I swear to God, those fries gave me bloat that can only be solved by chemical deliciousness."

Kent gives me a quick nod and starts to walk away, no good-bye, no nothing, just trying to get out of there as fast as he can.

I duck around Lindsay and call out, "Bye, Kent! See you later!"

He turns around quickly, surprised, and gives me a huge smile. "Later, Sam." He touches his head, a salute, like one of those guys in an old black-and-white movie, and then he lopes off back into Main.

Lindsay watches him for a minute, then looks at me and narrows her eyes. "What's up with that? Kent stalk you into submission yet?"

"Maybe," I say, because I don't care what Lindsay thinks. I'm buzzing from his smile and being so close to him. I feel light and invincible, the best kind of tipsy.

She stares at me for one beat longer and then just shrugs. "Nothing says 'I love you' like a brick through the window." Then she slips her arm through mine. "Yogurt?"

And that, for all her million and one faults, is why I love Lindsay Edgecombe.

THE ROOT AND BUD

"Come on, Sam." Lindsay's looking up at Kent's house greedily, like it's made out of chocolate. "Your face looks fine."

I'm checking my makeup for the fiftieth time in the flip-down mirror. I put a final slick of lip gloss on and fish a gummy

368

piece of mascara from the corner of my eyelashes, practicing the speech I've rehearsed in my head. *Listen, Kent, this may sound random, but I was wondering if you, you know, wanted to hang out sometime. . . .*

"I don't get it." Ally leans forward from the backseat, her Burberry puffy jacket crackling. "If you're not going to do it with Rob, what are you freaking out about?"

"I'm not freaking out," I say. Despite the fact that I've put on cream blush and moisturizer with a slight tint, I look vampire-pale.

"You're freaking out," Lindsay, Elody, and Ally say at the same time, and then start laughing.

"Sure you don't want a shot?" Ally pokes my shoulder with the vodka bottle.

I shake my head. "I'm good." I'm too nervous to drink, weirdly. Besides, this is the first day of my new beginning. From now on I'm going to do things right. I'm going to be a different person, a good person. I'm going to be the kind of person who would be remembered well, not just remembered. I've been repeating this over and over, and just the idea of it is giving me strength, something solid I can hold on to, a lifeline.

It's helping me beat back the fear and the buzzing sense somewhere deep inside me that I've forgotten to do something, that something's off.

Lindsay puts her arms around me and plants a kiss on my cheek. Her breath smells like vodka and Tic Tacs. "Our very own designated driver," she says. "I feel like an after-school special."

"You *are* an after-school special," Elody says. "The warning kind."

"You should talk, slutsky," Lindsay says, turning around to peg Elody with a tube of lip gloss. Elody catches it and squeals triumphantly, then dabs some on her lips.

"Well, I'm the freezing kind," Ally says. "Can we go in, please?"

"Madame?" Lindsay turns to me, flourishing her hand and bowing slightly.

"All right. Let's do it." I keep on running lines in my head: *You know, catch a movie, or go get something to eat or whatever . . . I know it's been a couple of years since we really talked. . . .*

The party is loud, a giant roar. Maybe it's because I'm sober, but everyone looks ridiculously packed together, hot and uncomfortable, and for the first time in a long time, I feel shy walking in, like people are staring at me. I keep my mind on what I'm here to do: find Kent.

"Crazy." Lindsay leans forward and circles her hand in the air, gesturing to all the people smashed together, moving an inch at a time, like they're all connected by an invisible rope.

We push our way upstairs. Everyone's eyes look bright, like dolls' eyes, from alcohol and maybe other stuff. It's kind of creepy, actually. Even though I've been in school with all these people forever, they look different, unfamiliar, and when they smile at me I just see teeth everywhere, like piranhas getting ready to eat something. I feel like a curtain has dropped away and I'm seeing people for who they really are, different and sharp and unknowable. For the first time in days, I think about the dream I was having for a while, where I'm walking through a party and everyone looks familiar except for one thing, something off. I wonder if the real point of that dream was not that other people were transforming, but that I was. Lindsay keeps one finger jabbed into the small of my back, encouraging me to keep moving, and I'm glad for it. That little point of connection gives me courage.

I push my way into the first room at the top of the stairs, one of the biggest, and my heart drops all the way into my stomach: Kent. He's standing in the corner talking to Phoebe Rifer, and instantly my mind goes fuzzy, a big useless snowstorm. My mouth feels like it's stuffed with cotton and I totally regret not taking at least one shot, just so I won't be so aware of how weird and tall and awkward I feel, like I'm Alice in Wonderland and have gotten too big for the room.

I whirl around to say something to Lindsay—I don't know what, but I need to be *talking* to someone, not just standing there gaping like some kind of overgrown vegetable—but she's vanished. Of course. She must have gone to find Patrick. I ball my hands into fists and close my eyes. That means any second now, in *three, two, one* . . .

"Sam." Rob doesn't put his arms around me, and when I turn around, he's looking down his nose at me like I smell. It's insane, but I've actually *forgotten* he was going to be at the party. I haven't been thinking about him at all. "I didn't think you were going to show."

"Why wouldn't I?" I fold my arms across my chest after Rob flicks his eyes not so subtly down to my boobs.

"You were acting all crazy today." There it is: the slur coming out. "So what? Are you going to apologize?" He grins, lazy and sloppy. "We can figure out a way for you to make it up to me."

Anger bubbles up inside of me. He's looking me up and down like his eyes are fingers and he's trying to touch all of me at once. I can't believe how many nights I spent on his basement couch, letting him slobber on me. Years and years of fantasy fall away in that one second.

"Oh, yeah?" I'm struggling to control my temper, but I can't keep the edge out of my voice. Fortunately, Rob's too drunk to notice. "I'd like that. To make it up to you, I mean."

"Yeah?" Rob's face lights up and he takes a step closer to me, wraps his arms around my waist. I shudder inwardly but force myself to stay put.

"Hmmm." I dance my fingers up his chest, sneaking a glance at Kent, who's still talking to Phoebe. I'm momentarily distracted—Phoebe has the personality of a freaking noodle, for God's sake—but I snap my eyes back to Rob's face and force

myself to flirt. "I think we need a little one-on-one time, don't you?"

"Definitely." Rob lurches a little to one side. "What were you thinking?"

I reach up on my tiptoes so I'm whispering in his ear. "There's a bedroom on this floor. Bumper stickers all over the door. Go inside and wait for me. Wait for me *naked*." I pull away, giving him my sexiest smile. "And I promise to give you the best apology ever."

Rob's eyes are nearly bugging out of his head. "Now?"

"Now."

He detaches himself from me and takes a stumbling step in the direction of the hallway, then something occurs to him and he spins around. "You'll be there soon, right?"

This time there's nothing forced about my smile. "Five minutes," I say, holding up my right hand with my fingers splayed. "I promise."

When I turn away from Rob it's a struggle to keep from bursting out laughing, and all the nervousness I feel about talking to Kent dissipates. I'm ready to march right up to him and shove my tongue down his throat if I have to.

Except that he's gone.

"Shit," I mutter.

"That's no way for a lady to talk." Ally comes up behind me, raising her eyebrows as she takes a swig from the bottle. "What's wrong with you? Attack of the Cokran Crisis?"

373

"Something like that." I rub my forehead. "Have you, um, seen Kent McFuller?"

Ally squints at me. "Who?"

"Kent. McFuller," I say a little louder, and two sophomores whip around and stare at me. I stare right back until they look away.

"The host with the most." Ally raises her bottle. "Why, did you break something already? It's a pretty good party, don't you think?"

"Yeah, good party." I try not to roll my eyes. She's too tipsy to be useful. I gesture toward the back of the house. Lindsay and Elody should be in the back room, and Kent must be close. "Let's circulate."

Ally takes my arm. "Yes, ma'am."

I spot Amy Weiss—probably the biggest gossip in the entire school—making out with Oren Talmadge in the doorway like she's starving and his mouth is stuffed with Cheetos. I drag Ally toward them.

"You want to circulate with *Amy Weiss*?" Ally hisses in my ear. Freshman year Amy spread the rumor that Ally let Fred Dannon and two other boys touch her boobs behind the gym in exchange for a month's worth of math homework. I've never been sure whether the story was true or not—Ally swears it wasn't, Fred swears it was, and Lindsay guesses that Ally only let them look, not touch—but in any case Ally and Amy have been unofficial archnemeses since then.

"Pit stop." I tap Amy's shoulder and she extricates herself from Oren's mouth.

"Hey, Sam." Her face lights up. She glances quickly at Ally, then back to me, snaking her arms around Oren's neck. Oren looks extremely confused, probably wondering what happened to the suckfish on his face. "Sorry. Am I blocking the hallway?"

"Just your butt is," Ally says cheerfully. I squeeze her arm and she yelps. The last thing I need is for Amy and Ally to get into it.

"You know there's a much better spot," I say, "if you and Oren want . . . you know, more *privacy*."

"We want privacy," Oren pipes up.

I smile at him. "Open bedroom. Bumper stickers on the door. *Extra*-soft bed." I raise my fingers to my lips, blow a kiss to Amy. "Have fun."

"What was that about?" Ally explodes as soon as we're out of earshot. "Since when are you and Amy BFF?"

"Long story." I'm feeling good, powerful, and in control. Things are turning out the way they should. I put my hand on the door to Kent's room as I pass it. *Sorry, Rob.*

Ally and I weave through the hallway. I'm scanning the crowd for Kent, ducking into various side rooms, getting more and more frustrated when I don't see him.

We hear someone scream and then there's an explosion of laughter. For a moment my heart stops and I think, *It can't be, not tonight, not again, not Juliet,* but then I hear Oren yell, "Dude, pull your *pants* up, for God's sake." Ally pokes her head out of the doorway of the room we're in and looks back in the direction of Kent's room. Her eyes get so big and round she looks like a cartoon character.

"Um, Sam? You might want to see this."

I peek out into the hallway. Rob is booking it toward the stairs—or trying to, at least. It's a little hard for him to move quickly since he's (a) absolutely surrounded by people gaping at him and (b) more than a little unsteady on his feet—wearing nothing but his boxer shorts and his New Balance sneakers with mismatched socks. And his hat, of course. He's clutching the rest of his clothes in front of his crotch and keeps barking at people, "What the hell are *you* looking at?"

I would feel bad for him if it weren't for the sneakers. Like what, he couldn't be bothered to take them off? He was too busy planning his method of attack on my bra or something? Plus, when he's almost at the stairs, he lurches accidentally into a sophomore, but instead of pulling away he wraps her in a drunken hug. I can't hear what he says, but when she untangles herself I can see she's giggling, like getting mauled by a half-naked, sweaty senior who's blitzed out of his mind is the best thing that's happened to her all day.

"Yup," I say to Ally. "We're definitely broken up. It's official."

She's looking at me strangely. "Kent."

My heart flutters. "What?"

"It's Kent."

My brain taps out again. She knows. It's obvious that I've been completely obsessing over him; maybe Lindsay said something after she found us together outside the cafeteria. "I—the Rob thing has nothing to do with—"

Ally shakes her head, jabs a finger over my shoulder. "Kent. Behind you. Weren't you looking for him earlier?"

Relief washes over me. She doesn't know. Then a tiny twinge of disappointment too. She doesn't know because there's nothing *to* know. *He* doesn't even know. I spin around and search the hall for him.

"In there." Ally points to a door ten feet down the hall. From our angle it's impossible to see more than a few feet into the room, which, from the huge desk blocking over half of the doorway, looks to be a storage space or a study. People are flowing in and out.

"Come on." I haul Ally off again, but she breaks free.

"I'm going to go find Lindsay." She's clearly tired of whatever mission I'm on. I nod and she scoots off toward the back room, using the vodka bottle like a cattle prod, poking people out of her way. A hand clamps down on my arm and I jump.

I turn around: Bridget McGuire and Alex Liment.

"You have Mrs. Harbor for English, right?" She doesn't wait for me to answer before launching into her spiel. "Do you know if she handed out the essay assignments for *Macbeth*? Alex missed. Doctor's appointment."

Because I didn't go with Lindsay for frozen yogurt after all—something was tugging at me, making me want to stay close to school, to the center of things—I'd almost forgotten about Bridget and Anna and Alex. And now the look on Alex's face—the little, crooked smile that used to creep onto Rob's face whenever he'd successfully gotten an extension from one of his teachers for some completely fabricated reason—makes me want to smack him. I think of Anna with her coal-black eye makeup and her improvised lunchroom on the floor of the abandoned bathroom. Even Bridget isn't so bad. Annoying, yes, but pretty and nice and the type of person who probably spends her free time volunteering with sick children.

I can't take it. I can't let him get away with it.

Bridget's still babbling about Alex's mom being a health nut. I interrupt her. "Does anybody smell Chinese food?"

Bridget wrinkles her nose, clearly disappointed that I haven't been listening. "*Chinese* food?"

I make a big show of sniffing. "Yeah. Like, like"—I stare directly at Alex—"like a big bowl of orange beef."

His smile droops a little, but he shrugs and says, "I don't smell anything."

"Oh my God." Bridget cups a hand in front of her mouth. "It's not my breath, is it? I totally had Chinese food last night."

I keep staring at Alex. "What's wrong with you?" I ask, not even bothering to keep the edge out of my voice.

He blinks. "What?"

Bridget looks confused, and for a moment the three of us stand there, not saying anything. Alex and I have locked eyes, and Bridget is looking back and forth between us so rapidly I'm worried her neck's going to snap off.

Then I smile. "You know, *health*-wise. Why did you have to go to the doctor?"

Alex relaxes visibly. "No big deal. My mom wanted me to get some weird shot. And you know, just a general checkup and stuff."

"*Mmm-hmmm*. I hope they were thorough." I shoot a pointed glance at his crotch. Fortunately Bridget is staring at him, watching him turn red, and doesn't see.

"Um. Y-yeah. Pretty much." He squints at me like he's just noticed me for the first time.

"I've been looking for a doctor," I breeze on. I feel bad for Bridget, but at the same time, she deserves to know what her lame excuse for a boyfriend is up to. "It's *so* hard to find a good one, you know? Especially one that doubles as a restaurant with a $4.99 lunch special. That's rare."

"What are you talking about?" Bridget's voice is a squeak. She whips back to Alex. "What is she talking about?"

A muscle is ticking in Alex's jaw. I can tell he wants to curse me out but knows that would make it worse, so he just stands there glaring.

I put my hand on Bridget's arm. "I'm sorry, Bridget. But your boyfriend is really a slimeball."

"What is she talking about?"

Bridget's voice shoots up another octave, and as I walk away I hear Alex start trying to calm her down, no doubt feeding her lies as quickly as he can come up with them. I should feel good about what I've done—he deserves it, after all, and in a weird way I'm only setting things right—but as soon as I walk away I feel strangely deflated. The feeling of control vanishes and in its place comes a tingly feeling of anxiety. I flip back through the day's events like I'm scrolling down a computer screen, trying to find some lapse, something I've forgotten to do or say. Maybe I should have gone to Juliet's house earlier, to check up on her. Then again, I'm not really sure what I would have said. *Hi. Can you verify for me that you're not going to throw yourself in front of any cars tonight? That would be great. No explosives, either. This is* my *life you're playing with.*

The music's so loud, the notes are hardly distinguishable from one another. I fantasize about taking Kent's hand and pulling him away somewhere quiet and dark. The room downstairs, maybe, or the woods, or someplace farther. Maybe we'll just get in the car and drive.

"Sam! Sam!"

I look up. In the back room Lindsay's climbed onto one of the couches, waving at me over the tide of bobbing heads. Ally's next to her, and several feet beyond them I see Elody whispering something to Steve Dough.

I hesitate, a sense of hopelessness washing over me. It's ridiculous for me to talk to Kent. I have no words to describe how wrong I've been about him, about Rob, about everyone. I don't think I can explain to him how I've been changing. And maybe it's all a lie, anyway. Maybe it's impossible to change.

In that moment, while I'm teetering between two doorways, the people around me get all quiet and hushed, faces growing slack. Up on the couch Lindsay falters, her hand flapping uselessly to her side. Next to her, Ally begins opening and shutting her mouth like a fish. The buzzing is all through my body now, like the hum of an electrical wire.

And there she is, marching down the hallway. After all that: Juliet Sykes on a mission.

In a second the despair, the hopelessness, the sense of forgetting things or missing the point somehow, all gets transformed into rage. When she sees Lindsay she stops and opens her mouth, going straight into her "you're a bitch" routine, but I don't even let the first word escape from her mouth before I'm charging forward, grabbing her arm, and half dragging her backward down the hallway. She's too surprised to fight me.

I pull her into the nearest bathroom—"Out," I order two girls who are primping in front of the mirror—and slam the door and lock it. When I turn around to face her she's staring at me like *I'm* the psychopath.

"What are you doing?"

She must misunderstand my question. "It's a party," she says

381

with soft insistence. When she's not busy freaking out and calling me a bitch she has a nice voice, musical like Elody's. "I'm allowed to be here like everybody else."

"No." I shake my head, pressing fingers to my temples to keep them from pounding. "I mean, what are you *really* doing? Why are you here?"

Her eyes flutter to the doorknob behind me. I move over so it's wedged into my lower back. If she wants to get out, she'll have to move me out of the way.

Apparently she doesn't like her chances, because she takes a long, slow breath. "I came to tell you something. You, and Lindsay, and Elody, and Ally."

"Oh, yeah? What's that?"

"You're a bitch," she says quietly, not like an accusation at all, more like something she's sorry about.

At the same time she says it, I say it with her. "I'm a bitch."

She stares at me.

"Listen, Juliet"—I rake my hands through my hair—"I know we haven't always been nice to you or whatever. And I really feel bad about it—I do." I try to gauge what she's thinking, but it's like something has shut down behind her eyes, a button switching off, and she just stands there staring at me dully. I rush on, "The thing is, we never really meant anything by it, you know? I don't think I—we—really thought about it. It's just the kind of thing that happens. People used to make fun of me all the time." She's making me nervous, just staring like that, and

I lick my lips. "*All* the time. And, like, I don't think it's really because people are mean or bad or whatever. I just think . . . I just think . . ." I'm fighting to find the words. Memories are colliding in my head: the sound of people singing as I walked down the hall, the smell of ice cream on Lindsay's breath the day we threw Beth's tampons out the window, riding a horse through a blur of trees. "I just think that people *don't* think. They don't know. We—*I*—didn't know."

I feel pretty proud of myself for getting all of that out. But Juliet hasn't moved or smiled or even freaked out. She's so still she could be carved out of stone. Finally a little tremor goes through her, a personal earthquake, and her eyes seem to focus on me.

"You haven't always been that nice to me?" she says dully, and my stomach sinks. She didn't hear a word I said.

"I—yeah. And I'm sorry about that."

Her eyelids flutter. "In seventh grade you and Lindsay stole all my clothes from the locker room so I had to walk around in my sweaty gym clothes for the rest of the day. Then you called me Stinky Sykes."

"I—I'm sorry. I don't remember that." The way she's staring at me is awful, like she's seeing in and through and beyond me to some void.

"That was before you came up with Psycho, of course." Juliet's voice has lost its musical quality. It's completely tone-less. She raises her arm and mimes slashing a knife through the air, emitting a series of high-pitched shrieks that send chills up and down my arms, and for a moment I think maybe she *is* crazy. Then she drops her arm. "Real funny. *Psycho killer, qu'est-ce que c'est.* Catchy."

"People used to tell this really dumb joke about me. Kind of sing it when I walked by. What's red and white and weird all over . . ." I'm hoping to make her laugh or twitch or something, but she just keeps staring at me with that dumb, animal look on her face, a blank.

"I never sang it," she says, and then, like she's forced to keep reciting everything we ever did, continues. "You took pictures of me when I was showering."

"That was Lindsay," I say automatically, getting more and more uncomfortable. If she would get angry, it would be one thing—but it's like she's not even seeing me, like she's just reading off a list she's looked at a million times.

"You posted the pictures all over the school. Where *teachers* could see."

"We took them down in, like, an hour." I'm ashamed as soon as I say the words. As though the fact that we took them down makes it better.

"You hacked into my Yahoo account. You published my—my private emails."

"That wasn't us," I say quickly, feeling a rush of relief that this, at least, was not our fault. To this day I'm not sure who did hack her account, and circulate email exchanges between Juliet and some guy named Path2Pain118 she'd obviously met in a chat room. There were dozens of emails, all of them long rants about how much high school sucked and how awful everybody was. The hacker had forwarded the emails to almost everyone in school after giving them a new subject line: *Future School Shooters of America.* I shiver, thinking about how easy it is to be totally wrong about people—to see one tiny part of them and confuse it for the whole, to see the cause and think it's the effect or vice versa. And though I've now been at Kent's house five times in six days I feel disoriented, confused by the bright bathroom light and Juliet's impassive face and the sounds of the party coming through the door.

Juliet keeps going on like I didn't even speak. "You started the rumor that I lost my virginity for a pack of cigarettes."

Ally. That was Ally. I can't say it. It doesn't matter, anyway. It was us. It was all of us. Everyone who repeated the story and whispered "slut" and made a smoker's hacking cough whenever she walked by.

"I don't even smoke." She says this with a smile, like this is the funniest thing in the world. Like this, her whole life, is one big joke.

"Juliet—"

"My sister heard that rumor. She told my parents. I—" Finally she loses it a little, balling her hands into fists and squeezing them against her thighs. "I've never even kissed anyone." This comes out as a fierce whisper—a confession—and the intensity of it, the sadness and regret, makes a black well of anger break somewhere inside of me.

"I know, okay? I know we did horrible things. I know we've been shitty and things are bad and—" I break off, the words getting tangled in my throat. I'm on the verge of tears, full of blind fury that hits me like a cloud, blots out everything but a single burning point of frustration: I can't make her see, can't make her see that I'm trying to make things right. I feel like I'm watching both of our lives swirl down the drain, mine and hers, wrapped around each other. "What I'm saying is, I want to make it up to you. I'm trying to *apologize*. Things—things are going to get better."

She presses her lips together, staring at me mute and white-faced, and I have to tense every muscle in my arms to keep from reaching out and grabbing her shoulders, shaking her.

"I mean . . ." I'm going on blindly now, groping, grabbing at words and ideas as they come buzzing up to me through my anger, trying to get through to her. "You got those roses today, right? Like a whole bunch of them?"

An enormous shudder goes through her. And now a light snaps on in her eyes again, but instead of gratitude, there's hatred burning there.

"I knew it. I knew it was you." Her voice is so full of rage and pain I rear back like she's hit me. "What was that? Another one of your little jokes?"

Her reaction is so unexpected it takes me a few seconds to

think of a response. "What? *No.* That wasn't—"

"Poor little Psycho." Juliet narrows her eyes, almost hissing at me. "No friends. No roses. Let's screw with her *one* more time."

"I didn't want to screw with you." I have no idea what's happening or how things have gone so badly wrong. "It was supposed to be nice."

I don't know that she even hears me. She leans closer. "So what was the plan? What were you going to do with that 'secret admirer' crap? Bribe one of your friends so he'd pretend to like me? Ask me out? Maybe even to go to prom? And then— what? On the night that we're supposed to go, he just won't show up? And it will be *so goddamned funny* if I freak out, if I go crazy, if I cry or break down in the hallways when I see him in school." She jerks away. "Sorry to disappoint you, but you're repeating yourselves. Been there, done that. Eighth grade. Spring Fling. Andrew Roberts."

She slumps forward as though her speech has exhausted her, the anger and the burning light disappearing simultaneously, all the expression going out of her face, her hands uncurling.

"Or maybe you didn't have a plan," she says, this time quietly, almost sweetly. "Maybe there was no point to it at all. Maybe you just wanted to remind me that I have nobody, no friends, no secret admirers. 'Maybe next year, but probably not,' right?" She smiles at me again, and it's much worse than her anger.

By this point I'm so frustrated and bewildered I have to

fight back tears. "I swear, Juliet, that wasn't the point. I just—
I thought it would be nice. I thought it would make you feel
better."

"Make me feel better?" She repeats the words as though
she's never heard them before, and now her eyes have a dreamy,
faraway look. Every trace of anger and emotion is gone. She
looks peaceful, even, and I'm struck by how beautiful she
is—up close, just like a supermodel, with that ghostly pale skin
and those huge blue eyes, the color of the sky very early in the
morning.

"You don't know me," she says in little more than a whisper.
"You never knew me. And you can't make me better. Nobody
can make me better."

This reminds me of what I said to Kent only two days ago—
I don't think I can be fixed—but now I know I was wrong.
Everyone can be fixed; it has to be that way, it's the only thing
that makes sense. I'm trying to figure out a way to tell Juliet
this, to convince her of it, but very calmly, and with that floating grace she's always had, she puts her hand on one of my
arms and moves me gently but firmly out of the way, and I
find myself stepping aside and letting her reach for the door
handle. The tears are pushing at the back of my throat, and I'm
still struggling for words, and the whole time it's like her face
is growing paler and paler, glowing almost, like the sheer white
point of a flame; and I have this idea that I'm already seeing her
sputter out, her life flickering in front of me, a TV on static.

She pauses with her hand on the door, staring directly in front of her.

"You know, I used to be friends with Lindsay." She's still speaking in that horrible, calm voice, as though she's talking from a distance of miles and miles. "When we were younger we did everything together. I still have a friendship necklace she gave me, one of those hearts split down the middle. When you put them together the necklace spelled 'Best Friends Forever.'"

I want to ask what happened, why they stopped being friends, but the words are stuck behind the lump in my throat. And I'm scared of interrupting. As long as Juliet's talking to me, she's safe.

"That was right before her parents got divorced." Juliet shoots a quick glance in my direction, but her eyes seem to go directly over my face without actually registering it. "She was so sad all the time. I used to go to her house for sleepovers, and her parents would be arguing so badly we'd have to hide under her bed and stuff pillows everywhere to muffle the sound. She called it 'building a fort.' She was always like that, you know, always trying to make the best of things. But when she thought I was asleep, she would cry and cry and cry. She started having nightmares, too. Really bad ones. She'd wake up screaming in the middle of the night."

Juliet's staring at the door again, smiling a little. I wish I could walk back into her memories and see what she's seeing, fix whatever is broken there. "She started to wet her bed again, you know? Because everything was so bad with her mom and dad. She was humiliated, of course. She swore me to secrecy—said she'd never speak to me again if I told anybody. We used to wake up in the morning and some of the pillows in the fort would be damp. I would pretend not to notice. One morning I came into the bathroom to brush my teeth, and she was sitting in the tub, scrubbing a pillow with so much bleach it made my eyes sting. She must have been scrubbing for half an hour. The pillow was all white-splotched and ruined, and her fingers were raw and red. They were burned, almost. But it's like she couldn't even see it. She just wanted it to be *clean*."

I close my eyes, feeling the floor sway underneath me, remembering coming into the bathroom of Rosalita's and seeing Lindsay on her knees, the chunks of food in the toilet. The mixture of shame and anger and defiance on her face.

"One time the fighting got so bad we even ran away from her house. We were only seven or eight, but we walked all the way to my house. It was March and pretty cold. The plan was for Lindsay to move into my room. I wasn't going to tell anyone, just keep her safe and bring her food. Mostly she wanted gummy bears and Snickers bars. She loved chocolate then, and candy. Anything sweet, really."

Without meaning to, I let out a little, strangled sound. I don't know if I can listen anymore. I have the feeling that this is it:

this bathroom, this story. That this is the root and bud of it all, the beginning and the end.

But Juliet keeps going in that strange, measured tone, as though we have all the time in the world. "Of course it didn't work. We got upstairs and into the bedroom, but then we started arguing about who should sleep in the little trundle bed and who should get the big one, and my mom heard us. She was horrified that we'd walked all that way. She was screaming and crying that we could have been kidnapped or killed or whatever. I remember being really embarrassed." Juliet turns her hands upward, stares at her palms. "It was nothing compared to Lindsay's freak-out, though, when my mom said she had to go home. I've never heard anyone scream that loudly."

She's silent for so long I think she's done. Her words keep buzzing in my head, flitting around and arranging themselves like clues in a crossword puzzle. *She was always like that, you know, always trying to make the best of things. . . . She must have been scrubbing for half an hour. . . . Her fingers were raw and red.* I feel like I'm on the verge of understanding something I'm not sure I want to know. The room feels tiny and stifling. There's a crushing weight on my chest. I'm tempted to make a run for it, push past her into the party and go get a beer and forget about Juliet, forget about everything. But I'm rooted where I am. I *can't* move. I keep seeing the endless darkness of my dream rising in front of me. I can't go back to it.

"It's funny when you think about it," Juliet says. "We did everything together, Lindsay and me. We even joined Girl Scouts together. It was her idea. I didn't want to do all that— cookies and campfires and stuff. We went away on a camping trip at the beginning of fifth grade. We slept in the same tent, of course."

I watch Juliet's hands. They're trembling ever so slightly but so quickly you can barely see it, like the wings of a humming-bird. Out of the corner of her eye Juliet catches me looking, and she brings her hands down to her thighs, gracefully but with finality.

"You remember the name they gave me in fifth grade, right? The name Lindsay gave me? Mellow Yellow?" She shakes her head. "I used to *dream* that name, I heard it so often. Sometimes I forgot what my real name was."

She turns to me and her face is radiant, almost glowing, gor-geous. "The funny thing is, it wasn't even me. Lindsay was the one who wet her sleeping bag. In the morning the whole tent smelled. But when Ms. Bridges came in and asked what had happened Lindsay just pointed her finger at me and screamed, *She did it.* I'll never forget her face when she screamed it—*She did it!* Terrified. Like I was a wild dog and I was going to bite her."

I press back against the door, grateful for something to lean on. It makes perfect sense, of course. It *all* makes perfect sense now: Lindsay's anger, the way she always held up her fingers in the shape of a cross to ward Juliet Sykes off. She doesn't *hate* her. She's afraid of her. Juliet Sykes, the keeper of Lindsay's oldest, maybe her worst, secret.

And it all seems absurd now, the chance and randomness of it. One person shoots up and the other spirals downward— random and meaningless. As simple as being in the right place, or the wrong place, or however you want to look at it. As simple as getting a craving for Diet Pepsi one day at a pool party, and getting swept away; as simple as not saying no.

"Why didn't you say anything?" I ask, even though I already know the answer. My voice comes out hoarse from the effort of swallowing back tears.

Juliet shrugs. "She was my best friend, you know? She was always so sad back then." Juliet makes a noise that could be a laugh or a whimper. "Besides," she says more quietly, "I thought it would pass."

"Juliet—" I start to say.

She shakes her shoulders like she's brushing off the weight of everything, the conversation, the past. "It doesn't matter now," she says quickly, and just like that she snaps the door open and slips out.

"Juliet!"

There's a huge clot of people standing by the door, and when I come out I'm pressed backward momentarily as two juniors scuffle for the bathroom, both of them yelling, drunk. "I was here first!" "No, I was!" "You just got here!" A few people give me dirty looks, and then Bridget McGuire charges past all of them, face red and blotchy and tear-streaked. When she sees me she sobs out, "You—" but she doesn't finish her sentence, just swoops around the juniors and locks herself in the bathroom.

"Jesus Christ, not again," someone yells.

"I'm going to pee my pants," one of the juniors moans, crossing her legs and hopping up and down.

Alex Liment is right behind Bridget. He pushes up to the bathroom door and begins rapping on it, calling for her to come out. I still haven't moved. I'm pressed up against the wall, penned in by people, paralyzed by how wrong everything is. I remember a story I once heard about drowning: that when you fall into cold water it's not that you drown right away but that the cold disorients you and makes you think that down is up and up is down, so you may be swimming, swimming, swimming for your life in the wrong direction, all the way toward the bottom until you sink. That's how I feel, as though everything has been turned around.

"You're really unbelievable."

I'm suddenly aware that Alex is talking to me. His lips are curled back, showing all his teeth.

"You know what you are?" He puts one hand on either side of my head so he's blocking me in. I can see sweat on his forehead and smell weed and beer on his breath. "You, Samantha Kingston, are a bitch."

Hearing that jolts me, wakes me up. I have to focus. Juliet is off somewhere in the woods, in the cold. She's probably making for the road. I can still find her, talk to her, get her to *see*.

I put both hands on Alex's chest and shove him. He stumbles backward.

"I've heard it before," I say. "Trust me."

I force my way through the hallway and am halfway down the stairs when someone calls my name. I stop dead so that the people behind me bump each other like dominoes and start cursing at me.

"Jesus Christ, *what*?" I whirl around and see Kent, who leapfrogs over the banister and swings down onto the stairs, nearly taking out Hanna Gordon.

"You came." He lands two stairs above me, a little out of breath. His eyes are bright and happy. His hair is falling over his forehead, picking up light from the Christmas bulbs strung everywhere, bits of it the color of chocolate and some of it caramel. I have an almost uncontrollable urge to reach over and push it back behind his ears.

"I said I would, didn't I?" There's a dull pain unfurling in my stomach. All I wanted all night—all day—was to be standing this close to him. And now I have no time. "Listen, Kent—"

"I mean, I thought you were probably here when I saw Lindsay, et al. You guys usually travel in packs, you know? But then I was looking for you—" He stops himself, blushes. "I mean, not *actively* looking. Really just kind of perusing the

395

crowd, you know, as I was walking around socializing. That's what you're supposed to do when you host. Socialize. So I was just keeping an eye out—"

"Kent." My voice comes out sharp, mean, and I close my eyes just for a second, imagining what it felt like to lie with him in total darkness, imagining the touch of his hand on mine. It suddenly occurs to me how impossible all of this is—with me and him. When I open my eyes he's just standing there, waiting, a little crease in his forehead: so adorable and normal, the kind of guy who deserves the kind of girl who wears cashmere sweaters and is really good at crossword puzzles, or plays the violin, or volunteers at soup kitchens. Someone nice and normal and honest. The pain in my stomach intensifies, as though something's caught in there, snapping away at my insides. I could never be good enough for him. Even if I lived the same day into infinity, I could never be good enough.

"I'm sorry," I force myself to say. "I—I can't talk to you right now."

"But—" He tucks his hands into the cuffs of his shirt, looking uncertain.

"I'm sorry." It's better, I almost say, but I figure there's no point. I don't look back, either, even though I can feel him watching me.

Outside I pull on my fleece, zipping it all the way up to my chin. The rain drives down my neck and spots my leggings immediately. At least tonight I'm wearing flats. I stick to the driveway. The pavement is icy and I have to reach out and brace myself against the cars as I pass. The cold tears at my lungs, and it's so strange, but in the middle of all this I have the stupidest, simplest thought—*I should really jog more*—and as soon as I think it I almost come undone, torn with the dual desire to laugh and to cry. But the thought of Juliet crouching by Route 9, watching the cars whiz past, waiting for Lindsay, keeps me going.

Eventually the sounds of the party drop away, and then it's silent except for the driving rain, like thousands of tiny shards of glass falling on the pavement, and my footsteps ringing out. It's dark, too, and I have to slow down, moving from one car to the next with my hands, the metal so cold under my fingers it feels hot. When I find the Tank, hulking above all the others, I fish through my bag until my fingers close around cold metal and a rhinestone-encrusted key chain that reads BAD GIRL. Lindsay's car keys. I blow air out of my cheeks. This, at least, is a good thing. There's no way Lindsay can leave without me. Her car won't be on the road tonight, no matter how long Juliet waits. Still, I lock and double-lock the doors.

Then the cars drop away, too, and I shuffle forward at a crawl, mentally cursing myself for not bringing a flashlight, cursing February 12, cursing Juliet Sykes. I see now that the roses were a stupid idea, an insult, even. I think of Juliet and Lindsay all those years ago in a tent, when Lindsay raised a finger and pointed, terrified, humiliated, and it all began.

And for years Juliet kept Lindsay's secret. *I thought it would pass.*

At the same time the more I think about it—the rain beating furiously—the angrier I get. This is my *life*: the whole big, sprawling mess of my life in all its possibilities—first kisses and last kisses and college and apartments and marriage and fights and apologies and *happiness*—brought to a point, a second, an edge of a second, razored off in that final moment by Juliet's last act: her revenge against us, against me. The farther I get from the party, the more I think, *No. It can't happen this way. No matter what we did, it can't happen this way.*

Then the driveway opens up suddenly, and Route 9 is there, shining ahead of me like a river, liquid silver lit up by pools of light. I don't even realize I've been holding my breath until I exhale and I'm gasping, grateful for the light.

I wipe the rain out of my eyes and turn left, scanning the edge of the woods for Juliet. A little part of me is hoping that talking to me did make her feel better—maybe she went home, after all, maybe it meant something. At the same time, the way that she spoke in that low, flat voice comes back to me, and I know that wherever she was in that bathroom, it wasn't with me. She was lost somewhere, trapped in a fog, maybe of memories, maybe of all the things that could have happened differently.

A car roars behind me, making me jump. On the landing I

lose my footing and go on hands and knees to the ice as the car speeds by, followed closely by a second car, its engine as loud as thunder. Then honking, waves of sound rolling toward me, getting louder and louder. I look up and see the headlights of a car bearing down on me. I try to move and can't. I try to scream and can't. I'm frozen, the headlights growing as big as moons, floating there. At the last second the car swerves a little, passing so close to me I can feel the heat of the engine and smell the exhaust and hear a line of music pumping from the radio. *Light it, blaze it, tear it up.* Then it's gone, still honking, passing away into the night as the bass from the speakers grows dimmer and dimmer, a distant pulse.

My palms are cut up from the pavement, and my heart is pounding so quickly I'm pretty sure it's going to leap out of my chest. Slowly, shaking, I stand up. Another car passes on the other side of the road, this one at a crawl, water from its tires pinwheeling in both directions.

And then, fifty feet ahead of me, I see a figure in white emerge from the woods, unfolding from a crouch like a long, pale flower. Juliet. I start going toward her, slowly now, trying to avoid the slick patches of dark ice. She stands there, perfectly still, like she doesn't even feel the rain. At a certain point she even lifts up her arms, parallel to the ground, as though preparing to take a dive off the high board. There's something beautiful and terrifying about seeing her in that position. It reminds me of when I was little and we would go to church on

Christmas and Easter, and I was always afraid to look at the pulpit, where there was a wooden statue of Jesus mounted on the cross.

"Juliet!"

She doesn't respond; I'm not sure if she doesn't hear or is just ignoring me. I'm fifteen feet away, then ten. There's a low rumbling behind me. I turn and see a big truck bearing down through the darkness. Again I have a random thought—*he should totally have his license suspended, he's going way too fast*—and when I turn around again I see that Juliet is staring up the road, tensed, arms at her thighs, and she reminds me of something, but it takes me a second to realize what it is, just like it takes me a second to realize what's going on—*she looks like a dog about to go after a bird*—and then everything clicks together, and as she begins to move, a white blur, I'm moving too, running as fast as I can and closing the distance between us as she's sprinting out across the nearest lane. The truck blasts its horn, a sound so large it seems to fill the air with vibration, and then I slam into her with all my weight, and we roll, tumbling, backward into the woods. I'm screaming and she's screaming and pain blooms in my shoulder. I roll over onto my back, the black branches overhead a thick net.

"What are you *doing*?" Juliet's yelling, and when I sit up her face has finally lost its composure and is twisted with anger. "What the hell are you doing?"

"What am *I* doing?" My anger flares up too. "What are *you* doing? Jumping in front of random trucks—I thought the whole *point* was to wait for Lindsay—"

"Lindsay? Lindsay Edgecombe?" Juliet's anger drops away and she looks completely confused. She brings her hands up to her head, squeezing. "I don't know what you're talking about."

I'm suddenly uncertain. "I—I thought. You know, like this was your big revenge—"

Juliet laughs, but there's no humor in it. "Revenge?" She shakes her head, and again that veil seems to drop over her face. "Sorry, Sam. For once this isn't about you." She stands up, not bothering to wipe off the thick tracks of mud and leaves that are clinging to her. "Now please leave me alone."

My head is spinning and I'm having trouble focusing on her, like we're separated by miles instead of a few feet. The rain is coming down harder now, jagged pellets of it. Little snatches of things are whirling around in my head: Lindsay patting the hood of the Tank proudly, saying, "I could go head-to-head with an eighteen-wheeler and never feel it"; the owner of Dunkin' Donuts calling out, "That's not a car, it's a truck"; the randomness of things, the way everything can change in a second; the right place at the right time, or at the wrong time; time; that enormous truck coming at us, its big metal grill shining like teeth, the impression of lights and hugeness. The only thing you can see: headlights, size, a sense of power. Not revenge. Chance. Stupid, dumb, blind chance. Just a part of the strange mechanism of the world, with its fits and coughs and starts and random collisions.

"But why . . . ?" I struggle to my feet. "Why did you come here? What was the point?"

She doesn't look at me, but she shrugs slightly. "There was no point, really. I just wanted to say it. I was always afraid to say it before—what I really thought of you. I'm not afraid anymore. Of you, of anybody, of anything. I'm not even afraid of—" She breaks off, but I know what she was going to say. *Not even afraid of dying.*

But I know what she's saying isn't totally true. Her decision to come to the party was more than that. Things are clicking into place, making a horrible kind of sense: she needed us here, needed that final push. I close my eyes against the memory of a wet and stumbling Juliet being shoved from person to person like a pinball. And tonight, I guess, she just needed to tell her story—needed to remember how bad things have been. I wonder if the day when we all slept over at Ally's—the day that things ended differently for her, the day that they ended alone, with a gun—it took her longer to work up the courage. If she came to the party, unnoticed, ignored, and found she didn't have the strength to go through with it. If later that night she sat and stared at the gun in her lap, and conjured up the faces of all the people who'd tormented her over the years.

Vicky Hallinan's face hovers in the darkness suddenly,

twisted into a grimace, and I snap my eyes open. Maybe before you die it's your ghosts that you see.

"This isn't the way," I say weakly, feeling like the rain has seeped into my brain and made it soggy and useless. I can't remember anything I was planning to say to her. I repeat it a little louder. "This isn't the way."

"Please," Juliet says quietly. "I just want to be alone."

"What about your family?" I say, my voice rising hysterically as I realize I'm losing her again, losing my chance. "What about your sister?"

She doesn't answer me. She's staring at the road, still. The rain has soaked her shirt so I can see her shoulder blades jutting out of her back like the wings of a baby bird, and I think of the moment when Ally's mom came into the den and told us, "Juliet Sykes shot herself," and I thought it was so wrong— that she, of all people, should have jumped or leaped or fallen through the sky. I again have the fantasy I did then, that she'll suddenly sprout wings and go soaring up into the air, out of harm's way.

The road has been unusually clear of traffic, but now from both directions I make out the growl of engines. Loud ones. Big ones.

"Juliet." I take a step forward and grab her arm tightly. "I can't let you do this."

She turns to me, staring at me with eyes so empty it takes my breath away. They're pools, liquid, nothing. Looking at her reminds me of that stitched-together mask with the holes cut away for eyes: monstrous, deformed, patched together, with eyes that look into and look out at nothing. I'm so startled I loosen my grip. There's a roaring in my ears, and I dimly have a sense of cars, but I'm transfixed. I can't stop staring at her.

"It's too late," she says, and in that second when I'm not holding on tightly enough she wrenches away from me and hurtles onto the road just as two vans converge, about to pass each other, and all I see is the shine of metal and something white suddenly launched into the air, and for a second I feel an overwhelming sense of joy, and I think she's done it, she's flying, and time seems to stop with her glittering in the air like a beautiful bird. But then time resumes, and the air doesn't hold her, and as she drops there's a piercing sound splitting the darkness and again it takes me a long time to realize it's me, screaming.

GHOSTS AND HEAVEN

An hour and a half later I'm parked in Lindsay's driveway, and the two of us are watching the rain turn to snow, watching the world go quiet as, in a moment, thousands of raindrops seem to freeze in the air and come drifting silently to earth. I've already dropped off Elody and Ally. On the way home from the party nobody spoke. Elody leaned back against the seat, pretending to sleep, but at one point I glanced in the rearview mirror and saw the glitter of her eyes, watching me.

"Jesus. What a night." Lindsay leans her forehead on the window. "So crazy, you know? I never would have thought . . . I mean, she was obviously screwed up, but I didn't ever think she would . . ." She shivers, shoots a look at me. "And you were *there*."

When the police came, and the ambulances—followed by all the people at Kent's party, drifting through the woods, quiet, suddenly sober, attracted by the sound of the sirens like moths to a flame—they found me standing by the side of the road, still staring. I'd even been interviewed by a female police officer with a big mole exactly at the point of her chin, which I had focused on like a single star in a dark sky, something to orient me.

Was she drunk?

No.

Was she on anything else? Don't be afraid to tell me.

No. At least—I don't think so.

Lindsay licks her lips, fidgets her hands in her lap. "And she didn't . . . she didn't, like, *say* anything? She didn't explain?"

It's the same thing the police officer asked me earlier: the final question, maybe the only one that matters. *Did she say anything to you? Anything at all to give you a sense of how she was feeling, what she was thinking?*

I don't think she was feeling much of anything.

To Lindsay I say, "I'm not sure it's the kind of thing you can explain."

She keeps pressing it. "But I mean, she must have had problems, right? Stuff at home, right? People don't just *do* that."

I think of Juliet's cold, dark house, the TV shadows climbing the walls, the unknown couple in the hard silver frame.

"I don't know," I say. I look at Lindsay, but she keeps her eyes averted. "I guess we'll never know now."

I feel a sense of emptiness so deep it stops feeling like emptiness and starts feeling like relief. I imagine this is what it would be like to get carried off on a wave. This is what it would feel like in the moment that the thin, dark edge of shore ducks its head beyond the horizon, when you roll over and see only stars and sky and water, folding in on you like an embrace. When you spread your arms and think, *Okay*.

"Thanks for dropping me off." Lindsay puts her hand on the door handle, but makes no further motion to get out. "Are you sure you're going to be okay?"

"I'll be okay."

I watch patterns of snow coming down at an angle as though flowing, cresting, breaking on a massive current, a tide that leaves the world glittering. It's beautiful. All I can think is that it's the first of many things Juliet won't see.

Lindsay is chewing on a nail, a habit she's always claiming to have kicked in third grade. The automatic garage light has clicked on and her features are all dark.

"Lindsay?"

She jumps like we've been silent for hours and she's shocked to see me still in the car. "What?"

"Remember that time in Rosalita's? After you came back from New York? When I walked in on you in the bathroom?"

She turns to stare at me, not saying anything. Her eyes are a deeper dark than the rest of her face, two spots of total blackness.

"Was that really the only time?" I ask.

She hesitates for just a second. "Of course it was," she says, but her voice is a whisper and I know she's lying.

And now I realize Lindsay's not fearless. She's terrified. She's terrified that people will find out she's faking, bullshitting her way through life, pretending to have everything together when really she's just floundering like the rest of us. Lindsay, who will bite at you if you even look in her direction the wrong way, like one of those tiny attack dogs that are always barking and snapping in the air before they're jerked backward on the chains that keep them in one place.

Millions of individual snowflakes, spinning and twirling and looking, all together, like rolling waves of white. I wonder if it's true that they're all different. "Juliet told me." I lean back against the headrest and squint so that everything disappears but the whiteness. "About the Girl Scout trip. When you were in fifth grade—when you were still friends."

Lindsay's still not saying anything, but I can feel her trembling a little next to me.

"She told me it was really you who—*you* know."

"And you believed her?" Lindsay says quickly, but she does it automatically, dully, as though she doesn't expect it to do any good.

I ignore her. "Remember how everybody used to call her Mellow Yellow after that?" I open my eyes and look at her. "Why did you tell everyone it was her? I mean, in the moment, okay, I get it, you were scared, you were embarrassed, but afterward . . . ? Why did you tell *everyone*? Why did you *spread* it?"

Lindsay's shaking is getting worse now, and for a second I think she won't answer, or she'll lie. But her voice is steady when she speaks, steady and filled with something I don't recognize. Regret, maybe.

"I always thought it wouldn't last." She sounds as if it still amazes her after all these years. "I thought eventually she'd tell everybody what really happened. That she would stick up for herself, you know?" Her voice breaks a little, a note of hysteria creeping in. "Why didn't she ever stick up for herself? Not once. She just—she just *took* it. Why?"

I think of all the years that Lindsay's been holding on to this secret knowledge, this secret self who cried every night and scrubbed pillows clean of pee—the scariest secret of all, the past we're trying to forget.

And I think of all the times I sat in squirming silence, terrified I would say or do the wrong thing, terrified the dorky, lanky, horseback-riding loser inside me would rise up and swallow the new me, like a snake feasting on something. How I cleared the shelves of my trophies and dumped my beanbag chair and learned how to dress and never ate the hot lunch, and, above all, learned to stay away from the people who would drag me down, and carry me back to that place. People like Juliet Sykes. People like Kent.

Lindsay rouses herself and pops the door open. I cut the engine and get out of the car with her, throwing the keys over the roof. She catches them in one hand. Headlights flare to life, and I turn, squinting, holding up a hand in the general direction of the car idling behind me. I mouth, "Two minutes."

Lindsay nods toward Kent, who is parked behind us, waiting to drive me home. "You're sure you're all good? To get home and everything, I mean."

"I'm sure," I say. Despite everything that has happened tonight, the thought of sitting next to Kent for a whole twelve minutes on the way to my house fills me with warmth. Even though I know it's not right—even if I know, somewhere deep inside me, that it won't work out, that it can't work out for me with anyone anymore.

Lindsay opens her mouth and closes it. I can tell she wants to ask about Kent but thinks better of it. She starts to walk up toward the house, hesitates, and turns.

"Sam?"

"Yeah?"

"I'm really sorry. I'm really sorry about . . . everything."

She wants me to tell her it's okay. She needs me to tell her that. I can't, though. Instead I say, quietly, "People would like you anyway, Lindz." I don't say, *if you stopped pretending so much*, but I know she understands. "We'd still love you no matter what."

She balls up her fists and squeezes out, "Thanks." Then she turns and heads up to the house. For a second the light falling on her face makes her skin look wet, but I'm not sure whether she's crying or whether it's the snow.

Kent leans over and opens the door for me and I slide in. We back away from Lindsay's house and turn onto the main road in silence. He drives slowly, carefully, twin funnels of snow lit up by the headlights, both hands resting lightly on the steering wheel. There's so much I want to say to him, but I can't bring myself to speak. I'm tired and my head hurts, and I just want to enjoy the fact that there's only a few inches separating our arms, the fact that his car smells like cinnamon, the fact that he has the heat on high for me. It makes me feel drowsy and heavy in my limbs, even as my insides are alive and fluttering and 100 percent aware of him, so close.

As we get near my house he slows down so we're barely crawling, and I'm hoping it's because he doesn't want the drive to end either. This is the moment for time to stop, right here— for space to yawn open and fall away like it does at the lip of a black hole, so that time can do its endless loops and keep us forever going forward into the snow. But no matter how slowly Kent goes, the car moves forward.

Soon my street sign appears crookedly on the left, and then we're passing the darkened houses of my neighbors, and then we're at my house.

"Thanks for driving me home," I say, turning to him as he turns to me and says, "Are you sure you'll be okay?"

We both laugh nervously. Kent pushes his bangs away from his eyes, and they immediately flop back into place, making my stomach dip.

"No problem," he says. "It was my pleasure."

It was my pleasure. Only Kent could say it and make it not sound like something cheesy from an old movie, and my heart aches frantically for a second as I think of all the time I wasted, seconds and hours spun out of my fingertips forever like snow into the dark.

We sit for a minute. I'm desperate to say something, anything, so I don't have to get out of the car, but the words don't come and the seconds run by.

Finally I blurt out, "Everything tonight was awful except for this."

"Except for what?"

I tick my index finger once between us. You and me. Everything was awful except for this.

A light comes on in his eyes. "Sam." He says my name once, just breathes it, and I never knew that a single syllable could transform my whole body into a dancing, glowing thing. He reaches out suddenly and puts a warm hand on either side of my face, tracing my eyebrows, his thumb resting lightly for one single miraculous second on my bottom lip—I'm tasting cinnamon on his skin—and then he drops his hand and pulls away, looking embarrassed.

"Sorry," he mumbles.

"No . . . it's okay." My body is humming. He must be able to hear it. At the same time it feels like my head is going to lift off from my shoulders.

"It's just . . . God, it's so awful."

"What's so awful?" My body abruptly stops humming and my stomach goes leaden. He's going to tell me he doesn't like me. He's going to tell me he sees through me again.

"I mean, with everything that happened tonight . . . it's not the right time . . . and you're with Rob."

"I'm not with Rob," I say quickly. "Not anymore."

"You're not?" He's staring at me so intensely I can see the stripes of gold alternating with the green in his eyes like spokes of a wheel.

I shake my head.

"That's a good thing." He's still staring at me like that, like he's the first and last person who will ever stare at me. "Because . . ." His voice trails off, and his eyes travel slowly down to my lips, and there's so much heat roaring through my body I swear I'm going to pass out.

"Because?" I prompt him, surprised I can still speak.

"Because I'm sorry, but I can't help it, and I really need to kiss you right now."

He puts one hand behind my neck and pulls me toward him. And then we're kissing. His lips are soft and leave mine tingling. I close my eyes, and in the darkness behind them I see beautiful blooming things, flowers spinning like snowflakes, and hummingbirds beating the same rhythm as my heart. I'm gone, lost, floating away into nothingness like I am in my dream, but this time it's a good feeling—like soaring, like being totally free. His other hand pushes my hair from my face, and I can feel the impression of his fingers everywhere that they touch, and I think of stars streaking through the sky and leaving burning trails behind them, and in that moment—however long it lasts, seconds, minutes, days—while he's saying my name into my mouth and I'm breathing into him, I realize this, right here, is the first and only time I've ever been kissed in my life.

He pulls away too soon, still cupping my face. "Wow," he says, out of breath. "Sorry. But wow."

"Yeah." The word catches in my throat.

We stay there like that, staring at each other, and for once I'm not feeling anxious or worried about what he's thinking. I'm just happy, held in his eyes, buoyed up in a warm, bright place.

"I really like you, Sam," he says quietly. "I always have."

"I like you too." Don't worry about tomorrow. Don't even think about it. I shut my eyes briefly, pushing away everything but this moment, his warm hands, those delicious green eyes, the lips.

"Come on." He leans forward and kisses my forehead once, gently. "You're tired. You need to sleep."

He gets out of the car and scoots around to the passenger side to open the door for me. The snow has begun to stick, a blanket over everything, blurring the edges of the world. Our footsteps are muffled as we make our way up the front path and onto the porch. My parents have left the porch light on, the only light in a dark house on a dark street—maybe the only light in the world. In its glow the snow looks like falling stars.

"You have snow in your eyelashes." Kent traces a finger over my eyelids and over the bridge of my nose, making me shiver. "And in your hair." A hand fluttering, the feel of fingertips, a cupped palm on my neck. Heaven.

"Kent." I wrap my fingers around the collar of his shirt. No matter how close he's standing, it isn't close enough. "Are you ever afraid to go to sleep? Afraid of what comes next?"

He smiles a sad little smile and I swear it's like he *knows*. "Sometimes I'm afraid of what I'm leaving behind," he says.

Then we're kissing again, our bodies and mouths moving together so seamlessly it's like we're not even kissing, just thinking about kissing, thinking about breathing, everything right and natural and unconscious and relaxed, a feeling not of

414

trying but of complete abandonment, letting go, and right then and there the unthinkable and impossible happens: time does stand still after all. Time and space recede and blast away like a universe expanding forever outward, leaving only darkness and the two of us on its periphery, darkness and breathing and touch.

SEVEN

The last time I have the dream it goes like this: I am falling, tumbling through the air, but this time the darkness is alive around me, full of beating things, and I realize that I'm not surrounded by dark but have only had my eyes closed all this time. I open them, feeling silly, and at the same time a hundred thousand butterflies take off around me, so many of them in so many brilliant colors they are like a solid rainbow, temporarily obscuring the sun. But as they wing higher and higher they reveal a landscape below us, all green and gold and sun-drenched fields and pink-tinged clouds drifting underneath me, and the air around me is clear and blue and sweet smelling, and I'm laughing, laughing, laughing as I spin through the air because, of course, I haven't been falling all this time.

I've been flying.

And when I wake up it's wonderful, like I've been carried quietly onto a calm, peaceful shore, and the dream, and its meaning, has broken over me like a wave and is ebbing away now, leaving me with a single, solid certainty. I know now.

It was never about saving my life.
Not, at least, in the way that I thought.

AND ON THE SEVENTH DAY

I remember I once saw this old movie with Lindsay; in it the main character was talking about how sad it is that the last time you have sex you don't know it's the last time. Since I've never even had a first time, I'm not exactly an expert, but I'm guessing it's like that for most things in life—the last kiss, the last laugh, the last cup of coffee, the last sunset, the last time you jump through a sprinkler or eat an ice-cream cone, or stick your tongue out to catch a snowflake. You just don't know.

But I think that's a good thing, really, because if you did know it would be almost impossible to let go. When you do know, it's like being asked to step off the edge of a cliff: all you want to do is get down on your hands and knees and kiss the solid ground, smell it, hold on to it.

I guess that's what saying good-bye is always like—like jumping off an edge. The worst part is making the choice to do it. Once you're in the air, there's nothing you can do but let go.

Here is the last thing I ever say to my parents: *See you later.* I say, *I love you,* too, but that's earlier. The last thing I say is, *See you later.*

Or actually, to be completely accurate, the last thing I say to my father is, *See you later.* To my mother I say, *Positive*, because she's standing in the kitchen doorway holding the newspaper, her hair messy, her bathrobe hanging wrong, and she says, *Are you sure you don't want breakfast?* Like she always does.

I look back when I'm at the front door. Behind her my father is at the stove, humming to himself and burning eggs for my mother's breakfast. He's wearing the striped pajama pants Izzy and I got him for his last birthday, and his hair is sticking out at crazy angles like he's just put a finger in an electrical socket. My mom puts a hand on his back while she squeezes past him, then settles at the kitchen table, shaking out the newspaper. He scoops the eggs onto a plate and sets it in front of her, saying, "Voilà, madame. Extra crispy," and she shakes her head and says something I can't hear, but she's smiling, and he leans down and kisses her once on the forehead.

It's a nice thing to see. I'm glad I was looking.

Izzy follows me to the door with my gloves, grinning at me and showing off the gap between her two front teeth. A feeling of vertigo overwhelms me when I look at her, a nauseous feeling lashing in my stomach, but I take a deep breath and think of counting steps, think of running leaps, and my dream of flying.

One, two, three, jump.

"You forgot your gloves." Lisping, smiling, wisps of golden hair.

"What would I do without you?" I crouch down and squeeze her in a hug, as I do seeing our whole life together: her tiny infant toes and scalp that smelled like baby powder; the first time she tottered over to me; the first time she rode a bike and fell and scraped her knee, and when I saw all that blood on her, I almost died from fright, and I carried her all the way home. And I see beyond it, strangely, glimpses of her in the other direction: Izzy grown tall and gorgeous with one hand resting on a steering wheel, laughing; Izzy wearing a long green dress and picking her way in heels toward a waiting limousine on her way to prom; Izzy loaded down with books as the snow swirls around her, ducking into a dorm, her hair a golden flame against the white.

She squeals and squirms away. "I can't breathe! You're crushing me."

"Sorry, Fizzer." I reach back and unhook my grandma's bird necklace. Izzy's eyes go huge and round.

"Turn around," I say, and for once she's totally quiet and does what I say with no complaints, standing perfectly still while I lift her hair and fix the charm around her neck. She turns back to me, her face very serious, waiting for my opinion.

I give the necklace a tug. It falls halfway down her chest, sitting just to the right of her heart. "It looks good on you, Fizz."

"Are you giving it to me—for real real? Or just for today?" Her voice is a hush, like we're discussing state secrets.

"It looks better on you, anyway." I put a finger on her nose, and she twirls away with her hands in the air like a ballerina.

"Thanks, Sammy!" Except, of course, it comes out *Thammy*.

"Be good, Izzy." I stand up, throat tight, an aching in my whole body. I have to fight the urge to get down on my knees and squeeze her again.

She puts her hands on her hips like our mom does, mock-offended, sticking her nose in the air. "I'm always good. I'm the best."

"The best of the best."

She's already turned around, running and sliding in her slippered feet back toward the kitchen, yelling, "Look what Sammy gave me!" with one hand cupped around the charm. Tears are blurring my vision so I can't see her clearly, just the pink of her pajamas and the golden ring of her hair.

Outside the cold burns my lungs and makes the pain in my throat worse. I take a deep breath, sucking in the smells of wood fires and gasoline. The sun is beautiful, long and low on the horizon like it's stretching itself, like it's shaking off a nap, and I know underneath this weak winter light is the promise of days that last until eight P.M. and pool parties and the smell of chlorine and burgers on the grill; and underneath that is the promise of trees lit up in red and orange like flames and spiced cider, and frost that melts away by noon—layers upon layers of life, always something more, new, deeper. It makes me feel like crying, but Lindsay's already parked in front of the house, waving her arms and yelling, "What are you doing?" so instead I just keep walking, one foot in front of the other, one, two, three, and I think about letting go—of the trees and the grass and sky and the red-streaked clouds on the horizon—letting it all drop away from me like a veil. Maybe there will be something spectacular underneath.

A MIRACLE OF CHANCE AND COINCIDENCE, PART I

"And so, I was like, listen, I don't care that it's stupid, I don't care that it's, like, a holiday invented by Hallmark or whatever. . . ." Lindsay's rattling on about Patrick, punctuating her story by tapping the steering wheel with the heel of her hand. She's perfectly in control again, hair swept back in a ponytail just messy enough, lip gloss slicked on, a mist of Burberry Brit Gold clinging to the puffy jacket she's wearing. It's strange to see her this way after last night, but at the same time I'm glad. She's cruel and frightened and proud and insecure, but she's still Lindsay Edgecombe—the girl who freshman year took a key to Mari Tinsley's brand-new BMW after Mari called her a froshy prostitute, even though Mari had just been voted prom queen, and nobody, not even people in her own grade, would stand up to her—and she's still my best friend, and despite everything I still respect her. And I know that however wrong she's been—about a million things, about other people, about herself—she'll figure it out. I know from the way she looked last night, with the shadows making a hollow of her face.

Maybe it's just wishful thinking, but I like to believe, on some level, or in some world, what happened last night matters, that it didn't totally vanish. *Sometimes I'm afraid to go to sleep because of what I'm leaving behind.* Thinking about Kent's words makes shivers dance up and down my spine. This is the first time in my life I've ever missed kissing someone; the first time I've ever woken up feeling like I've lost something important.

"Maybe he's freaking out because he's too into you," Elody pipes up from the backseat. "Don't you think, Sam?"

"Uh-huh." I'm savoring my coffee, drinking it slowly. A perfect morning, exactly how I would have chosen it: perfect coffee, perfect bagel, riding around in the car with two of my best friends, not really talking about anything, not really *trying* to talk about anything, just babbling on about the same stuff we always do, enjoying one another's voices. The only thing that's missing is Ally.

I suddenly get the urge to drive around Ridgeview for a little bit longer. Partly I don't want the ride to end. Partly I just want to look at everything one last time.

"Lindz? Can we stop at Starbucks? I, um, kind of want a latte." I take a few gulps of my coffee, trying to drain it, to make this more believable.

She raises her eyebrows. "You hate Starbucks."

"Yeah, well, I got a sudden craving."

"You said it tastes like dog pee strained through a trash bag."

Elody gulps her coffee. "Ew—hello? Drinking. Eating." She waves her bagel dramatically.

Lindsay raises both hands. "That's a direct quote."

"If I'm late to poly sci one more time I swear I'll get detention for life," Elody says.

"*And* you'll miss the chance to suck face with Muffin before first," Lindsay says, snickering.

"What about you?" Elody pegs her with a piece of bagel, and Lindsay squeals. "It's a miracle you and Patrick haven't fused faces yet."

"Come on, Lindsay. Please?" I bat my eyelashes at her, then twist around to Elody. "Pretty please?"

Lindsay sighs heavily, locking eyes with Elody in the rearview mirror. She flicks on her turn indicator. I clap my hands and Elody groans.

"Sam gets to do what she wants today," Lindsay says. "After all, it's her *big* day." She emphasizes the word *big*, then starts cracking up.

Elody picks up on it right away. "I would say it was Rob's big day, actually."

"We can only hope." Lindsay leans over and elbows me.

"Ew," I say. "Perverts."

Linday's on a roll now. "It's going to be loooong day."

"A hard one," Elody adds.

Lindsay sprays some coffee out of her mouth and Elody shrieks. They're both snorting and laughing like maniacs.

"Very funny," I say, looking out the window, watching the houses begin to stream together as we come into town. "Very mature." But I'm smiling, feeling happy and calm, thinking, *You have no idea.*

There's a small parking lot behind the Starbucks in town, and we get the last spot, Lindsay slamming into it and nearly taking out the side mirrors of the two cars on either side of us, but still yelling, "*Gucci*, baby, *gucci*," which she claims is Italian for "perfect."

In my head I've been saying good-bye to everything, all these places I've seen so often I start to ignore them: the deli on the hill with perfect chicken cutlets and the trinket store where I used to buy thread to make friendship bracelets and the Realtor's and the dentist's and the little garden where Steve King put his tongue in my mouth in seventh grade, and I was so surprised I bit down. I can't stop thinking about how strange life is, about Kent and Juliet and even Alex and Anna and Bridget and Mr. Shaw and Ms. Winters—about how complex and connected everything is, all threaded together like some vast, invisible netting—and how sometimes you can think you're doing the right thing, but it's actually terrible and vice versa.

We head into Starbucks and I get a latte. Elody gets a brownie, even though she's just eaten, and Lindsay puts a stuffed bear on her head and then orders a water without blinking while the barista stares at her like she's crazy, and I can't help but throw my arms around her, and she says, "Save it for the bedroom, babe," making the old woman behind us inch away. We come out laughing and I almost drop my coffee—Sarah Grundel's brown Chevrolet is idling in the parking lot. She's drumming her hands on the wheel, checking her watch, waiting for a spot to open up. The last spot—the spot we took.

"You've got to be freaking kidding me," I say out loud. She'll definitely be late now.

Lindsay catches me staring and misunderstands me. "I know. If I had that car I totally wouldn't rock it past the drive-way. I think I'd rather walk."

"No, I—" I shake my head, realizing I can't explain. As we pass, Sarah rolls her eyes and sighs, like, *Finally*. The humor of the situation hits me and I start to laugh.

"How's the latte?" Lindsay asks as we climb back in the car.

"Like dog pee strained through a trash bag," I say. We roll out of the spot, giving Sarah a little beep, and she huffs and zooms in as soon as we're out of the way.

"What's her drama?" Elody asks.

"PNS," Lindsay says. "Parking Need Syndrome."

As we pull out of the parking lot, it occurs to me that maybe it's not so complicated at all. Most of the time—99 percent of the time—you just don't know how and why the threads are looped together, and that's okay. Do a good thing and something bad happens. Do a bad thing and something good happens. Do nothing and everything explodes.

And very, very rarely—by some miracle of chance and coincidence, butterflies beating their wings just so and all the threads hanging together for a minute—you get the chance to do the right thing.

Here's the last thing that occurs to me as Sarah recedes in the rearview mirror, slamming out of the car, jogging across the parking lot: if you're one tardy away from missing out on a big competition, you should probably make your coffee at home.

When we get to school I have a few things to take care of in the Rose Room, so I split up with Elody and Lindsay. Then, because I'm already late, I decide to skip the rest of first period. I wander through the halls and the campus, thinking how strange it is that you can live your whole life in one place and never really look at it. Even the yellow walls—what we used to call the vomit hallways—strike me as pretty now, the slender bare trees in the middle of the quad elegant and sparse, just waiting for snow.

For most of my life it's always seemed like the school day dragged on forever—except during quizzes and tests, when the seconds seemed to trip over themselves trying to run away quickly. Today it's like that. No matter how badly I want for everything to go slowly, time is pouring away, hemorrhaging. I've barely made it into the second question of Mr. Tierney's quiz before he's yelling, "Time!" and giving all of us his fiercest scowl, and I have to turn in my quiz only partially completed. I know it doesn't matter, but I've given it my best shot anyway. I want to have one last day when everything is normal. A day like a million other days I've had. A day when I turn in my chem quiz and worry about whether Mr. Tierney will ever make good on his threat to call BU. But I don't regret the quiz for long. I'm past regretting things now.

When it's time for math I head down early, feeling calm. I slide into my seat a few minutes before the bell and take out my math textbook, centering it perfectly on my desk. I'm the first student to arrive.

Mr. Daimler comes over and leans against my desk, smiling at me. I notice for the first time that one of his incisors is extra pointy, like a vampire's. "What's this, Sam?" He gestures at my desk. "Three minutes early and actually prepared for class? Are you turning over a new leaf?"

"Something like that," I say evenly, folding my hands on top of my textbook.

"So how's Cupid Day treating you?" He pops a mint in his mouth and leans closer. It grosses me out, like he thinks he can seduce me with fresh breath. "Any big romantic plans tonight? Got someone special to cozy up next to?" He raises his eyebrows at me.

A week ago this would have made me swoon. Now I feel totally cold. I think about how rough his face was on mine, how heavy he felt, but it doesn't make me angry or afraid. I fixate on his hemp necklace, which is, as always, peeking out from under his shirt collar. For the first time he strikes me as kind of pathetic. Who wears the same thing for eight straight years? That would be like if I insisted on wearing the candy necklaces I loved when I was in fifth grade.

"We'll see," I say, smiling. "What about you? Are you going to be all by your lonesome? Table for one?"

He leans forward even more, and I stay perfectly still, willing myself not to pull away.

"Now why would you assume that?" He winks at me, obviously thinking that this is my version of flirting—like I'm going to offer to keep him company or something.

I smile even wider. "Because if you had a real girlfriend," I say, quietly but clearly, so he can hear every word perfectly, "you wouldn't be hitting on high school girls."

Mr. Daimler sucks in a breath and jerks backward so quickly he almost falls off the desk. People are coming into class, now, chattering and comparing roses, ignoring us. We could be talking about a homework assignment, or a quiz grade. He stares at me, his mouth opening and shutting. No words come out.

The bell rings. Mr. Daimler shakes his shoulders and stumbles away from the desk, still staring at me. Then he turns a complete circle as if he's lost. Finally he clears his throat.

"Okay, everyone." His voice breaks and he coughs. When he speaks again it's a bark. "Everyone. Seats. Now."

I have to bite the edge of my hand to keep from cracking up. Mr. Daimler shoots me a look of total disgust, which makes the urge to laugh even harder to resist. I look away, turning toward the door.

Right at the moment that Kent McFuller walks through it.

We lock eyes, and in that second it's like the classroom folds in two and all of the distance disappears between us. A zooming, rushing feeling comes over me, like I'm being beamed up into his bright-green eyes. Time collapses, too, and we're back on my porch in the snow, his warm fingers brushing my neck, the soft pressure of his lips, the whisper of his voice in my ear. Nothing exists but him.

"Mr. McFuller. Care to take a seat?" Mr. Daimler's voice is cold.

Kent turns away from me and the moment is lost. He mumbles a quick sorry to Mr. Daimler and then heads for his seat. I turn around, following him with my eyes. I love the way he slides into his seat without touching his desk. I love the way, when he pulls out his math textbook, a bunch of crumpled sketches come with it. I love the way he keeps nervously fiddling with his hair, running his hands through it even though it swings back into his eyes immediately.

"*Miss* Kingston. If I could trouble you for just a second of your *precious* time and attention."

When I turn back to the front of the room, Mr. Daimler is glaring at me.

"I guess for a second," I say loudly, and everybody laughs. Mr. Daimler folds his mouth into a thin white line but doesn't say anything else.

I flip open my math textbook, but I can't focus. I drum my fingers on the underside of the desk, feeling antsy and exhilarated now that I've seen Kent. I wish I could tell him exactly how I feel. I wish I could explain it somehow, that he could *know*. I watch the clock anxiously. I can't wait for the Cupids to come.

Kent McFuller is getting an extra rose today.

After class I wait for Kent in the hall, butterflies making a mess of my stomach. When he comes out he's carefully holding the rose I've sent him, like he's afraid it will break. He glances up, serious and thoughtful, his eyes searching my face.

"You going to tell me what this is about?" He doesn't smile, but there's a teasing lilt to his voice and his eyes are bright.

I decide to tease him right back, even though being so close to him is making it hard to think. "I don't know what you're talking about."

He holds the rose out and flips the note open so I can read it, though, of course, I know what it says.

Tonight. Leave your phone on and your car out, and be my hero.

"Mysterious," I say, holding back a smile. He looks ten times more adorable when he's worried. "Secret admirer?"

"Not so secret." His eyes are still roving over my face like there's the answer to a puzzle written there, and I have to look away to keep from grabbing him and pulling him toward me. He pauses. "I'm having a party tonight, you know."

"I know." I rush on. "I mean, I heard."

"So . . . ?"

I give up on playing with him. "Listen, I may need you to pick me up from somewhere. Twenty minutes, tops. I wouldn't ask unless it was important."

He crooks one side of his mouth into a smile. "What's in it for me?"

I lean forward so my mouth is inches away from the perfect shell of his ear. The smell of him—freshly cut grass and mint— is addictive. "I'll tell you a secret."

"Now?"

"Later." I pull back. Otherwise I won't be able to stop myself from kissing his neck. I don't know what's wrong with me. I was *never* like this with Rob. I can barely keep my hands to myself around Kent. Maybe dying a few times messes with your hormones or something. I kind of like it.

His face gets serious again. "What you wrote here . . ." He fingers the note, folding it and unfolding it, his eyes dazzling, swirling with gold. "The last bit . . . the hero thing . . . how did you—?"

My heart is beating frantically, and for one second I think he knows—I think he remembers. The silence is heavy between us, everything past and remembered and forgotten and wanted swinging there like a pendulum. "How did I what?" I can barely breathe the words.

He sighs and shakes his head, gives me a weak smile. "Nothing. Forget it. It's stupid."

"Oh." I realize I've been holding my breath, and I exhale, looking away so he won't see how disappointed I am. "Thanks for your rose, by the way."

Of all the roses I've gotten it's the only one I kept. *It's my favorite*, I'd said, when Marian Sykes delivered it to me.

She looked up at me, startled, and then looked around, as though I couldn't possibly be talking to her. When she realized I was, she blushed and smiled.

You have so many, she said shyly.

The problem is I can never keep them alive, I said. *I have, like, a black thumb.*

You have to cut the stems on an angle, she said eagerly, then blushed again. *My sister taught me that. She used to like to garden.* She turned away, biting her lip.

You should take them, I said.

She stared at me for a second as though suspecting a joke. *Like, to keep?* she said, reminding me of Izzy.

I'm telling you, I can't have any more flower homicides on my conscience, I said. *You could take them home. Do you have a vase?*

432

She paused for a fraction of a second more and then broke into a dazzling smile, transforming her whole face. *I'll keep them in my room*, she said.

Kent cocks one eyebrow. "How do you know that I'm the one who sent it?"

"Come on." I roll my eyes. "No one else draws weird cartoons for a living."

He puts a hand on his chest, acting offended. "Not for a living. For the love of it. Besides, they're not weird."

"Whatever. Then thanks for your totally normal note."

"You're welcome." He grins. We're standing close enough that I can feel the heat coming off him.

"So are you going to be my knight in shining armor or what?"

Kent does a little bow. "You know I can't resist a damsel in distress."

"I knew I could count on you." The hallways are empty now. Everyone is at lunch. For a moment we just stand there smiling at each other. Then something softens in his eyes and my heart soars. Everything in me feels fluttering and free, like I could take off from the ground at any second. *Music,* I think, *he makes me feel like music.* Then I think, *He's going to kiss me right here, in the math wing of Thomas Jefferson High School,* and I almost pass out.

He doesn't, though. Instead he reaches out and touches my shoulder once, lightly. When he removes his fingers I can still feel them tingling on my skin. "Until tonight, then." A flicker of a smile. "Your secret better be good."

"It's amazing, I promise." I wish I could memorize every single thing about him. I want to burn him into my mind. I can't believe how blind I was for so long. I start to back away before I do something wildly inappropriate, like jump on top of him.

"Sam?" he stops me.

"Yeah."

His eyes are doing that searching thing again, and now I understand why he told me before that he could see through me. He's actually been paying attention. I feel like he's reading my mind right now, which is more than a little embarrassing, since most of my thoughts for the moment involve how perfect his lips are.

He bites his lip and shuffles his feet a little. "Why me? For tonight, I mean. We haven't really talked in, like, seven years. . . ."

"Maybe I'm making up for lost time." I keep backing away from him, skipping a little.

"I'm serious," he says. "Why me?"

I think of Kent holding my hand in the dark, leading me through rooms crisscrossed with moonlight. I think of his voice lulling me to sleep, carrying me off like a tide. I think of time stilling as he cupped my face and brought his lips to mine.

"Trust me," I say, "it can only be you."

Kent's Valogram was only the first of several adjustments I made in the Rose Room this morning, and as soon as I enter the cafeteria I can tell that Rob got his. He breaks away from his friends and lopes up to me before I can even make it over to the lunch line (where I'm planning on ordering a double roast beef sandwich). As always, his stupid Yankees hat is barely balanced on his head, twisted around to the side like he's in some rap video from 1992.

"Hey, babe." He goes to put his arm around me, and I step away casually. "Got your rose."

"Thanks. I got yours too."

He looks around, sees a single rose looped through the handle of my messenger bag, and frowns. "Is that mine?"

I shake my head, smiling sweetly.

He rubs his forehead. He always does this when he's thinking, like the act of actually using his mind gives him a headache. "What happened to all your roses?"

"They're in storage," I say, which is kind of true.

He shakes his head, letting it go. "So there's a party tonight. . . ." He trails off, then tips his head and smirks at me. "I thought it would be fun to go for a bit." He reaches out and clomps a hand on my shoulder, massaging me hard. "Like, you know, foreplay."

Only Rob would think that pounding foamy beer from a keg and screaming at each other counts as foreplay, but I decide to let it go and play along. "Foreplay?" I say, as innocently as I can.

He obviously thinks I'm being flirtatious. He smiles and tilts his head backward, looking at me through half narrowed eyes. I used to think it was the cutest thing when he did this; now it's a bit like watching a linebacker try to samba. He might have all the moves down, but it just doesn't look right.

"You know," he says quietly, "I really liked what you wrote in your note."

"Did you?" I make my voice a purr, thinking about what I scrawled out this morning. *You don't have to wait for me anymore.*

"So I was thinking I'd get to the party at ten, stay for an hour or two." He shrugs and adjusts his hat, back to business now that he got the flirting out of the way.

I feel suddenly tired. I'd been planning to mess with Rob a little—to get back at him for not paying attention, for not being there, for not caring about anything except partying and lacrosse and how he looks in his stupid Yankees hat—but I can't keep up the game anymore. "I don't really care what you do, Rob."

He hesitates. This was not the answer he was expecting. "You're sleeping over tonight, though, right?"

"I don't think so."

His hand flies up to his forehead again: more rubbing. "But you said . . ."

"I said you didn't have to wait for me anymore. And you don't." I suck in a deep breath. *One, two, three, jump.* "This isn't working out, Rob. I want to break up."

He takes a step backward. His face goes completely white, and then he turns bright red from the forehead down, like someone's filling him with Kool-Aid. "What did you say?"

"I said I'm breaking up with you." I've never done anything like this before, and I'm surprised by how easy I'm finding it. Letting go is easy: it's all downhill. "I just don't think it's working out."

"But—but—" he sputters at me. The confusion on his face is replaced by rage. "You can't break up with me."

I unconsciously shuffle backward, crossing my arms. "Why's that?"

He looks at me like I'm the dumbest person alive. "*You*," he says, almost spitting the word, "cannot break up with *me*."

Then I get it. Rob *does* remember. He remembers that in sixth grade he said I wasn't cool enough for him—remembers it, and still believes it. Any sympathy I still feel for him vanishes in that moment, and as he's standing there, bright red with his fists clenched, it amazes me how ugly I find him.

"I can do it," I say calmly. "I just did."

"And I *waited* for you. I waited for you for *months*." He turns away and mutters something I don't hear.

"What?"

He looks back at me, his face twisted with disgust and anger.

437

This cannot be the same person who a week ago nestled against my shoulder and told me I was his personal blanket. It's like his face has dropped away and there's a totally different face underneath.

"I said I should have screwed Gabby Haynes when she asked me to over break," he says coldly.

Something flares in my stomach, leftover pain or pride, but it passes quickly enough and is replaced again by a feeling of calm. I'm already gone from here, already flying over this, and I can suddenly understand exactly what Juliet feels, must have felt for some time. Thinking about her brings my strength back, and I even manage to smile.

"It's never too late for second chances," I say sweetly, and then I walk away to have my last lunch with my best friends.

Ten minutes later, when I'm finally sitting down at our usual table—scarfing an enormous roast beef sandwich with mayonnaise and a plate full of fries, hungrier than I've been in a long time—and Juliet comes through the cafeteria, I see she has placed a single rose in the empty water bottle that is strapped to the side of her backpack. She's looking around, too, her face cutting the curtain of her hair in two, checking each and every table she passes, searching, looking for clues. Her eyes are bright and alert. She's chewing her lip, but she doesn't look unhappy. She looks *alive*. My heart skips a beat: this is the important thing.

As she weaves past our table, I see a folded note fluttering just under the petals of her rose, and even though I'm too far away to read it, I can see what's written there clearly, even when I close my eyes. A single phrase.

It's never too late.

"So what's up with you today?" Lindsay asks on the way to The Country's Best Yogurt. We've almost reached the Row, the line of small shops clustered at the crest of the hill like mushrooms. The blanket of dark clouds is being drawn over the horizon inch by inch, bringing the promise of snow.

"What do you mean?" We're walking arm-in-arm, trying to stay warm. I wanted Ally and Elody to come along, but Elody had a Spanish test, and Ally insisted that if she missed another English class she'd probably get suspended. I didn't make a big deal out of it.

A day like any other.

"I mean, why are you acting so weird?"

I'm trying to formulate an answer and Lindsay goes on, "Like, zoning out at lunch and stuff." She bites her lip. "I got this text from Amy Weiss. . . ."

"Yeah?"

"Amy Weiss is obviously crazy, and I would never believe anything she says, especially about you," Lindsay qualifies quickly.

"Obviously," I say, amused, pretty sure I know where this is headed.

"But . . ." Lindsay sucks in a deep breath and says in a rush, "She says she was talking to Steve Waitman, who was talking to Rob, who said that you broke up?" Lindsay shoots a glance at me and forces a laugh. "I told her it was bullshit, obviously."

I pause, choosing my words carefully. "It's not bullshit. It's true."

Lindsay stops walking and stares. *"What?"*

"I broke up with him at lunch."

She shakes her head like she's trying to dislodge the words from her brain. "And, um, were you planning on *sharing* this little piece of news at some point? With your *best friends*? Or were you just counting on it to make the rounds eventually?"

I can tell she's really hurt. "Listen, Lindsay, I was going to tell you—"

She presses her hands to both ears, still shaking her head. "I don't understand. What happened? You guys were supposed to—I mean, you told me you wanted to—*tonight*."

I sigh. "This is why I didn't want to tell you, Lindz. I knew you'd make a big deal out of it."

"That's because it *is* a big deal."

Lindsay's so outraged she's not even paying attention as we pass Hunan Kitchen: she's too busy glaring at me like she expects me to suddenly turn blue or combust, like I can never be trusted again.

It occurs to me she's *really* going to feel that way after I do what I'm about to do, but it can't be helped. I turn to her, putting my arms on her shoulders. "Wait here for a second, okay?"

She blinks at me. "Where are you going?"

"I have to stop in Hunan Kitchen for a second." I brace myself, waiting for her to freak out. "I kind of have something for Anna Cartullo."

I'm prepared for her to scream or stalk off or throw gummy bears at me or *something*, but instead her face goes totally blank like the power switch has been flipped off. I'm kind of worried she may be going into shock, but the opportunity is too good to pass up.

"Two minutes," I say. "I promise."

I duck into Hunan Kitchen before Lindsay—and her attitude—can come back online. A bell jingles on the door as I walk in. Alex looks up, worried for a second, and then plasters a smile on his face.

"What's up, Sam?" he drawls. Idiot.

I ignore him and go straight to Anna. She has her head bent, pushing the food around her plate. It's a lot safer than eating it, that's for sure.

"Hey." I'm nervous for some reason. There's something unsettling about her quietness, the way she lifts her eyes and stares at me with no expression. It reminds me of Juliet. "I just came by to give you something."

"Give me something?" She curls her lip back, skeptical, and the resemblance to Juliet is no longer so strong. She must think I'm crazy. As far as she knows we've never exchanged a word in our lives, and I can only imagine what she thinks I want to give her.

Alex is looking back and forth from Anna to me, as confused as she is. I'm aware of Lindsay watching me through the grimy window, and the fact that three people are staring at me like I've lost it is a little overwhelming. I reach into my bag, hands trembling a little bit.

"Yeah, listen, I know it's weird. I can't really explain it, but . . ." I pull out a big book of M. C. Escher sketches and put it on the table next to the bowl of sesame chicken. Or orange beef. Or cooked cat. Or whatever.

Anna freezes, staring at the book like it's going to bite her.

"It just seemed like the kind of thing you'd like," I say quickly, already backing away from the table. Now that the hard part is over I feel a thousand times better. "There's over two hundred drawings. You could even hang some of them up, if you had a place to put them."

Something tenses in Anna's face. She's still staring at the book on the table, her hands resting on her thighs. I can see how tightly she's curling her fists.

I'm just about to turn and jet out the door when she glances up. Our eyes meet. She doesn't say anything, but her mouth relaxes. It's not quite a smile, but it's close, and I take it as a thank-you.

I hear Alex say, "What was that about?" and then I'm out the door, the bell sounding a shrill note behind me.

Lindsay's still standing there exactly as I left her, eyes dull. I know she's been watching through the window.

"Now I know you've gone crazy," she says.

"I'm telling you, I don't know what you're talking about." I feel exhilarated now that it's over with. "Come on. I'm fiending me some yogurt."

Lindsay doesn't budge. "Lost it. Flipped your lid. Gone bat shit. Since when do you bring Anna Cartullo presents?"

"Listen, it's not like I got her a friendship bracelet or something."

"Since when do you even *talk* to Anna Cartullo?"

I sigh. I can tell she's not going to give up on this. "I talked to her for the first time a couple days ago, all right?" Lindsay's still staring like the world is melting away before her eyes. I know the feeling. "She's actually pretty nice. I mean, I think you might like her if—"

Lindsay makes a high-pitched squealing noise and claps her hands over her ears again like the very words are torture. She keeps on shrieking like this while I sigh and check my watch, waiting for her to finish her performance.

Eventually she calms down, her squealing dying away to a gurgling noise in the back of her throat. She squints at me.

I can't help but giggle. She looks like a total freak.

"Are you done?" I ask.

"Are you back?" She peels one hand off her ear tentatively, experimenting.

"Is *who* back?"

"Samantha Emily Kingston. My best friend. My hetero-sexual life partner." She leans forward and raps once on my forehead with her knuckles. "Instead of this weird lobotomized boyfriend-dumping Anna Cartullo–liking pod who's impersonating her."

I roll my eyes. "You don't know everything about me, you know."

"I apparently don't know *anything* about you." Lindsay crosses her arms. I tug on the sleeve of her jacket, and she trudges forward reluctantly. I can tell she's actually upset. I put my arms around her and squeeze. She's so much shorter than I am that I have to take mini-shuffling steps so our paces are matched up, but I let her set the rhythm.

"You know what my favorite flavor of yogurt is," I say, hoping to appease her.

Lindsay heaves a sigh. "Double chocolate," she grumbles, but she's not pushing me off of her, which is a good sign. "With crushed peanut butter cups and Cap'n Crunch cereal."

"And I *know* you know what size I'm going to get."

We're at the door to The Country's Best Yogurt now, and I can already smell the deliciously sweet chemical-y aroma wafting out to us. It's like the smell of the bread baking at Subway. You know it's not the way nature or God intended it to smell, but something about it is addictive.

Lindsay looks at me from the corner of her eye as I pull my arms off her. Her expression is so mournful it's funny, and I choke down another laugh.

"Better be careful, Miss Jumbo Queen," she says, tossing her hair. "All that artificial yumminess is going straight to your hips."

But her mouth is crooked up into a smile, and I know she's forgiven me.

FRIENDSHIP, A STORY

If I had to pick the top three things I love about each of my friends, here's what they would be.

ALLY:

1. Spent all of sophomore year collecting miniature porcelain cows and reading obscure facts about them online after one of them—a real one, I mean—wrapped its tongue around her wrist while she was on vacation in Vermont.
2. Cooks without recipes, and is totally going to have her own cooking show someday, and has promised we can all come on and be guests.
3. Sticks her tongue out all the way when she yawns, like a cat.

ELODY:

1. Has perfect pitch and the clearest, richest voice you can imagine, like maple syrup pouring over warm pancakes, but doesn't ever show off and only sings on her own when she's in the shower.

2. Once went a whole school year wearing at least one green item of clothing every single day.

3. Snorts when she laughs, which always makes me laugh.

LINDSAY:

1. Will always dance, even when nobody else is, even when there's no music—in the cafeteria, in the bath-room, in the mall food court.

2. Toilet papered Todd Horton's house every single day for a week after he told everyone that Elody was a bad kisser.

3. Once broke into a full-on sprint while we were cut-ting across the park, pumping her arms and legs and zooming across the fields in her jeans and Chinese Laundry boots. I started running too but couldn't catch up to her before we were both doubled over, huffing out the cold autumn air, my lungs feeling like they were going to explode, and when I laughed and said, "You win," she gave me the strangest look over her shoulder, not mean, just like she couldn't

believe I was there, then straightened up and said,

"I wasn't racing you."

I think I understand that now.

I'm thinking about all these things at Ally's house, feeling like I haven't said them enough, or at all, feeling like we've spent too much time making fun of one another or bullshitting about things that don't matter or wishing things and people were different—better, more interesting, cuter, older. But it's hard to find a way to say it now, so instead I just laugh along while Lindsay and Elody shimmy around the kitchen and Ally frantically tries to salvage something edible from two-day-old Italian pesto and some old packaged crackers. And when Lindsay throws her arms around my shoulders and then Ally's, and then Elody scoots around to Ally's other side, and Lindsay says, "I love you bitches to death. You know that, right?" and Elody yells, "Group hug!" I just barrel in there and put my arms around them and squeeze until Elody breaks away, laughing, and says, "If I laugh any harder I'm going to throw up."

THE SECRET

"I just don't get it." Lindsay's pouting in the front seat, halfway down Kent's driveway, where the line of cars ends. "How do you expect us to get *home*?"

I sigh and explain it for the thousandth time. "I'll get us a ride, okay?"

"Why don't you just come in with us now?" Ally whines from the backseat, also for the thousandth time. "Just leave the damn car."

"And let you drive home, Ms. Absolut World?" I twist around and stare pointedly at the vodka bottle she's holding. She takes this as a cue to toss back another gulp.

"I'll drive us home," Lindsay insists. "Have you ever seen me drunk?"

"It doesn't matter." I roll my eyes. "You can't even drive sober."

Elody snorts and Lindsay wags a finger at her. "Watch out or you'll be walking to school from now on," she says.

"Come on, we're missing the party." Ally finger-combs her hair, ducking so she can check herself out in the rearview mirror.

"Give me fifteen minutes, tops," I say. "I'll be back before you even make it to the keg."

"How will you get back here?" Lindsay's still eyeing me suspiciously, but she opens the door.

"Don't worry about it," I say. "I hooked up a ride earlier."

"I still don't see why you can't just drive us home later." Lindsay's grumbling, still unhappy about the arrangements, but she climbs out, and Ally and Elody follow. I don't bother answering. I've already explained, and explained again, that I may be ducking out of the party early. I know all of them assume it's because Rob will be there and I'm afraid I'll freak or something, and I don't correct them.

I'm planning to drop the car in Lindsay's driveway, but after I pull out onto Route 9, I find that, without meaning to, I steer toward home. I'm feeling calm, blank, like all of the darkness outside has somehow seeped in and turned everything off inside me. It's not an unpleasant feeling. It's kind of like being in a pool and kicking up onto your back until you find the perfect balance where you can float without thinking about it.

Most of the lights are off at my house. Izzy's gone to sleep several hours ago. There's a faint blue light glowing in the den. My father must be watching TV. Upstairs a bright square of light marks the bathroom. Through the shades I can see a figure moving around, and I imagine my mom dotting Clinique moisturizer on her face, squinting without her contacts, the tattered arm of her bathrobe fluttering, a bird wing. As usual they've left the porch light on for me, so that when I come home I won't have to fumble in my bag for my keys. They'll be making plans for tomorrow, maybe wondering what to do for breakfast or whether to wake me up before noon, and for a moment grief for everything I am losing—have lost already, lost days ago in a split second of skidding and tearing where my life ripped away from its axis—overwhelms me, and I put my head down on the steering wheel and wait for the feeling to pass. It does. The pain ebbs away. My muscles relax, and once again I'm struck by the rightness of things.

449

As I'm driving back to Lindsay's, I think about something I learned years ago in science class, that even when birds have been separated from their flock they will still migrate instinctively. They know where to go without ever having been shown the way. Everyone was talking about how amazing that was, but now it doesn't seem so strange. That's how I feel right now: as though I am in the air, all alone, but somehow I know exactly what to do.

A few miles before Lindsay's driveway, I pull out my phone and punch in Kent's number. It occurs to me that he may have thought I was kidding earlier today. Maybe he won't pick up when he doesn't recognize the phone number, or maybe he'll be so busy trying to keep people from puking on his parents' Oriental carpets he won't hear it. I count the rings, getting more and more nervous. One, two, three.

On the fourth ring there's the sound of fumbling. Then Kent's voice, warm and reassuring: "Hunky Heroes, rescuing distressed women, captive princesses, and girls without wheels since 1684. How can I help you?"

"How did you know it was me?" I say.

There's a surge in the music and the swelling of voices. Then I hear Kent cup his hand over the phone and yell, "Out!" A door shuts and the background noise is suddenly muffled.

"Who else would it be?" he says, his voice sarcastic. "Everyone else is here." He readjusts something and his voice becomes louder. He must be pressing right up to the phone.

The thought of his lips is distracting. "So what's up?"

"I hope your car's not blocked in," I say. "Because I'm in desperate need of a ride."

On the way back to Kent's, we're mostly quiet. He doesn't ask me why I was standing in the middle of Lindsay's driveway, and he doesn't press the issue of why I've chosen him to be my ride. I'm grateful for that, and happy just to sit in silence next to him, watching the rain and the dark brushstrokes of the trees against the sky. As we turn into his driveway, which by this point is almost completely packed with cars, I'm trying to decide exactly what the rain dancing in the headlights looks like. Not glitter, exactly.

Kent puts the car in park but leaves the engine on. "I still haven't forgotten that you promised me a secret, by the way." He turns to look at me. "Don't think you're getting off so easy."

"I wouldn't dream of it." I unbuckle my seat belt and inch closer to him, still watching the rain out of the corner of my eye. Like dust, kind of, but only if dust were made of solid white light.

Kent folds his hands in his lap, staring at me expectantly, his mouth just curved into a smile. "So let's hear it."

I reach across Kent and pull the keys out of the ignition, cutting the lights. In the resulting darkness the sound of the rain seems much louder, washing all around us.

"Hey," Kent says softly, his voice making my heart soar again, making my whole body light. "Now I can't see you."

His face and body are all shadow, darkness on darkness. I can just make out the lines of him, and, of course, feel the warmth from his skin. I lean forward, catching my chin on the roughness of his corduroy jacket, finding his ear, accidentally bumping it with my mouth. He inhales sharply and his whole body tenses. My heart is fluid, soaring. There's no longer any space between heartbeats.

"The secret is," I say, whispering right into his ear, "that yours was the best kiss I've ever had in my life."

He pulls back a little so that he can look at me, but our lips are still just inches away. I can't make out his expression in the dark, but I can tell that his eyes are searching my face again.

"But I've never kissed you," he whispers back. Around us the rain sounds like falling glass. "Not since third grade, anyway."

I smile, but I'm not sure if he can see it. "Better get started, then," I say, "because I don't have much time."

He pauses for only a fraction of a second. Then he leans forward and presses his lips to mine, and the whole world powers off, the moon and the rain and the sky and the streets, and it's just the two of us in the dark, alive, alive, alive.

I don't know how long we're kissing. It seems like hours, but somehow when he pulls away, breathing hard, both hands holding my face, the clock glowing dully on the dashboard has only inched forward a few minutes.

"Wow," he says. I can feel his chest rising and falling quickly.

We're both out of breath. "What was that for?"

I force myself to pull away, find the handle in the dark and pop the door open. The cold air and the rain *whooshes* in, helping me think. I suck in a deep breath. "For the ride and everything."

Even in the dark I can see his eyes sparkling like a cat's. I can hardly bring myself to look away. "You really saved my life tonight," I say, my little joke, and then before he can stop me, and even though he calls my name, I jump out of the car and jog along the driveway toward the house, for the very last party of my life.

"You made it!" Lindsay squeals when I find her in the back room. As always the music and heat and smoke is impassable, a wall of people, perfume, and sound. "I totally thought you would flake."

"I knew you'd show," Ally says, reaching out and squeezing one of my hands. She drops her voice, which at this volume means she screams a little quieter. "Did you see Rob?"

"I think he's avoiding me," I say, which is true. Thank God.

Lindsay twists around, calling for Elody—"Look who decided to grace us with her presence!" she screams, and Elody scans our faces before registering that I haven't been at the party the whole time—and then turns to me, slipping her arm around my shoulders. "Now it's officially a party. Al, give Sam a shot."

"No, thanks." I wave away the bottle she offers me. I flip open my cell phone. Eleven thirty. "Actually, um, I think I'm going to go downstairs for a bit. Maybe outside. It's really hot up here."

Lindsay and Ally exchange a glance.

"You just came from outside," Lindsay says. "You just *got* here. Like five seconds ago."

"I was looking around for you guys for a while." I know I sound lame, but I also know that I can't explain.

Lindsay crosses her arms. "Uh-uh, no way. Something's going on with you, and you're going to tell us what it is."

"You've been acting weird all day." Ally bobbles her head.

"Did Lindsay tell you to say that?" I ask.

"Who's been acting weird?" Elody's just made her way over to us.

"Me, apparently," I say.

"Oh, yeah." Elody nods. "Definitely."

"Lindsay didn't tell me to say *anything*." Ally puffs up her chest, getting offended. "It's obvious."

"We're your best friends," Lindsay says. "We *know* you."

I press my fingers against my temples, trying to block out the throbbing sounds of the music, and close my eyes. When I open them again, Elody, Ally, and Lindsay are all staring at me suspiciously.

"I'm fine, okay?" I'm desperate to prevent a long conversation—or worse, a fight. "Trust me. It's just been a weird week."

Understatement of the year.

"We're worried about you, Sam," Lindsay says. "You're not acting like yourself."

"Maybe that's a good thing," I say, and when they stare at me blankly, I sigh, leaning forward to wrestle them all into a group hug.

Elody squeals and giggles, "PDA much?" and Lindsay and Ally seem to relax too.

"I promise nothing's the matter," I say, which isn't exactly true, but I figure it's the best thing to say. "Best friends forever, right?"

"And no secrets." Lindsay stares pointedly at me.

"And no bullshit," Elody trumpets, which isn't part of our little routine, but whatever. She's supposed to say, "and no lies," but I guess one works as well as the other.

"Forever," Ally finishes, "and till death do us part."

The last part falls on me to say, "And even then."

"And even then," the three of them echo.

"All right, enough mushy crap." Lindsay breaks away. "I, for one, came to get drunk."

"I thought you didn't get drunk," Ally says.

"Figure of speech."

Ally and Lindsay start going back and forth, Ally dancing away with the vodka bottle ("If you don't get drunk, I don't see the point of drinking and wasting it") as Elody wanders back over to Muffin. At least the attention is off me.

"See you later," I say loudly to all of them in general, and Elody glances over her shoulder at me, but she may be looking at someone else. Lindsay flaps a hand in my direction, and Ally doesn't hear me at all. It reminds me of leaving my house for the last time this morning, how in the end it's impossible to understand the finality of certain things, certain words, certain moments. As I turn away my vision gets blurry, and I'm surprised to find that I'm crying. The tears come without any warning. I blink repeatedly until the world sharpens again, rubbing the wetness off my cheeks. I check my cell phone. Eleven forty-five.

Downstairs I stand just inside the door, waiting for Juliet, which is a bit like trying to stay on your feet in the middle of a riptide. People swarm around me, but hardly anybody looks my way. Maybe they're getting a weird vibe off me, too, or they can tell I'm focused elsewhere. Or maybe—and this makes me sad as soon as I think it—they can sense, somehow, that I'm already gone. I push the thought away.

Finally I see her slip through the front door, white sweater tied loosely around her, head stooped. Instantly I jump forward and put a hand on her arm. She starts, staring at me, and though she must have imagined coming face-to-face with me tonight, the fact that I've found her, and not the other way around, throws her off guard.

"Hey," I say. "Can I talk to you for a minute?"

She opens her mouth, shuts it, then opens it again. "Actually,

I, um, kind of have somewhere to be."

"No, you don't." In one movement I draw her away from the crowded entrance and toward a little recessed area in the hall. It's a little easier to hear each other here, though it's so squished we have to stand nearly pressed chest-to-chest. "Weren't you looking for me, anyway? Weren't you looking for *us*?"

"How did you—?" She breaks off, sucks in a breath, and shakes her head. "I'm not here for you."

"I know." I stare at her, willing her to look at me, but she doesn't. I want to tell her that I get it, that I understand, but she's examining the tiling on the floors. "I know it's bigger than that."

"You don't know anything," she says dully.

"I know what you have planned for tonight," I say, very quietly.

Then she looks up. For a second our eyes meet, and I see fear flashing there, and something else—hope, maybe?—but she quickly drops her eyes again.

"You can't know," she says simply. "Nobody knows."

"I know that you have something to tell me," I say. "I know that you have something you wanted to say to all of us—to me, to Lindsay, to Elody, and Ally, too."

Again she looks up, but this time she holds my gaze, eyes wide, and we stare at each other. Now I know what the look on her face is, behind the fear: wonder.

"You're a bitch," she whispers, so quietly I'm not sure I even hear the words or am just remembering them, imagining them in her voice. She says it like she is reciting the lines to an old play, some long-neglected script she can't manage to forget.

I nod. "I know," I say. "I know I am. I know I have been—we all have been. And I'm sorry."

She takes a quick step back, but there's nowhere to go, so she ends up bumping up against the wall. She flattens herself, hands braced against the plaster, breathing hard, like I'm some kind of a wild animal that might attack her at any second. She's shaking her head quickly from side to side. I don't even think she knows she's doing it.

"Juliet." I reach out, but she shrinks an extra half inch into the wall, and I drop my hand. "I'm serious. I'm trying to tell you how sorry I am."

"I have to go."

She seems to break away from the wall with effort, like she's not sure she'll be able to stand without it. She tries to squeeze past me, but I shuffle around so we're face-to-face again.

"I'm sorry," I say.

"You said that." Now she's getting angry. I'm glad. I think it's a good sign.

"No, I mean . . ." I take a deep breath, willing her to understand. *This is how it's supposed to be.* "I have to come with you."

"Please," she says. "Just leave me alone."

"That's what I'm telling you. I *can't*." As we're standing there

I realize we're almost exactly the same height. We must look like the dark and light sides of an Oreo cookie, and I think how just as easily it could have been the other way around. She could be blocking my path; I could be trying to slip around her into the dark.

"You don't—" she starts, but I don't ever hear what she's about to say. At that second someone yells, "Sam!" from the stairs, and as I turn around to look up at Kent, Juliet darts past me.

"Juliet!" I whip around but not quickly enough. She's swallowed by the crowd, the gap that allowed her to break for the door closing just as quickly as it opened, a shifting Tetris pattern of bodies, and now I'm running up against backs and hands and enormous leather bags.

"Sam!"

Not now, Kent. I'm fighting my way toward the door, every few steps being carried backward as people drive relentlessly toward the kitchen, holding up cups that need to be refilled. When I'm almost at the door, the crowd thins and I surge forward. But then I feel a warm hand on my back, and Kent's spinning me around to face him, and despite the fact that I need to catch Juliet and the fact that we're standing in the middle of a billion people, I think about how good it would feel to dance with him. Really dance, not just grind up on each other like people do at homecoming—dance the way people used to, with my hands on his shoulders and his arms around my waist.

"I've been looking for you." He's out of breath and his hair is messier than usual. "Why did you run away from me before?"

He looks so confused and concerned I feel my heart somersault in my chest.

"I don't really have time to talk about this right now," I say as gently as possible. "I'll catch up with you later, okay?" It's the easiest way. It's the *only* way.

"No." He sounds so emphatic I'm momentarily thrown off guard.

"Excuse me?"

"I said, *no*." He stands in front of me, blocking my path to the door. "I want to talk to you. I want to talk now."

"I can't—" I start to say, but he cuts me off.

"You can't run away again." He reaches out and places his hands gently on my shoulders, but his touch makes a current of warmth and energy zip through me. "Do you understand? You can't keep doing this."

The way he's looking at me makes me feel weak. The tears threaten to come again. "I never meant to hurt you," I croak out.

He releases my shoulders, pushing his hands through his hair. He looks like he wants to scream. "You act like I'm invisible for years, then you send me this adorable little note, then I pick you up, and you kiss me—"

"I think *you* kissed *me*, actually."

He doesn't miss a beat. "—And you completely blow me away and rip my world up and everything else, and then you go back to ignoring me."

"I blew you away?" I squeak out before I can stop myself.

He stares at me steadily. "You blew *everything* away."

"Listen, Kent." I look down at my palms, which are actually itching to reach out and touch him, to smooth his hair back and tuck it behind his ear. "I meant everything that happened in the car. I meant to kiss you, I mean."

"I thought I kissed you." Kent's voice is even and I can't tell if he's joking or not.

"Yeah, well, I meant to kiss you back." I try to swallow the lump in my throat. "That's all I can tell you right now. I meant it. More than I've ever meant anything else in my life."

I'm glad I'm staring down at my shoes because at that second the tears push out of my eyes and start running down my cheeks. I quickly wipe them away with the back of my hand, pretending to be rubbing my eyes.

"What about that other thing you said in the car?" Kent doesn't sound angry, at least, though I'm too scared to look at him. His voice is softer now. "You said you didn't have much time. What did you mean?"

Now that the tears have found a way out, there's no stopping them, and I keep my head bowed. One of them splatters on my shoe, leaving a mark in the shape of a star. "There are things going on right now. . . ."

He puts two fingers under my chin and tilts my face up toward his. And then I really do stumble. My legs just give out underneath me, and he scoops one arm behind my back to keep me upright.

"What's happening, Sam?" He brushes a tear away from the corner of my eye with his thumb, his eyes searching my face, doing the thing where I feel like he's turning me inside out and looking straight into my heart. "Are you in trouble?"

I shake my head, unable to speak, and he rushes on, "You can tell me. Whatever it is, you can trust me."

For a moment I'm tempted to let myself stay this way, pressed against him; to kiss him over and over until it feels like I'm breathing *through* him. But then I think of Juliet in the woods. I see two blinding beams of light cutting through the darkness, and the low sound of roaring, like a faraway ocean, an engine jumping to life. The roaring and the lights fill my head, pushing everything else out—the fear, the regret, the sadness—and I can focus again.

"I'm not in trouble. It's not about me. I—I have to help someone." I break away from Kent gently, detaching his arm from my waist. "I can't really explain. *You* have to trust *me*."

I lean forward and give him a final kiss—just a peck, really, our lips hardly brushing together, but enough for me to feel that sense of soaring again, strength and power flowing through me. When I pull away I'm expecting more argument, but instead he just stares at me for a beat longer and then whirls around and disappears toward the stairs. My stomach plummets and for one split second I ache for him so badly—I *miss* him—I feel like my whole chest has caved in. Then I think of the dark, and the lights, and the roaring, and Juliet, and before I can think of anything else, I fight the final few steps to the door and step out into the cold, where the rain is still coming down like shards of moonlight, or like steel.

A MIRACLE OF CHANCE AND COINCIDENCE, PART II

"Juliet! Juliet!" I know she's gotten a fair start and won't be able to hear me, but it makes me feel better to call her name, makes the darkness all around me not feel so close and heavy.

Of course I've forgotten the flashlight. I begin my combo shuffle-run down the icy driveway, wishing I'd decided to wear sneakers instead of my favorite olive leather wedge-heeled Dolce Vita boots. At the same time, these are shoes to die for—to die *in*.

The lights of the house have winked out behind me, swallowed by the curves of the road and the tall spikes of the trees, when I think I hear someone calling my name. For a second I'm sure I've imagined it, or it's only the sound of the wind through the branches. I pause, hesitating, and then I hear it again. *"Sam!"* It sounds like Kent.

"Sam! Where are you?"

It *is* Kent.

This throws me. I was pretty sure when he stalked away from me at the party that that would be the end of it. I never expected he would actually follow me. I consider turning around and going back to him. But there's no time. Besides, I've said everything I can. For a moment, standing there in the freezing cold with the air burning my lungs and the rain pouring into my collar and down my back, I close my eyes and remember being with him in the warm, dry car surrounded on all sides by pouring rain. I remember the kiss and a feeling of lifting, as though we were going to be swept away at any moment by a wave. When I hear him call my name again it sounds closer, and I imagine him cupping my face and whispering to me. *Sam.*

Someone screams. I snap my eyes open, my heart surging in my chest, thinking of Juliet. But then I hear a few voices calling to one another—distant, still, a confusion of sounds—and I could swear that among them I hear Lindsay's voice. But that's ridiculous. I'm imagining things, and I'm wasting time.

I keep going toward the road. As I get closer I hear the roar of vehicles, the hiss of wheels against asphalt, both sounding like waves on a beach.

When I find Juliet she's standing, drenched, her clothes clinging to her body, her arms floating loosely at her sides like the rain and the cold doesn't bother her at all.

"Juliet!"

She hears me then. She swivels her head sharply, like she's

being called back to earth from somewhere else. I start jogging toward her, hearing the low rumbling of an approaching truck—*going way too fast*—behind me. She takes a quick step backward as I pick up speed, pinwheeling my arms to keep from toppling over on the ice, her face coming alive when she sees me, full of anger and fear and that other thing. Wonder.

The engine is louder now, a steady growl, and the driver leans on his horn. The noise is huge: rolling, blasting around us, filling the air with sound. Still Juliet hasn't moved. She's just standing there, staring at me, shaking her head a little bit, like we're long-lost friends in a random airport somewhere in Europe and have just bumped into each other. *It's so weird to see you here. . . . Isn't it funny how life works? Small world.*

I close the last few feet between us as the truck surges past, still blasting its horn. I grab onto her shoulders, and she takes a few stumbling steps backward into the woods, my momentum nearly carrying her off her feet. The sound of the horn ebbs away from us, taillights disappearing into the dark.

"Thank God," I say, breathing hard. My arms are shaking.

"What are you *doing*?" She seems to snap into herself, trying to wrench away from me. "Are you *following* me?"

"I thought you were going to . . ." I nod toward the road, and I suddenly have the urge to hug her. She's alive and solid and real under my hands. "I thought I wouldn't get to you in time."

She stops struggling and looks at me for a long second. There

465

are no cars on the road, and in the pause I hear it sharply, definitively: "Samantha Emily Kingston!" It comes from the woods to my left, and there's only one person in the world who calls me by my full name. Lindsay Edgecombe.

Just then, like a chorus of birds rising up from the ground at the same time, come the other voices, crowding one another: "Sam! Sam! Sam!" Kent, Ally, and Elody, all of them coming through the woods toward us.

"What's going on?" Juliet looks really afraid now. I'm so confused I loosen my grip on her shoulders and she twists away. "Why did you follow me? Why can't you leave me alone?"

"Juliet." I hold up my hands, a gesture of peace. "I just want to talk to you."

"I have nothing to say." She turns away from me and stalks back up toward the road.

I follow her, feeling suddenly calm. The world around me sharpens and comes into clearer focus, and every time I hear my name bouncing through the woods it sounds closer and closer, and I think, *I'm sorry*. But this is right. This is how it has to happen.

How it was supposed to happen all along.

"You don't have to do this, Juliet," I say to her quietly. "You know it's not the right way."

"You don't know what I have to do," she whispers back fiercely. "You don't *know*. You could never understand." She's staring at the road. Her shoulder blades are jutting out underneath her soaked T-shirt, and again I have the fantasy of a pair of wings unfurling behind her, lifting her away, carrying her out of danger.

"Sam! Sam! Sam!" The voices are close now, and diagonal beams of light zigzag through the woods. I hear footsteps, too, and branches snapping underfoot. The road has been unusually clear of traffic, but now from both directions I make out the low growl of big engines. I close my eyes and think of flying.

"I want to help you," I say to Juliet, though I know that I can't make her understand, not like this.

"Don't you get it?" She turns to me, and to my surprise I see she's crying. "I can't be fixed, do you understand?"

I think of standing on the stairs with Kent and saying exactly the same thing. I think of his beautiful light green eyes, and the way he said, *You don't need to be fixed* and the warmth of his hands and the softness of his lips. I think of Juliet's mask and how maybe we all feel patched and stitched together and not quite right.

I am not afraid.

Dimly, I have the sense of roaring in my ears and voices so close and faces, white and frightened, emerging from the darkness, but I can't stop staring at Juliet as she's crying, still so beautiful.

"It's too late," she says.

And I say, "It's never too late."

467

In that split second she's launched herself into the road, but she looks back, startled, recognition lighting up her eyes. Then I'm hurtling out behind her. I slam into her back, and she goes shooting forward, rolling toward the opposite shoulder, just as two vans converge, about to pass each other. There's a furious high whine and someone—more than one person?—screams my name and a feeling of heat all through my body and the sensation of being lifted, thrown, by a huge hand, a giant's hand; the earth revolves, turns upside down and sideways, and then a fog of darkness eats up the edges of the earth, turning everything to dream.

Floating images, moving in and out: bright green eyes and a field of sun-warmed grass, a mouth saying, *Sam, Sam, Sam,* making it sound like a song. Three faces blooming together like flowers on a single stem, names ebbing away from me, a single word: *love.* Red and white flashes, tree branches lit up like the vaulted ceiling of a church.

And a face above mine, white and beautiful, eyes as large as the moon. *You saved me.* A hand on my cheek, cool and dry. *Why did you save me?* Words welling up on a tide: *No. The opposite.* Eyes the color of a dawn sky, a crown of blond hair, so bright and white and blinding I could swear it was a halo.

EPILOGUE

They say that just before you die your whole life flashes before your eyes, but that's not how it happens for me.

I see only my greatest hits. The things I want to remember, and be remembered for. The time in Cape Cod when Izzy and I snuck down to the bay at midnight and tried to catch crabs with leftover hamburger meat, and the moon was so fat and round it looked like something you could sit on. When Ally tried to make a soufflé and came marching into the kitchen with a roll of toilet paper on her head like a chef's hat, and Elody laughed so hard she peed a little bit and swore us all to secrecy. Lindsay throwing her arms around us and saying, "Love you to death," and all of us echoing, "And even then." Lying on the deck on hot August afternoons with the smell of grass shavings and flowers so heavy in the air, it's like you're tasting them. The time it snowed on Christmas, and my dad split up one of the old TV tables in the basement to use as firewood, and my mom made apple cider, and we tried to remember the words to "Silent Night" but ended up singing all our favorite show tunes.

And kissing Kent, because that's when I realized that time doesn't matter. That's when I realized that certain moments go on forever. Even after they're over they still go on, even after you're dead and buried, those moments are lasting still, backward and forward, on into infinity. They are everything and everywhere all at once.

They are the meaning.

I'm not scared, if that's what you're wondering. The moment of death is full of sound and warmth and light, so much light it fills me, absorbs me: a tunnel of light shooting away, arcing up and up and up, and if singing were a feeling it would be this, this light, this lifting, like laughing . . .

The rest you have to find out for yourself.

ACKNOWLEDGMENTS

In no particular order, many thanks . . .

To Stephen Barbara, the ultimate hustler and the greatest agent in the world; to Lexa Hillyer, for being the first to read any part of *Before I Fall* and love it; to the incredible Brenda Bowen, for being the first to believe in it; and to the wonderful Molly O'Neill, for her enthusiasm and for making *me* believe.

To Rosemary Brosnan, for her intelligence, acuity, and sensitivity; to everyone at HarperTeen, for the insane quantities of support and for giving me Magnolia cupcakes when I was jet-lagged.

To Cameron McClure of the Donald Maas Literary Agency, for her hard work and continued advocacy on behalf of the book.

To DUB Pies in Brooklyn for keeping me caffeinated and happy.

To Dujeous, for the generous use of their lyrics. Check them out at www.dujeous.net.

To Mary Davison, who might teach us all something about living life to the fullest.

To all of my amazing, brilliant friends, for inspiring and challenging me; and in particular to Patrick Manasse, for being a patient listener and a tough critic.

To Olivier, for being immensely supportive, even when I was struggling.

To Deirdre Fulton, Jacqueline Novak, and Laura Smith, a single word: *love*.

To my parents, for filling our house with books I could fall in love with—and later, for encouraging me to pursue my dreams—and always, for their constant love and support.

To my brilliant sister, for being someone I will always look up to.

And lastly, to Pete: For encouraging me to go to graduate school and helping me get on my feet once I did; for letting me frantically edit in Harbor Springs; for always being so proud of me; and because whatever I was writing, I was always trying to write my way back to you.

Bonus Material
from the Movie

Turn the page for Lauren Oliver's exclusive
interview with Zoey Deutch and Ry Russo-Young,
plus behind-the-scenes photos from the set.

In December 2015, I had the chance to go to Vancouver to watch a few days of filming for the *Before I Fall* movie, starring the unbelievably nuanced Zoey Deutch and directed by the sharp, incisive director Ry Russo-Young. I was, admittedly, nervous. I had no idea how I would react to seeing my book transformed into a living, breathing thing, and I found the set both chaotic and agonizingly slow.

But I was swept away by Zoey's performance—and by the performances of all the actors—and by Ry's choices, which had preserved so much of the book's heart while updating and sharpening its look and message.

Ry and Zoey were nice enough to agree to an interview.

What appealed to both of you about this project? Why did you take it on?

Zoey: I thought it was a truly beautiful script and moving story, and I love Ry Russo-Young. It felt like a departure from the normal young adult fare.

Ry: I had a similar experience to Zoey. The story truly surprised me with its unexpected depth and humanity. The book reminded me of how I felt emotionally and psychologically when I was a teenager—I don't see enough movies about teenage girls whose problems aren't trite or cliché. Sam is struggling with the complexities of life, confronting her demons, and it's rare to see such a thoughtful treatment of that on film. It seemed like a great opportunity.

Zoey, you shot the movie in blocks, meaning you often had to shoot very different Sams on a single day, as in short succession her feelings and responses to the same scenes change. How did you handle this?

Zoey: A lot of planning and preparation! Ry and I spent an immense amount of time creating shorthands for the different days and Sams.

What are some of your favorite moments in the movie? Were there any particularly challenging moments?

Zoey: It would be hard to pick one "favorite moment," but something that struck me was how elegant the structure of the film is—the way it's bookended with the same images, and bittersweetness.

In terms of challenges, one thing that was comical is that *Before I Fall* is all about time, and while we were shooting we had very little of that. We were always at the mercy of time. In particular, I remember having to quickly shoot all the wakeups; it was very delicate work, and Ry and I wanted to make sure we were gauging each wakeup correctly while not giving in to the rushed nature of shooting.

4

Ry: I could literally name ten favorite moments right now but will limit it to just one. On day six, it's a tiny thing but when Sam sees Kent in the hallway at school, she tells him she has a secret and as she says this, she's walking backward with this tiny bounce in her step. This little move that Zoey made up, besides being adorable, says so much about where the character is at in this moment in the story; it's brilliant and I smile every time I see it on screen.

Overall, we had such a great family on the film, with Halston, Cynthy, Medalion, Logan, Elena, Kian, and little Erica, who played Izzy. It was fun exploring with all these young actors and actresses and helping them find the moments of truth. Many of my favorite moments involve the way they play off each other in scenes, the unexpected creative laugh or glare I never saw coming until I watched it on the monitor.

And I think we all learned from the masterful Jennifer Beals. Another favorite moment is when she hesitates three times in Sam's doorway. She just nailed the conflicted feelings of being a rebuffed parent. Our editor, Joe Landauer, has a particular eye for this kind of nuance.

Any set stories you feel like sharing? Late-night shoots? Especially challenging shoots?

Zoey: I remember one night shoot in the forest, Ry and I were cuddling for warmth in between setups and rewriting the day six scene between Sam and Juliet . . . It was freezing, but it makes me smile.

Ry: I remember that too! We shot the movie in the mountains around Vancouver in November and December, often shooting overnight in the cold and the rain. The car crashes alone took a week of night shooting. So it was a particularly hard movie for the cast and crew. Cozy moments like that helped us all get through.

What are you proudest of about the movie?

Zoey: The thing I am probably most proud of is that many people have told me after they saw *Before I Fall*, they immediately called their wife, or husband, sister, brother, daughter, or person they deeply care about, to tell them "I love you." That feels very special to me.

Ry: Agreed. And I'm proud that the movie seems to affect people regardless of their demographic. You don't need to be a teenage girl to have the film speak to your experience. A friend's sixty-year-old father saw the film and was crying, he loved it; that's a big achievement in my book.

Logan Miller is a cutie. I hear you guys had a lot of fun on set. How did you guys first begin to bond?

Zoey: I initially recommended him for the part before he auditioned. I just thought he'd be a great Kent. We did have a lot of fun, unfortunately very loudly and obnoxiously, so here's my formal apology to the rest of the cast and crew who had to deal with us. Sorry.

The relationship between Sam, Lindsay, Elody, and Ally feels so real. Can you talk about working with the other actresses, and do you yourself have strong female friends that gave you inspiration?

Zoey: It was important to feel that Sam was a follower and not a leader, that she was not the alpha, maybe not even the beta. That was something Ry and I were very careful and calculated about achieving.

Any favorite lines?

Zoey: My favorite line in the movie is probably the last one Sam says. It's devastating and poignant.

Ry: "Maybe for you there's a tomorrow. Maybe for you there's one thousand or three thousand or ten."

If you had one day to live what would you do?

Zoey: I would be with my family and dog. I'd eat all my favorite meals, cuddle, and laugh.

Ry: Same minus Zoey's dog. I'd probably watch some of my favorite movies too.

If you hope viewers take anything away, what would it be?

Zoey: Gratitude!

Ry: An appreciation of their own life: its fragility, silliness, fun, warmth, pain, and kindness. I think we made a movie that has a lot of heart and my hope is that it brings out kindness in those who watch it.

From Page to Screen
On the Set of *Before I Fall*

Zoey Deutch, director Ry Russo-Young, and Halston Sage
share a smiley moment between takes, with producer
Jon Shestack in the background.

On Day Five, Sam (Zoey Deutch) skips school to spend the day with little sister, Izzy (Erica Tremblay).

A tender moment between Sam (Zoey Deutch) and
Kent (Logan Miller), away from the crowds at the party. *Swoon*.

Read on for an excerpt from **REPLICA**,

Lauren Oliver's masterful bestselling novel

with two narratives in one:

Lyra's story and Gemma's story.

See how **LYRA'S** story begins . . .

ONE

ON VERY STILL NIGHTS SOMETIMES we can hear them chanting, calling for us to die. We can see them, too, or at least make out the halo of light cast up from the shores of Barrel Key, where they must be gathered, staring back across the black expanse of water toward the fence and the angular white face of the Haven Institute. From that distance it must look like a long green jaw set with miniature teeth.

Monsters, they call us. Demons.

Sometimes, on sleepless nights, we wonder if they're right.

Lyra woke up in the middle of the night with the feeling that someone was sitting on her chest. Then she realized it was just the heat—swampy and thick, like the pressure of somebody's hand. The power had gone down.

Something was wrong. People were shouting. Doors slammed. Footsteps echoed in the halls. Through the windows, she saw the zigzag pattern of flashlights cutting across the courtyard, illuminating silvery specks of rain and the stark-white statue of a man, reaching down toward the ground, as though to pluck something from the earth. The other replicas came awake simultaneously. The dorm was suddenly full of voices, thick with sleep. At night it was easier to speak. There were fewer nurses to shush them.

"What's wrong?"

"What's happened?"

"Be quiet." That was Cassiopeia. "I'm listening."

The door from the hall swung open, so hard it cracked against the wall. Lyra was dazzled by a sudden sweep of light.

"They all here?" It sounded like Dr. Coffee Breath.

"I think so." Nurse Don't-Even-Think-About-It's voice was high and terrified. Her face was invisible behind the flashlight beam. Lyra could make out just the long hem of her nightgown and her bare feet.

"Well, count them."

"We're all here," Cassiopeia responded. One of them gasped. But Cassiopeia was never afraid to speak up.

"What's going on?"

"It must be one of the males," Dr. Coffee Breath said to Nurse Don't-Even-Think-About-It, who was really named Maxine. "Who's checking the males?"

"What's wrong?" Cassiopeia repeated. Lyra found herself touching the windowsill, the pillow, the headboard of bed number 24. Her things. Her world.

At that moment, the answer came to them: voices, shrill, calling to one another. *Code Black. Code Black. Code Black.*

Almost at the same time, the backup generator kicked on. The lights came up, and with them, the alarms. Sirens wailed. Lights flashed in every room. Everyone squinted in the sudden brightness. Nurse Don't-Even-Think-About-It stumbled backward, raising an arm as though to shield herself from view.

"Stay here," Dr. Coffee Breath said. Lyra wasn't sure whether he was speaking to Nurse Don't-Even-Think-About-It or to the replicas. Either way, there wasn't much choice. Dr. Coffee Breath had to let himself into the hall with a code. Nurse Don't-Even-Think-About-It stayed for only a moment, shivering, her back to the door, as if she expected that at any second the girls might make a rush at her. Her flashlight, now subsumed by the overheads, cast a milk-white ring on the tile floor.

"Ungrateful," she said, before she, too, let herself out.

Even then they could see her through the windows overlooking the hall, moving back and forth, occasionally touching her cross.

"What's Code Black?" Rose asked, hugging her knees to her chest. They'd run out of stars ever since Dr. O'Donnell, the only staff member Lyra had never nicknamed, had stopped giving them lessons. Instead the replicas selected names for themselves from the collection of words they knew, words that struck them as pretty or interesting. There was Rose, Palmolive, and Private. Lilac Springs and Tide. There was even a Fork.

As usual, only Cassiopeia—number 6, one of the oldest replicas besides Lyra—knew.

"Code Black means security's down," she said. "Code Black means someone's escaped."